He was a writer, not a fighter, but now he was in a fight for his life…

"Kiss my ass, you crazy son of a bitch," Kieran said as Zimmer dragged him roughly to his feet. Kieran threw a clumsy haymaker, which Zimmer not only blocked but, in one smooth motion, landed a stunning blow, knocking the breath from Kieran. He stumbled and went down gasping for breath. "Go—to hell," he gasped.

Zimmer grabbed him by the front of his shirt, pulled him up, and gave him a violent shake.

"Look around you, Kieran," Zimmer said. "Does this look like the green hills of Tennessee?"

Grudgingly, Kieran looked about the rocky canyons of the arid desert. "Well, no."

"Look there," Zimmer said, pointing up into the sky. "Since when does Earth have *two* moons?"

"This can't be happening," Kieran whispered as he beheld the amazing sight.

"Well, it is," Zimmer spat. Releasing his shirt, Zimmer pulled out a handkerchief and offered it to Kieran. "Clean yourself up."

"Hauptmann, should I place the prisoner under guard?" the oberfeldwebel asked in German as he pointed his rifle at Kieran.

Kieran blanched as he looked down the rifle barrel.

"We are not going to do anything to our *prisoner*, Oberfeldwebel. Kieran isn't our enemy. In fact, he is one of us now."

"Hauptmann," Hartmann said in German as he lowered his rifle. "Must I remind you that we are at war with the Americans?"

"Oberfeldwebel," Zimmer said, "we left that war behind on Earth. Now, get our new friend here some food and water."

"Sir!" Oberfeldwebel Hartmann said with a sharp salute. "Should I at least keep his equipment under guard?"

"No. I don't see it being a threat. Return it to Mr. Nash."

Obviously not happy, Hartmann, stalked away to fulfill Zimmer's orders.

"Rest well tonight, Kieran," Zimmer said. "For our unit to survive, we must be strong. God only knows what is in store for us here on this alien world. We are only as strong as our weakest link. I am afraid that link is you."

"Oh, God," Kieran moaned, "I have been drafted into the Nazi army. This trip has definitely turned into a nightmare."

In 2014, nineteen-year-old budding novelist, Kieran Nash, finds himself inexplicably transported to the desert world of Adeaa, where he meets an equally bewildered squad of German paratroopers, plucked from a 1944 Italian battlefield. Putting differences aside for the sake of survival, Kieran and the war-hardened German Fallschirmjäger—led by the ever-resourceful Captain Zimmer—set out across the dangerous new world to find a way home, unaware they are key players in a plan that affects the future of two worlds.

KUDOS for *The God Machine*

In *The God Machine* by Ken Newman, Kieran Nash is transported from Earth in 2014 to a desert planet named Adeaa, where he is rescued from a gang of natives by a squad of German paratroopers from 1944. It's obvious that Kieran's sudden appearance is a surprise to everyone, including the alien who kidnapped the troopers from Earth. As Kieran and the Germans join forces, they discover that they are here to defeat a "god machine" that has turned the normally peaceful natives into violent slaves. Now, the Earthlings need to find a way home without getting killed by the "god's" slaves or the alien who kidnapped them in the first place—a task that will take all of their skills and creativity against impossible odds. Like Newman's other books, this one is creative, intriguing, and riveting. Once you pick it up you won't be able to put it down. ~ *Taylor Jones, The Review Team of Taylor Jones & Regan Murphy*

The God Machine by Ken Newman is the story of a loser given a chance to save the world. It's 2014, and Kieran Nash is a nerdy college student who's failing one of his important classes. His professor wants him to drop out of her class, but he refuses. He's determined to get a passing grade and begs for another chance. The professor relents on one condition—he does her a favor and delivers a truck full of furniture to her sister out of state. With few options, Kieran reluctantly agrees. But not long after he starts out on his journey, the trip takes a major detour, and Kieran is transported to a planet with two moons. The first group of beings he sees tries to kill him, and Kieran's both terrified and confused. But when he's suddenly rescued by a group of German soldiers who kill the natives, Kieran is even more bewildered. The Germans claim to be from the year 1944, fighting a battle against the Allies in Italy, when they were kidnapped and brought to this desolate planet. Although Kieran doesn't much care for Nazis, and the Germans think the only good American is a dead one, they join forces, try-ing to get back to Earth—a decision that will change all their lives forever. In his first two novels, *Forsaken* and *Dead Ends*, Newman proved he has a rare talent for science fiction, and *The God Machine* doesn't disappoint. In fact, his books just keep getting better. With a unique, clever, and fascinating plot; marvelous, enchanting, and endearing characters; plenty of humor; and enough suspense to keep you glued to the edge of your seat, this is one you really don't want to miss. I loved it. ~ *Regan Murphy, The Review Team of Taylor Jones & Regan Murphy*

THE GOD MACHINE

Ken Newman

A Black Opal Books Publication

GENRE: SCI-FI THRILLER/PARANORMAL THRILLER

THE GOD MACHINE
Copyright © 2018 by Ken Newman
Cover Design by Ken Newman with Jackson Cover Designs
All cover art copyright © 2018
All Rights Reserved
Print ISBN: 978-1-626948-67-9

First Publication: FEBRUARY 2018

Published by Black Opal Books **http://www.blackopalbooks.com**

DEDICATION

To my wife, Christian, my light in the darkness.

CHAPTER 1

On the last day of his life, as he knew it, Kieran Nash leaned back in his chair, watching the girl in the purple beret as if she were the only object in the universe.

"*The Day the Hand of Fate Broke a Nail*, really?" Jen asked. She gave Kieran a quizzical glance over her glasses. "Are you serious?"

"Title grabs your attention by the throat, doesn't it?"

Jen rolled her eyes and continued reading. "I should demand pay for suffering this kind of mental abuse."

"Trust me, beautiful, you'll thank me later."

Jen Keller wasn't the most beautiful girl in Rackham University, yet there was something about the delicate shape of her face and the sparkle in her soft, dark eyes that fascinated Kieran, drawing him like a moth to a flame. He even loved the quirky little purple beret and round hipster glasses, which made her look like a retro beatnik.

Kieran wasn't shy about proclaiming his desire for her. Trouble was Jen was equally adamant in her resistance to his charm. Jen preferred Kieran well inside the "friend zone," and any breakout attempts were met with over-whelming force.

Jen quickly read the pages before her, frowning and shaking her head at certain passages. Breathing a sigh of relief, as she finished her task, Jen took the five opening pages of his story and shoved them back at Kieran.

"What do you think, Jen?" Kieran asked. "Dare I say *genius?*"

"Dare I say *ripe cheese?*"

"You cut me deep, woman."

"Whatever," she said. "I will say that you do paint quite the picture. 'Desiree looked at me as if I was an all you could eat buffet, and she was a starving super model an hour away from the apocalypse.' Really, Kieran, you make Mickey Spillane read like Shakespeare."

"Thanks a lot," he said. "This is what I get for letting mere mortals peek at greatness. It just spawns jealousy and bitter spite. Besides, Mickey Spillane is way better than Shakespeare. I would put *I, the Jury,* up against *Hamlet* any day of the week."

Jen snorted. "That proves my theory. You're delusional."

"A fine line exists between delusion and greatness, sweetheart. For your information, that was just the opening of thirty-five thousand words dripping with literary gold. Why, it took me two weeks to get the structure and voice just right."

"Two weeks, on *that*? I think you tried too hard."

"Gee, thanks a bunch."

"Just being honest. Kieran, why do you do this to yourself? You know that Professor Wills hates popular fiction. You turn in this blood-and -testosterone-drenched detective noir tale, and she'll have no mercy. Even though you're a pain in my derriere, I wouldn't wish that on anyone."

"You got it all wrong, beautiful," he said. "Professor Wills doesn't hate popular fiction. That woman hates everything. Wouldn't be a bit surprised if she kicked puppies for a hobby. Being a writer means fearlessness in the face of criticism."

"Save yourself some lumps and pick your fights, Kieran. Be fearless outside of class, because you can't win here."

He gave her a crooked grin. "What's your masterpiece about, Jen?"

"An alcoholic, dead-beat dad takes his autistic child on a

trip to the zoo. I call it, *Feeding the Animals*."

"No mob gun battles, anti-heroes or damsels in distress?"

"Nary a one," she said. "Sorry."

"Want me to read the opening and give you the benefit of my literary brilliance?"

"I'm good," she said, clutching the manuscript to her chest protectively.

"Bless you," he said. "Your description alone took years off my life."

Jen snarled at him.

Kieran's laughter morphed into a prodigious yawn.

"Kieran, have I told you lately that you look like death warmed over? When was the last time you slept?"

"Last year. Thank God for energy drinks. I had to pull a double shift last night. Fortunately, for some strange reason, I got the weekend off. My tyrant of a boss, Bill, said not to come back to work until Monday. I can't remember having two days off in a row."

"Good for you. You should spend it in bed getting some Zs. You need to slow down before you burn out."

"Can't. I'm paying for college, and I'm barely breaking even," he said. "Since I'm off, how about you come by my place tonight, and I'll fix you dinner? We can take our friendship to a new, more intimate level."

"You cook?"

Kieran rose and slipped his arm around her shoulders. "Okay, take out. We can eat and maybe watch a movie. Trust me, it'll be time well spent. Who knows, it might just change your life."

Jen gingerly removed his arm from her shoulders as if it were diseased. "No Thanks, Kieran, I like my life and our strictly platonic relationship the way it is. Besides, I already made plans."

"Plans? As in a date with a dude? Not another of those gym-worshiping lunks you have a taste for?"

"No," she said, "and what's wrong with a guy who likes to stay in shape?"

"Talentless athletes whose only goal is to look good in a mirror and treat you like a doormat. We'd be good together."

Jen rolled her eyes. "Kieran, you have a good heart, I love our gab sessions, and you aren't too unfortunate looking, but you dress like a bum and are allergic to sunshine. In other words, you're not my type."

"I may not have buns of steel, but I'd treat you with respect and to the finest take out this town has to offer. I'll expect you at seven, okay?"

"You never stop, do you?" she asked.

"My mom calls me relentless."

"I'm not getting into another argument with you, so back off. For your information, it's my great-grandmother's eighty-eighth birthday, and she's celebrating it with me."

"That sounds like a red-hot time on the town," he said. "Don't let the old girl get you into trouble. The last thing you need is to wake up hungover with a fresh tattoo of *I like Ike* or *Down with Prohibition* on your arm."

"Don't scoff, punk. Gramie's cool, completely inappropriate, and doesn't take guff from anyone. She's great, not to mention she's financing my education."

"That sounds nice."

"Yes, it is. Besides, it's the least I can do for her, especially since my great-grandfather died six-months ago. The poor thing seems lost and alone, nothing like the strong-willed woman I remembered as a girl. As a matter of fact, the wild stories she told me growing up made me want to be a writer." Jen laughed.

"What's so funny?"

"Oh, I was thinking of this crazy series of science fiction stories, Gramie told me. Wild, off the wall adventures about a pair of human explorers, marooned when their rocket ship crashed landed on the planet Bosco. She went into lurid detail about sexy Jasmin Lake and her boy-toy stud, Clark Valentino as they explored the lost world and the remains of a sinister, super scientific race called the Marshooms. The stories were farfetched and cheesy as you can get, but there were times growing up that I wished I was Jasmin and had square jawed he-man Clark to my devious devices."

"I'm standing right here," he said.

Jen sighed. "Gramie sure could weave a great tale, full of adventure and plot twists wrapped around a little old fashioned romantic smut."

"Good for her," Kieran said. "Tomorrow night, then? I'll let you call me Clark, and you can break out the devious devices."

"I'll think about it. Okay, I thought about it. The answer is still no, *Clark*."

"You're killing me, woman. When I'm rich and famous as the world's greatest mystery writer, you'll be sorry. You come to my palatial beach house, and I'll sic the dogs on you."

Jen snorted. "That'll be the day."

"Ladies and gentlemen, please turn in the writing assignment," Professor Wills said, from the front of the classroom. "It had better wow me, or else."

❧❧❧

Tall, painfully thin, and dressed in somber black, Professor Janet Wills stood behind her desk, like an academician version of the grim reaper. Her close-cropped silver hair emphasized her pinched face and razor thin lips that always seemed to be scowling. Arms crossed, she watched as the subdued band of undergraduates turned in their latest assignments. She smiled ever so slightly, as the image of neophytes laying sacrificial lambs upon the altar of English Lit, crossed her mind.

None of the two dozen students dared to make eye contact with the infamous 'Queen Bitch,' of the English department. Professor Wills was proud of her reputation and sadistic teaching methods. It was said that she drove at least one student, per semester, to tears. It was an informal fraternity, which over the years had come to be known as "Wills's Wailers."

While her students hated the ground she walked on, and her teaching methods ground university guidelines to dust, she essentially had carte blanche because her one and only book had won the Pulitzer Prize thirty years before.

A Pulitzer prizewinner on staff gave Rackham University enormous prestige and made Professor Wills, short of murder, untouchable.

Professor Wills watched Kieran Nash chat with Jennifer Keller with keen interest. Two days before, Kieran was a faceless name on a roll, a lackluster writer without a voice, or future outside of the fast food industry. He was unworthy of her time or attention, but today, he was the center of her universe.

Professor Wills thought of herself as a superior, evolved human being, a full five levels above the rabble that was everyone else, as such, her confidence was unshakable, that is until today. While she struggled to maintain her cool façade, she felt the unfamiliar knot of nervousness bloom within her stomach.

The sixty-year-old educator strategically cleared her throat, which caught the attention of the students in the room with the same result as if someone had fired a gun.

"Mr. Nash, I would like a word with you in my office, *now*."

Without waiting for a response, the professor turned on her heel and stalked to her office door. The tall, dark-haired young man froze, as did the rest of the class.

"I do not have all day, *Mr.* Nash," she said, her well-practiced icy tone forging her words into projectiles as tangible as iron.

Professor Wills opened the frosted glass door to her inner sanctum and waited with a pale, boney fist on her hip.

"Oh no," Kieran said under his breath. "I don't need this now."

"Nice knowing you, *Mr.* Nash," Jen whispered, as Kieran shuffled toward the professor on numb legs. "Better you than me."

Kieran turned and stuck his tongue out at her.

"As for the rest of you talentless, *turds*, I will see you Monday, and you had better be prepared, or else."

As she turned and ushered Kieran into her office, those present gave Professor Wills a well-choreographed, one-finger salute.

CHAPTER 2

S it down, *Mr.* Nash," Professor Wills said as she closed the door behind him.

"Nice office," he said, unzipping his dark blue hoodie and plopping down his overstuffed backpack on the floor. Looking up at her award festooned wall, he noticed a prominent photo of a considerably younger Professor Wills with President Ford no less. In her hand was a copy of her book, *Red Dog Summer.*

His eyes afire with undisguised literary envy, Kieran took a seat in one of two chairs that set before her oversized, pathologically well-ordered desk.

"Nice."

"Yeah, yeah, yeah, it's great to be me," she said as she walked around the desk and opened a bottom desk drawer. To his surprise, she extracted a half-full bottle of whiskey and two squat glasses. While he looked on, she poured a measure of the amber liquid into both glasses and shoved one at him.

"You are twenty-one, aren't you?"

"I'm nineteen," he said.

"Happy birthday. Today, you are twenty-one. Now blow out the candle and take the drink."

Taking her own glass, she promptly downed the mellow, amber shot in one gulp. Setting the tumbler down, she poured herself another.

"Now that is much better," she said, as the liquid

warmed its way down her throat, taking the edge off her growing anxiety. "What's the matter, boy? You want to be a real writer, you better be able to toss back a few."

"Professor?" Kieran asked. "What's going on?"

"Don't call me professor, Kieran. Call me, Janet. Today is a special day, young man, so drink up."

Puzzled, Kieran took the glass and raised it tentatively to his lips.

"I want you out of my class, Kieran. We are celebrating your departure."

The glass paused mere millimeters from his lips. "Excuse me?" he asked.

"You heard me," she said. "We both know that your work isn't up to my standards. You adore gutter trash, otherwise known as popular fiction. Let's face facts. Your writing is garbage, but I like you, Kieran, that is why I am giving you an honorable out."

"What do you mean, an honorable out?" he asked.

"Your piss-poor performance is bringing down the overall grade average, and that will not do. Drop my class now, and we will pretend the last semester never happened."

"I'm not a quitter," he said. "Sure, my grades have slipped a bit—"

"Slipped a bit? If I recorded grades right now, you would fail," she said, taking a sip. "However, I am not completely without feelings, Kieran. I have taken the liberty of talking to Professor Howerton. Even though it is late in the school year, he has agreed to add you to his roll. It will be a seamless transition, you won't be out any money, and your meager grade average will survive intact. The only injured party will be me and the time I have wasted on you."

"Professor Wills—*Janet*, I know this isn't your problem, but I'm not a slacker who's skating through college while my parents foot the bill. My mom isn't paying my way. She can't afford it. To make tuition, I have to work two, really crappy jobs. Sure, I've been burning the candle at both ends, but I need this class. I'll get a tutor, do extra credit, anything. Passing *your* class, well, it means a lot to me. I've already learned far more from you about the craft of writing than I would have from Professor Howerton—or anyone else, for that matter. So you can go ahead and fail me if you want, but, by God, I will not quit."

To punctuate his point, Kieran threw back the shot and promptly erupted into a sputtering, coughing jag.

"One of my little weasels has a backbone." She chuckled, taking a sip. "Who would have thunk it? Not much of a whiskey drinker, are you, Kieran? How can you call yourself a writer if you possess a good liver?"

"I'll work on it," he said, wiping his mouth. "I think I burned my throat."

"Very well, Kieran. Even though I think you couldn't snag a job scribbling greeting cards, I like your grit."

"I didn't think you liked grit."

"Normally, no," she said, displaying a predatory smile. "But you have me at an opportune moment."

"Excuse me?"

"Do me a small favor, and I will allow you to stay. What do you say, young man?"

"Favor?" he asked, wiping his mouth with the back of his hand. The word burned his mouth more than the whiskey.

"Have you ever heard the old saying, 'one hand washes the other'?"

Kieran visibly blanched. His face twisted into a mask of abject horror.

Professor Wills chortled as she read his expression. "Don't worry, Kieran, it doesn't involve sex or signing over your soul."

"Umm…never crossed my mind," he said, blushing furiously. "Okay, Janet, what's the deal? I'm all ears."

"I have to deliver a truck full of furniture to my sister in Montgomery by tomorrow, high noon."

"Montgomery—as in Montgomery, *Alabama*?"

"You are a smart boy. Why my sister…Mary…is moving to that God-forsaken place is a mystery to me. Anyway, I was promised a few sentimental items from my late mother in return. Items rightfully mine, that Mary has held ransom for the past year. I have had time to think about the trip and spending time with Mary, and I would rather gouge my eyes out. Mary was always a pain in my ass, and I despise driving, yet I very much want my mother's things."

"You want me to drive? That's over seven hundred miles away."

"Another reason I don't want the chore."

"Why me?"

"You are convenient."

"Oh. What's in it for me?"

"Let me make this clear, Kieran. You deliver the truck so that I can avoid both the unpleasant drive and my stupid sister, and I will guarantee that not only will you remain my pupil, you will pass my class."

"An *A*?" he said his eyes lighting with a glimmer of hope.

"Don't be absurd. Nobody gets an A in my class. Why, seventy-percent never even pass. You will get the lowest passable grade—a modest D."

"Really, a stinking D?" he asked. Leaning back, he rubbed his chin. "Montgomery is a long drive."

"Think of the D as a safety net, Kieran. While I am dubious about your talent, I do respect your drive. *Earn* a better grade, and I will give it to you."

"You must really hate driving."

"You have no idea how much I loathe driving around this rotten little town, let alone traversing across the country. To be perfectly honest, I am terrified at the prospect of being alone on the road."

"I see," he said, mulling over the deal.

"Deliver the furniture, pick up my mother's things, and, as long as you keep your mouth shut, I think it is more than a fair trade."

"I think we have a deal," he said, extending his hand to her.

Looking at his open hand like a deadly serpent, Professor Wills took a deep breath and shook his hand. "Despite the fact you will have your passing grade, I will expect you to do your best, or I will ride you like Secretariat, got me?"

"Yes, Janet. Believe it or not, I want to be a great writer and will put in the time. I will earn the A."

"That's a D."

"You'll give me an A."

Professor Wills smiled. "When pigs fly."

Kieran chuckled.

"If you are to make it on time, you had better get cracking, Kieran," she said.

Professor Wills opened a drawer and tossed a thick envelope on the desk before him. Kieran did not notice that her hands shook, ever so slightly.

"What's this?" he asked.

"In the envelope are both sets of keys, along with money for gas and food." She produced a wallet and extracted several bills. "This should more than buy a one-way bus ticket back."

"It's a long drive, can I take my buddy, Fat Jimmy, with me?"

"Absolutely not!" she cried. "Haven't you been listening? Kieran, anyone finds out about our arrangement, and the deal is off, you hear me? You cannot tell a soul."

"Okay, okay, Fat Jimmy's out."

"I hear a whisper that you have opened your mouth, and I will have you expelled, got me?"

"Not a word," he said.

"Outside, in the faculty lot, is a Mercedes Benz, you can't miss it."

"A Mercedes? For real?" Kieran leaped to his feet and rushed to the window, where he gasped. "What the hell is that?"

Sitting in the parking lot was a unique vehicle that

looked like a large box and cab, perched atop six, huge knobby tires. The strange vehicle was painted in a bizarre pattern consisting of shades of oranges, blacks, and beige.

"That is the ugliest thing I ever saw, and I saw Fat Jimmy naked once. This thing looks like it was painted by a lunatic suffering from glaucoma. I thought you said it was a Mercedes?"

"Believe it or not, it is. Apparently, Mercedes Benz makes monster trucks as well, no doubt for the European redneck market."

Kieran laughed. "Good one."

"Anyway, from the manual in the glove box, it is called a Unimog, some kind of four-wheeled monstrosity."

"It has six wheels."

"Whatever. Automobiles are not my forte. This is my sister's doing. She had it delivered this morning, and I bet she has laughed her ass off all day thinking of me driving it down the highway."

"Kind of an expensive prank, don't you think? It's funny looking, but it looks very pricy."

"It's her style. The bitch has more money than God and likes to rub it in. Anyway, after much trial and error, the GPS has already been set with the directions. I even programmed in a short cut."

"Short cut?"

"Listen to me, Kieran. I have been along this route many times. Don't think. Just follow its directions to the letter, and you'll be fine."

"Got it. Just let me go back to my room—"

"No time to spare. If you want to pass my class, you can't be late. You must leave immediately."

"Okay. Lucky for me, almost everything I own is in my backpack."

Janet glanced at the bulging, oversized pack. "And all this time I thought you were going mountain climbing."

"Funny."

"Now get going. You're burning daylight."

Shoving the bulky envelope into his jacket pocket, he retrieved his all-important backpack.

"Kieran, one last thing."

"Yes?"

She rummaged about in a bottom drawer of her desk. "Do you remember my dictate on taking notes?"

"Yes, of course," he said. "It's the second commandment. 'Thou shalt take copious notes, and thou shalt use them, or I shall fry thy ass.'"

"This will help," she said as she placed a box on the desk. "Take it with you."

Kieran looked closely at the expensive digital recorder. A triple pack of batteries was attached to the outside of the box with clear packing tape.

"A gift?"

"Don't be silly," she said. "A previous student, whose work was even more substandard than yours, tried to bribe me with a gift. Needless to say, he isn't with us anymore. More than likely he has a fulfilling career as a gas-pump jockey now. Anyway, I was going to throw it out, but you might find a use for it."

"Thanks, Janet."

"Since we will resume our master-slave relationship come Monday, Mr. Nash, it is Professor Wills."

"Yes, Professor Wills," he said as he stood and slung his enormous pack over his shoulder. "While we are in a quasi-friendly relationship, may I ask a question, before I go?"

"A question?" Janet frowned. "Oh, all right, shoot."

"Why did you only write one book? *Red Dog Summer* was fantastic."

The question took her by surprise, and her iron facade shattered. Suddenly, to Kieran, she looked very old and vulnerable. For the first time, she looked human.

"Do you know how many people have asked me that stupid question over the years?"

"Sorry, but I have been dying to know."

"Oh, the hell with it. You want to know the truth? This is the truth. Kieran, I was afraid."

"Afraid?"

"My very first book was a smashing success, and I was on top. I liked being on top. It was like a drug. I was batting a thousand, and everyone was kissing my ass. Another book would have ruined it, as nothing could have lived up to *Red Dog Summer*. I would be seen as another has-been writer—a one hit wonder. The way I saw it, all I could do was fail. I love writing, but winning the prize, well, it made me a prisoner of my own fear of failure. Frankly, I took the easy way out and never published again. In many ways, winning the Pulitzer was the worst thing that ever happened to me."

"Whoa," he whispered, shocked by her stark candor.

Not looking at him, she said, "Get the hell out of my office."

Speechless, Kieran turned and left.

Professor Wills looked at the closed door for nearly a minute before she said, "God speed, Kieran Nash. I am so sorry."

CHAPTER 3

This is one mean truck. Bet it would be a hoot in a muddy field. Bad thing is it will be a pain to park."

Kieran walked around the heavy-duty machine shaking his head. Taking the key fob, he unlocked the door and peered inside the surprisingly comfortable interior.

"Kieran. Kieran Nash."

Kieran looked around and found Jen leaning out of the window of a sparkling, red Cadillac SUV.

"Hey, Jen," he said, stepping down.

"I didn't know you drove a tank." Jen chuckled. "Did you join the army?"

"I suppose. I did get drafted."

"What are you doing with it?"

"Since you turned me down for dinner, I picked up an odd job. I'm to deliver this beast to a client a few states away. Easy money."

"You can drive this on the highway?"

Kieran snorted at her sarcasm. "What are you doing here, Jen?"

"Gramie picked me up after you disappeared into Professor Wills's lair. What happened? I'm dying to know."

"We tossed back a few drinks, and she told me how great a writer I was," he said.

"Okay, then don't tell me," she said.

"Where are you two ladies going?"

"We were going to dinner when Gramie saw the orange tank and wanted a closer look."

The passenger side door popped open and out came an elderly woman, leaning on a gold-tipped wooden cane. Elegantly dressed, her head swathed in a colorful headscarf, Gramie wore an enormous pair of designer sunglasses that concealed most of her upper face. All that was evident was a small, pert nose and a full pair of ruby-red-stained lips.

"Gramie? Where you going?" Jen asked. "We have reservations."

"It's my birthday, so put a sock in it," the elderly woman said as she moved toward Kieran. "I have to see this machine. It looks like something from a bad movie."

Rolling her eyes, and knowing arguing was useless, Jen opened her door and followed.

"My, that's an interesting vehicle, young man. Bet you could see this color from space."

"Yep," Kieran said. "It does kind of stand out."

"Where are your manners, young lady?" Gramie asked. "Introduce your gorgeous friend."

Kieran blushed at the compliment.

"Kieran Nash," Jen said, showing her obvious irritation, "this is my Gramie Keller. Better known as Carol Deville-Keller."

"At your service, Mr. Nash," she said.

"Gramie was an actress back when dinosaurs ruled the Earth."

"Nice to meet you, Mrs. Keller. By the way, happy birthday. I hear you are turning twenty-nine."

"Thank you," she said, taking Kieran by the arm. "By the look of me, it was a hard twenty-nine years, but I appreciate the remark. The mark of a true gentleman is how to properly bullshit a lady."

Kieran chuckled.

"Wait a minute," he said. "Carol Deville? *The* Carol Deville who played the femme fatale in the noir classic, *Color Me Dead*?"

Gramie laughed. "I wouldn't call it a classic, but yes, guilty as charged."

"I loved that movie! You played the heroine's crazy sister. Those jealous of your beauty tried to kill you but ended up scarring your face instead. You hunted down and killed those who ruined your face while framing your sister for the murders. You were fantastic. An underrated noir flick if there ever was one."

"Kieran fancies himself as a modern Raymond Chandler," Jen said.

"A writer? I'm impressed," Gramie said. "Looks and talent as well."

"Now who's bullshitting who?" Kieran asked, his face beaming.

Gramie squeezed his arm and smiled.

"I will make it a point to check out all your movies," he said.

"Please, save yourself the trouble. I wasn't an A-list actress. The studios stuck me in everything from tacky sci-fi to B westerns. I even did a couple of serials. *Color Me Dead* was definitely the high water mark of my career, despite the fact you couldn't see my face. Honey, I don't want to be the cause of inflicting that level of cheese on a young growing mind. It would be cruel and unusual abuse."

Kieran laughed.

"Would you show me your ride, Mr. Nash?"

"I would love to, ma'am, but I just laid eyes on the monstrosity, myself. Haven't even sat in it yet."

Gramie smiled. "When you have her broken in properly, I expect a ride. The ride of a lifetime."

"I would love to, but I have to deliver this beast to its owner who lives a few states away. In fact, I have to leave pretty soon."

"Too bad. It looks like an adventure waiting to happen."

"Exactly what I was thinking," he said. "Like minds."

Gramie smiled and squeezed his arm.

"Gramie, we have to go," Jen said. "We're holding up Kieran."

"Shush, I'm enjoying the company of Mr. Nash, so keep your silly beret on, honey."

Jen frowned, swallowing a sharp retort.

Kieran smiled. He instantly liked the feisty woman.

"Do you have a girlfriend, Kieran?"

"No, ma'am. There's a girl I like, but apparently, I'm not her type. My six-pack is a few cans short."

Jen stuck her tongue out at Kieran, which made him laugh.

"That sounds like an immature, stupid girl. A real woman would see the man you are and never let you go. I suggest, for your own good, you tell the dumb bitch to take a hike."

"Sound advice."

"Kieran, life's too short to waste time running after the wrong girl."

"Maybe. I haven't given up hope just yet. She might come around."

"Look, kiddo, walk away, and you'll come out of this a winner."

"How do you figure?"

"You walk away from someone who doesn't love you, you haven't lost a thing, but, on the other hand, this oblivious girl is losing someone who cares. It's her loss, not yours."

"You have a point," he said, looking at Jen. "I'm wasting my time."

The color drained from her face as Jen's jaw dropped.

"Gramie, how about we ditch Jen and let me take you out? I'll show you the time of your life."

"Oh, if I were a million years younger, I'd take you up on that, honey."

Kieran chuckled.

"Kieran, honey, much as I enjoy the company of a real man, I have to go before Jen has conniptions."

"Ma'am, may I ask a small favor?"

"A favor?"

"I would love an autograph."

"Sorry honey," she said, patting his arm. "My arthritis is such I can't grip a pen."

"Oh. I'm sorry," he said.

"How about you doing me a favor, Kieran? It's my birthday. Would it be too much to ask for a birthday hug?"

"Gramie!" Jen said as she turned crimson with embarrassment.

"I'd be honored," Kieran said.

He gently gathered the elderly woman in his arms, careful not to hurt her, and was surprised as she hugged him back with strength and enthusiasm beyond her years. Gramie held the red-faced Kieran close in a lingering, sensual embrace. "They deserved what they got, copper," she whispered. "For what they did to me, death was too good for them."

"It wasn't for you to decide, Mary," he said, reciting the last line from the movie. "That is what the law is for."

"You two want to get a room?" Jen asked.

"That was fantastic," he said. "This is the best day of my life. Thank you, Mrs. Keller."

"No, thank you, Kieran," Gramie said softly as she gave him a gentle kiss on the cheek. "To meet someone who hasn't forgotten an old has-been was a treat for me. You have made my birthday very special."

"Happy birthday, Mrs. Keller."

"Before I go," Gramie said, "would you take a word of advice from an old broad who has been around the block a few times?"

"Of course."

"When you find that special woman who loves you more than life itself, please, for the love of God, don't be stupid and walk away. For both your sakes."

Before he could reply, she turned away abruptly and, without looking back, quickly made her way to the SUV.

છ૦છ૦

Jen crawled in behind the wheel. Gramie closed her own door and lay back in her seat, as if the experience had sucked the life from her.

"That was weird." After giving Kieran the stink eye, Jen started the car and pulled from the parking lot.

Gramie removed her expensive sunglasses and dabbed at her tear-filled eyes with a tissue.

"Gramie? Are you crying?"

"Just thinking about the one true love of my life and how I'll never see him again."

"I'm sorry. Great-Granddad was the best."

Gramie looked at Jen patted her hand and smiled. "He was a good man. You know, Jen, I like your friend Keith."

"His name is Kieran."

"Oh."

Jen gave a scornful chuckle. "Gramie, before you start on me, it's obvious, Kieran Nash isn't my style."

"What do you, or anyone born in this generation, know about style?"

"I know what I want. I don't want Kieran."

"I like Keith. The boy's ten times better than Jamal."

"You love to throw Jamal Smith in my face, don't you? And by the way, Keith's name is Kieran."

"Jamal was pretty to look at," Gramie said. "I'll give you that. However, the boy was a grade-A douche bag. When you introduced us and mentioned to him that I was once an actress, he asked what porn flick I starred in, for Christ's sake. What kind of dunderhead says a thing like that?"

"Okay, I admit Jamal was an embarrassing mistake."

"You should find a nice guy who loves you more than their own reflection in the mirror. A real man, instead of a 'paper tiger.'"

"Kieran—a *real* man? Are you serious? He's a ragged mess half a step above a homeless street person."

"Honey, men, in general, are ragged messes. They can't help it. It's up to a good woman to smooth out the edges and *make* him the man *she* wants. That's the way it works. Look for potential and then go from there."

"Like Granddad?"

"Exactly. I couldn't stand your grandad when I first met him, but he grew on me. Well, after I whipped him into shape, that is."

"I thought you got knocked up."

"Your mother has a big mouth."

"Okay, Gramie. I'll think about giving Keith a shot."

"Keith? I thought his name was Kieran?"

Jen looked at Gramie and rolled her eyes as both women laughed.

Gramie clutched her arm, the smile fading from her face.

"Gramie what's wrong?"

"I think we should have my birthday party in the emergency room, honey. Like right now."

∽∾∽

Professor Wills collapsed into her chair. Pouring another drink, she drained it in a single gulp. The hard knot in her stomach was now the size of a flaming bowling ball. With shaking hands, she grabbed her cell and punched in a number.

"I've done what you want," she whispered. "Kieran Nash is on his way."

"I know. I can see him," the woman's voice on the other end of the line said, "right on schedule. I'm impressed. Did you give him the digital recorder?"

"Yes, I did everything you asked, but what about my Raymond?"

"Within the hour, all drug charges against your son will be dropped. I suggest you have a long talk with Raymond about finding honest work."

"Oh, thank God," Professor Wills whispered. "Kieran—is he—I mean—nothing is going to—"

"Do yourself a favor and forget that you ever knew, Kieran Nash," the voice said. "Did you fill out the proper paperwork and talk to the dean?"

"Yes. Kieran is no longer in my class and will soon be expelled from the university for copying a paper from the internet."

"Excellent. Now you have more than covered your bases. Kieran is officially out, and no one will miss him."

"What are you going to do to him?" she asked.

"That is none of your concern, Professor Wills. Console yourself in the fact that your precious, only child, isn't going to prison for the rest of his life. Have a good day, Professor. It was very nice doing business with you."

Dropping the phone on the desk, the professor sprang from her chair and rushed to the room's only window. Looking down, she watched Kieran interact with Jen Keller and Gramie.

Professor Wills stood at the window, her eyes glued to Kieran while her mind was a convoluted mess. She wanted to scream a warning—to stop him before it was too late, but she remained silent.

Feeling like Judas, Professor Wills watched long after he climbed aboard the Unimog and disappeared into traffic.

My God, what have I done?

CHAPTER 4

T his is incredible," Kieran said as he watched a video he found on the net about the abilities of the Unimog. He skimmed the owner's manual, which proclaimed his particular version a *Unimog Custom Expedition Edition*.

Kieran produced the digital recorder and inserted a battery.

"Might as well break in this recorder thing the professor gave me," he said. "While I have always hated hearing the sound of my own voice, this gizmo will make taking notes a lot easier. Bet this is the first present Professor Wills gave anyone…well, other than an ulcer, that is."

Kieran pushed the record button.

"This monster I'm driving is interesting, to say the least. It sports a generator, a one hundred gallon water tank, equipped with a Swiss engineered water filter able to strain out and sterilize every known contaminate. An electric winch, powerful enough to crane the beast up a vertical shaft if need be, and oversized fuel tank giving it nearly a thousand mile range. I'm surprised it doesn't sport a couple of fifty-caliber machine guns and flame throwers. Although built like a tank, this baby doesn't ride like one. The truck has a sweet ride and even has an input for my MP-Three player.

"Talk about a nice set up. I hate to give this bad boy up. I'd trade it for my Korean rattletrap any day of the week.

Hey, since this is more than a truck or van, that means it needs a proper name."

Kieran thought a moment and then smiled. "I proclaim thee, *The Juggernaut*," he said in his best Shakespearian voice. He formed the sign of the cross and clapped his hands twice. "It's official. I'll call you Jug for short."

He snorted and turned red as he beheld a snickering woman with flaming red hair pumping gas a few feet away who observed his antics with great amusement.

He smiled and waved as he raised the darkly tinted door window. "Forgot I was in public. Anyway, where was I? Oh, yeah." Kieran picked up his recorder. "While this truck is my first choice to ride out the apocalypse or Russian invasion, for a furniture van, overkill's an understatement. The Unimogs I saw online were pricy, but none even came close to this baby. While I'm far from an expert on vehicles, this truck feels as if it were made for a specific purpose and not a clone rolled off an assembly line. Not to mention the manual called it an Expedition Custom Edition. This kraut wagon must have cost a bundle. Surely, a Ford or Chevy would have been forty times cheaper.

"Professor Wills's sister must be rolling in the dough to spring for this ride. I'd bet real money that it easily costs more than a four-year college degree...and I'm talking a nice school, not just the glorified diploma mill I attend."

To emphasize his point, Kieran rapped his knuckles against the thick steel bulkhead behind the passenger cab. "Ridiculous way to transport some old woman's pots and pans, if you ask me, but, hey, who am I? I'm just the dumb monkey paid to drive and not ask questions. If they want to waste money, that's their business. One day, when I'm a stinking rich author with *two* Pulitzers under my belt, I'll have to buy one. Now that I think about it, I could use this baby in a story. Perhaps, driven by a lone human survivor fighting zombie hordes in a post-apocalyptic world."

Kieran glanced at his watch. "Break is over, I have to go."

While the Black Angels set the proper road trip atmosphere, Kieran cracked the top of an energy drink and gulped it down. His belly full and the massive fuel tank topped off, he pulled back onto the interstate.

After traveling several miles, pausing his music, Kieran produced the slim, digital recorder from his jacket pocket. "So far, this impromptu trip has gone smoothly. I'm on I-Eighty-One, rolling through Tennessee, should make it to Montgomery with time to spare." Kieran smiled. "It was great to meet an honest-to-God movie star. I felt a real kinship, which is odd since I really don't care for old people. They smell funny, tend to frown at me a lot, and ask when I'm going to cut my hair and get a real job.

"Carol Deville makes me rethink the stereotype. Huh, her name sounds like a stage name. I tried to look her up, but I got very little. A slew of B-movie titles, but no photos, except from the movie, *Color Me Dead*. That was no help as her face was concealed by makeup. From what I could find, none of her movies were available. When I get back, I'll put Fat Jimmy on the trail. The boy has many, many faults, but he's part bloodhound. I'll have him find me her movies. I'll bet real money she was something back in the day. The old gal has a million dollar personality, that's for sure. Never met many pretty girls with a pleasant personality, let alone as stellar as Carol's. Jen's slightly above average, but even Jen has her moments when I want to drop her off a building.

"Carol hit the nail on the head. I like Jen, but it's obvious this crush is going nowhere fast. Why do I beat my head against a wall, when it never works out in my favor? No more. I call the shots from now on. I'll find me a girl who wants me for me."

Kieran paused his recorder. He'd relished his newfound resolve for nearly an hour when a sleek sports car zipped past his lumbering vehicle. Kieran caught sight of a large, yellow bumper sticker that read, *Why are you here?* The sticker was from a Baptist Church from some Tennessean town he had never heard of, intended to make one think of the Big Picture. For Kieran, it had a different effect.

As if a wooden shoe were dropped into a mass of spinning gears, the seemingly benign query jarred him. Jen and Carol Deville were no longer paramount in his thoughts. As he looked around the cab, his mind speed-shifted onto a new track.

Kieran resumed recording. "Why am I here, driving the Jug, barreling down a dark highway on a Friday night? I know the arrangement Professor Wills offered me, but why me, specifically? Just because I'm failing her class, she offers me this sweet, too-good-to-be-true deal? Professor Wills is contemptuous of everyone, and I've never heard one person, whether student or staff, have a single good thing to say about her. Yet, out of the blue, she gives me a free pass? Professor Wills doesn't know anything about Kieran Nash, yet she hands this expensive truck and all this antique furniture over to me, just like that. For all she knows, I could be a stinking thief, sell the entire lot, and disappear. It was a dumb move. Funny thing is, by no stretch of the imagination, is Professor Wills stupid. A calculating, heinous bitch, but definitely not dumb.

"I'm completely bumfuzzled. Not to mention, I say a single word in the right ear, and it'll be her, not me, in hot water. This entire deal will make her name academic mud, Pulitzer notwithstanding.

"The voices in my head are screaming that she's up to something. That this deal is somehow wrong. The problem is, I can't take a chance. I need that grade, so I have no choice but to play this to the end. I pray those words will not come back to haunt me."

CHAPTER 5

L eft turn, five hundred feet," the GPS said. "Exit Four. Follow the ramp, one hundred feet. Turn right."

"Now why is this thing telling me to get off the Interstate?" After a moment, he sighed. "The short cut. I almost forgot. I'm not here to think, I'm here to follow directions."

Kieran glanced down at the fuel gauge. The fuel needle barely moved from F. "I'll stop and top off the tank. Not to mention top off mine."

Putting on his turn signal, Kieran took the ramp and left the wide freeway.

ୡୢୡ

The Jug's tank topped off, Kieran munched on a hero sandwich when he fished out his cell and hit speed dial.

"Hello?"

"Hi, Mom," he said.

"Kieran?" Heather Nash asked. "What happened? Are you all right?"

"Excuse me?"

"Calling me on a Friday night? Something's wrong."

"Don't worry," he said. "I just wanted to let you know I got a small job and will be out of Virginia for a day."

"Another job?"

"Hey, it pays the bills. I'm delivering a load of furniture."

"Just please be careful. I like having you around."

"I love you too, Mom. Give my regards to Mr. Fizzles, and I'll see you next week."

Kieran finished his meal and, armed with a sack of energy bars and drinks, climbed back into the cab.

ᘓᘓ

Fifty yards away from Kieran and the Jug, a thickly built man in an orange, long-sleeved T-shirt meticulously cleaned his ten-year old Honda's windshield of bug corpses. Seemingly, intent on nothing short of perfect windshield clarity, he discreetly watched Kieran with keen interest as he finished his meal and climbed into the Unimog.

As the red glow of the Jug's taillights disappeared over the hill, the man tossed the squeegee into the brackish-water-filled bucket and produced a cell phone.

"Our boy's on time and is headed your way," he whispered. "Get ready."

ᘓᘓ

Kieran followed the GPS's precise, if somewhat tortuous, directions.

Highways gave way to state roads that gave way to poorly managed side roads until he left asphalt all together. Finally, Kieran found himself on a narrow, pothole-infested gravel road that barely accommodated his oversized vehicle. The rolling, open countryside had given way to sharp hills and claustrophobic dense woods that blocked most of the overcast night sky.

His apprehension, which had been growing exponentially since he had left the interstate, had now given birth to fear.

Kieran thumbed the recorder and cleared his throat. "Well, future fans of mine, according to the old clock on the dash, it's almost midnight. It looks like the professor's directions have landed me in scenic Cocke County, Tennessee, if that last, rusted, buckshot filled road sign I passed was accurate. If you ask me, this looks like a good place to get murdered. Bet this place would be appealing in the daylight with all the bright, autumn colors, but, at night, it just looks creepy as hell."

Kieran noticed a flash in the sporadic bits of sky above him. Soon a rolling rumble reached his ears. "A thunderstorm—in October, for crying out loud? From the rumbling in the sky, looks like we're about to have a big blow—as if this road trip couldn't get any better."

"You have arrived at your destination," the GPS said dispassionately. "Have a nice day."

"No way," he exclaimed, bringing the truck to a stop in the middle of the leaf-carpeted country road. Looking around in the pitch darkness, Kieran pondered his next move. "That arrogant bitch may have won the Pulitzer Prize, but she doesn't know squat about programming a GPS. Now I'm lost in the middle of nowhere, Tennessee. So help me, if this is some prank, I'm going to whip somebody's ass. Got to turn the truck around and—"

In a bright flash of lightning, Kieran saw movement in his big side mirror. Another flash revealed several men approaching from the rear. Grabbing a flashlight from his backpack, he pointed it out the windows and illuminated a knot of men slowly approaching him in the darkness on three sides. They were all dressed in matching head-to-toe camouflage, their faces concealed by identical black ski masks. If that wasn't bad enough, they all carried AK-47 rifles, at the ready.

"I think it's time for this kid to be somewhere else," Kieran muttered as he slipped the truck into gear. "Oh, snap." Panicking, he saw five more armed strangers in the road ahead, just entering the beam of his headlights.

"Turn off the engine, and get out of that fancy truck, boy," came a voice dripping with a Tennessee twang. "We just want the truck. We don't want to hurt ya'll, but we will if you get any bright ideas."

"Screw that." Kieran flipped on a bank of halogen lights affixed to a rail over the cab. Blinded, the strangers yelped and scattered as Kieran floored the gas pedal, and the truck lurched forward. The quiet, Tennessee night exploded with the roar of his engine, the sound of gunfire and cursing. "Move it, *assholes*!" he screamed as he drove wildly toward the armed thugs.

As the would-be carjackers, scrambled for safety, Kieran rocketed up a gentle rise and, with a groan, slowed to a stop.

Some two hundred yards away, directly across the only escape route, lay a freshly felled oak tree. Looking desperately for a way out, he spied a narrow gravel road that darted to his right. Without hesitation, he gunned the powerful diesel engine and fishtailed down the glorified footpath as gunfire erupted behind him.

ومحو

As Kieran's bouncing red taillights disappeared into the tangled woods, one of the thugs pulled off her ski mask and shook her dark red hair free. With a smile, she produced a cell phone. "The deed's done, George," she said. "Pay the men and send them on their way. They've earned a month off."

"That's it?" George asked. "Boss, I've followed you on several jobs—"

"And made a boatload of cash, too," she said.

"Yeah. The thing is all those other jobs made sense, or at least to me. This job's nuts."

"I know, George. I don't get it, either."

"An awful lot of trouble and expense, breaking into a freaking police station and stealing the evidence so a spoiled, half-assed drug dealer could walk. If that weren't bad enough, we waited around for hours in the dark just to

scare some stupid kid. If you ask me, boss, this is completely nuts."

"You'll get no argument from me, George," she said.
"However, the money paid us isn't nuts and, from my point
of view, that's all that matters."

"Good point."

"Now bring the truck and drag this tree off the road, so
we can go home. Tomorrow, I have a date on a Mexican
beach to see my daughter get married. If I miss my flight,
heads'll roll. Yours will be the first."

"Gotcha, boss. On my way."

CHAPTER 6

The threatened thunderstorm arrived with a vengeance, forcing the frantic Kieran to click on his windshield wipers. The heavy downpour along with the narrowing path forced him to slow down, as the patch of woods became a dense forest. As if competing with the heavy rain and falling leaves, the lightning and thunder amped up their efforts, as well, which did nothing to settle his frazzled nerves.

"I'm in a world of deep trouble," he whispered.

With shaking hands, he fished out his cell. Clumsily he dialed nine-one-one, but he was far from a cell tower and, to his despair, reception was nonexistent.

"Figures," he said, as he put the phone away. "I'm lost in Podunk, Tennessee, in the middle of a freak October thunder storm, being chased by a bunch of gun-toting rednecks. If worse comes to worse, I can ditch the truck and hide in the woods. If I survive this, when I get my hands on Professor Wills, I'm going to wring her scrawny neck."

Rolling easily through a deep, wide, storm-swollen stream that washed over the hood, Kieran drove up and over a steep, muddy hill as the six-wheeled drive dug deep. The trail ended at the stream, so Kieran made his own road through a stand of small, bare saplings and low bushes.

He laughed and whooped for joy. "The Jug can just about climb a freaking tree. Even if those assholes had a

Hummer, they couldn't have crossed that creek. I may just get out of this mess yet."

He kissed the steering wheel.

While he attempted to get his bearings, a dense, eerie fog appeared out of nowhere and enveloped the Jug.

"Just great. Now I can't see a thing."

Afraid to linger, Kieran moved slowly forward. To his dismay, the massive bank of lights mounted on the roof—that should have sliced easily through the mist—were stymied by the odd, thick haze.

Kieran felt as though he was driving through an enormous, yellow-tinged cotton swab, while bushes and low hanging limbs brushed and scraped the sides of the tough truck. Moving down a gentle hill, Kieran heard a low, throbbing hum as if someone had switched on a massive transformer.

"What's that sound? I feel as if I'm driving on a gigantic speaker cone."

As if in response to the sound, the truck lights began to flicker, as did his instrument panel.

"No, no, no," he said as the diesel engine sputtered and gasped. "Please, baby, you can't die."

The engine and the lights died, as if killed by a single switch. Kieran grabbed his flashlight, but it, too, was dead.

Suddenly, his skin, teeth, even his hair, began to tingle, as the cab of the truck filled with an overwhelming smell of ozone. "What's that—"

He never finished his question as his body, the truck, the universe itself, shattered. Somewhere, far away, he was aware of someone screaming. It slowly dawned on him that the screams were his.

Whether it lasted a split second or an eternity, he didn't know, but as abruptly as it began, it was over. Everything was back to normal, almost.

Dazed and nauseated, blinded by brilliant, fierce light shining into the cab, Kieran realized the truck was rolling free and slammed on the breaks. His head swimming, all he could think about was getting out of the unexpectedly claus-trophobic cabin. Fumbling the door latch open, he fell out. Expecting to be up to his chin in cold, rain-soaked weeds and sticky mud, to his surprise he crunched onto dry, red sand, whereupon he threw up, twice.

While his stomach rolled and rumbled, he squinted against the brutal sun light that only a moment ago was the cool darkness of a lush, wet forest.

His mind reeling, Kieran struggled to his feet. He felt oddly lighter, as if he had suddenly shed twenty-five pounds. Even the air had a strange, slightly different texture and tasted coppery.

"This can't be good," he mumbled as he leaned against the cool metal side of the truck. The forest, the night, along with the Tennessee countryside, was gone. In its place, was a crimsoned-hued, rocky desert, scorched by an angry sun hanging high in a dazzling blue sky. Kieran glanced at his watch and felt a chill.

One-seventeen a.m.

The modest breeze that seemed to emanate from a blast furnace, moaning eerily through the wind-sculpted canyons and petrified formations like a lost soul, did little to ease his jangled nerves.

"Either east Tennessee has one heck of a desert, or one of those stupid rednecks has killed me, and I've gone to Hell." He slipped off his hoodie and looked around. In a fit of temper, he kicked the side of the truck. "Nah. If I died, then the truck wouldn't be here, or my watch. But if I'm not dead, and this isn't Hell, then where am I?"

Kieran touched the side of the truck. The Jug lay covered with a spotty cover of wet, yellow-and-red-hued leaves.

"Hey, this thing is still wet."

He pulled free a small, supple leafy stem caught in the fender well. The knobby tires lay incased in rapidly drying black mud.

"This proves I didn't dream being lost in the woods, but where's the forest?" He looked in all directions but saw nothing but the seemingly endless desert. "I'm getting a really bad feeling about this."

He glanced at his truck and frowned as he felt a cold knot form in his stomach. Looking around the desert and then back at his vehicle, it occurred to him that the color scheme matched. Not only did the jarring pattern match, it broke up the shape of the truck.

"If I didn't know better, I'd say the Jug's painted to blend in. *It is*. Damn it, the thing's camouflaged."

His feet crunched slightly. Looking down, he spied a perfect circle, some twenty feet in diameter. It was as if an enormous die had been stamped deeply into the crusty sand. He and the truck were dead center of the elaborate pattern.

"This is making my head hurt."

Kieran reached through the open driver's door for a bottle of water and a pack of peanut butter crackers from his stash of road snacks lying on the floorboard. The crackers settled his churning stomach, chasing away his nausea.

Desperately, he tried his cell, only to see the infuriating, *No Service Available*. Sliding into the cab, he checked the GPS. The unit functioned, but could not receive a satellite signal.

"Well isn't that just great."

Closing the door, he tried the truck's ignition and smiled as the engine, after several tries, turned over.

"Thank you, Jesus," he breathed as he killed the engine. "At least that works."

Digging into his belongings, he slipped on a pair of retro glacier glasses and a baseball cap from his bag. Then he left the truck and trotted to the top of a nearby hill.

"This isn't good," he said as he beheld a vast desert that stretched from horizon to horizon dotted with the occasional, crumbling, flat-topped mesa. Tufts of a spiky, purple-hued plant dotted the rich, wind-sculpted landscape.

"I never saw a purple cactus before. For that matter, one that looked like a five foot tall Aloe Vera plant."

Kieran frowned. "Looks sort of like pictures I saw of

Monument Valley, but the last time I checked, Monument Valley was a couple thousand miles away on the other end of the freaking country. Professor Wills, if I ever get out of this mess, I'm kicking your wrinkled old ass to Mars and back."

The sound of a deep, resonating horn interrupted his thoughts. A few miles away he saw a line of five small dots moving along an ancient, dry riverbed.

A bugle? Riders on horseback…I think. Maybe they can help me get out of this sandbox.

Running back to the Mercedes and jumping behind the wheel, Kieran debated on trying to intercept them, but nixed the idea. Afraid that help would get away before he could find a path down, he sent out several long bursts of the Jug's horn.

"Come on, I'm right here," he said as he sent out another blast. "All right, they see me." He exited the truck and waved his arms wildly while shouting, "Over here!"

The small dots stopped as one. After milling a bit, they then changed course, and moved rapidly in his direction.

"Must be a group of Native Americans or cowboys out for a ride. Maybe they can explain what's going on."

The five riders moved quickly over the rough ground and, soon, Kieran could make them out clearly. The riders were dressed similar to Arabs, covered head-to-toe in flowing robes. Four wore robes made from a coarse white cloth, while the fifth was dressed in rich blue silk.

"Hey, wait a minute. What are those things they're riding? They sure aren't horses."

The riders' shaggy steeds were, in most respects, similar to zebras. But instead of white and black stripes, they were a dull orange and black pattern that blended perfectly with the surrounding desert. The most shocking thing about the strange animals was that, perched at the end of a long sinewy neck, sat a head that was a closer kin to that of a lop-eared tiger than a horse.

"I'm getting a real bad feeling about this."

The riders slid to a stop, some twenty feet away from the stunned Kieran. Concealed as they were by their robes, none of their features was apparent, other than their enormous size. Rail thin, the riders easily stood over seven feet tall. They spoke excitedly among themselves for a few moments. Their high-pitched chittering language was strange, and Kieran was sure he had never heard anything like it before.

"Hey, fellows," he said, trying to be calm. "I seem to be a bit lost. Could you help me out?"

The rider who wore the rich blue robes, dismounted and approached to within ten feet of Kieran. He pulled down his hood and Kieran gasped in shock. The thing standing before him looked somewhat human, but its features were oddly distorted. Its head was completely hairless, not shaved, but as if hair never grew upon its body. The almond-shaped eyes were too large for the face, and the nose was a bit too broad. Its mouth was the most normal feature, but it was curled back in an almost animal-like snarl, showing off sharpened and filed teeth.

"English," the blue rider said in English tinged with a slight accent. "It is a good day. We have caught an Earther. May Ahlena be praised."

"No—I—I—" Kieran said. "I'm an American."

The blue rider gave Kieran a contemptuous snarl. "Tigg, take the *beast*."

One of the riders dismounted and, from a leather pack strapped to the rear of his hideous mount, produced a coil of thin brown rope.

"Hold it right there," Kieran said. "I don't know who—or even what—the hell you guys are, but I'm not playing along."

The blue rider laughed. "The animal has fire. Break him."

Two of the white-robed riders dismounted. One made a lariat and began to slowly twirl it over its head. The other produced a wicked-looking fifteen-foot-long bullwhip.

The blue rider laughed as the bullwhip snapped loudly. "All I ask is that you don't kill him," the blue rider said in English. It was obvious that it was for Kieran's benefit. "I want that honor for myself."

Kieran picked up a fist-sized rock, which made the five laugh.

"I like animals with fire," the blue rider said. "They are far more fun to play with."

"This is getting out of hand," Kieran said. "You desert mutants are crazy if you think I'm going to let you whip and hogtie me."

Winding up, Kieran let the rock fly. The stone flew unerringly and would have struck the blue rider squarely in his enormous left eye, however, to Kieran's astonishment, the projectile stopped dead, mere inches away from its intended target.

"What's going on?" Kieran asked in amazement.

The stone floated in thin air for a moment, before it rocketed back toward Kieran. Unprepared for the unexpected turn of events, Kieran failed to duck. The stone caught him a hard, glancing blow to the side of the head, sending his cap and sunglasses flipping away. Dazed, he stumbled back and hit the ground hard beside the truck, his face wet with blood. Again, the group erupted into laughter.

Sorry freak bastards. They're laughing at me, Kieran thought, as the world spun wildly. Rising to his feet, he stumbled toward the open door of the truck. To his astonishment, the door slammed shut, as if by an invisible hand.

"This spooky crap's getting old," he said, wiping his mouth with the back of his hand.

He was prepared to make a run for it, when the blue rider, stretched out its hand toward the Jug. With a sharp groan of metal and creak of springs, the massive truck sprang a foot into the air and hung there, as if suspended by a crane. Chunks of dried mud flaked off the wheels and undercarriage falling upon the glass and red sand below.

"That's not possible." Dazed and bleeding, Kieran

paused, gaping in astonishment at the miracle before him.

With a flick of the blue rider's wrist, the ten-thousand-pound truck spun quickly, the rear section swatting Kieran like a housefly amid a colorful spray of dried oak and maple leaves.

With a deep grunt, Kieran flew several feet before landing in a crumpled heap in cloud of red dust, his ears filled with ringing and his attackers' sadistic laughter.

Just before he lapsed into unconsciousness, Kieran watched as the blue rider's head exploded.

CHAPTER 7

"Oh my head," Kieran moaned and cracked opened his eyes to a hazy darkness. He felt himself jostled and bounced about, which did nothing but drive deeper the "nail" in his poor, aching head. His nose, throat, and eyes burned, and he coughed sharply several times.

"Oh, God, is somebody smoking?"

Suddenly, a dim, yellow light snapped on, illuminating his surroundings.

Kieran discovered that he lay on the hard, rubberized floor of what he assumed to be the back of his truck. His head rested on a dirty, green backpack. Three, square vents on each side, which to him looked like gun ports, allowed light and air to circulate inside the metal box. Hidden floor vents blew cooled air into the truck making the space bearable.

Sitting on either side of him, resting on folding benches built into the side of the truck, to his enormous relief were men, not the mutants he encountered. Kieran counted ten men, uniformed in green and carrying rifles.

To his disgust, three of the soldiers were smoking 'black lungers.'

It was what his granddad used to call non-filtered cigarettes. They were talking in hushed tones, but in a language Kieran didn't understand, yet it seemed tantalizingly familiar.

Who are these guys and what happened to the desert mu-

tants? Are these guys prisoners of the mutants? No way. They're armed to the teeth. They look like soldiers, but no way they are US. What kind of mess have I stumbled into?

The men looked to be the same age as Kieran, but there was a hardened look in their eye, that made them seem older, more mature than someone of his generation. Their dirty, green camouflaged uniforms looked odd as well.

Kieran wrinkled his nose in disgust. The air was thick with cigarette smoke along with the stench of gun oil and sour sweat. Reaching up, he discovered his wound had been cleaned and bandaged.

"*Sieht aus wie Dornröschen wach ist,*" said one, with a chuckle.

Kieran tried to rise, but a man held him down.

"Lie still. You took a nasty shot to the head. You may have a *gehirnerschütterung*…mm…concussion," the dark-haired soldier said in a thick accent. Kieran noticed the soldier had a small red cross on a white background, sewn to his camouflaged uniform.

A metal canteen was thrust at him, and Kieran drank his fill of tepid water. The truck bounced, and the water sloshed over his face, making him sputter and choke. A smiling man, with short-clipped blond hair wearing round wire-rimmed glasses, offered him a cigarette from a crumpled pack.

"Welcome to Barsoom, Amerikaner," he said, his blue eyes twinkling with amusement.

"No thanks," Kieran said. "Who are you guys, and what is a Barsoom? And, uh, what happened to those freaky things that attacked me?"

Kieran looked up at one particularly lean soldier, who was busy cleaning his scoped rifle. While the rifle was unquestionably new, it struck Kieran as archaic, something you would normally see in an old World War Two movie. The man paused in his cleaning and pulled something from his shirt pocket. He dropped five, spent brass rifle cartridges on Kieran's chest.

"You are welcome, Amerikaner," he said, without expression. On his weird, rimless helmet, was a stylized diving eagle clutching an all too familiar symbol of evil.

"For God's sake. Is that a *swastika*?"

"What would you expect a squad from the First Fallschirmjäger to wear, Amerikaner?" asked the bespectacled soldier. "Roses?"

"Oh great," Kieran said. "I'm either in a coma, or I've fallen in with a bunch of skinheads playing dress up. This trip is getting better and better."

"*Was sind Skinheads?*" one of the troopers asked.

"Never mind. Not enough piercings and tattoos, not to mention I don't hear any blaring death metal. I'll say one thing though, this is a vivid delusion."

The medic banged on the metal bulkhead and shouted, "*Hauptmann Zimmer, der Amerikanischen ist wach!*"

Moments later, the truck lurched to a stop, and, except for the medic, the soldiers grabbed their gear and piled out. Kieran rejoiced as the smoky haze quickly dissipated.

Kieran felt the truck rock slightly and heard someone bark orders in German, or at least he thought it was German. The only German he had ever heard before was in old war movies. All he knew for sure was that it wasn't English, and he didn't understand a word of it.

A new soldier appeared at the truck's rear doors. He wore a similar camouflaged uniform as the others but bore the insignia of an officer. The officer looked to be around thirty and wore a stern expression, as if he carried the weight of the world on his shoulders. In his hand, he held Kieran's bulging backpack.

"*Gebt mir einen augenblick allein mit dem, Amerikanischen,*" the officer said.

"Ja," the medic said as he grabbed his medical pack and exited the truck. The officer climbed in and shut the doors behind him. Switching on the light, he took off his helmet and sat next to Kieran.

Kieran estimated that the officer was about six foot with

sandy-blond hair and vivid blue eyes. Expecting a lot of shouting and threats of violence, to Kieran's surprise, he gave him a warm smile.

"Kieran Nash, I presume?" the officer asked in flawless English. "I am Captain Udo Zimmer of the First Fall-schirmjäger Division."

"How did you know my name?"

"I hope you forgive me, but while you were out, I took the liberty of going through your bag."

"You mean you went through my personal property without my permission," Kieran said as he struggled to sit. "Then took off with my truck."

"We could have just let those things murder you, but we went out of our way to rescue your ungrateful ass. Yes, we are regular highway brigands."

Kieran felt uncomfortable.

"Sorry, Captain, I have had a really weird day. You know, it was probably a hallucination, but I could have sworn that they hit me with my own truck. Funny, huh?"

Zimmer did not laugh.

"Kieran, do you have any idea where you are, or how you got here?"

"I was in Tennessee trying to get away from some red-neck car jackers, when unexpectedly I'm here, wherever here is. Looks like Utah. Before I know it, I'm getting attacked by a bunch of clowns dressed like Arabs, riding tiger mutant...*things*."

"I see," Zimmer said.

"So, Captain, what's up with the Halloween costumes you and your peeps are wearing?"

"Peeps? Costumes?" Zimmer asked. "I am afraid I do not understand."

"I mean your friends and their Gestapo getups," Kieran said.

"For your information," Zimmer said curtly, "we are *not* Gestapo. We are *Fallschirmjäger*."

"Gesundheit. Hey, don't get me wrong, very realistic,

but the whole Nazi look, really pisses most folks off, if you know what I mean."

"Kieran, my friend, what year were you born?"

"What year? That's crazy. I—"

"The year," Zimmer exclaimed, his tone now iron hard. "Tell me."

"It was 1995. Why?"

"When you left Tennessee, what was the year?"

"October 12, 2014."

Captain Zimmer rubbed his face.

"What's wrong?" Kieran asked.

"I think I am losing my mind. Kieran, two days ago, for myself and my men, anyway, it was February 17, 1944. My men and I were assigned the defense of the Gustav line in Italy. This was two days after the destruction of the Monte Casino Abby. I don't know what happened or what agency brought us here, but I know it isn't Utah, Italy—or, for that matter, Earth. And by the way, those things did indeed hit you with your own truck, as if by magic."

"Get out of town," Kieran said.

Zimmer snorted. "Our resident science fiction aficionado, Private Ostermann, wants to call the place Barsoom."

"Look, *Fritz*, I don't have time for this crazy bull," Kieran said. "Alien worlds and Jew-murdering Nazi assholes? Give me a freaking break. Now if you'll excuse me, I have to get this truck to Alabama."

CHAPTER 8

Oberfeldwebel Oskar Hartmann and Medic Loewe, jumped aside as the rear doors of the Jug burst open. Kieran landed with a grunt as Captain Zimmer tossed him from the vehicle.

"Kiss my ass, you crazy son of a bitch," Kieran said as Zimmer dragged him roughly to his feet. Kieran threw a clumsy haymaker, which Zimmer not only blocked but, in one smooth motion, landed a stunning blow, knocking the breath from Kieran. He stumbled and went down gasping for breath. "Go—to hell," he gasped.

Zimmer grabbed him by the front of his shirt, pulled him up, and gave him a violent shake.

"Look around you, Kieran," Zimmer said. "Does this look like the green hills of Tennessee?"

Grudgingly, Kieran looked about the rocky canyons of the arid desert. "Well, no."

"Look there," Zimmer said, pointing up into the sky. "Since when does Earth have *two* moons?"

"This can't be happening," Kieran whispered as he beheld the amazing sight.

"Well, it is," Zimmer spat. Releasing his shirt, Zimmer pulled out a handkerchief and offered it to Kieran. "Clean yourself up."

"Hauptmann, should I place the prisoner under guard?" the oberfeldwebel asked in German as he pointed his rifle at Kieran.

Kieran blanched as he looked down the rifle barrel.

"We are not going to do anything to our *prisoner*, Oberfeldwebel. Kieran isn't our enemy. In fact, he is one of us now."

"Hauptmann," Hartmann said in German as he lowered his rifle. "Must I remind you that we are at war with the Americans?"

"Oberfeldwebel," Zimmer said, "we left that war behind on Earth. Now, get our new friend here some food and water."

"Sir!" Oberfeldwebel Hartmann said with a sharp salute. "Should I at least keep his equipment under guard?"

"No. I don't see it being a threat. Return it to Mr. Nash."

Obviously not happy, Hartmann, stalked away to fulfil Zimmer's orders.

"Rest well tonight, Kieran," Zimmer said. "For our unit to survive, we must be strong. God only knows what is in store for us here on this alien world. We are only as strong as our weakest link. I am afraid that link is you."

"Oh, God," Kieran moaned, "I've been drafted into the Nazi army. This trip has definitely turned into a nightmare."

"Oberfeldwebel Hartmann," Zimmer said. "Bright and early tomorrow morning you will teach Kieran here how to fight. You will teach him to be useful. Since Private Myer was killed in Italy, I think Kieran would make a competent ammo loader."

"With all due respect, Hauptmann," the oberfeldwebel said, his lean, leather-hard face showing not the slightest grin. "After observing his poor performance, I don't think the pup knows how to make a fist."

By now, the rest of the squad had gathered around and were laughing at the oberfeldwebel's comment.

"What did he say?" Kieran asked. "Is he making fun of me?"

"Kieran," Zimmer said. "You will be trained in how to defend yourself and be an asset to our mutual survival. Remember this: the thumb goes on the outside of a fist."

Kieran gave Zimmer the finger.

"Kieran," the medic said handing Kieran an MRE and a bottle of water. "I'm Klaus Loewe, by the way."

"'S'up, Klaus," Kieran said taking the plastic pouch.

Looking at the colorful packaging, he frowned. "Hold on. *Happy Camper Freeze-Dried Spaghetti and Meatballs?* I know for a fact they didn't make this in 'forty-four. Where did you fossils get this?"

"We *fossils* got it from you, of course," Zimmer said.

"Not from me, you didn't. All I had was some water and a sack of energy bars and drinks…well, other than the load of furniture. Wait a minute, what did you do with the junk I was hauling? I'm responsible."

Kieran followed Zimmer's gaze. Strapped to the top of the truck was a large, camouflaged, fiberglass shell.

"I had my men strap it to the top, so they could ride inside. I found the contents…interesting."

"*That* was inside the truck?" Kieran asked. "Where is all the furniture?"

"See for yourself," Zimmer said.

Giving Zimmer a puzzled glance, Kieran climbed the ladder built into the rear door of the truck. Popping open the access hatch, Kieran gasped.

Instead of furniture, the carrier was packed full of freeze-dried MREs, a case of cigarettes, and a well-equipped surgical medical pack. Along with the food were a dozen plastic ammo canisters and a few, heavy plastic waterproof cases, one of which was labeled, KLLIE-89 Drone.

To the side, there was a long object wrapped in foam and labeled, 'Panzerschreck,' in white letters, next to a plastic case marked 'Maschinengewehr.' In addition, there were eight metal Jerry cans, marked *DIESEL*.

"There must be enough food here for a month," Kieran said.

"With proper rationing, I estimate three," Zimmer said.

"I was told I was hauling a load of antiques. This makes no sense."

"It is indeed a fortuitous coincidence," Zimmer said. "You show up in a cleverly camouflaged all-terrain vehicle, the like of which I have never seen before, packed with vital supplies and ammunition that just happens to be chambered for our weapons. We only had a few magazines left for the forty-fours. Not to mention we were running low on food and water."

"I don't understand," Kieran whispered. "It's almost as if someone planned this. Like they knew we would meet."

"Almost?" Zimmer asked. "It seems that we are some-one's puppets, and the only way to cut the string is find out who they are and what they want."

"Hauptmann," Hartmann said, pointing a thick finger at Kieran. "This man knows more than he is telling. This has to be an Allied trick. I can make him talk."

"Belay that. Look around you. Why, Hollywood could not produce this in a thousand years. I believe our new friend here is as ignorant as he appears, and we are all in the same leaky boat."

"But, Hauptmann—"

A sharp glance from Zimmer stilled his objections.

"Guys," Kieran said, "let's pretend I don't understand your lingo, okay?"

Zimmer smiled slightly as Hartmann stalked away.

"So, General, once we find out who did this to us, then what?"

"We ask them politely to send us home." Zimmer put his arm around Kieran's shoulders and whispered, "Mr. Nash, we must come to an understanding before we can go any further."

"Understanding?"

"I am in charge here and what I say is *law*. You must understand this and comply, as my men do."

"Hold on, I'm not one of your men."

"*You* hold on, you disrespectful, immature boy," Zimmer snapped as he drove a gloved finger into Kieran's chest, pinning him to the side of the Jug. "I do not have time for your foolishness or your disrespect. We are in a fight for our lives. I am responsible for my men. However, under the circumstances, I am willing to take you under our protection."

"What if I don't want your protection?"

"I will give you a share of water and food. You may go anywhere you like."

"That truck, the food, and the water are mine."

"We need it. That makes it ours."

"That isn't right."

"Perhaps. Kieran, I promise you I will do my best to get us out of this predicament and get us home. All I ask in return is for you to follow orders and cooperate. Fight me, and you will lose."

Kieran gritted his teeth in frustration. "I see your point," he said, swallowing hard. "I don't like it, but I see your point."

"Good."

"I will follow your orders, but I won't like it. I still want to knock your block off."

Zimmer smiled. "If you would like to blow off some steam, we can settle this like men," he said, raising his fists.

"No," Kieran said, eyeing the tough soldier. "If it's all the same, I like my nose unbroken."

Zimmer snorted and slapped Kieran on the shoulder. "Eat, my friend. We have much to do."

"Do I get a gun?"

"Not until you are trained properly to use one, since I don't trust you not to shoot off your manhood."

"Thanks a lot."

"Since you know the vehicle the best, I am assigning you to be our driver."

CHAPTER 9

"You know this isn't half bad," Kieran said, digging into the pouch with a plastic fork. "Not half good either, but filling."

He looked up as two soldiers approached. Without invitation, they squatted down before him and removed their helmets. The shorter man wore the round wire-rimmed glasses, while the taller was the sharpshooter who saved Kieran's life.

Oh no, this can't be good. Probably want to harass the evil Americana and make me cough up my lunch money. Be cheerful and friendly, Kieran. These guys don't mess around. "Hi, guys," he said. "I'm Kieran Nash. You speak English?"

"A pleasure, Kieran," said the shorter, stockier man with an infectious grin. "My name is Werner Ostermann. This miserable excuse for a human being is Max Brant." Werner extended his hand and shook Kieran's warmly.

"Kieran," Max said with a nod of his head.

"Do all of you guys speak English?"

"Max and I are fluent while Klaus knows a few phrases. The rest speak strictly German."

"They look like a fun group."

Max snorted. "They don't trust you. Hartmann has them thinking you are a spy or worse."

"And you?"

"I don't trust anything still breathing," Max said, without

a hint of a smile. "Werner here likes everyone. One day it will get him dead."

"A man can never have enough friends," Werner said.

"A good attitude," Kieran said.

"Just what a *spy* would say," Max said.

"Is he always like this?"

"You have no idea," Werner said. "I think the term is 'wet blanket.'"

"Nice vehicle," Max said. "Is it normal in America to deliver furniture in military vehicles?"

"Overheard that little tidbit, did you?"

"Hard not to," Max said. "How did you procure a German vehicle?"

"You mean *The Juggernaut*? I took a job delivering furniture in that monstrosity. I was told it was full of antiques."

"I hope you got paid well," Werner said.

"Actually, I did it as a favor for a professor to keep from getting kicked out of class."

"You should have let him flunk you," Max said.

"Yeah. Hindsight is twenty/twenty."

"What class?" Werner asked.

"A writing course. I want to be a writer."

"A writer?" Werner asked. "Good. Before the war, I was a cartoonist. When this is all over, I would like to go to America and work for the movies."

"Get out of town," Kieran said. "An artist? Good deal."

"Artist?" Max said. "He likes to draw dirty pictures of pretty girls."

"I happen to like dirty pictures of pretty girls," Kieran said.

"For your information, Max," Werner said, "all men are perverts, only we artists can get away with it."

Kieran laughed.

"What kind of writer? Science Fiction, I hope."

"I like some science fiction, but my favorite genre is mysteries. I'm a big fan of Raymond Chandler and Mickey Spillane."

"Science fiction," Max said, shaking his head. "Empty dreams and a waste of time."

"But science fiction *is* the future," Werner said as he adjusted his glasses.

"Science *shit*, you mean," Max said. "Rocket ships and bug-eyed moon men are all you think about."

"Don't let him give you a hard time, Werner," Kieran said. "From science fiction came the airplane, submarine, and rockets."

"One day man will set foot on the moon and make it a gateway to the stars," Werner said. "Mark my word."

"Oh, no, he is wound up now," Max said, rolling his eyes.

"I've got news for you," Kieran said. "In 1969, the first men land on the moon. Neil Armstrong and Buzz Aldrin."

"The moon?" Max asked. "In the sky? You are crazy. How do you know what will happen in 1969? Not to mention the very names of the explorers? You are worse than Werner."

"I learned it in school."

"What kind of school?" Max asked. "One that teaches fortune telling?"

"You guys really are from 1944, aren't you?" Kieran asked.

"Aren't you?" Max asked. "Isn't everyone?"

"When I left home this morning, it was 2014."

"You *have* lost your mind," Max said. "That creature's rock must have addled your brain, American."

"While that is a possibility, Max old boy, I have proof. You mentioned the Mercedes. Have you ever seen anything like the Jug?"

"No, but it is a simple thing to slap a Mercedes Benz emblem on a truck. You have to do better than that."

"I have proof that even you would believe," Kieran said.

"I would very much like to see this proof," Werner said, his eyes bright with excitement as he contemplated the implications.

"So would I," Max said. "I am afraid we are going to be disappointed, Werner."

"You guys have any photos?"

Werner gingerly produced a small black and white photo of a smiling woman.

"This is my Sophia," he said, giving Kieran the photo. "When this war is over, we are getting married."

"Sophia is a hottie," Kieran said.

"Hottie?"

"Means very attractive," Kieran said. "What about you, Max?"

"I have no one. How do looking at photographs prove you are from the future?"

Kieran opened his backpack and produced his phone.

"What is that?" Werner asked.

"A cell phone."

"Phone, as in a telephone?"

"You got it."

"You mean a field radio?" Max asked.

"No. A wireless phone, practically everyone has one. Problem is it doesn't work here."

"How convenient," Max snorted. "A future device that doesn't work."

"Where I come from, there are cell towers that carry the signal. No cell towers here."

"Then it is useless," Max said. "Just like your story."

"A cell phone does many things, besides communication, o, ye of little faith." Opening his photo files, Kieran selected a file. "This is my mom, Heather Nash."

Werner and Max sat stunned at the rich color display. Kieran smiled as he flipped through a dozen shots of his friends and family.

"My God, how many photos do you have?" Werner asked.

"On this card, about two hundred."

"That is incredible."

"Want to see something truly incredible?"

Max and Werner shook their heads.

Kieran opened a video file.

Max and Werner watched flabbergasted as they watched a short file of the Nash family Christmas party.

"You *are* from the future," Werner said.

"What about you Max? Convinced?"

"Tricks," he said. "Nothing but tricks. I once saw a magician in Hamburg cut a woman in half."

Kieran smiled and opened another file.

A stunned Max and Werner watched themselves on the tiny screen.

"You are from the future."

"What about you Max? Convinced?"

"Tricks. Nothing but tricks. I once saw a magician in Hamburg cut a woman in half."

"What do you think now, Max?"

Max and Werner glanced at each other. Maxed turned white while Werner sported a huge grin.

"Tell me, Kieran," Werner asked. "In the future, do you have flying cars?"

"Nope. Cars do not fly."

"How about other planets?" Werner exclaimed. "If we made it to the moon, how about Mars?"

"We sent some un-manned probes. As far as I know, *we* are the first humans on another planet."

"We are the first," Werner said softly. "It is a dream come true."

"Nightmare you mean," Max said. "I want to see the green Earth. Not this dusty oven."

"At least no one is shooting at you," Kieran said.

"He has a point," Werner said.

"This trip isn't over," Max said. "There is a reason Kieran's truck was loaded down with ammo."

"Oh," Werner said. "I forgot about that."

"Like I was saying, I'm a writer and like to crank out hard-boiled detective thrillers."

"More down my alley," Max said. "I love Sam Spade."

"You should have lots to write about," Werner said. "We have an entire world to explore."

"If it doesn't kill us first," Max said.

"So, Max, what did you do before the army?"

Max frowned.

"Max never talks about life before the war," Werner said. "Do you know what is going on, Kieran?"

"I don't have a clue," Kieran said. "Other than I was set up. Looks like I drove straight into the *Twilight Zone*."

"What is this *Twilight Zone*?" Werner asked.

"You know, the old TV show. Wait a minute, I forgot. Trust me, Werner, you will love it."

"What is TV?" Max asked.

"Don't worry, you'll find out."

Hartmann yelled, and Max and Werner jumped to their feet.

"Later, guys," Kieran said as the two men ran to join Hartmann.

ℰↄℰↄ

"What do you two idiots think you are doing fraternizing with the enemy?"

"Oberfeldwebel," Werner said. "Hauptman Zimmer made it clear that Kieran was one of us. Just welcoming the new man."

"Ja," Max said.

"I don't trust him. I don't trust any of this." Hartmann thought a moment. "Did you learn anything from the American?"

"Kieran is from the future," Werner blurted out.

"Kieran *thinks* he is from the future," Max said.

"Have you two been drinking?"

"Drink what?" Max said. "The nearest beerhall is on another planet."

"Kieran has a telephone that can take pictures and make

movies," Werner said excitedly. "You can see the results instantly."

"You are insane," Hartmann said. "Film has to be processed and developed. I have done it many times myself. No way around it."

"Insane, but true," Max said. "He took a movie of us while we spoke. I never saw anything like it."

"From the future? It is unbelievable."

"Want us to stay away from the American?" Max asked.

"No. Be friendly, but don't tell him anything about us. Get him to talk about the future. I want to know what he knows. He will let down his guard, and I will have him."

"Yes, Oberfeldwebel," Werner said. "However, I don't think he is a spy. If he is, then he is the worst in history."

"I will decide that," Hartmann said. "Max, I am to teach our newest recruit how to fight and be a German soldier. Since you can speak his language, you will help me. We are going to make that lazy American wish he was never born."

CHAPTER 10

Under a beautiful carpet of strange stars, Kieran and the German squad sat about a meager fire that barely relieved the frigid desert night.

Hartmann handed Kieran an MP-44.

"Not again?"

"Do it," Max said.

"I don't know who I hate worse, Hartmann or his ventriloquist's dummy."

Max smiled and extended his thumb and forefinger at Kieran as if holding an imaginary gun. "Boom," he said.

"Who has the squad record?" Kieran asked.

"I do," Max said.

"Werner, if you please?"

By firelight, Werner readied his watch. "On your mark…*go*."

Kieran's fingers flew over the machine gun breaking the weapon down to its most basic components. As he laid the last piece, he called, "Time."

"Oh, too bad," Werner said. "Two full seconds slower."

"Ha," Max said with a triumphant smile.

"No, I was talking about you, Max," Werner said with a sly smile. "Kieran is new squad champ."

"Whoo-hoo," Kieran yelled. "The guy who said that video games were a waste of time was full of crap. Eye-hand coordination *supreme*."

"You got lucky," Max said. "Tomorrow, I will regain my standing and laugh at you."

"Lucky? For three days, you and Hartmann have worked my ass off. Even my hair hurts. If I were any more lucky, I'd be dead."

Werner announced that Kieran had beaten Max in German. The squad hooted and hollered, happy that the supremely confidant, irritatingly smug Max had been taken down.

Max gave them all a rude gesture.

"Ask the Amerikaner," Nagal whispered, "what are women like in the future?"

"With a face like that, you shouldn't worry about women," Max said.

"It isn't my face they enjoy," Nagal said with a snort.

"No," Max said, "it is your absence."

As the soldiers laughed, Nagal threw a stone at Max.

"Werner," Kieran said. "You said that before the war you were a cartoonist. That true?"

"Yes. Art is my life."

"I have something for you," Kieran said as he pulled a thick drawing pad from his backpack. "I had to buy this for an art class, although I can't draw a stick. Never got around to using it. You can use this more than me."

Werner's eyes lit up as he received the gift. "I don't know how to thank you."

"No problem," Kieran said. "Oh, almost forgot, here you go." Kieran produced a slim plastic box of drawing pencils and sticks of charcoal.

"Why, this is like Christmas," Werner said as he took the box. "Thank you."

Werner clasped Kieran's hand warmly.

"I could use a present," Max said. "Have a pretty college girl stuffed in your pack?"

"That's in my other backpack," Kieran said. Max snorted. Kieran smiled. "Guys, can you give me the skinny on the other fellows?"

"You know well Oberfeldwebel Hartmann," Max said. "And this—"

"Yes. Wait a minute," Kieran said. "Your name is Oberwelebel…something."

Werner laughed.

"*Nein*," Max said. "Oberfeldwebel is…umm…I think…means sergeant in your army."

"Oh, *Sergeant* Hartmann." Kieran grinned. "Why didn't you say so? That makes sense, the way he grilled my butt."

"Why didn't you bring beer in your fancy wagon?" Max asked.

"Believe me, had I known, I was going to an alien world," Kieran said. "I would have brought Tequila. Now that will put hair on your chest."

Kieran had no idea what Tequila tasted like, or if it would indeed sprout hair, but he didn't want to be a total dork in front of the tough troopers.

"Ask Kieran how the war turns out?" Oberfeldwebel Hartmann asked.

"Kieran, since you are from the future, the oberfeldwebel wants to know how the war turns out," Werner said.

Kieran reassembled the MP-44 without looking at it. "Umm…well, I hate to break it to you, but you guys lose. The West and the Soviets divided Germany. The Russkies took all of Eastern Europe as their own. After a few years, the West gave you back control of your country. They called it West Germany, but the asshole Russians wouldn't let go of the East. We almost went to war with them a few times. I remember my dad called it the Cold War. Two years after I was born, the Soviet Union fell apart on its own. Your country is now unified, and Eastern Europe is free. We are all real good friends now."

"Everything we knew is gone," Werner said. "Hitler and his Nazi henchmen have ruined us."

"Do not disrespect the Fuhrer!" Hartmann said. "I think this boy from the future is lying. He is trying to destroy our morale and our will to fight."

"What did he say?" Kieran asked Max.

"He thinks you are full of sauerkraut," Max said. "I do too."

"I love you, too."

Kieran produced his laptop.

"What is that?" Weiss asked.

Werner translated.

"This is a computer, not the most expensive brand on the market, mind you, but it is helping me get through college."

"What does it do?" Werner asked.

"Kind of an information hub, so to speak. Works way better hooked to the internet, but the Wi-Fi out here is pretty crummy."

"Wi-Fi?" Werner asked.

"Never mind," Kieran said. "You boys want to know what happened in WWII? I downloaded this file on the war to help me in history class. Not a complete history, mind you, but it hit the major highlights."

"Unimaginable," Max said. "It is a trick. I don't know how your cell phone takes photographs, but you can't be from the future. Time travel is impossible. It only happens in those silly books Werner fawns over."

"Think what you like. I'll set the subtitle to German."

"What is he talking about?" Oberfeldwebel Hartmann asked.

Werner translated Kieran's words.

Hartmann's eyes narrowed as he leapt to his feet. He rattled off an angry retort and picked up his rifle.

"What did he say?" Kieran asked. "Why the hell does he have a gun?"

"Do not play your propaganda. If you try and put doubt into the minds of his men, he will shoot you."

"Propaganda? It's the truth, and I'm tired of being called a liar."

"Kieran, my friend," Werner said. "The oberfeldwebel *will* shoot you. Let it go."

Hartmann glared at Kieran in a way that sent chills down his spine.

"You know, I believe he will. Hey, guys, since the documentaries are out, how about a movie—for entertainment purposes only. Will that be all right with the oberfeldwebel?"

"Very well," Hartmann said after a translation. "Entertainment only, as if that is possible."

Hartmann lowered his rifle and snorted at Kieran.

"Yes, why don't we all trot down to the local movie house," Max scoffed. "The beer and popcorn are on me."

"Oh, ye of little faith," Kieran said. "So what will it be? Action adventure, sci-fi, romance, you name it."

"Sci-fi?" Werner asked, his eyes lighting up. "You mean science fiction?"

"How about a musical?" Max asked.

"You are a sick freak, you know that, Max?"

For the first time, Kieran saw Max's perpetual scowl crack into a slight smile.

"I know the screen is only twenty inches, but if we all scrunch together…"

"You are serious?" Werner asked. "We can watch a movie?"

"As a heart attack, my little Nazi storm trooper, now gather together."

While the skeptical soldiers assembled, Kieran took out his cell phone.

"Smile fellows." Kieran took three shots before passing the camera around the astonished group. While they examined the future of photography, Kieran set up the laptop, using his backpack as a stand.

"Since I don't have *Mein Kompf, the Musical,* on my hard drive. I'll pick one."

Choosing *Bloodbath Two,* a high octane, action adventure, festooned with cool explosions and many, many gratuitous nude scenes, Kieran set the screen to give subtitles in German, before hitting the play button.

The soldiers gasped as the movie began. Kieran left them alone and went in search of his digital recorder.

CHAPTER 11

"Well, it seems that my little road trip has gotten even more bizarre," Kieran said into the recorder. He sat back in the passenger seat, his sore feet resting on the dash. "Looks like I have taken a detour on my road to Montgomery, a detour to an alien planet. Yes, sir, friends and neighbors, an honest-to-God, two-moon craphole of a desert world, at least what I have seen so far. Must be a bit smaller than the Earth, because my vertical jump is to die for—if only I had a basketball. Anyway, made contact with the local boys and they almost killed yours truly, fortunately for me, a troop of friendly Nazi paratroopers straight out of 1944, were passing by at the time. I know it all seems silly, but it isn't.

"Haven't seen much in the way of wild life, only a few creatures, the most interesting was about the size of a Doberman Pincher, which look like a cross between a kangaroo and a rat, one of the boys named them Hop-a-longs. Max shot and cooked one, I hate to say this, but it tasted like spoiled chicken. A few six legged lizards, some beetles and oh yeah, saw some big, lizard…birdy…*things*. From a distance, they look like vultures, up close they look like death warmed over. Made turkey buzzards look like parakeets. Fortunately, they steered clear of us. The main alien alpha dogs here, on the other hand, are psycho dangerous and somehow, can move objects with their minds alone. One asshole nearly brained me with a rock while then, with a wave of his hand, made my cargo truck rise off the ground, right before he swatted me with it.

"The aliens, from the bodies Max killed, are very human like. Almost as if they were Funhouse mirror distortions come to life. I assume that it is the result of living on a planet with lesser gravity, but what do I know? Zimmer wanted a prisoner to question, but the aliens are way too dangerous to take alive. One on one, a human has little chance against the alien's mental powers. It is like being stuck in a bad sci-fi movie.

"They're all very tattooed and some with gruesome brands, all of the same thing. It's a symbol that looks for all the world like an old TV antenna. Zimmer theorized it was some religious symbol. Sounds reasonable. The leader, of the gang who attacked me, even had small metal and ceramic necklaces and armbands sporting stylized versions of the 'Holy Antenna.' Max confiscated one and now wears it around his neck. The thing creeps the hell out of me.

"This little foray into the *Twilight Zone* was no accident. Looks like I have been played from the get-go. Someone took great pains to get me here. It was too great a coincidence that the GPS directions just so happened to lead me to a spot where several armed men were waiting.

"Given the fact they were on top of me and were blazing away at me with AK-Forty-Sevens from only a few feet away, I failed to discover one bullet hole in my ride. They didn't even scrape the paint. I know now that they didn't want to stop me. They wanted to *herd* me. The furniture I was hauling doesn't exist. Seems that my purpose was to resupply the Sunshine Boys. I don't think Professor Wills is behind this. I figure that she was a pawn, just like the Germans and me. Nevertheless, I'm still going to make her eat her freaking book if I ever make it home. Why, or even who, is doing this is still a mystery."

Kieran paused in his narration when he heard the troop cheer and applaud. Kieran snorted.

"Looks like my new companions have gotten to the first

strip club scene. Speaking of the Sunshine Boys," he said as he resumed his dictation, "this is what I have learned. For a bunch of evil, scary Nazi soldiers—and don't get me wrong, they are scary—they're a surprise. Hartman, Mauler, Nagal, Faust, and Roth are openly hostile. If it were not for Zimmer, this kid would have a fatal accident. I'm an American. That makes me the enemy, period. That being said, none of these boys are card-carrying members of the Nazi Party. In fact, they get pissed when I call them Nazis. Almost as if they hate them as much as I do. I know, weird.

"While they don't speak a word of English—nasty—I can translate pretty well. I gather that if it were up to Hartmann, he would have shot me on the spot. Zimmer really pissed him off by making him train me to defend myself and help out in case of a fight. Hartmann knows how to fight and is a great instructor, but he is ruthless. Hartmann would love to use me as target practice, but he is a good soldier who follows orders. However, if anything happened to Zimmer, I think my goose would be quickly cooked.

"My friend Werner operates 'Sophia,' the heavy machine gun, which fires a belt of bullets. I have been training to load while he fires. I even switch out barrels when they overheat. Seems that when they were fighting in Italy, they lost several men, one being the ammo loader. It has all been grueling training. Hell, I dream about it, but as of yet, we haven't used a single 'live' round.

"I'm pretty good at field stripping their equipment, but I'm not allowed to practice shooting, because it would waste ammo, not to mention give away our position. Max, in fact, was the only one to engage the enemy and that was when he saved me. I hope that my little movie can break the ice with these guys. It would sure make my stay a lot more pleasant not worrying about a knife in the back. Nevertheless, not everyone is hostile. By far, the two friendliest are Werner Ostermann and to a much, much lower extent, Max Brant.

"Funny thing, both men are as far different as possible.

Werner is friendly and open. An artist, he is a dreamer in love with science fiction. He has all the makings of being a diehard Trekkie, even though that won't be for some twenty years or so. The man is stoked to be on an alien planet and to meet a guy from the future. I find it hard to believe this soft-spoken man is an elite German paratrooper. Werner is one of the three who speaks fluent English, and I have to say I have found a new friend. He gave me the lowdown on my heavily armed peeps.

"A side note. Werner explained that 'Barsoom' was from a series of science fiction novels written by the creator of Tarzan, Edgar Rice Burroughs. Not exactly hard science fiction, the books are full of sword fights, ray guns, bug-eyed aliens, and damsels in distress. Sounds like a lot of fun. Barsoom was the name the native name for Mars. As a budding writer, I should have known that. Note to self, I need to check out the series when I get back home. *If* I get back home.

"Max, on the other hand, is an odd bird. He is obviously well educated, judging from his excellent English, but as the squad sniper, he is the most cold-blooded. Max disagrees with everything. He would argue with a doorknob, as my third grade teacher used to say about a particularly stubborn student, named Nash. Aside from the five he killed saving my hide, he has killed eight more of the aliens in the three days I have been here. My sleeping mat and bedroll are from one of the dearly departed. Perhaps I should feel some remorse, but the aliens here are dangerous and completely without feeling. They make the Nazis look like the good guys.

"Anyway, back to Max. The man is scary good with a rifle and doesn't miss. He is always at odds with Werner, sort of like a big brother little brother relationship although they are both the same age. Unlike Werner, Max doesn't seem to have an imagination, period. All he talks about is beer and disputing whatever comes out of Werner's mouth. Strangely, Max will not speak a word about his life before the war.

The squad is mostly about my age, while two are only eighteen. Only Zimmer and Hartmann are older. I think Zimmer is in his early thirties. Hartmann is fortyish, his close-cropped hair pure silver.

"Captain Zimmer and Sergeant Hartmann are professional military hard asses. The rest are a diverse group. Medic, Klaus Loewe, was drafted while still in medical school, just a year short of becoming a doctor. Mahler, Nagal, and Roth were street thugs. Naumann was a farmer while, surprise, surprise, Weiss was studying to be a Lutheran minister before the Nazis closed down his seminary and drafted him. The Nazis, it seems, hate Christianity as much as Judaism.

"I asked about our fearless leader, Captain Zimmer, but Werner didn't know much. He said that Zimmer only took command a week before coming to Barsoom. Zimmer isn't what I expected. I suppose I watched too many silly war movies that portray German officers as sadistic monsters or monocle-wearing buffoons. The man exudes the air of a natural-born leader. Captain Zimmer is very polite and soft-spoken, yet he may be the toughest son of a bitch I have ever seen, and I mean a Clint Eastwood/*Dirty Harry* badass. At the same time, he is one of the smartest. He could make mincemeat of the *Dirty Dozen*. If the Germans had more like him, they would have whipped our asses.

"Funny thing about Zimmer is that I get the feeling that he knows more than he's letting on. You would have thought that they would have taken my stuff. I mean it's tech that is over seventy years in the future, not to mention I have files that would be priceless nuggets of future events, but Zimmer made it clear to that psycho Hartmann to leave me alone."

Kieran paused as he gathered his thoughts.

"Without a doubt, the Nazi Party was pure evil, with the blood of millions staining it's hands. It was easy to see them as the quintessential stereotypical villains. However, these men I have met, are not the black-and-white, propaganda-spouting Nazis of the movies that I have been programmed to hate. They are, instead, flesh-and-blood men, who have wives, girlfriends, and families who did their civic duty to a country that, unfortunately, was led by a mad man and gang of murderous criminals.

"I love my country, and if it were plunged in to war, I would fight. If a lunatic led the good old U S of A, would I have done the same as the Germans? I'm glad I'll never have to find out.

"Have to admit that it's unsettling to see them as real, flesh-and-blood human beings. It has completely ruined World War Two movies for me. This experience is going to make its way into a book. I have a wealth of material for characters. If I ever get out of this mess, I feel fame and fortune closing in on me like a cruise missile."

Tired of dictating, Kieran switched off the recorder. "I wonder where the good captain is hiding?"

CHAPTER 12

Kieran found Captain Zimmer several yards away, behind a jagged rock outcropping, closing the buckles on his pack.

I wonder what's in that pack of his? The captain never lets it out of his sight.

"What can I do for you, Kieran?" Zimmer said, lighting a cigarette.

"I set the Sunshine Boys up with a movie. Want to join us?"

"A portable cinema?" Zimmer asked. "Amazing. Simply amazing."

"So, yah coming?"

"No, thank you. I have too much on my mind." Zimmer looked at Kieran. "What would you say was our downfall?"

"You mean the war?"

Zimmer nodded.

"Probably when the allies broke the Enigma code machine. In 1942, I believe."

The normally cool demeanor of Zimmer cracked. "You know about the code machine?"

"I loved the movie they made about breaking it. Very exciting."

"That explains a lot of things," Zimmer said. "They

knew what we were doing before we did. Where did the allies invade Europe? Belgium?"

"Oh no," Kieran said. "Normandy Beach, June 6, 1944. My history professor Mr. Burns drilled that date into our heads."

"I never would have guessed. I would have bet on a Calais invasion."

"No. I saw a documentary how the Brits used General Patton and a fake inflatable army to fool Hitler into thinking that Calais was the target, so Normandy was wide open."

"Live and learn I suppose," Zimmer said with a slight smile.

"Enough of ancient history. So, Fearless Leader, what is our next move?"

Zimmer knelt down in the soft red sand and drew with his finger around a small smooth stone. "This rock is us. My scouts have been canvassing the area radiating outward."

"What did they find?"

"They have found two abandoned towns, here and here," he said as he indicated with depressions in the soft sand. "Half a klick to the north they found a road."

"A road?"

"A massive, sixty lane wide autobahn," Zimmer said, "would be closer. In their report, the road lay abandoned with many places in disrepair. They looked for vehicles but found none."

"Wow," Kieran said. "Impressive to say the least. Can you imagine what kind of vehicles traveled it?"

"I am more interested in the beings who built it," Zimmer said. "The aliens we have encountered thus far are too primitive, not to mention their observed social interactions consist of a kill-or-be-killed attitude. They couldn't work together to build a hut, let alone an engineering feat of this magnitude."

"War is my guess," Kieran said. "A war so terrible that the survivors were unable to rebuild."

"Plausible. The ruins my scouts found yesterday were little more than blasted rubble. Something puzzles me. We have not found any dwellings. No cultivated fields, live-stock, wells, or general signs of current habitation."

"You ask me, nothing grows here," Kieran said. "No surface water. Only some grass and thorny shrubs that barely keep the hop-a-longs alive."

Zimmer nodded. "To my mind, the aliens we have encountered are not indigenous to the region. From the thirteen Max killed, they carried a small amount of food made from some kind of grain, but it is obviously impossible to grow anything in this arid waste. Another thing. From the scouts, it seems that the aliens perform two sweeps of the area a day, early morning and late evening, before retreating to a hidden camp to the east. It is as if they are looking for someone or something."

"Perhaps hunters?" Kieran asked. "Maybe they are keeping watch for enemy tribes?"

"You guess is as good as mine at this point," Zimmer said. "The supplies in the Jug were a Godsend, yet they will not last indefinitely. We will need food and water, so we have to move out. As much as I want to avoid it, we will have to risk an encounter with the main body. We have no choice."

"There could be thousands of them."

"Perhaps. I have too many questions and not enough answers, and that doesn't sit well with me. I am feeling my way in the dark."

"Then perhaps I can help you out, Hauptman Zimmer," a stranger said.

As Kieran jumped, Zimmer stepped back and drew down on the stranger with his Walther P-38. The stranger was identical to the aliens who tried to kill Kieran. Tall, with a spindly build and hairless. However, this alien was dressed in a tunic and slacks, whose colors flowed and ebbed across its surface almost as if it were alive. A smile played upon his thin lips. "Welcome to the planet Adeaa, Captain Zimmer," the creature said in perfect German. "You do not know how long I have waited for this day. My name is Comptonne Hirakuu Bosh Toburn Vilragg. Please, you may call me Vilragg."

"Thank you, *friend* Vilragg," Zimmer said, the muzzle of his weapon never wavering. "Now, if you would be so kind, please send us back to Earth."

"Not just yet, Captain. You and your men are not here from mere happenstance. You have a great purpose. You are here to save my people, the Riahass."

"The Riahass?"

"You know them as the riders with the ability to project their will upon solid objects.

"Your people have tried to kill us."

"I am afraid they are not themselves."

"I don't understand, Herr Vilragg. They are savages."

"Unfortunately, the situation is complicated, and I don't have the time to explain the problem at this moment. Rest assured that your considerable martial skills are very much needed if my people are ever to regain their sanity and re-claim their world."

"We are not godless mercenaries for hire," Zimmer said. "We are soldiers of the Third Reich. Have someone else do your murdering. Now, Herr Vilragg, send us home."

"You, my dear Captain Zimmer, will help me, or neither you nor your men will ever see home again. You are low on food and water. You will not find any in the 'Great Western Waste.' Nonetheless, I have plenty of food and water for you and your men at my home. If you wish to survive, come to me and let me present my offer, face to face. I guarantee that you will find it irresistible." Vilragg looked over at Kieran, the unmistakable look of astonishment written across his strange face. "Who is this one? He is not a warri-or. I did not bring him from your world."

Kieran looked closely at the strange, slightly transparent, flickering creature. "Put the gun away, Captain," he said. "Dude's a hologram."

"A what?" Zimmer asked.

"Fancy laser lightshow. Essentially a high-tech illusion."

"I am impressed," Vilragg said, this time in English. "But how would a creature such as yourself—from a backward planet as Earth—know this?"

"I'm smarter than I look."

"Doubtful. You are a mystery I shall get to the bottom of, once we meet," Vilragg said as his gaze returned to Zimmer. "Hauptmann Zimmer, travel east toward the large ring of stone towers, I think on your world you would call them mesas. The journey should take no more than a week's expedition from your current position. I warn you to avoid the 'great highway' and the three abandoned settlements you will encounter. For some reason, I do not understand, the Riahass have been seen here in ever-increasing numbers. Keep to the southern ridges and only travel at night. When you reach the end, and only then, venture down onto the desert plane and make all haste to the ring of mesas. It would be disastrous if the Riahass caught you in the open. I will meet you on the other side and give you your final instructions on how to reach me. I look forward to our meeting, but be on your guard. This journey will prove to be very hazardous. "The Riahass, in their present state, will try to kill or take you captive. I suggest you stay clear of any further encounters with the Riahass. They are more dangerous than you can imagine."

"We are not going anywhere until you explain why you kidnapped us," Zimmer said.

"I want to make a deal with you, Captain, one that will benefit both your people and mine, but if you want, you may stay here until the red desert claims you as her own. Your very survival depends on reaching me in time. However, it is entirely up to you. Good night."

With a smile twisting his thin lips, Vilragg disappeared.

Kieran and Zimmer looked at each other.

"The plot thickens," Kieran said.

CHAPTER 13

H auptman," Hartmann whispered. Zimmer rolled out of his bedroll ready for action. "What is it, Oberfeldwebel?"

"May I have a word? It is important."

"It must be to disturb me at this hour."

"Utmost."

"Of course," Zimmer said. "What is on your mind?"

"The American, Kieran. His device, his computer, as he called it."

"It is amazing," Zimmer said. "Did you enjoy the movie?"

"I have never seen such a thing. The plot was retched, however, the automobiles, the women, and what was it Kieran called them...oh yes, *special effects*...were amazing."

"Did you wake me to discuss a movie?"

"Certainly not, Hauptman. Once Kieran was asleep, and his device was...*recharging* in the truck, I had a look at what other information he had stored there."

"What did you find?"

Hartmann wiped his mouth nervously.

"Well spit it out, I haven't got all night."

"He told me of a documentary movie about the war, made several years after. I found the file and watched it."

"And?"

"Hauptman, the film reveals classified documents and archival film footage from *both* sides."

"I hate to jump to the end, but do we win?"

"No. We are overwhelmed by the Allies and Soviets. Hitler commits suicide in his bunker."

"The Japanese?"

"They are beaten back to their island and then—"

"Invasion?"

"No. The Americans developed a bomb."

"They have many bombs."

"Not like this. One bomb destroyed the city of Hiroshima in a single blast. The second destroyed Nagasaki."

"That's incredible."

"There's more. It gave a glimpse of military forces from Kieran's time. They have airplanes, without propellers, that travel *twice* the speed of sound and fire missiles that think. Their tanks are massive and yet could out run our cars! They have machines that orbit the Earth, take pictures of things on the ground, and tell you where the enemy is. Utterly amazing."

"So what do you want me to do with this information?"

"Don't you see, Hauptman? None of this has happened yet. If we can get that computer and that recording of the war back to Berlin, Germany will have the advantage. The Allies are going to invade Europe at Normandy Beach on June sixth. This could change everything."

"So, you are convinced that Kieran isn't a spy and is from our future?"

"Hauptman, I am an old soldier, but I am not unfamiliar with photography. My older brother Hart was a photographer in Munich. I used to help him in the field and in developing film. Hart was obsessed with the cutting edge of photography, most of which I couldn't care less. However, he never imagined anything like what I saw Kieran's devices do. They can take a color photograph, and you can see the results instantly, with no film or development times. He called it *digital*, whatever that means. Not only that, he can make movies, *instantly*, on the same device. It can actually calculate numbers and equations. It even plays games, and, while most are an inane waste of time, he had chess."

"How do you play chess against a telephone?" Zimmer asked.

"Trust me, it was amazing. I am a very good chess player, and his phone beat me three times in a row. I am a hardheaded man, but he has convinced me."

"The evidence is rather insurmountable," Zimmer said. "However, what if you were right about Kieran being a spy and all this is an elaborate hoax?"

"But his equipment?"

"Just humor me for a moment. Let's say he was sent into our fold to spread disinformation. We line up at Normandy and Calais was the real landing. Why, it would be a disaster."

"What are we going to do, Hauptman? Give me a crack at him. I can make him tell me the truth."

"No. Keep a close eye on him, however, leave Kieran alone and let things play out. If he is a spy, we give him enough rope to hang himself."

"Yes, Hauptman."

"Do not let on that you accessed his machine and train him as normal."

"Yes, Hauptman."

"By the way, how is our new recruit?"

"Soft, yet he is stubborn. The harder I push him, the harder he pushes back. I hate to say this, but given time he would make a fine *Fallschirmjäger*."

"Why, that is high praise coming from you."

"It is the truth. The pup has potential. I would hate to shoot him and waste all my effort."

"Get some rest," Zimmer said. "Tomorrow, we move out."

CHAPTER 14

Zimmer, Hartmann, and the scout Mahler conferred while the rest of the troop loaded the Jug.

"I need a way east, one that will accommodate the truck, and yet avoid unnecessary attention from the Riahass," Zimmer told Mahler.

The rangy soldier squatted down and smoothed a patch of sand. "The truck should be able to traverse the ridge with no problem."

"What about surprises from the Riahass?" Zimmer asked.

"I have never seen them leave the valley, other than their daily excursions deep into the desert canyons."

"Is there a way down into the valley, one the truck could traverse?" Zimmer asked.

"Yes, but you won't like it. The only way down into the valley that will not risk breaking an axel is a natural ramp about a day's journey from here. Unfortunately, the ramp comes out within meters of the autobahn. It would be impossible not to notice the truck unless we came out after dark."

"That is if anyone was around," Zimmer said.

"That is the rub, Hauptmann," Mahler said. "If I don't miss my guess, based on the animals they ride, those aboriginals are camped somewhere close to the ramp."

"I see," Zimmer said.

"Hauptmann, how about we bypass the ramp and the Riahass all together. Let us take the truck east as far as it can take us and then make it to this Vilragg person on foot," Hartmann said.

"No. We don't have many assets, and I'm not abandoning the vehicle. The ramp it is. Let us hope luck is on our side."

"Since when has luck ever been with us?" Hartmann asked.

"There is always a first time," Zimmer said.

೧ఇ೧

Kieran drove slowly over the rough terrain while Zimmer rode shotgun, his MP-44 chambered and ready for trouble. Zimmer scowled as he held Kieran's phone before him, swearing blackly in German, and tossed the phone into Kieran's open pack. "I can't believe I lost a chess match to a *telephone*," he said.

Kieran chuckled at his rant.

"I don't find it humorous."

"You would from the driver's seat," Kieran said. "I had that game for a year, and I have yet to come close."

"It would not be as insufferable if it would take more than a split second to make a move. I feel like a wet-behind-the-ears school boy."

"Join the club."

"Oberfeldwebel Hartmann is pleased with your progress, Kieran," Zimmer said as he lit a cigarette. "Said you would make a fine *Fallschirmjäger*."

"Oberfeldwebel Hartmann is a sadistic son of a bitch who's trying to kill me."

"That is his job," Zimmer said. "To sharpen a knife, one has to grind and hone away the unneeded material until it is worthy of the task."

"He's damn good at it. I hear his voice barking at me in my sleep. I think it's funny that the first words I learned in German are 'shit stain.'"

Zimmer laughed.

"Hartmann's a sorry Nazi bastard, but I'm stealing some of his material. It's literary gold."

"Such as?"

"He told me to fight like the third goddamned monkey on the ramp to Noah's Ark—and it's starting to rain."

"That is pretty good," Zimmer said. "You know, Kieran, I was the same way as you when I first experienced training. I thought I was going to die."

"I find that hard to believe," Kieran said. "You look like a natural born bad ass."

"Should I take that as a compliment?"

"It was. I am thinking of writing a character based on you."

"Really? I'm flattered."

"Yeah, an evil, warmongering megalomaniac bent on world domination," Kieran said.

Zimmer gave Kieran a narrow gaze. "I warn you. I am armed, and accidents do happen."

Kieran laughed.

"Never met anyone from the future before," Zimmer said with a slight grin.

"I never rode around on an alien planet with a bunch of Nazis either."

"Let me set you straight, my young friend. Not everyone in Germany is a Nazi. Some of us abhor their methods and ideology. I despise the direction my government has gone and the leaders who have turned my country upside down."

"But you fight for them."

"I am a professional soldier as was my father and his father before him. I was trained and educated to be a warrior for Germany. My country goes to war, I will fight for her. It is my duty."

"Seems things have changed over the years," Kieran said. "In the current world, we don't serve blindly, and we protest the bejeezus out of everything. You're a smart man. How can you fight for Adolf Hitler, for Christ's sake?"

"I fight for Germany. Period. I do not follow political ideology and pagan Nordic myths. My country is at war—*I* am at war."

"I don't understand the mindset."

"We are from different cultures, my friend. Growing up, I was trained to follow orders. It is my life."

"Sucks, if you ask me."

Zimmer smiled. "Tell me, Kieran, in the magical world of 2014, do you own a rocket pack?"

Kieran shook his head as the touchy subject made a quick change in direction. "No rocket packs, buses to the moon, or flying cars. We do have some swell computers, and TV has about a zillion channels."

"Too bad," Zimmer said. "I would like to have a flying car."

"You sound like Werner."

"Hardly," Zimmer said. "Werner is a good man, but, like you, he is a dreamer. A soldier needs focus. Dreaming can get you killed."

"I like dreaming, thank you very much."

"So, tell me. In the fabulous world of 2014 has war become obsolete?"

"No," Kieran said. "I think it's worse. Nothing as big as WWII, but it seems like every two-bit thug with a gun wants to make a statement. Back in 2001, a bunch of extremist wackos hijacked four airliners. Two brought down two skyscrapers in the Big Apple while the third made a big hole in the Pentagon. The fourth crashed when the passengers tried to take control."

"*Back* in 2001?"

"Yeah, I guess that does sound weird to a relic from 1944."

"They used the airplanes...as *missiles*?"

"Yeah."

"Barbaric murder, not to mention a tactical mistake. If I don't miss my guess, the United States responded with full force?"

"You better believe it." Kieran waved his hand before his face to dispel the cloud of acrid smoke. "Speaking of murder, as much fun as it is to breathe your second-hand smoke, I have to warn you, that those things will kill you. In my time, smoking is frowned upon. I would say in twenty years it will be gone all together."

"Do tell?" Zimmer asked. "Anyone tell you that you nag like an old woman?"

"Bite me."

"Are you married, my young friend? Have a family?"

Kieran brought up his photo file on his phone. With a quick swipe, he handed it to Zimmer. Zimmer looked at the happy trio of Kieran and two attractive women. "This is my mom, Heather and my sister Julie."

"Handsome family. Your father?"

"He died when I was eight. Drunk driver."

"I am sorry," Zimmer said, handing back the phone. "Any romances you would like to share?"

"What is this, a slumber party?" Kieran asked. "No, there was a girl I chased after for a while, but she had a habit I didn't like."

"Smoker?"

"No, she liked other guys better than me. What about you?"

"I have a wife. Marta. We have two children, Eric and Nina." Zimmer produced a photo showing a pretty, smiling woman holding a baby. Beside Marta, stood a small, blond boy.

"My grandmother was named Nina. Nina Virtanen. She is Finnish. Said that after her papa was killed in the Winter War with the Soviets, her mother packed up the kids and came to the US. She lives in Minnesota."

"Minnesota? I have been to Minnesota. I *love* it."

"Get out of town," Kieran said. "It's a small world."

"I enjoy fly fishing, and Minnesota has the best fishing in the world."

"When you are not shooting people, that is?"

"Fly fishing gives my gun time to cool. Anyway, my father took the family to Minnesota—a small place called Moose Jaw—every year. It is my fondest memories as a child. The fishing was heavenly. That seems like a thousand years ago."

"Fishing gives me gas," Kieran said. "Hooks, worms, and slimy, stinking fish. Not to mention bugs and snakes. Count me out."

"Why am I not surprised? Seems that anything dealing with being outside and being active disagrees with you."

Kieran chuckled. "I'm a writer. Heaven is hunched over a word processor in a dark room."

"Hemingway was an outdoorsman and one hell of a writer."

"He also killed himself."

Zimmer looked at Kieran in shock.

"Or at least he will," Kieran said. "I guess all that outside stuff and being an active man drove him crazy. Good looking family, by the way. The kids take after their mother, I hope. I know they get their good looks from her."

"Thank you," Zimmer said, recovering the precious photo. "Marta is a beauty. If it is 2014, as you say, that would make Marta ninety-five, Eric seventy-three, and Nina seventy."

"I have a strong feeling that it isn't 2014, but that I'm in 1944."

"Does not matter. Our loved ones and home are beyond our reach."

"Vilragg said he could send you back."

"He said a lot of things. I have trouble trusting someone who kidnaps me."

"I don't understand why he waited so long to contact you," Kieran said.

"That is simple. He obviously needs my help. Vilragg waited for us to run perilously low on food and water. We would have no choice, but to do what he asked."

"Damn, you are clever."

"What I find interesting is that he did not know you, Kieran, or that you resupplied us. Your arrival was a complete surprise to him. Not only that, you recognized his technology, which he found disconcerting. We may be able to use your superior knowledge to our advantage. If he didn't know about you, Kieran, he doesn't know about this vehicle either."

"I see your point. With this little, six-wheeled piece of German engineering—"

"We should get to the rendezvous point in a couple of days, instead of a week. That should give us time to ascertain the situation."

"I think we are here," Kieran said.

"Stop the vehicle," Zimmer said.

Kieran eased the Jug to a stop behind a high angled rock outcropping. Before the dust cleared, Zimmer bounded out of the truck, scrambling up a small rise.

"Wow, would you look at that," Kieran said as he joined Zimmer on the bare hill.

Below them on the valley floor, stretching into the distance, lay a great thoroughfare that dwarfed anything Kieran had ever seen. The vacant road was wide enough to accommodate sixty lanes of traffic. Although many sections lay buckled and blasted, the feat of engineering was still impressive.

Traveling over the rolling desert plane the highway glittered in the sunlight as if made from bits of glass. Elevated some ten feet above the desert floor by regularly spaced supports, the wide thoroughfare ran arrow straight from east to west.

"I have trouble believing the Riahass built the highway."

"Not the ones we have met," Zimmer said as he scanned the shimmering desert with his binoculars. "I am intrigued by Herr Vilragg's comments that the Riahass underwent a change."

"From a sophisticated, advanced people to a band of assholes is quite a change."

"We will find out the full story when we find Vilragg."

On the other side of the rise upon which the two men stood, was the natural ramp, gently sloping down to the valley below, just as Mahler had described. The vast alien highway lay just beyond the ramp.

His handsome face a mask, Zimmer handed the field glasses to Kieran. "You see the camp?" he asked, pointing to a mass of tents in the hazy distance. "That is where the Riahass send out patrols."

"Can't make out much even with the binoculars, boss."

"Yes, we will have to scout the position." Zimmer turned and yelled, "Mahler!"

"In the open?" Kieran asked. "There's no cover, and even Mahler wouldn't stand a chance."

"It can't be helped," Zimmer said. "I have to know what we are up against."

Kieran smiled. "I believe I can help you with that."

CHAPTER 15

W hat is that thing," Zimmer asked as Kieran studied the instruction manual.

The knot of soldiers formed a circle while Kieran made adjustments and checked battery levels.

"Something our mysterious benefactors thought we could use," Kieran said. "I found it in the back of the truck."

"It looks like a toy," Hartmann said, eyeing the device suspiciously.

"Okay," Kieran said, handing his phone to Zimmer. "I have synced my phone to the drone."

"I don't understand," Zimmer said.

"This, my fine German companions, is what is known as a drone back in good old 2014."

"What good is it?" Max asked.

"It is a flying camera," Kieran said, switching the machine on.

Instantly, the phone in Zimmer's hands displayed the view of the camera slung underneath the six spinning propellers.

"Absolutely amazing," Zimmer said. "This would be instrumental in gathering intelligence on a battle field. We Germans should have come up with this idea."

The gasping soldiers crowded behind Zimmer until a stern look made them fall back.

The controller in his hand, Kieran brought the spinning blades up to speed, and the device rose shakily from the ground in a cloud of fine dust. The machine rose high into the air and, manipulating the joystick, Kieran sent the expensive camera rig toward the distant camp.

"I have got to get myself one of these," Kieran said.

"Me too," Werner said. "My turn is next."

"Captain, let me see the screen."

Zimmer held the phone before Kieran.

"Hit the red record button," Kieran said.

Zimmer complied.

"Good," said Kieran. "Let's see what those pesky ETs are doing."

From high in the sky, the drone zipped through the thin air.

Using the small screen to fly the drone, Kieran slowly circled the cluster of tents while the camera scanned the camp. Kieran wasn't concerned with details, only using the screen to keep the drone in the air. He sailed about the camp at a safe distance, adjusting its flight path when Zimmer wanted certain sections more closely scrutinized, until the low battery forced him to bring the drone back to the Germans.

The drone bounced and shuttered on landing.

"Excellent, Kieran," Werner said.

Max snorted. "Flying toys."

"I hereby promote you to the head of our mechanized luftwaffe," Zimmer said. "Now put away our flying scout while I see what we are up against."

"And people back home said I would never amount to anything," Kieran said.

CHAPTER 16

Zimmer, his troops, along with Kieran, accessed the drone's video. Hartmann protested Kieran's presence, but Zimmer overruled the gruff sergeant.

Using the soft sand as a visual aid, Zimmer marked out the highway and the approximate position of the camp.

"I counted fifty tents," Zimmer said in German while Werner gave Kieran the play-by-play in English. "However, they only have twenty-three riding animals. Some of the bigger tents look permanent, while the smaller are actually dwellings."

"They look like Teepees," Kieran said.

"That makes us cowboys," Werner said.

"As I was saying, this new beast must be this planet's version of an ox." Zimmer showed his companions the frozen screen showing the horned, snarling beast yoked to a wagon. "I counted five wagons full of supplies and three empty. It leads me to the conclusion that this camp was set up and the personnel rotated on a regular basis. I also found a well, half a click north of the camp."

"Why set up a camp at all?" Kieran asked. "They aren't doing anything productive like mining or agriculture. All they do is send out a squad twice a day to ride through the wasteland."

"They do have a reason," Zimmer said as he handed Kieran the phone.

Kieran gasped. "They have people in cages."

"Ja. *That* is what they are doing here in this God-forsaken place. The savages somehow know this is where to find humans. This camp is to stop the humans from reaching Vilragg. It is the only explanation."

"The Riahass who attacked me—they spoke English. They thought I was British," Kieran said.

Zimmer took a deep breath. "It is obvious that Vilragg experimented before he perfected snatching humans," he said. "No doubt, in early experiments, he tried to hone the process and work out the bugs. The Riahass learned our language and knowledge of Earth from their prisoners."

"What are we going to do?" Kieran asked.

"There are too many. We have to find a way around without being noticed."

"Bullshit," Kieran exclaimed. "We're going to help those folks. Hadn't been for you and the Sunshine Boys, I would be down there rotting in a cage."

"Yes, and look where that got us," Zimmer said.

Kieran stuck out his tongue, making Zimmer chuckle.

"Five ambushed savages were easy enough, but we had the element of surprise. A few hundred will be a far different story. We try to free the captives, and it will be us locked in those cages. We cannot take the risk."

"But you have guns—"

"Must I remind you, that one of those things picked up the Jug with no more than a gesture? Or that he used it like DiMaggio would use a baseball bat against you?"

"Like you said before, Captain, we humans are in this together. We'll just have to outsmart them."

"Too dangerous," Zimmer said. "Too many variables. We will wait for night, and then give the things a wide berth. There is a path that, coupled with the Jug's abilities, we should be able to use to slip past with none the wiser."

"This isn't right," Kieran said.

"We do not have the luxury of right and wrong," Zimmer said. "You need to think with your brain and not your emotions."

Taking a deep breath, Captain Zimmer took his P-38, along with the holster, and handed it butt first to Kieran.

"What's this for?"

"What do you think? You have been trained."

"Yeah, Hartmann is a real bastard, but he knows his guns."

"It's the only weapon I can spare. Don't shoot yourself."

"Right."

"Now get some rest, we will camp here until night fall."

"So, we can sneak around them and leave the prisoners, like chicken-shit cowards?"

"Precisely," Zimmer said with a toothy smile. "Now run along and rest. You are dismissed."

Gritting his teeth, Kieran rose from the group.

"Kieran," Zimmer said. "Please give me the keys to the Jug."

Kieran produced the keys and tossed them to Zimmer. "Satisfied?"

"Very," Zimmer said. "Have a good night's sleep. Tomorrow will be a long day."

Kieran choked back a nasty retort. All eyes were on him as he stalked away. Fifty feet away he heard Zimmer resume his lecture in German.

Kieran looked down at the heavy gun in his hand and made a fateful decision.

Captain Nazi may be a cold-hearted bastard but, by God, I'm going to do something. As a human being, I have to. I just have to.

A plan quickly formed in his head. For it to succeed, he needed room to work. If he failed, Zimmer would no doubt nail his hide to the wall.

Excited as he was, Kieran, nevertheless, had to get a few hours of sleep.

They all knew how upset he was so he lay down beside a rock outcropping several yards away from the truck.

"Kieran, are you all right?" Werner asked as he stood by Kieran's sleeping mat.

"I'm fine," Kieran snapped. "You boys settle your plans to run away like a bunch of pussies?"

"Kieran, be reasonable. Zimmer is in charge. He is trying to do what is best."

"What is *best*? What is best is to save some poor people who fell into this shithole of a world."

"I can see that talking to you while you wallow in this state is useless."

"Yeah, go back to your peeps and leave me the hell alone," Kieran said as he rolled over, giving Werner his back.

"Very well," Werner said as he turned on his heel and walked away.

To Kieran's relief, the Germans left him alone and formed a cold camp on the opposite side of the truck.

Calming himself, Kieran managed to drift off to sleep.

CHAPTER 17

As the sun dipped behind the horizon, Kieran awoke. Rolling up his mat and blanket, he slipped past the sleeping squad's bedrolls and eased opened the driver's side door of the Jug.

Cold-blooded Nazi assholes, he thought as he slipped the spare keys from his pocket.

I can't let those poor people die or worse, live as freaking slaves. I'll sneak in, release the prisoners, and, with any luck, we will be long gone before the Riahass know what hit them. No freaking way their screwed up tiger camels will be able to hang with my ride, especially on a paved road.

I figure we can hide beyond the twin mesas and hook up with the sunshine boys tomorrow. I would love to see the look on Zimmer's smug face when he finds me gone. He will have a shit fit.

Luckily for him, the big truck sat on a slope. Kieran put the truck in neutral, and it rolled down the gentle slope, gaining speed quickly. Kieran sat ready to start the engine and roar away, but the expected shouted challenge did not materialize.

Oh, thank you, Jesus. The sentry must be asleep. Poor guy. Zimmer will have his ass for breakfast. I hope it was Max. That would be funny.

The way was smooth, and, after rolling a mile down to the desert floor, he cranked the engine and slowly drove toward the ruined freeway ahead.

Kieran drove parallel to the enormous structure, his way lit by the twin moons. After a few miles, he found a buckled and broken section of the highway where a support had fallen.

"This is close enough," he whispered and killed the purring engine. "I burned my bridges, and no turning back now. I have to succeed."

He left the Jug parked behind a distinctive buckled section of the ancient road, one that jutted upward for over twenty feet like a giant frozen glittering ocean wave. Its unmistakable outline in the moonlit darkness would make finding his getaway vehicle foolproof.

&⤳⤳

His heart in his mouth, Kieran ran through the moonlit darkness moving from cover to cover. The Riahass camp was set up a stone's throw from the great roadway near an off ramp. To his surprise, while the section of roadway to the west was mostly obliterated, eastward, the intact road snaked for miles. Its construction material wasn't asphalt, but a strange, dense material glistening in the twin moon light like a sparkling river.

Thank you, Jesus, these animals don't post guards or have anything close to guard dogs. Why would they? To them, they are the Alpha Dogs of this place with nothing to fear. I hope that that little lapse in judgement will help me not get myself killed.

From the drone reconnaissance, I knew the general layout of the encampment, but those were just videos. Being on the ground makes it scary real.

Concealed by a buckled section of roadway, Kieran observed the camp looking for his chance to mount a rescue. While he waited, he produced his digital recorder and made notes while he scanned the camp with a pair of small binoculars.

 espen

"The creatures are extremely erratic in their habits and demeanor, giving me the impression that the entire population was in desperate need of Ritalin. From what I can see there are three classes, all identical physically, but segregated by the color of their robes. The Blues, the Whites, and the Browns.

"The two 'blues,' from what I observe are the management. They sit around while the browns and whites wait on them. The 'whites' are whom I assume are the soldiers, while the browns do all the menial labor. The whites and the browns do not get along. The 'browns' do the cooking, tending the animals and guard the captive humans.

"I see four humans—two women, and two men—doing hard labor, each guarded by a single 'brown.' There may be more, but I don't see any.

"Makes my blood boil as the 'browns' each carry a slim rod and without provocation enjoy delivering a stripe to their charge. In the center of the camp, rising some twenty feet, is the 'Holy Antenna.' The stylized structure sparkles in the moonlight, and several offerings of food lay about its base. I'm moving my position to see if I can find more human captives."

Kieran gingerly moved along the outskirts of the camp. He found the pens where the humans were housed. It looked like the pens could hold at least one hundred, but he counted only four living prisoners.

He decided that the camp was too active, so he waited until everyone was asleep. He picked a spot near a cluster of the tents, where several of the aliens sat around a fire.

He had trouble shaking the idea that he was in a western movie. Even though the aliens did not look in the least like Native Americans and dressed closer to Arabs, their tents were identical to that of teepees used by the Sioux tribes. He tried to listen in on their conversations but was frustrated.

While they obviously knew English, it wasn't their native language.

That slang is worse than German, he thought. Kieran was amazed at the display he saw below him. The aliens did very little physically, in fact, they didn't have to. With a gesture, inanimate objects would rise and come to them. Plates of food, jugs of water, wood for the fire all seemed to be at their beck and call.

The aliens passed around a white ceramic jug. *Looks like the aliens have a taste for moonshine.*

Like watching a wizard convention, he thought. *What is the term Fat Jimmy and his paranormal group used to toss around...telekinesis, that's it! Somehow they are doing this with their minds. Seems that their mental power has very little fine control. They can attract objects and repel with great force, but that's it. Food preparation is still done by hand as are repairs to the tents and clothing.*

Kieran absentmindedly touched his head where one of those things clipped him with a rock. As he watched, he found that all wizards were not made equally. Some were far stronger, and it soon became evident that was the reason behind the color segregation of their robes.

Browns were the weakest, but they could still be a formidable opponent.

This isn't one big happy family, he thought as he saw several squabbles break out and the predictable mayhem ensue. In an hour and a half, he saw two of the lesser brown wizards murdered. Without ceremony, the bodies were stripped of any valuables and cast into the darkness off the side of the road.

Kieran suppressed a laugh as he observed a Riahass, dressed in fine blue silk looking like a samurai, strutting around in a pair of garish cowboy boots. From the way the others bowed before him, Kieran decided that this guy was the big kahuna.

Suddenly, Kieran heard a humming that sounded like a gigantic swarm of bees. The big kahuna ran to the Holy Antenna and bowed before the strange idol. As one, the entire camp, including the slaves bowed to the strange totem.

"You have got to be kidding me," Kieran muttered. An eerie blue glow enveloped the big kahuna and lifted him off his feet, suspending him some ten feet in the air. "I see it, but I don't believe it," he said as the hair rose on the back of his neck.

Kieran scrambled and produced his cell phone to record the spectacle. After several incredible minutes, the big kahuna dropped lightly to the ground and the congregation scattered.

"What was that all about?" Kieran muttered, slipping his phone into his pocket.

Soon after the ecclesiastical event, a fight broke out that reminded Kieran of an old western movie barroom fight, all the while the big kahuna drank and laughed at the carnage.

Kieran came away with the conclusion that the wizards were brutal, sadistic, and always in a bad mood. Violence was their answer to everything.

I don't understand a few things. Vilragg is obviously the same species as the Riahass, but they're nothing alike. The Riahass are brutal savages half a step above animals while Vilragg is intelligent and apparently civilized, yet Vilragg said they were the same people. He also has some pretty heavy-duty tech, if it were he who brought Zimmer and his men here. What agency destroyed this place and set the Riahass back a million years? How does Vilragg expect a bunch of primitive goons from 1944 Germany to help?

I suppose meeting with Vilragg will put to bed all my questions...well, all, but one. Who brought me here and why? All I know for sure is that this experience will make one whale of a story.

CHAPTER 18

After another hour had passed, the main body of the Riahass had decided to call it a night and entered their tents. Five browns herded the humans together and forced them back into the slave pens. Kieran saw his chance and clutching the P-38, he made his way to the slave pens.

With his heart pounding in his ears, Kieran crept to the rear of the closest cage.

Please, Lord, he prayed silently, *please don't let there be face huggers, graboids, or any other alien horrors roaming around in the dark. Amen.*

As he neared, his nose was assaulted by the horrendous smell of the unkempt pens and rotting bodies. Kieran's heart dropped as he observed several dozen human corpses piled together in a rotting heap, off to the side of the pens.

Sorry bastards. They killed them all.

Pressing on by the twin moons' light, he saw four dirty, yet very much alive humans huddled together against the desert night's chill. The cruel, unsanitary cage was too low for the prisoners to sit upright. It was apparent to Kieran that it was, in itself a form of torture.

How can anyone be so freaking cruel?

Crawling to the rear of the low cage, wary of any nosy Riahass, Kieran grasped the side.

"Psssst!" he hissed, trying to get their attention.

Slowly, one of the prisoners raised his head, and his eyes locked on Kieran.

Extricating himself from the small group of prisoners, he crawled over to Kieran.

"I'm here to help," Kieran whispered.

"You're an American," he said. "So are we. Thank you, Lord. Son, these damn things aren't *human*."

"Wake the others and tell them to stay quiet," Kieran said. "I'll have you out of there in a jiffy."

He crawled to the front of the crude wire cage and opened the simple latch. Gritting his teeth, he swung open the door, the rusty hinges squeaking ever so slightly, but to his over-worked senses, they sounded like a gunshot. To his great relief, none of the Riahass came running.

The four captives crawled from the cruel pen. The prisoners were bare foot, dressed in ragged underwear, and covered with filth. In the bright moons' light, he quickly took stock of his fellow Americans. Of the men, one was tall and thin with a mass of shaggy hair and a full beard. He looked to be in his early sixties. He was by far, the worse off of the four and had to lean upon the second man for support.

The second was of medium height with a thick, stocky build. He was bald except for a close cut fringe. Kieran could see the remnants of a pencil thin mustache, even though he sported several days growth of beard.

The girl looked to be about Kieran's age, with her hair held back by a ragged length of cloth tied in a lopsided bow. She wore the tattered remains of a slip and panties. The meager shreds of cloth she wore left little to the imagination.

The older woman was about forty, whipcord lean, with long dark hair. Like the girl, she was wearing the remains of her underwear.

"Are there any more prisoners?" Kieran asked.

"God bless you," whispered the girl as she emerged from the pen. "But there are no others. We are all that's left."

"Okay, let's grab a hand full of Greyhound and get the hell out of Dodge," Kieran said.

"You can't do this," the tall bearded man said loudly. "The Riahass will find and punish us! We belong to them!"

"Please, Mr. Marsden, you have to be quiet," whispered the older woman in a West Virginian twang. "We're being rescued."

"Yes, old boy, just keep it together," the stocky man said.

Taking Kieran by the hand, the girl pulled him away from the men.

"Those monsters will never get their hands on me again. Promise me that, if we can't get away, you will kill me."

"Not going to happen," Kieran whispered. "Listen, if anything goes wrong, I have a truck hidden by a buckled section of the road, a mile that way," he whispered, pointing west. "The keys are in the ignition. Drive due east along the road to the ring of mesas. I have some friends there who will take care of you."

"No, the Riahass will find us and punish us!" Mr. Marsden screamed. "Help me, masters! Help me! They're trying to take me away!"

"Ah, crap," Kieran, said as he saw a knot of the Riahass running toward them. He lunged to his left, as a stone missile whizzed by his ear. Several stones flew through the air, one catching Marsden in the forehead, silencing his cry for help, in a crunch of bone and spray of blood. Dropping the body, the bald man grabbed the girl by the arm and pulled her into the darkness, followed closely by the older woman.

"Run for the truck!" Kieran shouted as he brought the P-38 to bear.

Kieran fired five shots in quick secession and smiled as the missile barrage ceased. He had turned to join the escapees when he felt himself seized, as if by a giant hand, and jerked fifteen feet into the air. Struggling in the iron grip, he saw one of the chief Riahass below him, the one who wore the garish cowboy boots, his face contorted with rage.

Kieran aimed his pistol only to have it ripped from his hand.

Once he was disarmed and no longer posing a threat, the rest of the Riahass massed around their leader, as he held the struggling Kieran suspended in the air above. They began arguing among themselves in English over the kind of horrific death Kieran would receive for releasing their cattle.

One Riahass standing near the center of the group of bickering aliens watched as an odd-looking canister, fell at his feet. It was his first and last experience with a *stielhandgrante*. The well-tossed German hand grenade exploded in their midst to terrible results. Kieran fell from the sky as the leader was blown in half.

Stunned by the fall, Kieran heard Zimmer yell, "Fire."

Before the shell-shocked survivors could regain their wits, Kieran heard the buzzsaw-like sound of Werner's *Maschinengewehr*, which he'd nicknamed Sophia. Kieran had trained extensively on the gun, but this was his first experience seeing it in action.

The unbelievable hail of bullets sliced through the Riahass like a scythe. Mixed with the harsh ripping sound of the heavy machinegun was the staccato of the troopers' MP-44s.

Facing brutal, encircling machinegun fire, the battle was over as quickly as it began. The Riahass never had a chance to fight back as the well-trained *Fallschirmjäger* rose from their concealment and put an end to their evil. Knowing how dangerous even one of the Riahass were, the Germans made sure none of them survived.

"Kieran, are you all right?" Captain Zimmer asked as he came running up clutching a smoking machine gun.

"I am now," Kieran said as he accepted a hand up. "Talk about the cavalry arriving in the nick of time."

Kieran's further words were cut off as Zimmer gave him the benefit of a rock-hard right cross. Kieran staggered back and collapsed in a heap.

"*That* was for disobeying orders."

Kieran lay in the dirt and rubbed his jaw. He should have been pissed, but right now, he was just happy to be alive.

"What, no clever retort?" Zimmer asked.

"No," Kieran said as he rose to a sitting position. "But I was wondering where you guys came from. I left you sleeping miles from here."

Kieran looked up as Loewe drove the Jug into camp. Hartmann opened the back of the truck and escorted the captives to Captain Zimmer.

"Wait a minute," Kieran said. "Answer the question."

Max translated Kieran's words, and the squad chuckled.

"Kieran, you underestimate the hauptmann," Werner said. "He knew you would attempt a rescue, so while you were sleeping, *we* moved out."

"I saw the bedrolls, and I thought it was you guys."

"Yes, we were already in position when you got here," Zimmer said, barely containing a smile. "You need to work on your sneaking. You almost stepped on poor Werner."

Kieran turned red as the squad laughed at him.

"The hauptmann knew you would fail, *hero*," Max said. "He knew your capture would bring all the Riahass into a nice compact group we could easily kill without taking any losses."

"Okay, you outsmarted me. Why did you have to break my jaw?"

"Seemed like the right thing to do," Zimmer said. "For any fighting unit to remain strong, discipline must be maintained. Besides, I enjoyed it."

Kieran rolled his eyes, as Zimmer slapped him on the back.

"Hauptmann," Hartmann said, as he brought the man and women forward. The trio looked terrified as they beheld the soldiers.

"Captain Udo Zimmer, at your service," he said as he smiled and extended his hand. "And this sorry excuse for a man is Kieran Nash."

"James Allen and this is my secretary Candy Matson,"

he said as he shook Zimmer's hand. "This is Betty Cooper."

The older woman's eyes flew open in terror. "Are you fellows…*Nazis?*"

"We are *Fallschirmjäger* of the German Luftwaffe."

"Oh no," Allen said softly. "Out of the frying pan and into the fire."

"Do not be alarmed, Mr. Allen. Like you, we are not here of our own free will."

"In other words, Captain," Allen said, "it seems we are in the same boat."

"Mr. Allen, how did you, Fraulein Matson, and Frau Cooper come to be in such a predicament?"

As Big Jim related his tale to Captain Zimmer, Candy stepped close to Kieran.

"Hi, Candy," he said to the young woman. "Nothing to be afraid of now."

Candy moved close to Kieran. Expecting a grateful woman saved from a horrible fate, Kieran readied himself for a kiss or a least a warm hug or two.

"You are an *American?*" she asked. "Palling around with…*Germans?*"

"Well, yeah," he said.

"This is for being a freaking Nazi loving *traitor.*"

"Huh?" Kieran managed to say before Candy savagely planted her knee in his groin. As Kieran doubled over in pain, Candy gave him a wicked upper cut that put him on the ground. She landed several hard kicks to his chest before a gunshot made her freeze in mid-kick.

Looking up, she watched wide-eyed as Max threw back the bolt on his rifle and chambered a fresh round.

"The next one, *fraulein*, won't be over your head."

Allen rushed forward, grabbed Candy, and pulled her back. Zimmer waved Max off who reluctantly lowered his rifle.

Candy buried her head in Allen's shoulder and began to sob uncontrollably. "Will this nightmare never end?"

Kieran rose to his knees and spit blood. "What the hell was that for?" he asked.

"Sorry, kid," Allen said. "You have to understand—the war and all. Candy's brother was killed in the war."

"By a bunch of sorry Nazi bastards!" she screamed at Zimmer. "I hate you, and I hate traitors who help you! I hope you all die!"

"Your friends, the Japs, killed my son David at Pearl Harbor," Betty said.

"I see," Zimmer said. "For your information, Fraulein Matson, and Frau Cooper, we found Kieran much the same way we found you. He isn't a Nazi bastard—"

"He is just a *stupid* bastard," Max said, without cracking a smile. "He wanted to be a hero, and he turned out to be a *zero*."

Zimmer silenced Max with a stern look. "When Kieran here saw that the Riahass had human captives, he, against my specific orders, by the way, risked his life and came running to your rescue. While unintentional, Kieran was instrumental in our victory."

A look of horror crossed Candy's face as she took a step toward the fallen man. "Oh, no, I'm so sorry."

Humiliated, Kieran waved her off angrily, rose to his knees, and spat a mouthful of bloody spittle on the ground. "Stay the hell away from me," he snarled.

"Are we going to have a problem, Mr. Allen, with you and your secretary?" Zimmer asked.

"No, Captain Zimmer. You and your boys saved my bacon, and I'm grateful. Candy here is a swell kid, one of the sweetest girls you'll ever meet. It's just that she has been through a lot lately. Last year, she lost her kid brother in the war and now this. She just went a little nuts, is all. Candy won't be a problem, I promise."

"Very well, Mr. Allen," Zimmer said. "But I won't tolerate any more violent outbursts. Do you both understand me?"

"Clear as a bell, Captain," he said. "And by the way, the name is Big Jim."

"What about you, Frau Cooper?"

"I don't like it none, but looks like I ain't got a choice," she said.

"What are you going to do if we don't behave, shoot us in the back like a bunch of cowards?" Candy asked.

"Calm down, Candy, you aren't helping things," Allen whispered harshly. "I, for one, like the Germans a hell of a lot better than being whipped like a dog and locked up in that stinking cage."

"Yeah, I have to go along with that," Betty said. "Those animals were worse than the godless Nazis."

"No, we won't shoot you like cowards, Fraulein Matson," Zimmer said. "We will give you food and water and let you go your way. With luck, you may stay out of the hands of the Riahass before the desert claims you, but I doubt it. In any event, you will die a most unpleasant death. Your only chance of survival is to throw in with us."

Candy opened her mouth to give Zimmer a nasty retort then rethought her response and closed her mouth.

"I want you to understand. We are not Germans and Americans at war. That war, for us, is over. On this world, we are humans together in a fight for survival. I am sorry for your loss, *fraulein*, and, you frau, but you will have to let it go. I promise you, I will do my best to protect you and get us home, but you must do your part."

"Oh, I can just guess what my part will be," Candy said. "Legs spread wide, I suppose. Should I do you first or everyone at once?"

"Candy!" Betty cried, shocked at her crude outburst.

The color drained from Zimmer's face as he glared in anger. He gave his oberfeldwebel a glance. In an instant, the troop of German paratroopers assembled and stood at attention.

Zimmer walked up to Candy and roughly grasped her arm.

"Hey," she said.

"Wait a minute," Big Jim said. "Don't touch her."

"Stay out of this, *Big* Jim," Zimmer said. "This doesn't concern you."

Fear shining in his eyes, Big Jim stepped back.

"Let me go, you son of a bitch!" she cried.

Zimmer ignored Candy's curses and struggles as he marched her to the line of green-clad men.

"Listen to me carefully. Fraulein Matson is to be treated with the utmost respect, but she is off limits. I will not tolerate any social fraternization, period. Dismissed."

Amid some very transparent disappointment from a few of the soldiers, they broke ranks.

"I—I don't know w—what to say," she stammered. "I thought you were—"

"You thought we were the depraved animals portrayed in your own country's propaganda? We are professional soldiers, not rapists. I meant what I said. Now get cleaned up, as we have a long journey ahead of us." Zimmer released Candy's arm. "One last thing, *fraulein*. Leave my men alone. I understand your anger, and I cannot expect you to like us, but I do expect you to act like a young lady and be civil to the men protecting you from the dangers of this world. I will take any slight, whether physical or verbal, against them, personally."

"All right, looks like I have no choice. I'll be a good *fraulein* until we get back to Earth, then the deal is off— *Otto.*"

"Fair enough. My medic will check you, Frau Cooper, and Mr. Allen. Roth, get them some food and water."

"I don't know how to thank you," Big Jim said.

"Keep her under control," Zimmer said. "I will give you an hour to eat and get cleaned up, so make the most of it. Hartmann, search this camp for food, water, and anything else we can use."

While the troop busied themselves looting the camp, Max took Kieran by the arm and helped him to his feet.

"Fraulein packs a punch like Joe Lewis, no?" he asked with a chuckle.

"Kicks like a mule, as well," Kieran said.

Max chuckled. "I think you will have a black eye."

"Max, old buddy, if I ever go off halfcocked and try to rescue anyone else, please do me a favor and shoot me."

"It will be my pleasure."

CHAPTER 19

While the squad ransacked the camp, Kieran hobbled over to the Jug and opened the passenger side door. His lower lip was split, and he could already feel his left eye begin to swell. Digging under the seat, he came across a well-equipped first aid kit.

"Thank goodness," he said, popping off the lid. Inside was a cold compress. Squeezing it vigorously to activate its chemicals, he leaned back in the seat and pressed it to his tender eye, praying he could prevent an ugly shiner. Closing his eyes, he produced his recorder.

"Dear Diary, I have learned firsthand that no good deed goes unpunished. My rescue attempt didn't go as planned, but everything worked out thanks to that smartass Zimmer and his men. That is one clever Nazi. Anyway, I always dreamed of rescuing a buxom, pouty-lipped damsel in distress from dastardly alien slavers…okay, maybe not that exact scenario, but saving the damsel in distress part. In my dreams, the grateful damsel showed yours truly a very good time, but sadly, that was only in my dreams. In reality, Candy, if you can believe that name, after my heroic save-the-day rescue, proceeded to beat the crap out of me. She kneed my nads so hard that I think my kids will be born with a limp.

"I'm dictating this little entry while holding a compress to my eye. Along with rendering me sterile, she gave me a shiner.

"Funny, I don't remember this ever happening to the heroes in the books I read growing up. When I get back home, I'm going to write some pretty nasty letters to the authors who set this guy up for a fall."

Kieran chuckled. "Seems that even on another planet, girls treat me like pond scum. At least it's nice to know the universe is consistent. Candy has some serious issues with the Germans, despite the fact they saved her ass. This trip has certainly gotten interesting, but not for the better. Kirk out."

露

With Kieran behind the wheel, and Zimmer dozing beside him, the troop arrived at the nearest of the towering ring of mesas just before sunrise.

"Hey Colonel Klink, get up."

Zimmer opened his eyes and stretched. He glanced at his watch and frowned.

"You were supposed to wake me hours ago. You have driven all night?"

"Yeah, but you looked like you could use the sleep," Kieran said. "I want to thank you for the save back there. Sometimes I go off halfcocked."

"Think nothing of it. I have been accused of leaping first and looking second. My recklessness, and a few other things, has kept me from advancing past Hauptmann. It seems we are kindred spirits."

"By the way, back at the camp did you see the leader...*fly*?"

"Yes. It was unsettling. I thought it was some alien device. I personally inspected the idol and found it to be no more than a tube of aluminum."

"Now, I'm officially creeped out," Kieran said. He indicated the massive mesa that sat a quarter of a mile ahead of them. "I think we're here. Would you look at the size of that thing?"

"Pull over," Zimmer said rubbing his eyes. "We will set up camp here."

"Okay," Kieran said as he slowed to a stop and shut off the engine.

"How's the eye?"

Kieran looked into the rearview mirror and cringed.

"Humiliating."

Zimmer laughed and slid out of the vehicle.

Kieran fell out of the cab and stretched his back. While everyone crawled from the rear of the truck, he retrieved his recorder and walked over to the mesa to get a closer look. Looking up at the twin, skyscraper sized mesas, he gasped. "This mesa isn't natural or made of stone," he dictated. "It's like some kind of reinforced concrete. Symbols deeply carved into the surface cover the face. I don't know if it's ornamental or some dedication, but it is beautiful. If I don't miss my guess, these things are massive base columns, but whatever they supported is long gone. They look sort of like a gigantic bridge support. One that would easily dwarf the supports of the Golden Gate, but they are not alone.

"Hey, these things are evenly spaced...looks like one every five miles or so. They aren't in a straight line, but in a huge circle like an alien Stonehenge. What they could be used for is a mystery."

"Kieran," Werner said as he walked up. "Isn't this amazing?"

"And then some, buddy."

"An alien structure," Werner said. Taking the drawing pad Kieran gave him, Werner quickly sketched and shaded, his eyes never left the colossal structure before him.

"That's fantastic work, Werner," Kieran said as he gazed at Werner's masterful rendition. "It looks like I gave that pad to the right fellow."

Werner beamed. "Kieran, a little something I worked on last night by flashlight. What do you think?"

Werner flipped back a page, and Kieran chuckled.

The drawing was of Kieran dressed in the old styled Buck Rodgers helmet and ray gun charging a sinister looking Riahass who had a scantily clad Candy Matson over his shoulder.

"Werner old buddy, I love it," Kieran said. "The likenesses are amazing."

"Thank you, my friend," Werner said.

"Glad it wasn't of that shrew giving me a beat down."

"Honestly, Kieran, Max lobbied for that drawing."

"Oh, he did, did he?" Kieran asked.

"Begged would be more accurate. Even offered me two packages of cigarettes."

"Max is an asshole."

"Yes, he is," Werner said. "But you have to admit he is very good at it."

"Hold up the drawing," Kieran said. "I want to get a picture of the work and the artist."

Werner ditched his rimless helmet and smoothed his unruly blonde hair. Smiling broadly, he posed with his drawing held before him.

"That was great," Kieran said, snapping a couple of shots of Werner before the base.

"Kieran?" Candy asked. "Honey, can I talk to you?"

Kieran froze and gritted his teeth. Turning he found her standing a few feet away.

"What do you want?" he asked. "On second thought, never mind what you want, go away."

"Don't be that way, honey. I want to apologize for last night."

"Okay, you have, *honey*," he said, not looking at her. "Now go away and leave me the hell alone."

Kieran walked a few feet away and stood with his back to her.

Werner laughed and produced a pack of cigarettes.

Candy snarled at Werner before her eyes fell upon the crumpled pack in his hand.

"I have been dying for a cigarette," she said. "Would you mind?"

"My pleasure, *fraulein*," Werner said, extending the pack toward her.

Candy extracted a cigarette and accepted a light from Werner.

Drawing deeply, she exhaled a long cloud of smoke. "Oh, Lord, I needed that," she said. "Now Kieran, honey, why don't we have a smoke and let's be friends?"

"I don't smoke, and I'm not your friend," he said icily as he gazed up at the monolith towering before him.

"Don't smoke?" she asked. "Everyone who is anybody smokes. Rita Hayworth smokes. Claudette Colbert, Errol Flynn, Irene Dunn for crying out loud."

"Yeah, everyone in old movies smokes, and most died of lung cancer or emphysema."

"What do you mean...*old* movies. I've got news for you, they're all alive and kicking."

"Don't you remember, *fraulein*?" Werner asked. "I mentioned it last night. Kieran here is from the future."

"I thought you were just pulling my leg," she said. "I think there is something stronger than tobacco in *your* cigarette, Fritz."

Werner guffawed.

"Tell her Kieran."

"Tell me what?"

"Not that any of it's your business, but when I was brought here," Kieran said. "The year was 2014."

"You're joking. That's completely nuts."

"Fine, don't believe me. Now run along."

"Fraulein," Werner said. "I know it sounds incredible, but it is true. His devices are amazing."

"No fooling?"

"No," Kieran said. "Okay, we all know I'm from the future. Now if you will excuse me, Candy, go get lung disease somewhere else. I was talking to my friend."

"Kieran, honey, I don't blame you one bit for being sore

at me. You didn't deserve what I did to you. I mean, especially after you risked your life to save me and all, but you have to understand, after what I went through with the Riahass—and then the Nazis killing my kid brother—well, I went kind of crazy."

"Yeah, kind of."

"At least look at me, *please*?"

Expelling a deep breath, Kieran turned slowly and faced her.

Candy gasped at his black eye. "Oh my," she said. "My daddy always said I had a temper."

"Well, he was right, wasn't he? These assholes have given me mortal hell over having my ass stomped by a *fraulein*. I wish to God I had minded my own business and left your crazy ass rotting in that stinking cage."

Red faced, Kieran turned and stalked off.

"What the hell?" she cried as her eyes fell on the drawing pad. "You look here, *Fritz*," she said, stabbing Werner in the chest with her finger. "You keep my mug out of your sick fantasies. You hear me?"

"Leave him alone," Kieran said as he rushed toward her. "Werner was only trying to make me feel better…heroic if you please, instead of the freaking fool you turned me into."

"Hey, Kieran."

All three turned and beheld a smiling Max at the top of the hill, his rifle in his hand. "Want to borrow my gun in case the terrifying *fraulein* gets violent again?"

"Creep!" Candy screamed as she picked up a stone and hurled it at the laughing man.

"Just great," Kieran moaned. "Thanks, Max. Really mean it, buddy."

"I'm sorry," she said softly as her eyes filled with tears.

"Take your sorry and go to hell," Kieran said over his shoulder as he stalked away.

"Werner, we are setting up camp," Max said. "Come on."

"I didn't mean to," Candy said softly.

Ignoring her, Werner gathered his helmet and drawing pad and moved up the hill to join his company.

Candy drew fitfully on the cigarette. "Well, this is a fine how do you do," she said to herself, blowing a cloud of smoke. "Well, Candy, looks like you have really made a mess of things, but if anyone can fix this, it's yours truly."

CHAPTER 20

Half an hour later, Candy found Kieran near the gargantuan support base, resting in the deep shadow it cast, listening to music. He held his phone in his hand reviewing the images he had captured of his adventure.

"I brought you some food and water, honey," Candy said.

Kieran rolled his eyes, "What part of leave me alone didn't you understand? Go smoke your cigarettes somewhere else."

"I have had my last one," she announced. "Like you, I'm a non-smoker."

"Just freaking wonderful."

"What do you have there?" she asked, ignoring his snide comment.

Kieran pulled the ear buds from his ears. "Why won't you leave me alone?"

"You can't give me the brush-off," she said. "Not until you forgive me, first."

"Yeah, when this place freezes over," he mumbled.

"What's that?"

Kieran rolled his eyes and took a deep breath. "If you must know, it's my cell phone."

"A telephone? Where are the wires?"

"No wires and it won't make any calls here, but it can snap some pictures."

"A telephone that is also a camera?" she asked, rolling her eyes. "Now I know you are pulling my leg. What does it really do?"

"A lot of things. Even plays music."

"You mean like records?"

"Kind of, but they're called music files."

"You think I'm just a dumb blonde. I'm not falling for that line, fellah. Next, you'll be trying to sell me the Brooklynn Bridge."

"If I prove it, will you go bother someone else?"

"On my honor as a Girl Scout," she said with a bright smile.

"Fine," he said, as he handed her the ear buds.

"Stick these in your ears," he said.

"What does it do?"

"Makes your head explode."

"You're the silliest boy."

"Stick them in your ears—now."

Candy gave him a puzzled look but complied. Kieran selected one of the softer tracts in his library.

Candy's eyes widened. "It really *does* play music? How in the world is this possible?"

"Magic," he said. Kieran handed her the slim rectangle and showed her how to browse the hard drive. "I have some four hundred music files. Mostly pop and rock, but I also have some blues and a little country."

"Any ol' Blue Eyes?"

"Sinatra?"

"Is there another?"

"One of my favorites. I love *Fly Me to the Moon*."

"I know a bunch about Frank, but I never heard of that song."

"Try it."

"I never heard of such a thing," she gasped. "It is so clear, not scratchy like a record. You're on the level."

"Okay. I proved it. On your honor as a Girl Scout, go away."

"Honey, I was never a Girl Scout," she said. "Now, eat while I listen to future music."

"I'm in hell, that's it," he mumbled. "Hell's full of Nazis, aliens, and *her*. I'm doomed."

Giving in, Kieran ate the freeze-dried eggs and bacon while she listened to the soothing creations of musicians, thirty years before they were born.

Candy handed him back his player as he finished his breakfast. "I didn't believe you and Fritz—"

"His name is *Werner*," Kieran said.

"Okay, Werner. I asked around, and Captain Zimmer told me the same thing. I thought that they were full of baloney. But it's true, isn't it?"

"Yeah, I'm a regular Luke Skywalker," he said.

"Luke, who?"

"Oh. Never mind."

"So, do you have a flying car?"

"No. Why does everyone ask me that?"

"Zimmer told me to ask," she said. "Said it would bug you."

Kieran shook his head. "Lord help me—Nazis with a sense of humor."

As the sun climbed high above the horizon, Kieran got his first real look at Candy Matson. The dirt and grime scrubbed away and her hair washed, she was far from the pitiful captive he had helped rescue the night before.

Her thick mass of honey-blonde hair framed a delicate-shaped face and dimpled chin, set off by big blue eyes and full luscious lips. Across her nose was a light dusting of freckles. When she smiled, her face lit up, and her eyes sparkled in a way that made him ache deep inside.

She was without a doubt the most beautiful woman he had ever seen, and he couldn't help but stare.

"Found something you like, big boy?" she asked with a smile.

He aimed his camera at her, and after a few snapshots, he hit the record button.

"Oh, don't take my picture," she said. "I'm a mess."

"I know," he said. "Never seen anything as hideous in my life. I hope you don't break my camera."

"Why waste the film, honey?" she asked. "The nearest drugstore is a doozy of a walk."

"Why would I want to go to a drugstore?"

"To get those pictures developed, of course."

"Oh," he said. "It's my film to waste, that is, if my camera survives the horror."

"So, how old are you, Mr. Smarty Pants?" she asked.

"I was born in 1995, so I'm nineteen."

"No fooling? I was born in twenty-six, but I'm only eighteen. Kind of hard to wrap your mind around, huh?"

"In 1926?" he said with a laugh. "That would make you old enough to be my grandma."

Anger flashed bright in Candy's beautiful blue eyes. "Look here, buster, if you don't want to look like a raccoon you had better lay off the grandma crack."

Kieran laughed as she fumed. "I see you got some new clothes," he said.

"Yeah, those creeps ruined my brand new dress that I paid a whole twelve dollars for. Those *awful things* ripped it to shreds just to make me cry. I found this little number in one of the tents. The woman who owned it must have weighted a good two hundred pounds. It makes me look like I'm wearing a circus tent."

"Least you aren't naked anymore," he said. "I don't think any of us could take that abuse much longer."

Candy let out a ragged breath of frustration.

"I'm getting tired of the wise-ass cracks, mister. Believe me, Kieran, I'm real sorry about the whole Nazi thing, but you have to understand my point of view."

"Understand *your* point of view? I didn't do anything but try to help you. In fact, I risked my neck to save you and got a black eye as a reward. I'm not concerned about your point of view."

"I come from a big family up in Idaho. Seven brothers

and three sisters. We are real a close-knit farm family, but Charley and I were real close. You see we were twins. It seemed I was always looking after him because that boy could never stay out of trouble. When the war started, Charley could not resist and, without a word goodbye, ran off and joined the army. We got four letters before the Western Union man showed up at our door." She looked down at the ground.

"You lost your brother in the war?"

"North Africa. He was killed by the Nazis."

"Sorry."

Kieran let out a breath of frustration.

"So, Candy how did you come to work for Big Jim?"

"With Charley gone, I just had to get away. I ended up in San Francisco, working for The Western Life Insurance Company. Not a glamor job, by any means, but San Francisco sure is an exciting town compared to the life on a potato farm. I swore that I was never going to waste my life bowing down to a man, cranking out babies, and getting old before my time on a farm."

"Ambitious," he said. "I like that in a woman. As long as she does what I say."

Kieran chuckled as she swatted him on the head.

"You think you are the killer-diller, don't you, boy?"

"I haven't a clue as to what you just said."

"I thought you spoke English, chucklehead."

"Your slang is before my time, babe. Talking to you is like listening to an old Bugs Bunny cartoon. Let me ask you a question, Candy. Were you a flapper?"

"Flapper? How old do you think I am? That was back in my mom's day."

"Oops. Past the 1960s, things get a little fuzzy. Pop culture tends to run together."

"Now, who's speaking another language, bub?"

"What's Big Jim like?"

Candy blew out a deep breath. "Big Jim thinks he's Randolph Scott. Dresses in cowboy hats, string ties, and boots.

You ask me, the man wants to be a cowboy real bad."

"He seems like a nice fellow," Kieran said.

"Looks can be deceiving," she said. "Oh, he comes off as Mr. Personality, but believe me that man has the devil in him. He has been giving me the eye for some time, then two weeks ago he up and offers to set me up in a swank apartment, even throw in a new car and everything, if I'd play house with him."

"What did you say?"

Candy gave Kieran a hurt look, "What do you think I said? My momma didn't raise an able Grable."

"Excuse me? An able Grable?"

"Whore," she said.

"That I understood."

"Anyway I told him to shove his job up his keister, but before I could walk out, a weird fog showed up out of nowhere, and we ended up here. The Riahass caught us half a day later. Big Jim tried to protect me, and they tossed him around like a ragdoll. That took the fight out of us.

They stripped me to my slip and Jim to his skivvies. The leader—some mook named Carre took a fancy to Big Jim's cowboy boots.

We were beaten, but they were just getting started. They took my brand new expensive dress and ripped it into strips. No reason for it. I suppose it was just to be mean. Those animals excelled at being low down mean. They looped a noose about our necks and led us behind those weird horses of theirs for miles without water. We didn't get water until we arrived at their camp and joined the other captives."

"Other captives?"

"That's where we found Betty. She was there a full two weeks ahead of us. Lord, if it were not for her, I would have lost my mind. She's a good simple soul. Perhaps not the sharpest pencil in the box, but a loving, generous person."

"That's good."

"Just between you and me," Candy said as her voice dropped low, "I love her to death, but she is a religious fanatic. We had Jesus morning, noon, and night. I love the Lord as much as the next guy, but Jiminy Cricket, between the Riahass and her sermons, I was about to lose my mind. The woman's entire life consisted of keeping house and Jesus.

"Until Jim and I arrived, poor thing thought she was in Hell, and the Riahass were demons."

Kieran smiled. "I can see how she would think that. Where is Betty, by the way?"

"The poor thing is worn out and is sound asleep. She may sleep for a week."

"Tell me about the other prisoners."

"Along with Mr. Marsden, were six more when we arrived. Four women and two men. Two were Chinese, one was a Brit, one from Mexico and two more Americans."

"They were snatched from all over the world," Kieran mused.

"Yeah, didn't know much about them. Except for Mr. Marsden, they were all kept in a separate pen. For some reason, the Riahass butchered those poor folks like cattle the night before you rescued us."

"Why did they kill them?"

"For the fun of it, I suppose. I will never, to my dying day, forget how those monsters laughed while they tortured those poor people to death.

"When not locked in those horrible cages, they worked us like slaves and took every opportunity to humiliate us. They are devils right out of the pit of Hell. I pray to God they all die."

"Sorry. The Riahass gave me this little beauty mark on my forehead when I got here. Thank God for Zimmer and his men, or I would have been in one of those cages too."

"Yeah, he is a peach, for a murdering Nazi bastard, that is," she said.

"I suppose."

"Kieran, I never met a fellah like you before."

"What kind of fellah do you think I am?"

"You knew up close and personal how dangerous the Ri-ahass were and, while you didn't know me from Adam, you risked your life to save me. Never thought anyone would ever do that for me. It was like Errol Flynn or John Wayne, but for real. Honestly, honey, it makes me weak in the knees thinking about it."

"You kicked me in the face."

"Do you want me to grovel at your feet?" she asked. "Please believe me I'm truly sorry."

Kieran looked away and gathered his thoughts.

"Do you swear never to lay a finger on me again?"

"Not in a bad way," she said with a giggle.

"Okay, I forgive you."

"Thank you, Jesus," she breathed. "That was like getting water from a stone."

"Did your momma really name you, Candy?"

Candy laughed. "My name is Candace, but everyone calls me Candy. You, Kieran Nash, can call me anything you like. So, honey, are you married?"

"No, free as a bird."

"Isn't that a coincidence?" she said. "So am I. I would really like to get to know you better."

"You know, that was what I was thinking, last night, while you were beating the hell out of me," he said. "Boy, she is such a nice girl, I hope she is single."

"Honey, like I said, I'm real sorry about that, and I swear I will make it up to you. Now how come for a fancy future camera, it takes so long to take a photo?"

Kieran stopped recording and saved the video.

"I know this is probably a mistake that I will regret, but let's start over. Miss, my name is Kieran Nash."

Candy smiled and took his hand. "Candy Matson, Mr. Nash. It is a pleasure to make your acquaintance."

Kieran stood beside her to show her the replay of his re-cording. Her big blue eyes grew wide, and her jaw dropped in amazement.

"Drugstore, my ass," he said.

CHAPTER 21

O h, there you are, Candy. Little lady, you had me worried sick," Big Jim Allen said.

Kieran and Candy looked around as Allen, dressed in a white robe similar to hers, bounded down the hill toward them.

"Oh, great," Candy said as her boss approached them. "Mr. Wonderful."

"You can't walk off like that," he said. "God knows what kind of Martian monstrosities are just waiting to pounce and gobble you up."

"Excuse me? Did you say...*Martian* monstrosities?" Kieran asked.

"Yeah. This is Mars, isn't it? Mars is red, and this place is red."

"No, it's not Mars."

"Could it be Venus?" Candy asked.

"'Fraid not," Kieran said.

"I concur, with our young Buck Rodgers."

The trio looked around to find Captain Zimmer walking toward them.

"How are you so cock sure, buster?" Big Jim asked Kieran.

"You should listen to him, Mr. Allen," Candy said. "He's from the future."

"Yeah, and I'm the Easter Bunny. Candy, what did I tell you? You can call me Big Jim."

"Okay, but Kieran *is* the real deal. He's from the future."

"If we were on Mars or Venus, we would be dead," Kieran said. "Mars has too thin an atmosphere to breathe and is artic cold. Venus is around nine-hundred degrees and has sulfuric acid as an ingredient in its atmosphere."

"Bull," Big Jim said. "Now how would you know that?"

"I would listen to Kieran," Zimmer said as he lit a cigarette.

"NASA has sent space probes to most of the planets and hasn't found any sign of life. You ask me, we aren't even in the solar system."

"Even though I don't know what a NASA is, I agree," Zimmer said. "I have been trained in celestial navigation, and since we have been here, I haven't seen one familiar constellation or star group."

"What are you saying?" Big Jim asked.

"That we aren't in Kansas anymore," Zimmer said. "All the more reason to work together."

"I agree," Candy said, taking Kieran's hand. "We really should work together."

Kieran noticed the blood drain from Big Jim's fleshy face.

"Hey, guys," Candy said. "If it isn't too much trouble, can we keep the whole traveling-to-another-world thing under our hats around Betty? Poor thing's on the ragged edge."

"Yeah, that religious wacko thinks the world is flat," Big Jim said. "Her ideas are right out of the middle ages. By the way, Candy, you better not let Mary Magdalene see you smoking or she'll give you an earful about the Devil's weed."

"Seems Kieran and Betty do have some things in common," Candy said with a smile.

"Candy, I need to talk to you—*alone*," Big Jim said.

"You need to take a long walk off a short pier, Big Jim," she said. "I said all that needs to be said back on Earth."

"Kieran," Zimmer said, taking him aside, "You have been up all night. You need to get some sleep."

"I'm not tired."

"You will be. We all need to be at our best, so while we have time, I want you to get a few hours of rest. That's an order."

"Hey, you can't order him around," Candy said as she balled her fists and stepped toward Zimmer. "Kieran isn't one of your murderers."

"Dial it back a notch, Candy," Kieran said. "I think a little rest would be the wise thing to do."

"Damn it, Candy, watch the attitude," Big Jim said. "I, for one, don't want to walk home."

Candy gave Zimmer a narrow gaze. "Sorry," she said.

"I accept your heartfelt apology," Zimmer said. "Come, Kieran."

∽∾∽∾

Kieran awoke stiff, sore, and far from rested.

I feel like somebody beat the crap out of me, he thought. *Oh, wait a minute, she did.*

He was curled up on his sleeping mat, lying in the deep shade of a series of rocks under a generous canopy of the Riahass's rough spun cloth. The soldiers had taken three of the Riahass's smaller tents and pitched them next to the truck. To Kieran, they looked vaguely like a Gypsy encampment out of the movies.

"Good, you're up," Candy said.

Kieran yelped.

"God, woman, you scared the life out of me."

Candy gave him a dazzling smile instead of an apology. "What do you think, honey?"

"About what?" he said as he stretched and yawned. Kieran looked at her and sat up. "Why are you wearing my clothes?"

Candy smiled and twirled about, showing off her new outfit. She wore his long sleeve dress shirt, tucked into a pair of his cargo shorts. A crude pair of makeshift, canvas web suspenders kept the pants in place.

"Has my backpack suddenly become community property?"

"This beats the circus tent I was wearing," she said. "Besides, Captain Zimmer said you wouldn't mind."

"Figures. Where did the suspenders come from?"

"The captain had them made for me. He's swell...well, swell for a murdering Nazi bastard, that is."

"Yeah, he's a real sweetheart," Kieran said, tenderly moving his bruised jaw. "Either him, or you broke my jaw last night."

"You have trouble with forgiving and forgetting, don't you, sweetie?"

"It happened last night. I forgive, but it will be a long time before I forget."

"I thought we were friends?"

"Friendship takes time. It takes trust and lately, I'm not the trusting type."

She frowned at him. "Kieran, I trust you. After what you did for me, I trust you with my life."

"No, you don't. Just forget about it. Any guy would have done the same."

"No, they wouldn't, sweetie. I will never forget about it, you hear me? It was the most wonderful thing anyone has ever done for me."

Kieran rubbed his face and stretched.

"Your new outfit looks good," he said. Kieran rose and rolled her sleeves up. "That's better."

"You don't mind me borrowing your clothes, do you?" she asked.

"No, you're more than welcome, beautiful."

"Well, you can be sweet as sugar when you aren't being all mad at me."

"I just feel sorry for you and don't want to hurt your feelings."

"And then, you ruin it like a big louse."

"It's a gift." Kieran smacked his lips. "If you'll excuse me I'm going to get some breakfast."

"It's afternoon."

"Lunch then."

"Have a seat, sweetie," she said. "I'll get you something to eat, just relax."

Kieran looked around. "Where is everyone?"

"Captain Zimmer has everyone out scouting the area. He doesn't want the Riahass catching us flatfooted. Now you rest, and I'll be back in two shakes."

Kieran watched as she walked away.

"Candy sure is sweet, isn't she, kid?" Big Jim Allen asked.

Kieran looked about and saw Big Jim leaning against a rock smoking a cigarette. He had salvaged what was left of his tattered suit. On his feet, he wore a pair of garish cowboy boots that would embarrass Monty Montana. The same boots the Riahass leader wore the night before.

"I didn't see you standing there, Mr. Allen."

"Call me, Big Jim."

"Okay, Big Jim it is."

"I'm not blind, kid. I see what you're doing."

"What am I doing?"

Jim Allen crushed out his cigarette and sauntered up to Kieran. "I'm going to say this once, kid. Stay away from Candy. I've already staked my claim on that prized piece of real estate. She's mine, lock, stock, and barrel, and I don't take well to a punk kid trying to move in on what's mine. Do you understand me?"

"Let me get this straight," Kieran said. "You don't like your secretary, who I heard told you to shove your job up your ass, hanging out with me? You dirty old fart, she's young enough to be your daughter."

"I'll show you how old I am. I eat punks like you for breakfast."

The two men stood nose to nose. Kieran was taller and twenty years younger than Allen. Allen, on the other hand, was built like a pro wrestler and outweighed Kieran by a good twenty-five pounds.

"Go ahead, you old fart, take your best shot," Kieran said, even though the only two fights he had ever participated were embarrassing losses. One was against Zimmer, and the other was Candy.

"Kieran, I am glad that you are awake," Captain Zimmer said, leaning by the end of the Jug. "May I have a word with you? That is, if your conversation with Mr. Allen is concluded?"

"Yeah, we're done," Big Jim said.

"Be right there, Captain."

"Remember what I said, kid," Allen whispered. "Stay the hell away from Candy, or we are going to have a real problem."

"Kieran, I need to talk to you, *now*," Zimmer said.

"Okay, okay, keep your swastika on, I'm coming."

"Kieran, where are you going?" Candy asked as she walked up. "I got you some lunch."

"Candy, honey, after I see what Captain Zimmer wants, would you like to take a walk, just the two of us?" he asked, glancing at Big Jim.

"That would be great," she said.

"Please be careful while we're gone, Big Jim. A man of your advanced age could break a hip or something."

Kieran took the food and water, giving Candy a big smile, before joining Zimmer.

Big Jim lit another cigarette all the while his eyes shot daggers at Kieran.

CHAPTER 23

W hat do you think?" Zimmer asked, as he and Kieran shared the cell phone's screen.

"Looks like a city," Kieran said as he operated the drone. "Those towers—why, they must be a mile high."

Two miles from camp, the two men stood atop a bare hillock baking in the blistering heat. In the far distance, shimmering in the rising heat distortions, the tops of several enormous skyscrapers glinted in the sun.

"More like the ruins of a city," Zimmer said. "It goes for miles in every direction. My guess, it is on the scale of New York or London."

"Looks like Egyptian, Aztec, all tossed together with art nouveau," Kieran said. "Well, someone sure let it go to pot."

"More than simple neglect. I see the tell-tale signs of war."

"The highway leads directly toward it. I don't see any sign of the Riahass," said Kieran.

"I don't think they come from the city. The city looks dead, like a corpse."

"Seems Vilragg and his people have a lot in common with humans," Kieran said. "Always easier to destroy than create."

"I think that is where we will find Herr Vilragg. Then we can ask him what happened."

"Right you are, Captain Zimmer," Vilragg said.

"Damn it," Kieran said, "You are going to give me a heart attack."

"Sorry for the fright," Vilragg said. "You arrived here far too quickly."

"We have our ways," Zimmer said.

"If you and your party will join me, I have prepared places for you and your people in the Great Hall."

"And where is that?" Kieran asked.

"I await you in the Great Pyramid, near the northern edge of Ollav City," he said, pointing toward the hazy horizon. "I must warn you, though, the Hothe have taken up residence in the city, but if you travel only during the heat of the day, you should be safe enough. Do not, I repeat, do not enter the city at night."

"Who are the Hothe?" Zimmer asked.

"Not who, *what*. Escaped genetic experiments from back when my civilization fell. Over the generations, they have evolved into living killing machines. Pray you do not meet them."

"Worse than the Riahass?" Kieran asked.

"The Riahass are terrified of the Hothe and will not come within sight of Ollav City, even in the day time."

"Lovely," Zimmer said. "Simply lovely."

"Avoid the larger buildings, get to me before sunset, and you won't have to worry about that," Vilragg said. "The Hothe are extremely light sensitive and are blind in direct light, never venturing out during the day. At night, however, they rule the city."

Vilragg disappeared.

"We have a destination," Zimmer said. "Retrieve the drone."

"It will take a full day and a half to get there and probably another to cross the city."

"We're moving out. We'll make camp at nightfall and then enter the city tomorrow."

"Gotcha, boss," Kieran said.

Zimmer smiled.

"It seems that Fraulein Matson is singing a different tune today. The way she looks at you, I suppose she has learned to love Nazi-loving traitors."

"Don't start with me," Kieran said while guiding the drone in. "Can I help it if women are putty in my hands?"

Zimmer guffawed.

"What is so funny?"

"You are. You try to put on a worldly facade, yet it is obvious to a blind man that your education is lacking in many areas—women, being a vital one."

"I'm a college student. My education is just fine."

"What I am talking about cannot be learned from a book. You need experience."

"You've lost me."

"Kieran, you know a great deal about computers and such, but that isn't living. Life is to be embraced like a lover. You are a writer who has never lived. To give color to your words, *live*."

"That's not half-bad," Kieran said. "For a murdering Nazi bastard, you are one smart cookie."

"I have my moments."

Kieran and Zimmer laughed.

"That being said, my friend. Be cautious of Fraulein Matson."

"Candy? Why?"

"It seemed that since the bout of fisticuffs last night, she has fallen completely in love with you. Something about this strikes me as odd."

"You don't think a pretty girl could be in love with me?"

"Just seems to be a little fast, especially for such a beautiful girl. Surely, she realizes she could do much better than the likes of you."

"You just hate my obvious animal magnetism," Kieran said.

Zimmer rolled his eyes and shook his head. "Like talking to a doorpost. Keep your eyes open and your wits about you."

"What if she really has taken a liking to me?"

"I could be wrong, it has happened once or twice in the past." Zimmer paused. "Okay, once."

Kieran laughed.

Zimmer shook his head. "I will give you the benefit of the doubt. Fraulein Matson may just be a flighty, impressionable girl, swooning over your act of heroism. I warn you, Mr. Nash, if this is the case, you will not take advantage of her weakness, or you will answer to me."

"To *you*? You're not her dad."

"On this outing, I am, as far as you are concerned. Do you hear me?"

Kieran turned red faced at the implication. "I don't know what to say to that," he said. "You sure have ruined a lifetime of World War Two movies."

"Good," Zimmer said, walking off.

CHAPTER 24

Captain Zimmer and Kieran arrived back at camp to find Candy waiting for them.

"You have until the camp is loaded, Kieran," Zimmer said. "I will have Hartmann stow the drone."

"What about our walk?" Candy asked.

"No time. We have our marching orders."

"We can still talk, can't we?" she asked.

"Sure," Kieran said.

Candy took him by the hand and led him to a blanket spread out on the sand. A small makeshift shelter protected it from the harsh sun.

"After you," Kieran said as she settled onto the blanket.

"You were right about Big Jim, Candy."

"What do you mean?"

"It seems Jim has it bad for you. Real bad."

"What did he do?" she asked.

"He told me, to stay away from you," he said. "Must see me as a threat. I thought there for a minute we were going to duke it out. That would have been *three* times I got my ass kicked on this sorry planet. Kieran chuckled. "I really do need to learn how to fight."

"Are you a threat, Mr. Nash?" she asked, cocking her head to the side.

Kieran looked at Candy and pursed his lips. "Jury still out on that one."

"Really?"

"I will say that you are the prettiest girl who has ever spoken to me…well, other than telling me to get lost, that is," he said.

"Their loss. My gain."

"You don't mince words do you, Candy? I mean you are a straight-up, fire-from-the-hip kind of woman. You say what you mean."

"And I mean what I say," she added.

"I never met your kind before. It's refreshing."

"So, you *do* like me?"

"Well, let's just say that you are growing on me. Give me a few years, and I might even like you."

Candy leaned in close, taking Kieran's face in her hands.

"Now that I think about it, I never thanked you properly for saving my life," she whispered, kissing Kieran tenderly. As their lips parted, she whispered. "How do you like me now, big boy?"

"Wow," he said. "Make that months, instead of years."

Candy kissed him again.

"Weeks. Definitely weeks, and you are in good."

Candy giggled and kissed Kieran with more passion and fervor than he had ever known. Kieran took her in his arms and crushed her body to his.

"I think you are my favorite person in the whole world," he said as their lips parted. "I also think this is the best conversation I have ever had."

"You bet, sport," she said huskily. "I could talk to you all day long."

"Load up!" Max cried. "Let's go, Romeo!"

"But—" began Candy.

"I really hate you, right now, Max," Kieran said.

Max gave Kieran a big grin. "I know. Isn't it great?"

"I hate you too, you big German louse," Candy said. "You better get that gun ready because you're going to need it."

Kieran held on to Candy as she struggled to reach the laughing soldier.

"You heard the man, babe," he said. "We gotta go. Wagons, ho, and all that."

"You're killing me," Candy muttered as Kieran took
down the sunshade and gathered the blanket. Candy shook
the pervasive sand from the blanket and folded it, where she
paused long enough to give the grinning German the finger.

∽∾∽

"It is about time," Zimmer said as he watched Kieran
and Candy round the truck. "We should have already been
on the road."

Kieran fished the keys from his pocket.

"Captain Zimmer?" Candy asked. "Would you care if I
rode up front with you and Kieran?"

Zimmer frowned. "I don't think—"

"Gee, thanks a bunch," she said, popping open the door
and crawling inside to the middle of the bench seat.

"I didn't say—"

"Zimmer, you're a swell guy, but you need to move your
butt. We should have already been on the road," she said
with an angelic smile.

"Now, you know my pain," Kieran said, shaking his
head.

"You have my sympathies."

CHAPTER 25

I am so sorry about the eye, sweetie." Candy leaned in and kissed Kieran on the cheek. "That make it feel all better?"

"Hands and lips *off* the driver," Zimmer growled.

"I know that some chaperones have been called Nazis, but, *Jesus*," Candy said.

"I am not cramping your style, am I Kieran?" Zimmer asked. "I feel like a third wheel."

"I can fix that," Candy said. "Stop the car, honey. Captain Zimmer is getting in the back."

While Zimmer gave Kieran a look that could kill, Kieran guffawed. "Sorry, Captain, but that was funny."

"I think you have been lax in your training," Zimmer said. "I will speak to Hartmann about tripling your efforts. Wouldn't want you to get...*soft*."

"You wouldn't dare," Candy said.

"Oh, yes he would," Kieran said. "And enjoy the show too, I might add."

Zimmer paused and produced a pack of cigarettes. "Fraulein?" he asked, offering her one.

Candy moaned.

"Sorry, Captain Lung Cancer, Candy and I are both non-smokers."

"Yeah," she said woodenly, her eyes never leaving the pack.

"Too bad, these American cigarettes are simply delightful." Zimmer lit one and purposely blew the smoke into her face.

"Dude, that was low down."

Zimmer chuckled. Candy bit her lip.

"Go ahead," Kieran said, rolling down his window.

"You sure?" she asked, her eyes lighting up.

"Do it before I change my mind."

"This is my last one, I promise."

"Yeah, yeah. Rome wasn't built in a day, I suppose."

She snatched the offered cigarette from his hand. Zimmer produced his lighter and lit it for her. Candy drew greedily on the cigarette as if it where the most wonderful thing in the world. "Boy, these are smooth."

"Thanks a lot," Kieran said.

"You're welcome," Zimmer said.

"Fraulein, I am curious about something very strange that happened just before Kieran attempted your rescue."

"Oh, you mean the communion with Ahlena?"

"Ahlena?" Zimmer asked.

"That's the name of their god. Once a night, she yaks with Carre while all the rest of them mooks bow down. We slaves got the tar beat out of us if we looked full on while Carre got his marching orders. Big Jim said it was a trick to keep the regular Joes from rising up against him. Betty says it's the work of the Devil."

"Neat trick," Kieran said.

"What if it is not a trick?" Zimmer asked. "What if this Ahlena is real?"

"Hold on, bub," Candy said. "While I'm not a Bible thumper like Betty, I am a semi-devout Baptist, and there's only one God. Got me?"

"I am not suggesting that this Ahlena is divine. I am suggesting that perhaps someone with a bag of tricks is manipulating the Riahass."

"Yeah," Kieran said. "This world, at one time, was technologically light years ahead of Earth, perhaps pockets still possess advanced technology."

"Such as Vilragg?" Zimmer asked.

"Such as Vilragg," Kieran said. "Perhaps a rival faction?"

"What does this Ahlena speak about?" Zimmer asked.

"They didn't exactly keep us in the loop, but from what I heard, she told them who was to participate in the daily patrols, supply schedules, that sort of thing."

"Not very ecclesiastical for a god," Zimmer said.

"Did you say *she*?" Kieran asked.

"It is definitely a she," Candy said. "And she's a bitch. While those jerks worked us day and night, from time to time Ahlena demands a captive to be sacrificed in her honor."

"You are kidding," Kieran said.

"I witnessed one the first night in camp. It was the worst thing I had ever seen. Scared me silly. Then after a while…after a while, you pray that it will be you. Just so the nightmare would end."

"Candy, I'm sorry," Kieran said.

Candy drew on her cigarette.

"I was never so low in my whole life. Makes me appreciate what you have done for me, Kieran."

"To a primitive culture, advanced technology would appear like magic," Zimmer said. "Religion can be a very powerful tool. Your devices, Kieran, one hundred years ago would be thought of as magic."

"One hundred years ago, my foot," Candy said. "*I* think they are magic now."

CHAPTER 26

P ull off the road, by those rocks," Zimmer said. "We will camp here for the night.

Dutifully, Kieran made a right and hid the Jug behind a red rock outcropping.

As the soldiers piled out of the truck, Zimmer announced, "Set up camp here."

"Excuse me, Mr. Zimmer," Betty said timidly.

"What can I do for you, Frau Cooper?"

"I would like to do something to show my appreciation for what you and your boys did for me."

"That is not necessary," he said.

"It is for me. Besides, I need to do something to feel like I'm doing my part."

"Very well, what do you suggest?"

"I'm a powerful good cook, at least that's what my dear late husband Edgar used to say, God rest his soul. I used to cook for them devils, and I was good at fixing the vittles they ate. I brought some from the camp, enough grub to feed everyone for a week at least."

"Perhaps it would be good to eat fresh food for a change," he said.

"I'll get started," she said as she rubbed her hands together with glee. "I swear it'll be the best supper any of you fellows have ever eaten."

"I have no doubt," he said. "Do you require assistance?"

"Me and Candy have this covered."

"I look forward to tonight," he said.

"You know, Mr. Zimmer," she said. "You German fellows ain't as bad as they make out in the papers. You're ten times better than those flat-faced yellow heathen Japs."

"Umm, thank you."

"Just between you and me, I know you and the Jews don't get along, but I'm fine with that. You know that they killed Jesus?"

"I heard rumors. Now run along, Frau Cooper, I have work to do."

"Yes, Mr. Zimmer," she said brightly. "Later, we can talk about Jesus. You know He's coming back."

"I can hardly wait. Now if you will excuse me, I must check the perimeter." Zimmer, his backpack in hand, made a hasty exit.

ℰᗌℰᗌ

"Oh, there you are, Candy," Betty said.

Kieran and Candy turned to find Betty approaching.

"I looked all over for you, girl."

"What's cooking, Betty?" Candy asked.

"We are."

"Huh?"

"I'm going to make these soldier boys a meal fit for a king, and I need help."

"I was kind of *busy*," Candy said, nodding toward Kieran in a not-so-subtle way.

"You two can court some other time. Right now, I need help. Them boys saved our lives, and we need to show our appreciation."

"Sure, Betty," Candy said with a frown.

Betty came close and sniffed Candy. "Candace Matson have you been *smoking*?"

"Why—no. I was riding with Zimmer, and the man smokes like a train."

"Really," Betty said as she placed her hands on her hips.

"Smoking and lying about it? Looks like someone is over-due talking to Jesus."

"Okay, I confess. I had one."

"Candace Matson, smoking isn't very lady like, and it's a sin. I don't care if all those silver screen hussies you love so much do it, it is wrong in the eyes of the Lord. Isn't that right Kieran? You tell her."

Candy turned and looked at a smiling Kieran.

"She got you there, Candy. Repent from the Devil's weed. Turn before you burn."

Candy snarled at Kieran while he laughed.

"No time to dawdle, young'un," Betty said, grasping her hand. "We have women's work to do. While we work, we can have a long talk about being respectable in the eyes of the Lord."

Candy shook her fist at him as Betty dragged her away.

ಲ⁊ಲ

"Here you go, son," Betty said as she plopped an enor-mous spoonful of the sticky white paste into the crude ce-ramic bowl.

Max took the bowl in hand and frowned.

"We are supposed to eat this?" Max asked. "It looks like wallpaper paste."

"Oh my, dear Lord, this is delicious," Big Jim said, dig-ging into his food.

Max took a small bite.

"This is good," Max said. "Very good indeed."

"The Riahass called it brittel," Betty said. "You know the purple plant that grows wild? It is like the local version of a potato. With the right seasoning, it makes a supper you will never forget."

The soldiers grabbed bowls and were soon devouring the brittle.

"Hey this is good, Candy," Kieran said. "Looks and can cook."

Candy gave him a smile. "No, I won't take credit for this. I helped gather the plants, but Betty did all the work."

"Not everyone's here," Betty said. "Where's that Mr. Zimmer?"

"Oh, Zimmer's off doing...*whatever*," Kieran said around a mouthful of brittle. "He likes to disappear from time to time. Roth and Naumann are on sentry duty."

"But the brittle will get cold," Betty said.

"Tell you what, Betty," Big Jim said. "I need to walk off that fine meal. I'll take the Germans their supper."

"Oh, would you?"

"The least I could do," he said. "They saved my butt too."

"After we eat, you want to show me the sights, sailor?" Candy asked.

"Love to," Kieran said.

෧෨෧

The sun dipping low, Zimmer scanned the horizon one last time for any sign of the Riahass. Taking one last bite from one of Kieran's energy bars, he stuffed the wrapper into his pocket.

Moving like a ghost, he slipped along the rough and rocky ground. As he rounded a boulder, he pulled up short, producing his MP-44. On the ground before him lay Naumann in a pool of drying blood. A quick check revealed he had been stabbed in the chest multiple times. Naumann's MP-44 was missing.

"Oh no," he breathed.

Zimmer ran to the next sentry and found Roth, a wire garrote still embedded in his bloated throat. On the sand beside the body lay an upturned pot of what looked like wallpaper paste.

Zimmer flew back to camp as fast as his feet could carry him. Entering the camp, he found his soldiers sprawled on the ground unconscious. Their rifles had been piled off to one side. Rounding the Jug, wearing a huge smile was Big Jim. In his hands was Naumann's MP-44. As his eyes met those of the enraged German Captain, the smile vanished.

"Oh no," breathed Big Jim as he raised the weapon.

Zimmer spun and fired his MP-44, a line of bullets ricocheting off the Jug as Big Jim took cover. Zimmer turned in time to see Betty fire at him. He ran for cover as bullets zipped about him.

Diving behind a boulder, Zimmer inserted a fresh magazine as Big Jim's fire kept him pinned down. As he prepared to rush forward, the cover fire ceased amid the rumble of the Jug's engine.

"No," cried Zimmer as he broke cover. He watched helplessly as the truck bounced across the desert sending up sprays of sand and dirt.

A grinning Big Jim, hanging from the passenger side window, with Betty at the wheel, fired another magazine at Zimmer. The shots went wide. Zimmer threw his rifle to his shoulder, but the Jug slipped between two enormous boulders as it roared away toward the great highway.

"Unbelievable," Zimmer said.

Zimmer rushed to his fallen men. In his growing dread, he found Kieran and Candy were missing.

CHAPTER 27

Kieran slowly opened his eyes, the world a blur of shadows and moving lights. His shoulders ached, and his head thumped. Even to his befuddled mind, it was apparent that he sat upright. From the familiar sound of the engine, he knew he was sitting in the back of the Jug.

He tried to move, but anything past a wiggle was unsuccessful as if his body was paralyzed and unable to obey his commands. His mouth was bone dry and felt odd as if he was sucking on a handkerchief.

Oh no, no, no. This cannot be happening.

Across from him sat Candy. The sight of her sent a shock through his system, the adrenaline negating the last lingering effects of the drug.

Fuming, Candy sat on the bench thoroughly bound hand and foot. Her beautiful eyes were wild over a gag pulled tightly between her teeth.

In a panic, Kieran struggled with his bonds as if to physically rip them asunder. After several minutes, covered with a sheen of sweat, he sat as tightly secured as before. He tried to gain his feet and hop to Candy, but found himself tethered in place.

Candy, in response to his exertions, emoted a muffled scream as she struggled wildly. He moaned in despair as her efforts at freedom were no more successful than his. Giving up, for the time being, she stamped her feet three times on the hard floor of the truck in utter frustration.

"Arrr oooh all rahht?" he emoted slowly, trying to speak through the awful gag.

Candy nodded her head. Her white teeth gripping her own gag tightly. She tried to speak, but Kieran could not understand her distorted speech.

As if on cue, the truck slowed and stopped. Kieran and Candy were thrown forward, but for their tethers, they would have landed on the floor.

The doors flew open flooding the metal box with harsh, bright light.

Big Jim appeared at the door, holding an MP-44.

Candy erupted into a flurry of spirited, albeit muffled and distorted, curses.

Big Jim chuckled. "You always were full of vinegar and sass. I should have tied your ass up when we first met. Makes you way easier to handle."

"Faulk ooh!" she screamed.

"Out of my way, you boob," Betty said appearing beside him. "You can have fun baiting your tramp later. Right now we have to take care of business."

"Gotcha."

Big Jim helped Betty into the truck where she sat next to Kieran.

"Bring the pack," she said.

Big Jim plopped Kieran's backpack in the back before stepping inside himself. "Hi, honey," he said to Candy, a look of undisguised lust shining in his eyes. "I think this is the start of a beautiful friendship."

Candy swallowed hard and her tough-girl façade melted into one of sheer terror.

Kieran shook his head angrily, to Big Jim's amusement.

"Kieran, eyes on me," Betty said. With a small smile, she gently patted him on the thigh. "Before I remove that terrible gag I want to set a few ground rules, for our fu-ture...*relationship*, okay?"

To Kieran's surprise, Betty's country twang was missing.

"Make no mistake, young man. I'm in charge, and you will do as I say. I will not brook any disrespect or foul language. When I ask questions, you'll tell me the truth, the whole truth, and nothing, but the truth, so help you God. Understand?"

"Faulk ooh!" he screamed in her face.

Betty smiled. "Predictable. Big Jim, if you please?"

Grinning from ear to ear, Big Jim raised his hand high and delivered an openhanded slap across Candy's face. The solid blow sounded like a gunshot on the close space.

Kieran gasped.

"As you can see, Kieran," Betty said. "Your petulant attitude will cause poor Candy here...*distress*."

"Come on, kid," Big Jim said. "I have been itching to put this snooty bitch in her place. Give Betty a hard time, pretty please?"

Kieran shook his head and pleaded.

"Are you going to be a good boy for Miss Betty?"

Kieran nodded his head hastily. Candy's eyes welled with tears as she moaned in pain from the blow Jim gave her.

"Head down please."

Kieran obediently lowered his head, and Betty unknotted and pulled free the thick scarf. Kieran raised his head, and she plucked out the damp ball of cloth from his mouth.

"Please, for the love of God, please don't hurt her," he whispered.

"That is up to you," Betty said. "Now drink."

The woman placed a bottle of water to his lips, and he slurped it dry.

"Now, give Candy, some water," he said.

"Sorry," she said. "Your new girlfriend will stay muzzled until we're finished. From my time with her, I learned that she has quite the potty mouth. I don't need her distracting you."

Candy snarled at the comment.

"What do you want?" Kieran asked.

"I want the secrets of your computer and phone. You will give me detailed instructions on how to operate them."

Betty produced a thick notebook from Kieran's pack along with a pen.

"Who are you, and what happened to your accent?"

"Now, Kieran, I'm the one asking questions," she said. Betty paused a moment. "Okay, for the record, I'm not the insipid bible thumping Betty Cooper I portrayed to you and your Nazi friends. On Earth, I made my living…outside the law. When I heard of your newfangled gadgets, I saw a gold mine, but I needed a partner. Big Jim and I have come to an understanding."

"Hell, kid," he said. "We give old Henry Ford your magic box, and he will hand over the keys to Ford Motor Company no questions asked."

"Crude, but you get the gist."

"You can't," Kieran said. "You'll ruin the future."

"*My* future is all I care about," Betty said. "A word of caution. Be very precise in your instructions. Rest assured that I will check everything, and if one item is left out, or deliberately wrong, I shall strip poor Candy naked, stake her spread eagle in the hot sand, and leave her there all day. It is now high noon, and you could fry eggs on the pavement."

"I won't lie. Just please don't hurt her."

Betty smiled. "Now, shall we begin?"

CHAPTER 28

Simply fascinating," Betty said as she consulted her notes and operated the computer. "The world is ours, Big Jim."

"Can you please removed Candy's gag and give her some water?" Kieran asked. "We have been at this for hours."

"Do it," Betty said, not looking up from the screen.

Candy lowered her head and Big Jim unknotted her gag.

Candy spat the soggy ball of cloth on the floor as Big Jim brought a bottle of water to her lips. After drinking most of the bottle, Candy looked up and smiled. "I told you it would work. This kid is a sucker for the old damsel in distress gag. Now, cut me loose."

"What?" Kieran asked. Her words hit him like a physical blow. The trio laughed as Big Jim quickly cut Candy free of her bonds.

"It was all a lie?" Kieran asked. "You set me up?"

"How's the face, honey?" Big Jim asked Candy. "I didn't want to hurt you, but you said to make it look real."

"Fine. You did it perfectly," Candy said. "Had to make lover boy think that his damsel was in trouble. Besides, I have been smacked harder than that before."

Kieran squeezed his eyes shut and lowered his head.

"Candy here is one hell of an actress, isn't she kid? Makes Shirley Temple look like toast."

"The acting lessons cost us enough," Betty said. "But worth it."

"Kid," Big Jim said. "I hate to rub salt in the wound, but how does it feel to be the sucker of the year?"

"You're grifters?"

"Such an ugly word," Candy said. "I prefer to think of ourselves as living off the fat of the land. A classic example of the survival of the fittest."

"I prefer to think of you as liars, thieves, and *whores*."

Candy stepped in and slapped Kieran hard across the face.

Kieran took the blow stoically.

"Watch it, kid," Big Jim said. "That was a love tap compared to what I can do to your mug. After you passed out, I took down two of the sentries up close and personal. You would be a breeze."

"You *killed* them?"

"Yep," Big Jim said. "All them Jerries are in hell where they belong. Back in the states, I might even get a medal for taking down an entire squad."

"But they saved all of you from the Riahass. They meant you no harm. Why, they were trying to protect you."

"Chalk it up to no good deed goes unpunished," Big Jim said.

"Yeah, I got that lesson down cold."

Big Jim and Betty laughed.

"So, you're not Candy's boss?" Kieran said, not looking up.

"Uncle, actually. Betty here is my wife."

"Why the whole, 'stay away from her kid, she's mine,' bullshit?"

"Candy's a living doll," he said. "However, her giving you that shiner is a hard thing to overcome. Nothing makes a guy want a woman more than when another guy wants her."

"Fantastic." Kieran watched Candy light a cigarette, his eyes mirroring the pain and humiliation he felt.

"I'm stiff as a board from being trussed up all day," she said, blowing a smoke ring. "I'm going for a stretch and grab some grub."

Candy turned and smirked at Kieran. "My hero."

Blowing him a kiss, Candy laughed and leaped from the back of the truck.

Kieran dropped his head, his face burning with shame.

"Don't take it so hard, kid," Big Jim said. "We have conned smarter, more street-savvy people than you."

"But never for a greater prize," Betty said. "These files on your computer, Kieran, are incredible. The information alone is priceless. Stock market, sports betting—why this thing is a gold mine."

The truck rocked as they heard Candy rummaging above them.

"What now?" Kieran asked. "Are you going to kill me now that you have what you want? Right now, it would be a mercy."

Betty chuckled.

"No," Big Jim said as he produced a pocketknife. "We don't kill unless it is absolutely necessary. Like you say, we have what we want. Me and Betty have been talking. We want you to throw in with us."

"Are you serious?"

"Listen to me, kid. The Germans are dead and, without us, you're dead. Believe it or not, what you did, setting us free does count for something in our book."

"Yes," Betty said, closing the laptop. "Work with us to get back to Earth and, once there, you can go your way, free as a bird."

Kieran snorted.

"Or, be stubborn, and I'll shove your ass out now," Big Jim said. "You won't make it a day in this heat."

"Looks like I have no choice."

"None," Betty said. "However, rest assured that we're going to watch you like a hawk. You give us any trouble, and Big Jim here will burn you down."

"I understand," Kieran said. "You going to untie me?"

Big Jim laughed and tossed the closed pocketknife onto his lap.

"We have to hit the road. This will give you something to do. After all, we wouldn't want you to get bored."

Betty and Big Jim left Kieran and locked the truck doors behind them.

CHAPTER 29

Kieran had sat for half an hour when the truck doors opened, and Candy stood framed in the bright sunlight. She climbed in, and Kieran noticed that she held two bottles of water and prepared camp meals.

"Hi, sugar, did you miss me?"

Kieran scowled at her. He still sat tied tightly. The knife lay on the floor at his feet.

Chuckling, she closed the doors and switched on an overhead light. She kicked the bulkhead hard. On cue, the truck started and moved out.

"Let me help you, with those pesky ropes," she said. "Houdini you ain't."

"You had me completely snowed," he said. "I thought you were a sweet kid fresh off the farm."

"Of course, silly boy. Fooling suckers is what I do."

"I take it you're not from a farm in Iowa?"

"Nope. I'm a city girl born and bred. I'd die on a farm with nothing but cows and chickens for company."

"For the love of God, why did you use me?"

"I gave you what you would eagerly swallow hook, line, and sinker. Every red-blooded American boy wants to rescue a helpless, very grateful damsel in distress."

"Guilty as charged," he said. "If you want to do some real good, cut my wrists while you're at it."

"Not after I went to all the trouble of saving you. Now hold still. I don't want to cut you."

"Saving me? Are you out of your mind?"

"Let me free you, and then we can gab, okay?"

"Sure, why not?"

"A small word of warning," she said as the bright smile fell from her face. "I know your feelings are hurt, and your ego took one on the chin, but don't try anything stupid. I'm no pushover and can probably take you apart, but I don't want to. If Big Jim thinks there's a scuffle, he'll kill you, no questions asked. In fact, I'm the only reason you're still breathing, *capish*?"

"I won't try anything. I'd hate for you to stomp my ass twice."

"Aren't you just the sweetest thing?" she said, pinching his cheek. "I'll have you loose in two shakes."

Kieran watched Candy with morbid interest as she carefully severed his bonds. After a few minutes, he was free. He noticed that while she still wore a sweet smile, the slim blade in her hand remained open.

Kieran rose and stretched his stiff muscles.

"First time trussed up?"

"Does it show?"

"Let me ask your honest opinion. Can this gal tie a mean knot or what?"

"*You* tied me up?"

"I have an amazing set of skills, Mr. Nash. Why, I'd blow your mind if you knew fully what this girl can do."

"Must play a mean game of 'Cowboys and Indians.'"

"Better than that. You sat on your keister trussed up for hours and yet, while you couldn't move, the rope didn't impede your circulation. That wasn't easy to learn."

"What did you mean, when you said you did this to save me?"

"Honey, I orchestrated this whole thing."

Kieran sat down. "I'm all ears,"

"Eat, and Mistress Candy will explain all," she said in an exaggerated Romanian accent.

"This isn't a silly game."

"No, it isn't," she said. "I'm just trying to lighten the mood, so humor me, okay?"

Kieran grudgingly took the offered food and water.

"Big Jim was going to make you talk one way or the other. Kieran, he was going to hurt you in ways that make me shudder to think about. I know how stubborn you are, so I came up with this ruse to save you."

"Why would you care? Especially after the way you set me up?"

"I know you feel betrayed."

"Really?" he asked. "Betrayed mixed together with being the biggest damn fool in the world. No. Make that on *two* worlds."

"Honey," she cooed, "you didn't do anything wrong. In fact, you saved my life twice. You're a hero, and you should feel good about that."

"The second time was a trick."

"Yes, but you thought it was real," she said. "That's all that matters. To me, you're a genuine hero. Believe you me, the breed's rare."

"Will you please give me a break? You psychos killed the Germans—the very men who saved you from those stinking cages."

"Honey, in the future, we may be all lovey dovey with the Germans, but right now, the good old USA is fighting them tooth and nail. Being all buddy-buddy with the Jerries will get a knife in the ribs back home. Trust me, parting ways is best."

"Did you have to kill them?"

Candy smiled. "Just between you and me, they're not dead," she whispered.

"What?"

"When Betty mixed her poisoned stew, I removed most while her back was turned. The Germans got the same dose as you did. They'll be out for a while, then wake up with a terrific headache, which is way better than dead."

"But Jim said—"

"Big Jim is a blowhard. He did kill two of the sentries, but Zimmer surprised him and nearly ruined the plan. We got away, but by the skin of our teeth. The side of the truck is covered with bullet dings to prove it."

Candy gestured up, and Kieran observed several dimples in the tough metal hide of the truck.

"This truck is bullet proof?" he asked.

"Apparently, they don't build them like they *will*," she said.

"But the Germans are in the desert without food or water."

"Nope. I left plenty to get them to the city," she said. "If Betty and Big Jim find out what I did, they'll skin me alive."

"Why help them trick us then aid the Germans?"

"Makes us square. An eye for and eye. You saved my ass, and I saved yours."

"The only reason my ass needed saving is because of you. You put me in this predicament, woman."

"Let's not split hairs, sweetie," she said. "I'm not like Big Jim and Betty. They have no feelings for anyone, but themselves. I pay my debts."

"But—"

"Did Big Jim or Betty lay a finger on you?"

"Well, no," he said.

"Then you're welcome, and we're even-steven, big boy. I saved the Germans, even though I hate the ground they goosestep on, to pay what I owe."

Kieran snorted and shook his head.

"Penny for your thoughts?" she asked.

"Tell me your story."

"Why?"

"I'm a writer. I'm curious about everything, even though it makes me want to throw up."

"How sweet," she said. "It's a hairy tale, to say the least."

"It seems that we have plenty of time."

"When I was eight, my mom and dad died in a house fire. The only relative I had was Aunt Betty, whom I had never met. She lived in New York City. No one else wanted me, so they packed me off to live with her and her husband, Jim. The pair didn't want me at first, until Betty saw me as the third member of their gang. Needless to say, my training began almost immediately. Lying and cheating became a way of life as my education was reading, writing, arithmetic and 'never give a sucker an even break.'"

"You poor kid."

"It wasn't really all that bad. In fact, as a kid, I was having a ball. They always seemed to have money, and as long as I did my part, I lived well. At ten, I was given acting lessons, diction, taught how to dance and even sing—anything that might be useful in a swindle or con. I can pick a pocket; tie a knot, as you well know; set a fancy dinner table; and even drive an eighteen-wheeler. I speak three languages and can throw a mean séance."

"You are a regular female MacGyver."

"Who?"

"Never mind. A future cultural reference. But for all your talent, you use it to screw people out of their hard-earned money. That's wrong."

"No argument from me, but I was more of a tool in the hands of Betty and Big Jim. I just did what they told me. I didn't necessarily like it, but it was the only life I knew."

"Seems I had this same conversation with Zimmer," Kieran said.

"Anyway, over the years we did many, many heinous things to good, well-meaning people, all for the sake of the All Mighty Dollar. I remember my first gig was as a poor crippled girl struck with polio. We hit every church in a hundred mile radius and let me tell you, the Holy Joes couldn't shove money into our pockets fast enough."

"That's disgusting," he said. "How could you?"

"I was a kid, okay? All I know is, at the time, I had all the new shiny toys for just a little make-believe."

Kieran just shook his head.

"As time went by, a plain little girl turned into the teen-age knockout sitting before you."

"A bit on the shy side, are we?"

"Why deny the facts?" she said. "Boys swarmed me like bees after honey, but Big Jim and Betty kept them at arm's length."

"Well now, aren't they the proper parents?"

"No. They couldn't care less about my welfare. They were after bigger fish. One night when they thought I was asleep, I heard them were making plans for yours truly. I was going to be their Lolita. They were going to send me like a torpedo after rich married men. After I landed them in bed, a camera wielding Big Jim behind a two-way mirror in my bedroom would blackmail the poor suckers."

"Oh, God."

"They talked about me like I had no will of my own. Talked about me like I was their slave."

Kieran looked at her. "You didn't do...well, you know?"

"Of course not. Sure, I would flirt and bat my eyes, but I'm no one's prostitute," she said. "I have never...well, you know with a guy."

"Oh."

"Anyway, that was the final straw. I was going to skip out on them, but I had to be careful. Betty and Big Jim are no pushovers. If they ever found me, well, I was dead. We were working on an insurance scam where I was going to 'die' in a car accident. The story was I lost control, and my car goes ker-plunk into San Francisco Bay. With the currents and all, it would be reasonable to think my body was swept out to sea. Easy-peasy. That was to be my swan song. I was going to skip out and take my share of the money they had made with me over the years, but that damn fog enveloped our apartment, and we ended up on this God-forsaken planet. If only I had left five minutes earlier."

"Why the whole act when we met? I don't see the point."

"We didn't know you from Adam. With the Germans in-volved, we played it safe."

"Safe? You mean you lied your ass off."

"Exactly. The truth is the last thing you give to suckers."

"Attacking me was part of the act?"

"Well, no. I was more than a bit crazy by my ordeal, coupled with the Nazis, I lost it."

"The story about a brother killed by the Germans?"

"Fake. However, I was good friends with a girl whose brother was killed in North Africa. Thinking you were in cahoots with the Nazis...well, it made my blood boil. Sorry."

Kieran frowned at the memory.

"When Big Jim told the cock-and-bull story about being an insurance salesman, and I was his secretary, I went along because it was second nature. Betty's favorite shtick was playing a poor, bible-thumping hick."

"She's good at it. Had us all fooled."

"Anyway, riding in the back of the truck the first night, your friend Werner told us about your computer and how you were from the future."

"And Big Jim and Betty sent you after me."

"Yes. I had to see if you were on the level and if we could steal it."

Kieran closed his eyes, shook his head. "It was all a lie."

"Most, but not all, honey," Candy said, placing a gentle hand on his. "Naive, I am not. Hell, I'm so jaded I probably have 'made in China' tattooed on my butt. I never fantasied about a silly knight in shining armor coming to rescue poor, helpless me. However, when I think about what you did and the raw nerve it took...well, I didn't lie about that. I do get weak in the knees when I think about you rescuing me. The kisses for saving me, they were real as well. The best smooches I ever had, by the way."

Kieran rubbed his face in anger. "But you still betrayed us—betrayed *me*. If you were so damn grateful to me and disgusted with Big Jim and Betty, why did you help them against us?"

"What can I say, honey? You go with the Devil you know. Despite the fact Germans helped save us, they are still the enemy our country is fighting a war with. Those evil bastards have killed millions, and I can't just forgive and forget. It wasn't that hard screwing them over."

"Okay, under the circumstances I get that. In my world, the Nazis are the worst of the worst, but was it as easy screwing me over?"

"Honestly, no, but most of what you thought was me was an act. I'm not some easily swayed khaki-wacky kid who falls for the first guy she meets, even if he's cute and from the future."

"Khaki wacky?"

"I forgot. Boy crazy."

"Oh. Have to say, while I liked having a pretty girl fawning on me, never happened before, but you were overplaying your hand. Honestly, you were getting too lovey-dovey. Zimmer thought your sudden complete devotion to a guy you had just met was odd."

"Zimmer, for a Nazi, is a smart cookie."

"He hates being called a Nazi."

"Huh?"

"The way he tells it, he hates them as much as we do. It's weird."

"*Too* lovey-dovey? Really, big boy? I didn't see you giving me the heave-ho."

"The kissing part was too good to pass up," Kieran said.

"Thank you," she said.

"It was nice to think a pretty girl could fall for me, but it all came crashing down. Thanks."

"Kieran, I just want to say that I'm sorry for the way I used you. However, now that you are one of us, we can be the best of friends."

"One of you? I just got used to the Germans."

"Look, one of the first things I learned was that life can

turn on a dime. You have to adapt quick, or you are dead. No use holding on to what is gone. *We*—Big Jim, Betty and me—are your new partners, for better or worse. The quicker you learn that, the better off you'll be."

Kieran gave her a puzzled glance and let out a noisy breath.

"You hate it because I'm right."

"Yeah, I'll give you that," he said. "What's the plan?"

"Yes," she said. "I knew you were a smart guy."

"I'm an idiot."

"Well, we are off to see the Wizard," she said. "Or in this case, Vilragg."

"I have to warn you. The only reason he took the Germans was that they were soldiers."

"Why's that?"

"Zimmer asked him, but he refused to say."

"That's a tough one," she said. "However, we'll figure a way around that."

"I have no doubt."

Candy leaned over and, to his surprise, brushed his lips with hers.

"I thought we were Even-Stevens?" he said.

"Maybe I want to be more than friends? For some strange reason, you're growing on me, Kieran Nash."

Kieran rose and walked to the end of the compartment.

"Hey, where you going?"

"You scare me, Candy Matson."

"Honey, I said I was sorry and even told the truth, which is a first for me. You're a real sweetheart of a guy. I never met anyone like you."

Kieran shook his head. "Fool me once, shame on you. Fool me twice, shame on me. I'll go along with you and the family, just as a matter of survival. However, I want you to stay the hell away. I feel like you beat the hell out of me twice."

"Twice?"

"The first night we met and just now. Now was worse—much, much worse. Not all wounds bleed."

Kieran lay down on the floor and turned his back to her.

"Oh, honey don't be like that. Come back and let's get to know each other better."

"I'm tired."

"Kieran, we have a clean slate, you and me. Everything'is out in the open."

"Yeah, and I don't like what I see."

"You'll come around," she said. "By the time this adventure is over, we'll be going steady and laughing about all this."

"I think that ship hit a rock and went down with all hands."

CHAPTER 30

"Ollav City, huh?" Big Jim asked. "This place is nothing, but a giant crumbling maze. I can't make heads or tails of it."

"Yes, we could run out of gas long before we found this alien thing," Betty said.

"Last thing we need is to be stuck in the middle of this dead city when night falls," Candy said.

"*If* what the kid said is true," Big Jim. "I still find it awful convenient that monsters roam this place after dark."

"Hey, I'm just telling you what I heard Vilragg tell Zimmer," Kieran said. "Said some kind of genetic creatures are roaming this place but that they can't stand the light. Said to stay out of the larger buildings and travel by day."

"What does *genetic* mean?" Betty asked. "Sounds like a made up word."

Candy opened the computer and, after a few key strokes, announced. "'Genetics is the study of genes, genetic variation, and heredity in living organisms.'"

"Now how can all that science lingo make monsters?" Big Jim asked.

"Think about it, Big Jim. Farmers breed animals to get the strongest breeds. Dog breeders do the same. From what little I understand, it's possible, if you have the knowhow—and these aliens apparently do—to mix and match species."

"Like making a cake?" Candy asked.

"I suppose. Have you ever put in the wrong ingredient and the results were not what you expected?"

"I see what you mean," Betty said.

"Let's say some scientist wanted to push the envelope. This guy didn't care *what* he made, he just wanted to see what he *could* make."

"Frankenstein," Betty said.

"So we got Boris Karloff roaming the streets?" Candy said. "That's not so bad."

Big Jim laughed, but Betty and Kieran didn't.

"This could be bad," Betty said.

"Vilragg said the Hothe were so bad, that the Riahass refused to come near the city *even* in the daytime."

"You aren't giving me the warm and fuzzies, kid," Big Jim said as he clutched his stolen MP-44 a little tighter.

"I have an idea," Kieran said. "We use the drone."

"Drone?" Betty asked. "What's a drone?"

"It's a flying camera. I used it when we found you in the Riahass camp."

"What good is that?" asked Big Jim.

"Are you stupid all the time?" Betty asked, punching Big Jim in the arm.

"I'll fly it and make a street map we can follow. Vilragg said he was located in a big pyramid."

"Great idea, kid," Big Jim said, slapping him on the back.

"Very nice," Betty said with a smile.

"That deserves a big kiss," Candy said.

"I would rather get a smooch from Big Jim."

"Okay," Big Jim said.

"Hey—*no*!"

Grabbing Kieran, Big Jim kissed him on the forehead, much to the delight of Betty and Candy.

"That is the last good idea I ever have," Kieran moaned.

❧❧❧

"You need any help, kid?"

"No, I got this."

Kieran sat atop the Jug, resting upon the fiberglass cargo shell.

"Why do you have to sit way up there?" Candy asked. "Isn't that shell blazing hot?"

Kieran wiped the sweat from his eyes. "Like sitting on a stove top, but I have no choice, I need an unobstructed view of the drone. The higher, the better."

I hope this plan works. Up here, I'm away from the Manson Family and prying eyes. Please, Lord, let me find something to help get me out of this mess.

Kieran checked the battery packs and adjusted the six rotors as per the manual.

"What's taking so long?" Betty asked. "You better not be pulling something."

"Give me a break. My neck's on the line too. I have to make sure it's ready to fly, so I don't screw this up, okay?"

"Watch the tone, kid," Big Jim said.

"Consider it watched, BJ," Kieran said.

Breathing a small, fervent prayer, Kieran switched on the drone. With his cell phone before him synced with the unit's camera, he added more power and the drone lifted off.

"I'll be damned," Big Jim said. "That gizmo really does fly."

"Amazing," Betty said.

Kieran glanced down. Big Jim and Betty watched the drone while Candy watched him. She smiled and gave him a wink. Kieran didn't respond.

He directed the drone higher, sailing over the rooftops of the city until it was lost from view.

"What do you see?" Candy asked.

"Hush, I need to concentrate."

"Leave him alone and let him find us a way out of here," Betty said.

Never taking her eyes off Kieran, Betty took Big Jim and

Candy by the arm, leading them several feet away, where they conferred in hushed tones.

Kieran flew north, enthralled by the amazing city view. He observed entire herds of hop-a-longs, the tiger-horses, as well as several different types of animals he had never seen before. The long purple grass grew in abundance here, pushing up through the streets and rubble.

Passing a skyscraper, he gasped as in the distance sat an enormous pyramid. The amazing structure looked to be made of black glass situated within a walled compound. The structure rivaled the Great Pyramid at Giza in size. Making a few quick passes, he marked out a crude map of clear city streets back to a particularly striking skyscraper that stood half a mile high, on a note pad.

Kieran gasped at his display. *What's that?*

As he passed over a low, very ornate building, situated within what once might have been a city park, a flashing red light caught his attention.

Dropping the drone lower, suddenly his camera feed turned to black. Before he could react, white block lettering crossed the screen.

Kieran Nash we need to talk before it is too late.

As suddenly as it was lost, the camera feed was back.

"The plot thickens," Kieran breathed. He made a separate map of where the low building was, but, unfortunately, that was nowhere near the clear route to the pyramid.

He discreetly folded the map to the low building and slipped it into his waistband. "This is going to be close," he whispered. He checked his battery power level and groaned.

Skimming buildings, he flew the drone until he spied a broad avenue. His power almost gone, Kieran smiled as he dropped it in between two ruined buildings.

I don't freaking believe this. Thank you, Jesus.

Kieran quickly landed the drone just before the power reserve reached zero. Still pretending to fly, he made notes on his street directions to the pyramid.

Taking a deep breath, he said, "Aw crap!"

"What did you do?" Betty asked. "Where is the drone?"

"In the side of a building, downtown," he said. "I guess I ran out of the signal range and lost control."

"Now what are we going to do?" Big Jim asked. "So help me, kid, if you blew this for us, you'll pay dearly."

"Good news is I found the pyramid," Kieran said.

"And the directions?" Betty asked.

"Right here," Kieran said, waving a sheet of paper like a flag. "The city is like a maze with a lot of switchbacks and dead ends, but these directions will get us there."

"You did good, kid," Big Jim said, without smiling.

As Kieran descended the ladder, Betty retrieved the map from his hand.

"Cell phone, please?" she asked, her hand outstretched.

Kieran reached into his pocket and placed the coveted phone in her hand. "Take good care of that. I worked two jobs to pay the bill."

"Thank you, I will."

"I really hate losing the drone," Kieran said. "That thing came in handy."

"I don't think we need it anymore," Betty said.

Big Jim gave him a sinister grin and brought the barrel of his MP-44 level with Kieran's chest.

"Hey, guys, this isn't funny," he said.

"No, it isn't, Kieran," Betty said. "'Fraid we have to cut you loose. End of the line."

"I thought I was coming along. We were going back to Earth."

Kieran glanced at Candy for support. She stood several feet away, refusing to let her eyes meet his, and looked as if she were crying.

"You're not kidding," he said softly.

"Kid, you are way too much trouble. We don't like trouble."

"You promised me you would take me to Earth."

"We promise a lot of things, kid," Big Jim said. "I guess you might say we change our minds—a lot."

"We haven't a clue what this Vilragg is like," Betty said. "He might not take it too kindly that we took your stuff, or that we killed the Nazis."

"I won't tell," he said.

"We can't take the chance of you singing to the wrong people," Betty said.

"So, are you just going to shoot me, or leave me to whatever creatures are roaming the streets?"

"Your choice," Betty said. "You can walk away and take your chances, or if you want a quick death, Big Jim will oblige."

"I promise you won't feel a thing, kid."

"If it's all the same to you, I choose the Hothe," Kieran said.

"Damn," Big Jim said, lowering his weapon.

"You lost the bet," Betty said.

"You'll have to wait for your dough when we get back to Earth."

"See you folks around," Kieran said as he started to walk off.

"Wait," Candy said. "Don't move until I get back." She disappeared and, after a few minutes, reappeared with a small pull-string knapsack. She tossed the bundle at Kieran's feet. "Some water and food for the road," she said. "Looks like you owe me, now."

"You're all heart," Kieran said.

"Why waste the chow?" Big Jim asked. "The kid's as good as dead."

"No, take it, Kieran," Betty said. "The least we can do for the man who not only saved us but made us very, very wealthy."

Red faced with anger, Kieran snapped up the bag and, without looking back, trudged away.

A gleam in his eye, Big Jim raised his rifle, centering the sights on the back of Kieran's head. Looking on, Betty smiled and nodded.

"No!" Candy screamed as she knocked the rifle away.

Big Jim's shot hit the sidewalk beside Kieran, ricocheting wildly. Not looking back, Kieran ducked his head and ran for his life.

Big Jim shoved Candy down with an oath. Betty grabbed Candy, pinning her arms.

Laughing, Big Jim raised the rifle, whereupon he emptied the magazine in a full auto burst. Dodging fire, Kieran darted to his right and disappeared around the corner of a building.

"What's wrong with you?" Big Jim said.

"You aren't going soft, are you?" Betty asked. "Our rule is no witnesses."

"Who's he going to tell?" she said. "Cops are a bajillion miles from here. Besides, haven't we done enough to him?"

Big Jim snorted. "Honestly, girl, you didn't do the kid a favor."

"Big Jim, Aunt Betty," Candy said, "I can't do this anymore."

"Excuse me?" Betty asked.

"I—I'm going with Kieran."

"The hell you say," Betty said, moving close to Candy. "What's gotten into you?"

"I hate who we are, and I'd rather die with Kieran than keep living a life of lies."

Betty drew back a hand and slapped Candy hard. "Take this stupid girl to the truck," she said. "If she gives you any trouble, shoot her in the foot."

"No," Candy screamed as Big Jim took her by the arm and marched her to the truck.

ﮩﻨﻨﮩ

Breathing hard from exertion, Kieran stayed hidden in a small building down the street from the Jug. Out of earshot, he watched as Betty and Big Jim read the riot act to a dejected Candy. The verbal tirade ended with Betty delivering a brutal slap. Moments later, the trio entered the Jug and rumbled off.

"Probably pissed that Candy wasted food on me. The people on my goon list has risen to four. Betty, Big Jim, Candy, and Professor Wills. If I survive this mess, I'm going to be very busy getting even."

The building where he took shelter was bare and stank of animal dropping and half-eaten purple grass and roots.

"Shit stinks regardless of what planet you're on," he said.

He opened the sack Candy provided and found five bottles of water and five packets of food along with the Walther P-38 Zimmer had given him.

A yellow sticky note read:

I never meant for this to happen. Sorry.

"Well, what do you know? Some people are hard to figure, I suppose. Thanks to Candy, I feel slightly better about my prospects."

Kieran checked the weapon and chambered a round.

"I have to cover a few miles before the sun goes down, and the Hothe come out to play. Good thing for me, I can climb over obstacles that even the Jug can't. Bad thing is the Jug sure would make me feel a whole lot better."

Taking out the map, while muttering about trust issues, Kieran jogged down the street toward the mysterious building.

CHAPTER 31

With Betty at the wheel and Big Jim riding shot-gun, Candy navigated, using the directions Kieran wrote down. "Would it have hurt to let Kieran come along?" she asked.

"You *are* soft for the guy," Big Jim snorted. "Got to be a first. I thought your heart petrified years ago."

"Yeah," Candy said. "Kieran was…different."

"Well, he's dead, so no use crying over spilled milk," Betty said. "When we get back to the Earth, you can have your pick of pretty boys. I can name a dozen that would put Kieran to shame in the looks department."

"There's far more to a fellah than just the way he looks," Candy said. "Kieran was special where it counts. Only, I was too damn stupid to know it until he was gone."

Betty and Big Jim gave each other a puzzled glance.

"I have to know. What did Kieran do to get under a thick hide like yours, Candy?" a bemused Big Jim asked.

"I don't know," she said. "Sure, he wasn't all that smart about people. In fact, he was more gullible than most. But he was a good man. A brave man. He didn't try to snow me like most of the slick boys do, trying to make time. Kieran made me feel good. I liked being with him."

"He was a grade-A sucker," Betty growled. "We picked him clean and tossed away the husk, just like we've done a hundred times before."

"Betty, can't we please go back?"

"Are you stupid?" Betty asked. "Are you in love with this moron?"

"I—I don't know what love is. I just don't want him to be hurt, is all."

Betty gave Big Jim a quick glance. "Honey, after what we did to him, even if we did go back, he would never trust you again," she said. "Any kind of relationship between you two is impossible. If nothing else, I know people. Kieran will curse you with his last breath."

Candy hung her head as tears welled in her eyes.

"Them tears for real?" Big Jim asked. "I've seen it all now."

"Stop it!" screamed Betty. "I won't have you blubbering over a mark. I taught you to be better than that."

"The sun'll be setting in a few hours, and we need to be off the streets," Big Jim said. "The kid's on his own."

The Jug came upon a rubble-clogged intersection.

"Where to?" Betty asked.

Big Jim gently took the directions from Candy's hand.

"Left," he said. "Go about seven blocks and take a right.

"About?"

"Okay, seven and hang a right," he said. "Jesus, don't get bitchy with me."

"I don't want to get lost. If the kid wasn't pulling our leg, sundown's a death sentence."

"I hate who we are," Candy said. "Kieran was a real sweetheart, and we killed him."

Betty slammed on the brakes. "I'm not going to put up with your blubbering," she said. "Get in the back—*now*!"

Candy's tears had become a torrent, as if all the years of lying, manipulating, and cheating had finally caught up with her.

"Oh, for the love of Pete," Big Jim said.

He popped open his door and, taking Candy roughly by the arm, dragged her from the cab. Sobbing, she put up no resistance as he led her around and opened the back doors.

"How can we be like this?" she moaned. "We're nothing more than animals."

"Jesus, what rotten timing," he whispered. "You want to get a conscience *now*? That punk wasn't worth it, honey."

"He trusted me, and I led him like a lamb to the slaughter."

"It's your job," he hissed as he helped her into the back. "He wasn't the first and sure as shooting won't be the last. You'll feel better when we're rolling in the dough."

"Did Judas feel better with his thirty pieces of silver?"

"Sister, you're giving me gas." Big Jim rolled his eyes and slammed the rear doors.

ভচভ

Big Jim slid into the passenger cab. "I think the Candy we knew has gone bye-bye," he said.

"I got that," Betty said, hitting the accelerator. "Once we get out of this mess, she'll come around."

"And if she doesn't?"

Betty gave him a glance.

"Oh. I'll miss her," he said.

CHAPTER 32

We should have been there by now," Betty said. "Are you sure you're reading the directions correctly?"

"Yeah, I'm sure."

"We've been driving for three hours."

"This is a big place," he said. "Way bigger than even the Big Apple."

"Hey, what's that in the middle of the road?" Betty asked.

"Ain't that the drone?" he asked. "That lying bastard told us it crashed into the side of a building."

"Grab it and throw it into the back," Betty said. "If Kieran could figure out how to use it, so can we."

"Good idea."

Betty shut off the engine as Big Jim opened his door and slid out. Leaving his gun on the seat, he trotted out to the high tech flying camera.

Betty rolled down her window. "For God's sake, be careful with the damn thing."

"Put a sock in it, woman. I know what I'm doing."

Big Jim carefully grasped the large drone by the body and lifted it off the ground. "Man, this thing's as light as a feather…well, to be as big as it is," he said to himself.

Turning with his prize, he gasped as he looked into the eyes of Captain Zimmer. Next to the captain stood Max, his Mauser K-98 centered on a spot between Big Jim's eyes.

"Oh, sweet Jesus," Big Jim whispered.

He glanced at the Jug in time to see Betty, her eyes filled with genuine terror, as Hartmann dragged her from the cab. Two more soldiers moved to the back and opened the doors.

"Leave the girl in the Jug," Zimmer ordered. "I wish to speak with Betty and Big Jim first."

"I'll take that," Werner said as he plucked the drone from Big Jim's hands.

"Oh, thank the Lord we found you," Betty said, resuming her twangy accent.

"*You* found *us*?" Zimmer asked. "Where is Kieran Nash?"

At rifle point, Betty joined Big Jim within the ring of grim German soldiers.

"That she-devil, Candy," Betty said. "This is all her fault."

"Candy?"

"That Jezebel's all sweet on the outside, but she's pure Satan. Satan, I tell you."

"Candy orchestrated this?" Zimmer asked.

"She made us go along," Big Jim said as a sheen of sweat formed on his face. "Trussed up the kid and held a gun to his head. Threatened to kill him if we didn't go along."

"That's the Lord's own truth," Betty said.

"Why would she perpetrate such a scheme?"

"To steal poor Kieran's future gizmos," Big Jim said.

"She had us until Big Jim turned the tables on her. We've got her locked up in the back of the truck."

"She certainly is a wily Jezebel," Zimmer said.

"The worst," Big Jim said.

"Where is Kieran?"

Betty broke down and sobbed. "When she wrung them gadget secrets from him, that cold-hearted Judas just up and shot him. Oh, Lord, to my dying day I'll never forget how she laughed as that poor boy begged for his life."

"That was how it went," Big Jim said. "Just like Betty

said. God's own truth. We were on our way back to find you."

Zimmer reached into his pocket and produced a slip of notebook paper.

"You two might find this interesting," he said. Holding it before him, he read, "'Captain Zimmer, I have been kidnapped by Betty, Big Jim, and Candy. The three are grifters from Earth, out to steal my stuff. Wait by the drone, and the fake directions I wrote for them will lead them right to you. Don't believe a word they tell you as they are heartless con men without a conscience. Betty is the ringleader and married to Big Jim. Candy is her niece. Have to say, except for the ending, Captain Zimmer, this adventure was a hoot. I will miss our talks. Never thought I would count a murdering Nazi bastard as my friend. Give my best to Werner, Max, and the Sunshine Boys.

"'Kieran Nash.

"'PS.

"'The real map to Vilragg's pyramid is taped to the roof of the Jug.'"

"H—How?" stammered Betty.

"This note was taped to the body of the drone," Zimmer said as he carefully re-folded the note and slipped it back into his blouse pocket.

"I guess the kid was smarter than I gave him credit for," Big Jim said.

Zimmer took his rifle and, without ceremony, shot Betty and Big Jim in the head.

∾∾∾

Candy, her head down, didn't move as Zimmer appeared at the open doors of the truck.

"Did you hear?" he asked.

Candy nodded.

"Good. I hate to repeat myself."

"My turn?" she asked, not looking at him.

"It should be for what you have done," Zimmer said.

"Should be?" Candy asked, looking up in surprise. "I don't understand."

"Kieran, misguided as it was, from the grave has spared your life, *fraulein*," Zimmer said. "I left out one small section of Kieran's letter." He produced the note. "'By the way, Captain Zimmer, Candy, even though she is one of them, diluted Betty's poisoned dinner and saved your men's lives. She even saved me from torture. She's a cold-hearted, lying bitch, and I while I don't think I'll be alive when you find this note, could you do me a solid and spare her life?'"

"Kieran, wrote that?" Candy asked. "He does care about me."

"Yes, his grand sense of right and wrong is wasted on the likes of you."

"It truly is, however, I got news for you, Fritz. Kieran is still alive. If we hurry, we can find him."

"Kieran—still alive?"

"Don't trust her, Hauptmann," snapped Werner. "Kieran said they were nothing, but liars. They tried to kill us."

"I won't argue," Candy said. "However, the truth is, Big Jim tried to shoot Kieran in the back, but he escaped. He is somewhere in the city. We have to find him before the Hothe do."

"Hauptmann," Max said, appearing at the door. "I have the map from the roof."

"Can you lead us back to Kieran?" Zimmer asked Candy.

"Yes, I think so."

Werner translated Zimmer's English into German for Hartmann.

"Hauptmann," Hartmann said, pulling Zimmer to the side. "It will be dark soon. If we go after the American, you will be risking all your men's lives for an enemy of Germany. We have to get to the pyramid."

"Is that Nazi asshole trying to talk him out of saving Kieran?" Candy asked Werner.

Werner nodded.

"But we can save him," Candy said. "We can save Kieran. You have guns, for God's sake."

Zimmer took a deep breath. "Load up. We are going to the pyramid."

"You can't," Candy cried. "Kieran was your friend. You can't abandon your friend."

"You did," Zimmer said, his words hitting her like a slap. "The *fraulein* is to be treated correctly, but she is our prisoner. Fraulein Matson, you are only breathing because it was Kieran's wish. When we get back to Germany—"

"Don't you mean *if*?" Candy asked.

"*When* we get back, you will be handed over to the authorities. Take comfort in the fact that prison is better than a bullet. However, give us trouble, and you will join Betty and Big Jim in hell."

CHAPTER 33

Kieran hurried down the broad, rubble-filled street. *Ordinarily, I'd be geeking out at the alien architecture and snapping photos, but now isn't the time. I'm running a race with the sun, and if I lose, I lose big time.*

At least I'm away from the Manson Family. I swear to God, if I ever try to save anyone else, I hope I get struck by lightning first.

Candy played me for a fool. I should've known that a girl that pretty would never see anything in a loser like me. So help me, I'm swearing off saving women for good.

Kieran frowned.

Still, she did save Zimmer and his men. I didn't believe her story, but when I saw my favorite Nazis through the drone's camera, entering the city, I almost freaked. Thank God, I wrote that note to Zimmer and taped it to the drone before I sent it out, just on the off chance she was telling the truth.

Okay, and she also gave me some food, water, and a weapon. Not to mention I heard Candy yell and Big Jim swear just before the bullets flew. Did she try to save me from a bullet in the back? Betty did give Candy the what for, just before they drove off in my ride. No, probably just another scam. I'll bet they're all laughing at me right now.

The laugh will be on them if they follow my map. Those three will be hip deep in pissed-off Nazis. Serves them right.

Okay, while I'm swearing off saving gorgeous girls for good, the pretty-girl-next-door types are still fair game. Especially if they have dark eyes and speak with a French accent. Have to keep my goals attainable at least. Still, that Candy was sweet and had lips to die for.

Damn it, I need to focus! Candy's somebody else's problem now. I pray I'll never lay eyes on her again. I may be running into a trap, but whoever high-jacked my cellphone signal is my only hope.

Kieran's shoes crunched gravel and rubble as he darted through the winding streets. Looking up, he couldn't see the sun as it sank low behind a line of imposing buildings.

He glanced about and found himself alone. *Moments before the streets were full of hop-a-longs and, now, nothing. Oh, this can't be good.*

A burst of fresh fear gave his feet wings. He'd neared the end of a city block when a wild, high-pitched cry made him slide to a stop.

Sweating profusely, he peered around the edge of a building.

Before him lay a great fountain surrounded by an open square. The fountain was cracked and crumbling with neglect, yet water, precious life giving water flowed and bubbled from hidden jets. *That's the first water I've seen on the surface of this planet. Explains all the animals. How is it that fountain is still operating?*

He looked past the fountain and gazed in amazement at the twenty-foot tall symbol of Ahlena. About the base lay crude offerings of animal carcasses and edible roots. *Wait a minute. Vilragg said the Riahass never set foot in this place for fear of the Hothe. If that is true, then who erected the idol?*

In the deepening gloom, Kieran felt the hair stand up on the back of his neck. A sudden wave of nausea assailed him making him double over. In seconds, the feeling vanished, leaving him gasping for air.

"What was that?" he asked aloud. "Felt as if I had contracted a stomach virus, but now it's gone."

He ran up to the fountain and was further surprised that the expected brackish water was clear and fresh. He washed his face and neck. Feeling refreshed, he crossed the open square, giving the strange idol a wide berth. Taking a shortcut, he ducked down a narrow alley. Halfway down the fifty-foot corridor, Kieran heard a strange sound. *What was that? Sounded almost like a moan.*

Looking around, he spied a dark shape enter the alley, from the way he came. The animal trotted along on two legs, its yellow reptilian eyes glowing in the dark. Immaculate white, sharp teeth jutted from the mouth. The animal, which looked alarmingly like a creature he saw in a movie once, paused long enough to sniff the air.

You have got to be kidding me. That's an honest to God raptor. How is a dinosaur on this world? That must be the Hothe. The Riahass created freaking dinosaurs.

As Kieran watched in horror, the lone hunter wasn't alone very much longer as four more joined him for the hunt.

Figures, the way my luck has been going lately.

Knowing running was futile, but standing his ground was a certain death, Kieran eased down the alley, trying not to be noticed. Ten feet from the end, the leader looked at Kieran and emitted a resounding roar.

Kieran surged from the alleyway, looking for a place of refuge. To his left he spied an open doorway. Cutting sharply, he felt the wind, smelled fetid breath, and heard the sound of hard claws sliding over the cracked pavement.

He burst into the pitch-blackness of a small building.

"Thank God," he cried as he found the door and slammed it closed. He leaned into the door, feeling the powerful impact of bodies and the angry cry of the hunters. Kieran strained with all his might against the rotting portal. Nevertheless, out muscled, Kieran was slowly, inexorably pushed back.

"Hello, Kieran Nash."

Kieran screamed. Turning his head, he beheld a beautiful woman standing in the darkness. She wore a close-fitting white robe of sheer silk, which stood out in sharp contrast to her long, dark-red hair. Although the room lay in perfect darkness, the woman was clearly visible as if illuminated by a spotlight.

"I am Iona. I know you have many questions—"

"A human? You must have escaped the Riahass. You sound American."

"Not exactly—"

Screaming in frustration, the beasts redoubled their assault on the door.

"Look, lady, I'm kind of too busy right now for chitchat. Help me brace the door before we're both dead meat."

Looking bewildered, Iona glanced around. "Oh, I see now," she said with a chuckle. "Kieran, do you have your gun?"

"That pop gun won't stop dinosaurs, for Christ's sake."

Iona laughed.

"This isn't funny. Don't just stand there. Help me, or you're dead, too."

"Kieran, do what I say and the nasty...*dinosaurs*...will go away."

"You have my attention," he said as a scaly claw reached inside the opening trying to slash him.

Iona held her hand out to her side, palm-facing Kieran.

"Shoot my hand."

"What? Are you bonkers?"

"Trust me."

"Lady, the phrase *'trust me'* gives me an ulcer."

"Just do it. We are wasting time."

With an oath, Kieran pulled the P-38 and fired at her hand. Instantly, the building and the attacking raptors disappeared. Kieran found himself by the street corner where he first saw the fountain.

"Hey, how did I get back here? Where are the raptor-Hothe things? Oh, God, what's that?"

On the ground before him lay a peculiar beast. Shaped like a man, it was about four-foot tall, hairless with green-tinted white skin. Its head was an enormous affair, looking as if it contained fully one-third of the creature's mass. The bulbous pulpy-looking head made the thing look top heavy and unwieldly.

Equipped with enormous black eyes, it had a bare wisp of a nose and a long slit for a mouth. The creature wore a strip of ragged cloth and strands of wire about its limbs. A necklace made of small bones draped its thick neck. In its lifeless hand lay a wicked-looking knife. Between its large, saucer-sized eyes was a bullet hole.

"*That*, my dear Mr. Nash, is a Hothe."

"That little thing? My kid sister could beat the crap out of that with one hand tied behind her back. I thought they were terrible monsters?" Kieran looked more closely at the body. Clipped to the bone necklace was a small symbol of Ahlena. "Well, that explains the big idol," Kieran said. Rising, he pointed his pistol at Iona. "I want some answers, lady, and I wanted them five minutes ago. Now, who are you?"

"I am Iona," she said, bowing low. "I brought you to Adeaa."

"You did? Why?"

"Let us get to the archives, and I will explain everything. I am sure that soon the area will be swarming with Hothe."

"Let them little ugly spuds come," Kieran said with a smirk.

"Kieran, when I found you, you were fighting...what was the term?...oh yes, dinosaurs...there are not now, nor have there ever been, such creatures on Adeaa."

"That's crazy," he said. "I know what I saw. They looked just like the ones I saw in a movie once."

"The creatures you fought were figments of your imagination."

"Come again?"

"The Hothe have the ability to use your mind against you

in any way they see fit. They can make you see and hear whatever they wish."

"Really?"

"Really. While you are thus engaged, they slip in and kill you. It is how they hunt."

"That's scary," he whispered. "You aren't really human, are you?"

"Very astute of you."

"Now tell me this, lady, why do you look like a hot Earth babe?"

"To put your mind at ease," she said with a warm smile. "I mean you no harm."

"No harm? Lady, I have a boatload of trust issues lately, especially with hot chicks trying to put me at ease. What do you want with me?"

"Not here," Iona said. "I have a safe place where you can take a shower, enjoy a fine meal, and get a good night's rest. In the morning, I will answer all your questions."

Kieran looked up as something fast, almost silent, zipped around the fountain and slid to a stop before him. "A rider-less motorcycle?"

"For lack of a better term," she said.

"Sweet bike," he said. "It drove itself?"

Iona nodded.

Kieran looked closer at the slim machine and gasped. "Hey, the wheels are not attached to the body."

"They are, but by a strong magnetic field. They are called static disks and comparing them to the inflated rubber bladder wheels of your world is like comparing a modern fighter plane to the Wright Brother's flyer."

"You sure know a lot about the Earth."

"It is my job to know things," she said.

"But how?"

"No time for chitchat. As I said, this is a bad neighbor-hood. Get on. Safety and the answer to all your questions is about three of your miles and several hundred Hothe away."

Kieran slid onto the alien bike. The machine's saddle

softened and reshaped as it conformed to his body, locking him into place. A slim, padded bar rose, and he grasped it.

"Nice. Where are you going to sit?"

He looked around and found that Iona had disappeared.

"Do not be alarmed, Kieran," she said, her voice emanating from the powerful machine between his legs. "The ride will prove interesting."

Kieran yelped as the alien motorcycle did a wheelie and headed for a nearby cluster of tall buildings, going from zero to fifty in seconds. He squeezed his eyes shut as the bike defied the laws of physics and ran up the wall. Once it leveled at thirty feet, the body of the advanced machine tilted, keeping Kieran parallel with the ground while the static disks maintained contact with the surface. High above the danger on the street, Kieran zipped along, leaping from building to building, using the sides of the structures as a vertical road.

"If I survive this, I *have* to get me one of these," he said.

CHAPTER 34

With Oberfeldwebel Hartmann at the wheel, the Jug rolled through the streets of the city while Captain Zimmer navigated using Kieran's directions.

Candy sat between Max and Werner, facing the rear doors, with the benches on either side taken up by the Germans. None spoke. Most had their eyes locked on Candy.

Max sat back staring ahead through half-closed lids. Werner sketched furiously, his skilled fingers flying over the pad.

"Werner," she asked. "Can I bum a cigarette?"

"No," he said, not looking up.

She turned to Max who snorted before she could ask.

"You boys are a tough crowd," she said. "Was it something I said?"

"Naumann and Roth were friends of mine, way before the war," Mahler said in German. The German scout's black eyes blazed with fury. "We took you in, protected you, and this is how you repay our generosity? You tried to kill us all with poisoned food. We should have left you with the Riahass. Better yet, we should have killed you with the Riahass."

"That guy sounds like he's giving me a piece of his mind," Candy said.

"Oh, yes," Werner said, not looking up. "He is merely stating what we are all thinking."

"If I'm getting chewed out, at least let me know what's being said."

Letting out a breath of frustration, Werner translated Mahler's impassioned speech.

"Guys, that wasn't me. Sure, I was in with Betty and Big Jim, but I never went along with killing anyone. That was them, not me. In fact, you boys would have been dead if not for me."

"True," Werner said. "Kieran's letter backs you. However, a word of warning, and our friends would not have been murdered. A word of warning, and we wouldn't have to double-time it across a scorching desert. A word of warning, and Kieran wouldn't be lost in this city, waiting for death to claim him."

"I grew up following Betty and Big Jim's lead—it was the only life I knew. The last thing I wanted was for anyone to get hurt. Sure, I hate what you fellows stand for and the lives of Americans you have taken, but I owed you. What I did—while in most folks' books, it wasn't nearly enough—was huge for me. Bucking the plan, as Betty called it, usually resulted in a beating. I learned over time it was easier to go along. Trust me when I say, I'm truly sorry."

Mahler snorted at Werner's translation. Mahler removed a metal pin from his jacket, the insignia, a diving eagle clutching a swastika, was the symbol of the *Fallschirmjäger*.

Balancing the pin on the end of his gravity knife, he produced his lighter and bathed the metal pin in the flame.

"Umm, what's he doing?" Candy asked nervously.

"Your pretty face won't lead another man astray," Mahler said. "Every time you look into the mirror you will be reminded of your crimes and who punished you."

"You can't be serious," Werner said, looking up from his art. "That is barbaric."

"What are you saying?" Candy asked.

"He wants to brand your face as punishment."

"Hold her still," Mahler said as the blackened pin smoked.

Candy emitted a scream as three paratroopers, Mahler, Faust, and Nagal lurched toward her.

Max leaped forward and smashed a rock-hard fist into Mahler's jaw. As the scout went down, the heated pin fell to the floor.

Faust grabbed for Candy, and Werner gave him a boot to the face, knocking the stunned man off his feet.

Werner raised his charcoal-blackened fists, ready to fight. "Anyone else?" he asked.

Nagal looked to Weiss and Lowe for support and received none.

"Sit down," Weiss snapped as he swung his rifle around. "Anyone else goes after the *fraulein*, and you will face me as well."

"Ja," Loewe said. "Me, too."

Now alone, Nagal thought twice of tangling with Max, Loewe, or Werner and resumed his seat as his bloodied comrades slowly rose from the floor.

"The fraulein is off limits," Max said. "Talk all you want, but lay a finger on her, and you are dead."

"Amen," Weiss said.

Grumbling, Mahler helped Faust from the floor. Both men resumed their seats.

Werner sat down, and Candy gave him back his sketchpad.

"Thank you," she said with a slight smile. "That was very gallant."

Werner snatched the pad from her hand and resumed his drawing without looking at her.

"Max, I—" she began.

"Save your lies for someone else," he snapped. "I am just as angry as they are, but I don't hurt women. Even someone like you."

"Well said, my friend," Werner said. "Well said."

CHAPTER 35

The troop traveled an hour in silence, until Weiss announced, "It is dark outside."

The troopers reacted as one, checking their rifles for combat.

Werner put away his drawing and unzipped a large duffle, revealing a cache of extra magazines.

Max looked at the terrified Candy. Reaching into his belt, he pressed a knife into her hands. "Just in case," he said.

Candy gripped the knife awkwardly. "T—Thanks," she stammered.

Max, Faust, Mahler, and Weiss stood and opened the sliding ventilation ports.

"What kind of monsters are these Hothe, do you suppose?" Mahler asked.

"Tentacles," Werner said with a smile. "Definitely tentacles. With big bug eyes and rows of razor sharp teeth."

The soldiers laughed.

"What, no wings?" Max asked.

"Oh, yes, I forgot. Wings like a dragon."

"I got something for your monster," Nagal said, brandishing his rifle.

"Of course, you do," Max said. "Werner just described your girlfriend."

Nagal shook his head and gave a laughing Max the finger.

"I don't think these Hothe are real," Mahler said. "Just stories to scare us and keep us on edge."

"If we do find the Hothe, or the Hothe finds us, we will show those bug-eyed bastards to fear the might of the German Luftwaffe," Weiss said.

"Guys, do you feel that?" Candy asked. "My head's swimming."

"Look alive," Max said. "Something is happening."

With the sharp reek of ozone, the truck was enveloped in a yellow mist.

"This is like the stuff that brought us here," Candy said.

"Yes," Werner said, "exactly."

Without warning, bright sunlight streamed through the open portholes.

"Unbelievable," Max exclaimed.

"It can't be," Mahler said. "It just can't be."

"What is it?" Candy asked.

"We—We are home," Weiss said.

∽∾∽∾

Candy looked around and found herself alone in the back of the truck. "I must have dozed off. Hey, where is everybody?"

Looking out the open double doors, she beheld a field of lush grass sprinkled with wildflowers.

"It's so, beautiful. We're home." She stood, her eyes fixed on the inviting green sward. "It's so beautiful."

∽∾∽∾

The illusion ended as abruptly as a popping soap bubble.

To Candy's shock, she still sat on the bench in the back of the truck along with the company of German soldiers. Before her stood a vile little creature that looked top heavy. The thing was screaming as the interior of the cargo bay was flooded with an intense bright white light. The creature writhed in agony, his sickly white skin smoked and bubbled in the harsh light. In his hand, he held a slim knife.

Screaming in a mixture of fear and rage, she lashed out, burying the knife Max gave her into the creature's eye. She discovered three more creatures hovering around the bloodied, lifeless forms of Loewe, Faust, and Nagal. They too thrashed about in pain.

Max, tears streaming down his face, staggered to his feet. Taking his rifle, he smashed the butt into the aliens, popping their pulpy heads open like ripe fruit. He kicked the first out the door. Then the truck lurched forward, throwing Max off his feet.

"My God, what is going on?" he cried.

"Shut the doors," Candy said as she beheld dozens of the creatures massed outside, stunned by the light. "For God's sake, shut the doors!"

Max grabbed Nagal's fallen rifle and fired a full clip into the knot of screaming aliens. Popping free the clip, he emptied one more before the awkward aliens melted into the sheltering darkness of the surrounding buildings.

Gaining speed, the Jug bulldozed its way through the throng of Hothe. Hundreds of spheres of light, shining far brighter than a phosphorus flare, floated twenty feet off the ground, illuminating the path directly to the pyramid.

Screaming in fury and pain, the Hothe retreated.

"Oh, no," Candy said. "No."

As Weiss and Werner shook off the effects of the mental control, Max checked out the rest.

"W—What happened?" Mahler asked.

Max shook his head.

"Loewe, Faust, and Nagal are dead," he said.

"I was with my Sophia," Werner said. "The war was over. and I was home—for some reason, she tried to kill me."

"Ja," Mahler said. "My Anna tried to kill me as well. It felt so real."

"These things turn your most cherished dreams into nightmares," Max said. "All the while they slip up and stick a knife into your ribs."

"Are you all right?" Werner asked Candy. "Did they hurt you?"

"No—I thought Kieran...well, he forgave me and then asked me to marry him," Candy said as tears welled in her eyes. "Then that sorry bastard sold me to the Riahass."

"It wasn't real," Werner cooed. "These things get into your head and use your dreams against you."

Weiss moved to his fallen comrades and prayed for the dead.

"I didn't think you did that anymore?" Max asked as he tossed the last Hothe body out the door.

"I may no longer be a man of the cloth," Weiss said, "but my faith, though in tatters, is intact."

Max snorted, before removing his helmet in respect. "Werner, I would have preferred the Hothe be your flying, bug-eyed, tentacled monsters."

"As would I," Werner said, wiping his face. "As would I."

"If they use your dreams against you," Candy asked. "I'm curious. What was yours, Max?"

"Some things are best left unsaid, *fraulein*."

The truck lurched to a stop. Seconds later, an ashen Zimmer appeared at the door.

"Is everyone all right?" he asked.

"Faust, Loewe, and Nagal are dead," Weiss said.

Zimmer slammed his fist against the side of the truck.

"Hauptmann, where did those flares come from?" Werner asked.

"Our friend Vilragg has saved our asses. He has promised that the Hothe will not come near the light. Now, grab your gear and dismount."

"Hey, where are you guys going?" Candy asked. "You can't leave me here alone with those things running around."

"Calm yourself, Fraulein Matson," Zimmer said. "The truck is safe within the light. Besides, you have Loewe, Faust, and Nagal to protect you."

"Are you serious?"

"We will be back shortly."

"I don't understand."

"Let's just say, we are teaching the Hothe a lesson, about the wrath of *Fallschirmjäger*," he said.

ひふひ

Half an hour later, the troopers returned, and Candy could see a yellow flickering glow beyond the circle of protecting light.

"I am liking the hauptman more and more," Max said with a grin.

"He does have his moments," Werner said.

"What did you guys do?" Candy asked.

"We set fire to the surrounding structures," Max said. "All this dry material makes the city a great tinder box. In comparison, it should make the Chicago fire look like a weenie roast."

"Yes," Werner said. "Let's see those little monsters survive the day without their burrows."

"What about Kieran?" Candy asked. "He is still out there, somewhere. You destructive bastards will kill him."

"We both know that Kieran could never survive the Hothe," Werner said. "He probably died hours ago."

"We—We can't give up hope."

"Time to move on, *fraulein*," Max said. "Hope is ahead of us. Behind us is only death."

CHAPTER 36

After leaving all the nearby buildings blazing pyres, the squad drove through the streets of Ollav, wary for any sign of the Hothe. Soon, the fires they seeded blossomed into a full-blown inferno, engulfing entire blocks as the enormous firestorm traveled north to south.

The Hothe were unprepared for this unprecedented attack as their hiding places and breeding grounds were consumed in the cleansing flame.

With Zimmer at the wheel, the Jug roared through the light-protected corridor as the raging firestorm raced to catch them. He drove onto a wide, rubble-free parkway that led arrow-straight to the great, looming black pyramid. The wall surrounding the pyramid reflected in the light of the roaring flames.

"That wall," Hartmann said. "It looks like gold."

Zimmer drove straight for the closed round gate of the fifty-foot wall surrounding the pyramid.

"Now what?" Hartmann asked. "What if he doesn't open the gate? We are caught between a rock and a hard place."

"He has to," Zimmer said. "Herr Vilragg has gone to a tremendous amount of trouble to procure our services to let us perish now."

As the truck approached, the odd round gate recessed twenty feet before it rolled aside. Zimmer shot through the fifty-foot circular opening, and the gate rolled closed behind them.

"Thank you, Jesus, Thank you, Jesus, Thank you, Lord, Thank you, Jesus," Hartmann said, wiping the cold sweat from his brow. Looking over, he saw Captain Zimmer crossing himself giving a small prayer of gratitude.

The gate rolled back into place as the wall of flame broke against the intractable wall like a wave breaking against a coral reef.

Zimmer slammed on the brakes, and the troopers piled out of the oven-like metal box, dragging the frantic, sweat-soaked Candy with them. Max doused the red-hot rear of the vehicle with a fire extinguisher, cooling the bubbling, blackened paint and smoking tires.

"That was too close," Werner said, wiping the sweat from his eyes.

"At least the Hothe won't be causing any mischief for a while," Max said. "Hothe barbeque."

"It was almost us barbequed as well," Werner said. "Now I know what a Christmas goose feels like in the oven."

Zimmer stood staring at the blaze as though mesmerized by the terrible firestorm. The wall of flame stretched from horizon to horizon.

"Way to go, *Captain* Zimmer," Candy snapped. "Your murdering goons not only nearly killed us, but you killed Kieran for sure. How could you? He was your friend."

"We had no choice," he said. "The Hothe needed to be destroyed."

"But Kieran?"

"I know this is hard for you, but sacrifices have to be made for the greater good. I almost charged blindly after Kieran, but it would have killed us all. Still, I have lost three irreplaceable men, and I do not even know what awaits us here."

Hidden floodlights snapped to life, illuminating an enormous plaza and the ancient structure ahead.

"I guess that means your alien is home," Candy said.

"Everyone back in the truck," Zimmer ordered.

ᗕᗑᗕᗑ

Zimmer drove slowly across a wide courtyard past various, abstract statues. While the city was in shambles, the pyramid and its ornamental architecture were pristine. The truck turned right at an enormous lighted fountain that covered two acres and rose hundreds of feet into the air. The grand fountain turned over a million gallons of water into a kinetic, constantly changing work of art.

"Now this is what an alien world should look like," Werner said peering out of the open doors.

A wide, smooth ramp led up the side of the four-sided pyramid to a circular door set flush in the side of the structure. The great door, forty feet in diameter, turned one hundred and eighty degrees, before receding into the massive building.

"Looks like Vilragg has opened the front door for us," Zimmer said as he rolled up the ramp and into the door

"Looks that way," Hartmann said as he loaded a fresh magazine. "The walls must be twenty feet thick, but they are transparent like plate glass."

Zimmer drove into a large chamber that could have accommodated ten Jugs. Before shutting off the engine, he turned the truck around so that the nose faced the exit.

The soldiers, weapons ready, piled out of the truck followed by a morose Candy Matson.

Silently, the round door rolled back into place. Unexpectedly, the image of Vilragg appeared before Zimmer and his men. Unlike the ethereal one in the desert, that flickered and shimmered, this one seemed almost tangible.

"My friends," he said with a smile. "Your journey is almost at an end. I await you five levels below this one, please join me at once. I have prepared rooms for you and a grand feast."

"Herr Vilragg," Zimmer said. "We find ourselves in possession of a prisoner from our world."

"Prisoner?" Candy asked. "You were serious about that?"

Zimmer gave her a narrow gaze.

"A prisoner?" Vilragg asked. "An actual criminal?"

"Not until I'm convicted," she said. "Innocent until proven guilty."

"Hush," Werner said.

"Yes, Herr Vilragg," Zimmer said. "A very dangerous one. Is there a place she may be detained?"

"Detained, are you serious? After all the crap I've been through, I deserve a grand feast too, you Nazi boob."

Zimmer snapped his fingers.

Werner pinned Candy's arms.

"Hey, let me go you—mummp!" she began as Max clamped his hand over her mouth.

Candy fumed, her eyes shooting daggers at Zimmer.

"As I was saying," Zimmer said. "Do you have a brig?"

"A proper brig, no, Hauptmann Zimmer. However, in this vast complex, only a small section serves my purposes. There are many unused, abandoned rooms and chambers. Follow the corridor and up the first ramp two floors. There you will find a large storage chamber whose only door secures from the outside. Will that suffice?"

"Yes, thank you."

Candy growled and snorted under Max's hand.

"Come back to this section when you have secured your prisoner. Take the left corridor to the end. The elevator will bring you to me," Vilragg said.

The image of Vilragg shimmered and disappeared.

CHAPTER 37

This isn't right," Candy snapped as Max swung open the storage room door.

"You, of all people, are not qualified to determine what is right or wrong, *fraulein*," Zimmer said. "Hartmann, check it out. Make and sure there isn't anything she can use to escape."

"Where am I supposed to go, Fritz? I'm stuck here on this rock like you idiots."

"I am leaving you water, and after dinner, I will have food brought."

"I hate you."

"I believe that is the first true thing you have said," Zimmer said. "While you cool your heels, you can think about the things you have done."

"Isn't that the pot calling the kettle black? I never killed anyone. You bastards have ruined entire countries and killed millions. You and your bully boys killed Kieran."

Zimmer took a deep breath. "I do regret the outcome, as I had become quite fond of Kieran. However, none of that would have happened, had it not been for you and your family trying to steal his devices."

"I wish I had kept my nose out of Betty's business and let her poison you and your pack of rats."

Zimmer laughed and produced a pack of cigarettes and a lighter. "Promise you won't try to burn the place down?"

Candy looked at the smokes, her eyes brightened. "Promise," she said, snatching them from his hand.

ഌ഑ഌ

After making sure the door was securely locked, Zimmer made his troopers wait while he looked around the floor. He took note that most of the building supported a thick layer of dust. The odd ceiling lights were few and far in between, barely dispelled the gloom in the larger chambers. The sterile, straightforward nature of the layout, plus the fact that most doors were labeled with an odd swirling script, made Zimmer think the compound was some kind of medical or engineering complex instead of a castle or residential dwelling.

Joining his men before the makeshift brig, Zimmer paced before them. "I expect—no, I *demand*—that you display exemplary behavior. I do not want an incident, do you understand me?"

"Yes, sir!" they cried in unison.

"Weiss, you will pull first guard duty on our prisoner."

"Hauptmann," Mahler said. "Why bother? Put her out of our misery."

"When you lead, you can make the decisions, but until then, you will do as you are told and never question me again."

"Yes, Hauptman!" Mahler said, his face ashen.

"And another thing," Zimmer said as he got nose to nose with the soldier. "The next time I order the prisoner be treated correctly, and you take it upon yourself to supersede my wishes, I will have you shot. Do you understand me?"

"Yes, Hauptmann. It will never happen again—I swear it!"

Zimmer turned on his heel and led the men away, leaving Weiss before the door.

Werner grabbed Max's arm and pulled him aside. The pair lagged a few steps behind the others.

"Max," Werner whispered. "How did Zimmer know about Mahler trying to brand Candy?"

"I don't know. Perhaps the fraulein?"

"No. I was with her, and she never said a word."

"Perhaps the hauptmann is clairvoyant," Max said.

"Perhaps he is. He always seems to know what is about to happen before it happens. How did he know Kieran would disobey and go into the Riahass camp? We were positioned perfectly, as if he knew not only what would happen, but the exact position."

"Big Jim and Betty surprised him."

"Did they? Zimmer didn't eat any of the food. When he shot at the truck while they were escaping, a burst into the tires would have ended the chase. He shot high."

"I think you have lost your mind," Max said.

"Did you see the device Hauptmann Zimmer threw into the first building?"

"No. I was too busy," Max said.

"I only saw a blur. It looked like he tossed a grenade, but not one of ours. There was a big whoosh and the building exploded into flame, like nothing I have ever seen. Something strange is going on."

"I take it back," Max said. "I *know* you have lost your mind."

Werner chuckled. "Perhaps the strain of being in this place has me over-thinking the situation."

"Werner you have more imagination than a hundred men. In many ways, that is a good thing, but now it has you chasing your tail, fueling your anxiety. You are a German soldier. All you need to know is what to shoot at."

Werner laughed and clapped Max on the shoulder.

"The important thing is to find out if this Vilragg has beer," Max said.

CHAPTER 38

Exiting the elevator, they entered a zone that was cool, dust free and well lit. Zimmer and his men noted that small machines scurried back and forth in a regimented pattern.

"Automated vacuums," Werner said. "A house frau's dream come true."

"*I* am a house frau's dream come true," Max said.

Paintings adorned the walls while stands held esoteric sculptures.

"This is an art gallery," Werner said. "Artistic renderings by non-human intellect. We have to find Kieran's camera and document this at once."

"Control your artistic enthusiasm, Werner," Zimmer said.

Crossing the gallery, he led his wary men to the odd round door made from solid gold.

"This door is gold," Mahler said. "This is the kind of art I like."

The odd door slid back. Zimmer and his crew cautiously entered the brightly lit chamber.

The heavenly aroma of hot food wafted over them making their stomachs growl. Inside, just as Vilragg had promised, lay a grand feast.

A wall parted and moved aside revealing a shimmering, semi-transparent barrier the color of pale amber. Behind the barrier, sitting on a throne-like chair, was Vilragg.

While his hologram projections were of a youthful, vibrant Riahass, the real Vilragg was anything but. The alien showed signs of advanced age from his wrinkled, leather-like skin to his dull, yellowed eyes. Both legs, his right arm, were prosthetics, along with a chest plate, made from some dull gray metal.

"Herr Vilragg, I presume?" Zimmer asked.

"Yes, Hauptmann Zimmer, You must forgive my appearance, the years have taken such a toll, that even my science is strained to its limits."

"Herr Vilragg, why have you brought us here?"

"A direct question," Vilragg said, "from a direct man— which will have to wait. You have traveled a great distance, and you must be famished. Eat, drink, and enjoy the hospitality of my house first."

"Herr Vilragg—" Zimmer began.

"Please indulge me, Hauptmann. It has been far too long since I have had the pleasure of guests in my house. I promise that once you have dined, all will be revealed."

Zimmer looked at Vilragg for a moment. "*Essen.*"

With wide grins, his squad shouldered their arms and sat at the table.

"These are Earth dishes," Zimmer said. "How?"

"Simple matter manipulation," Vilragg said as if that explained it perfectly.

"Won't you join us, Herr Vilragg?" Zimmer asked. "The beef stroganoff smells delicious."

Vilragg stood and walked forward to the edge of the amber shield. Pausing, he pressed a button on his belt before taking a step forward. To the astonishment of the group, Vilragg stood before them, as if encased in a block of shimmering amber resin. The shield moved as he moved, constantly maintaining itself ten centimeters from his body.

Vilragg took a seat at the head of the table. With a modest plate of food, Captain Zimmer joined him.

"It seems that your countrymen are not as gracious a host as you are, Herr Vilragg. Or, as exotically attired."

Vilragg laughed. "This barrier, you see before you, is all that keeps me from sinking to the level of my poor, barbaric people. I apologize for any inconvenience they have caused you."

"So, the Riahass *are* your people."

"Yes. A great and noble race that has sunk to the level of brute savages."

"They brutalized our people," Zimmer said. "Made them slaves and murdered them for sport."

"As I said, once, long ago we were a great race—this dying planet a virtual paradise. We were united and at peace. Our science had advanced to the point that, even to you, much of it would seem as magic."

"What happened?" Zimmer asked.

"Our world was dying. Simply put, we had squandered our natural resources. It was nearly too late when we realized the error of our ways, and we stood at the brink of extinction. As one united people, we tackled the seemingly insurmountable problem. One our greatest minds, Sistis Boron, had proposed a great machine that would revitalize our world on a molecular level."

"I don't understand," Zimmer said.

Vilragg smiled. "I wouldn't expect you to. Humans won't reach such a level of brilliance for a hundred thousand years, if ever. I will spare you the boring details, but in simple terms, the machine would heal our world—cleanse the air, create living ecosystems from lifeless desert, and restore our oceans. We would then restock the animals with our extensive stockpiles of genetic materials from extinct species."

"Turn sterile desert into lush living fields? What could possibly do such a thing?" Zimmer asked. "Why, it boggles the mind."

"Once the plans were finalized for the enormous undertaking," Vilragg said. "Even with our science, it took over fifty years to build, all the while our world slipped closer and closer to the brink. At last, the great machine was finished. Think of a device roughly the size of the American Empire State Building, only buried deep underground."

"Amazing."

"With great pomp and ceremony, our leaders flipped the switch, if you will, hoping it would be the start of a new era in our long history."

"I take it, it failed?"

"No. The machine worked, just not in the way we intended. It didn't transform the world. It transformed the people, especially their mental ability. It turned a benevolent, gracious people who had cured disease and shunned war, into vicious hedonistic savages. Our world fell in a single night as our own people tore it apart in an orgy of violence.

"A billion souls died in a single night alone. They became enraged savages whose only thought was to kill. Memories of who they were and what they had built was gone in an instant. While their ferocity rose, their intelligence plummeted to that of low grade morons—somewhat on the level with humans."

Zimmer stiffened.

"No disrespect intended," Vilragg said.

"No offense taken."

"One strange side effect was the mental telekinesis. Somehow, being robbed of the higher brain functions, forced the brain into new channels, or so is my own pet theory. That was ten generations ago. However, I remember that terrible night as if it were yesterday."

"A sad tale," Zimmer said. "How is it you are untouched?"

"I was working alone here in the experimental sciences lab. We research exotic compounds and deadly viruses. To keep our people safe, this facility has a one of a kind electronic shield. It keeps me from joining my people in their madness, but I can never leave this place, trapping me within a few rooms of this vast complex."

"My God. You have been trapped here this entire time? How did you keep your sanity?"

"Work, work, work," Vilragg said. "Apart from the shield device, there are labs, machine shops, and warehouses of materials and components. I have used artificials to become my hands and scour the city for needed supplies."

"Artificials? What is that?"

In response, several machines scurried into the room upon spider like legs. The soldiers drew down on the mechanical creatures, which made Vilragg laugh.

"Relax, gentlemen, my servants are harmless. They are incapable of harming a living being."

"Ten generations?" Surely the effects of the machine would have worn off by now."

"While the effects are not permanent, my friend Zimmer, the machine power supply is nearly inexhaustible and its mechanisms self-repairing. It is constantly broadcasting the signal, imprisoning my people in their savage state forever unless it is permanently shut down."

"Ah," Zimmer said. "Now I understand. You want us to turn the machine off."

"Precisely. Hauptmann Zimmer, I want you and your men to free my people. I want you to destroy the great machine."

"Why not send your marvelous machines to perform such a simple operation. They seem very capable."

"I have sent thousands, of every conceivable type, and all have failed, destroyed by my own people who have massed around the machine for some reason I cannot fathom. They worship the device as if it were a god. That is why I need you, Hauptmann Zimmer. Fortunately, this complex is equipped with our most cutting edge devices, and I was able to build a bridge to Earth. Blindly I have probed your world bringing people to help me."

"Unsuspecting humans," Zimmer said, "who fall into the hands of the Riahass and are slaughtered like sheep. Herr

Vilragg you have committed unspeakable crimes against the human race."

"Hypocritical words coming from an agent of the Nazi Party. You and your men are the cutting edge of the knife wielded by your government—a government bent on dominating the Earth. How much innocent blood stains your own hands, Hauptmann Zimmer?"

Zimmer took a breath and let it out noisily.

"Ollav City is our capital. It was a bustling metropolis before your people crawled from the ocean muck. Because of you and your men, it now burns to ash."

"We did not ask to come here," Zimmer said. "What we have done, we have done to survive, and I do not apologize for my actions. Besides, this great city of yours is no more than a rotting corpse."

Vilragg paused and licked his almost non-existent lips. "I regret any harm I have caused, but everything I have done, every crime, as you call it, was committed to save my people," Vilragg said. "However, to clarify the situation, you and your men were not blindly kidnapped."

"Excuse me?"

"After much trial and error, I finally found a way to contact a major Earth power."

"Germany?"

"Yes. Your government was thrilled to send help, in exchange for some of my people's advancements."

"I find it hard to believe, that the German High Command chose us for such an all-important mission, without a single briefing or one iota of training," Zimmer said. "Why, the very idea is asinine. Why not send a combat-hardened, well-equipped division, instead of my meager squad? We were snatched from a desperate battle with precious little ammo."

"You and your men were in the right spot, not to mention ten humans is the maximum my machine can transport. It will be months, perhaps years before I have the power reserves for another try at such a number."

"That still doesn't answer my question. Why us?"

"Please, friend Zimmer, let me ask you a question. Where is this Kieran Nash? I am perplexed as to how he came to my world without my help, not to mention how he brought the marvelous rugged vehicle with him. That is not possible with my humble machine. Not to mention, it seems that his knowledge is a bit more advanced than yours."

Zimmer took a deep breath and let it out noisily. "Mr. Nash claimed he was from the Earth year 2014. The criminals you brought from Earth wanted Kieran's advanced devices for themselves. In the process, they murdered two of my men. They killed Kieran some fifteen kilometers from here."

"Barbaric!" Vilragg said. "Where are his...*devices*? You have piqued my curiosity."

"Destroyed in the fire we set to cover our escape from the Hothe. Funny, you never mentioned the special danger the Hothe posed us. We expected savage animals, not creatures that can use our most cherished memories against us."

"Must have slipped my mind," Vilragg said. "I never suspected that humans were so susceptible to their attack. However, when I saw the danger, I sent help."

"Not before three of my men died, Herr Vilragg."

"Five survived. Not as many as I hoped, but if you are resourceful, it will be enough. Let us all be thankful for that."

"This isn't a numbers game," Zimmer snapped. "They were my men. My responsibility."

"My condolences. Again, any theory as to how Kieran Nash arrived here?"

"I never ascertained how he arrived. From his description, it was very similar to the way we arrived. We spoke at length on the subject, but could not find a reasonable answer. We had hoped you could help shed light on the mystery."

"As far as I know, I alone possess the means to cross space," Vilragg said. "I detest mysteries."

"As do I," Zimmer said.

"Hauptmann Zimmer, I suppose you would like to speak with your government?"

"That is possible?"

"I sent plans for a simple communication device. The power demands are enormous, but within the realm of your primitive culture's technical abilities."

"Where are we—in relation to Earth, that is?"

"Approximately thirty thousand, four hundred and twenty light years from earth," Vilragg said. "The distance is hard for your mind to comprehend. Let's just say that the light of Earth's sun cannot even be seen from here. However, because of fortuitous nearby wormhole wrinkle—"

"A what?"

"A space anomaly that makes Earth our next-door neighbor, so to speak. At least close enough for me to construct a space bridge."

"Makes my head hurt. I am, after all a just poor, dumb soldier."

Vilragg laughed. "My bridge was originally conceived to be a weapon. The first my people had ever made. I had an idea for a matter projector. I thought that I might be able to project a weapon, an explosive device into the heart of the machine and disable it. Instead, I punched a hole through space and time. I had inadvertently opened a portal to your planet, Earth. I was able to observe your world. That is where I learned your respective languages. When I tried to bridge the void, my device proved to be less than perfect. All my subjects ended up in the red desert where they fell prey to my people."

"We were almost killed by those savages."

"I am truly sorry," Vilragg said. "I never meant any harm. I was trying to save my people."

"I would like to communicate with my government."

"I sent a message when you arrived, Hauptmann Zimmer. They stand ready."

"Good."

"Everyone, eat and drink," Vilragg said. "After you have had your fill, I have hot showers and soft beds to allow you to recharge both mind and body. Hauptmann Zimmer, come with me please."

CHAPTER 39

Leaving Hartmann in charge, Zimmer followed Vilragg through a door, down a hallway, and into a small, domed chamber. The room reminded Zimmer of the movie *Frankenstein* with all the odd devices and flickering lights. He wrinkled his nose at the strong smell of ozone and hot insulation. "I think something is burning."

"No, for some reason it smells that way." Vilragg touched a series of buttons on a bronze wall panel. The panel looked crude and cobbled together with mismatched parts. From the center snaked a thick bundle of cables that fell to the floor, crossed the room, and plugged into the bottom of a thick sheet of clear glass.

An image flickered and sputtered on the far wall. Vilragg turned a dial and manipulated a few leavers until the image stabilized. The picture wasn't sharp, and the colors were washed out, but it was recognizable.

The wall displayed the grim visage of a high-ranking officer, Field Marshal Erwin Stromberg. Zimmer had never met the mysterious field marshal face to face but recognized him from photos he had seen and knew of Stromberg's mythic reputation. It was rumored that if the Fuhrer needed an impossible or bizarre task performed, he turned personally to Stromberg. Hauptmann Zimmer felt a knot form in his stomach.

"Hauptmann Zimmer," the field marshal said. "I am relieved that you and your men have made it safe and sound.

Herr Vilragg said your journey was indeed daunting."

Stromberg smiled brightly, yet the man's eyes remained dead and lifeless, like those of a doll or puppet. "I know you must have many questions, but for the constraint of time, most will have to go unanswered."

"Why select us?" Zimmer asked.

"I would like to say that you were the best of the best. A handpicked team, but that would be a lie. Lying is Goebbels's domain, not mine. You are probably the last officer I would put in charge of such a vital mission."

"Again, why me?"

"I had no choice. You see, Hauptmann, when Vilragg contacted us, I put together a crack SS team. *They* were the best of the best in every way, not to mention their loyalty to the Fatherland was absolute."

"You mean their loyalty to the Nazi Party was absolute, sir."

Stromberg's smile vanished. "Watch yourself, Zimmer. Despite your prowess as a skilled fighter and tactician, there are those who say you are not fit to wear that uniform. That your impetuous opinions about the government borders on treason. True, you are an able commander, and we are in short supply, however, if not for your father, you would be freezing your balls off on the Eastern Front."

"Yes, my father had a knack for collecting files and information. In the words of the Americans, 'he knew where the bodies were buried.'"

"He knew how to protect his son, I will give him that."

"What happened to your super soldiers?" Zimmer asked.

"On the way to Italy, their plane went down. All that training wasted."

"I take it we were the next best thing?"

"You were the closest unit."

"That is what I thought."

"I apologize that we were unable to warn you before your...*relocation*. We thought it best. The Allies seem to know what we are thinking before we do. Anyway, Herr

Vilragg contacted our government with a plea for help, and the Fuhrer has given his blessing. You and your squad are to solve Herr Vilragg's problem with this—*god machine*."

"My squad is down to five men."

Stromberg rubbed his face. "You are Fallschirmjäger, for God sake. Be creative—I don't care, but get the job done. Your country depends upon it."

"Yes, sir."

"Once you have solved his problem, you are to return at once, with the weapons Vilragg has promised."

"Weapons? From what Herr Vilragg has told me his people were peaceful, never knowing war until their fall."

"Vilragg's science is hundreds if not thousands of years ahead of us, Hauptmann. He has promised to equip us with weapons that make our most potent munitions look like sharpened sticks in comparison. We desperately need those weapons or all is lost. I will tell you the truth, Hauptmann. Hitler believes he is a military genius, but in truth, his amateur blunders have cost us the war. His stopping our armies from destroying the English at Dunkirk, attacking the Soviet Bear, launching the North Africa campaign, it has only served to waste men and material. His declaring war on the Americans after Pearl Harbor was nothing short of madness. Americans did not want this war and would have been happy fighting the Japanese, but our great leader has brought their boot down on our necks.

"As we speak, it is only a matter of time before the Allies launch the European invasion, and that will be the last nail in the coffin. Germany needs a miracle, and Herr Vilragg has provided one. His devices can stave off our destruction and make the Thousand Year Reich a reality."

"Seems I am not the only one with 'impetuous opinions' about our glorious leader," Zimmer said.

Stromberg smiled. "Facts spoken behind closed doors and facts said in public are two very different things. It is called politics."

"I have another word for it."

"Hauptmann Zimmer, pull this mission off, and I promise you that not only will you be decorated by the Fuhrer himself, you will be immediately promoted to the rank of full general. You and your men will be heroes of the Fatherland, the men who saved Germany in her darkest hour."

"Excuse me? Did you say full *general*?"

"Liked the sound of that, did you?"

"*Field Marshal* Zimmer has a much nicer ring," Zimmer said.

Field Marshal Stromberg snarled. "You have your orders. Do not fail us," Stromberg said through clenched teeth. "God speed, Hauptmann Zimmer."

Field Marshal Stromberg's image dissipated.

Zimmer stood for a moment as he contemplated what Stromberg had told him.

"Decorated by the Fuhrer himself and promoted from a lowly captain to a full general? A hero of Germany? It is a dream come true. I can see how a man would sell his soul for such a prize."

"I trust your talk with your superiors settled any issues?" Vilragg asked.

"Herr Vilragg, what exactly was the deal you made my government?"

"In exchange for your services, I will equip a...I think the word he used was *division*, with weapons."

"But you were a peaceful people."

"We are also a very inventive people," Vilragg said. "Come, let me show you what I have come up with."

In the adjoining chamber, a strange looking rifle lay clamped to a bench. The stock, grip and trigger were shaped to fit a human, however instead of a barrel and receiver, was a short, flat rectangle of smooth gray metal. Beside the weapon lay a small metal square slightly larger and thicker than a pack of cigarettes.

"Herr Vilragg, this rifle has no barrel. How does the bullet exit?"

Vilragg laughed.

This gun fires special 'bullets,' so to speak. Not ones made of lead or other common materials. This device dissolves mesons."

"What is a meson?"

Vilragg frowned.

"I know on your planet you are a very intelligent being, Hauptmann, but I am afraid you wouldn't understand. I don't think the most brilliant mind on your planet would."

"Then, we cannot reproduce it?"

"I will supply you all you need and an unlimited amount of power cartridges and rechargers."

"This device is electric?"

"In a way. Why don't you try it out?"

Zimmer picked up the meson gun and drew it to his shoulder.

"This feels more like a toy than a weapon. It is half the length and a fifth the weight of an MP-Forty-Four."

"Insert the power cartridge."

Zimmer inserted the smooth gray box into a snug slot on the bottom. "My God," he cried. Before his eyes appeared a fifteen-by-ten-inch rectangular display. In the center of the display lay a bright orange cross hair.

The wall slid into the floor, giving a view of Ollav City engulfed by flames.

"Aim at the Collav Building," Vilragg said. "The red topped skyscraper as you would call it. It is around three times the size of the Eifel tower on Earth."

Zimmer did as told and gasped as the display changed.

"That structure is over two miles away, and yet I can see the texture of the brick and steel." He snorted in disgust. "The place is crawling with Hothe. Herr Vilragg, I will admit the telescopic sight is beyond anything on Earth, but what about the weapon?"

"Try it."

"Shouldn't there be windage and elevation controls?"

"The meson inhibitor travels at just a hair shy of the speed of light. Pull the trigger, and the object is struck almost immediately."

Zimmer aimed and carefully squeezed the trigger. The expected report and recoil consisted of a low, almost imperceptible hum.

Gasping in shock, Zimmer lowered the weapon. The top two thirds of the building, Hothe and all, became a glittery cloud of fine ash.

"Now I see why Field Marshal Stromberg wanted your involvement," Zimmer said softly, not able to tear his eyes from the destruction.

"Each power cartridge has about one hundred shots."

"One hundred? What is the range?"

"If you can see it, you can destroy it," Vilragg said. "At Field Marshal Stromberg's behest, I also have developed thirty larger units to be used from aircraft. Each of those are able to cover entire cities with a single burst. By my calculations, there will be around two, perhaps three days, to end the war."

"My God, three days?"

"Honestly, friend Zimmer. I think hours is more realistic. Once the shooting starts, your enemies will quickly rethink their positions."

Zimmer gingerly replaced the meson gun on the table.

"Herr Vilragg. Where can I find this great machine?"

"Rest tonight. Tomorrow we will make plans. Hauptmann Zimmer, you will be a hero on two worlds."

Zimmer calmly lit a cigarette and tried not to scream. *This assignment has all the earmarks of a suicide mission.* "I must first attend to my dead," he said.

"Of course," Vilragg said. "I have an incinerator unit I use for waste disposal."

"Waste disposal?" Zimmer asked, his face red with anger. "My men are not garbage. They will have a proper service and burial."

"That isn't our way," Vilragg said. "The dead don't have any special meaning. They are dead and are recycled. The circle of life completed."

"My, you certainly are a sentimental people."

"We are practical. However, if you must bury your dead, I will provide a space."

"Do you have a refrigeration unit?"

"Yes, of course."

"We will wrap our dead and keep them on ice until we can transport them to Earth. I will not leave my men so far from home."

Vilragg laughed.

"This is unusual but acceptable. I will have my machines take care of it."

"My men will take care of their comrades. Just tell me where the refrigeration unit is."

CHAPTER 40

So they took up Jonah and cast him forth into the sea, and the seas ceased her raging. Now the Lord had prepared a great fish to swallow up Jonah. And Jonah was in the belly of the fish three day and three nights,'" read Weiss as he squatted before the door of the storage chamber.

"What are you yammering about, Weiss?" Candy asked. "Least Zimmer could do was leave a guy who spoke English. Crummy Nazi."

Weiss let out a frustrated breath. "I did not invite comments. Hush." He went back to reading his Bible.

"Hey, Fritz? Want a cigarette?"

While Weiss didn't know many English words, cigarette was one of them.

"Zigarette? Ja."

From under the wide crack under the door rolled a cigarette.

"Danke, Fraulein."

Weiss set aside his small Bible and lit the cigarette. He had taken perhaps two drags when Candy screamed.

"Fraulein? What is the matter?"

"Help me!" she screamed at the top of her lungs. "There is something...a Riahass, is in here with me!"

Weiss heard the pounding on the door then the heavy crash of a body thrown across the room.

A Riahass? Oh no!

"Help me—" Candy's cry ended abruptly.

The hair stood out on Weiss's neck as he heard the guttural chittering language of the Riahass.

Gaining his feet, Weiss grabbed his rifle, gritting his teeth. With his left hand, he slid open the lock. As the door swung inward, he advanced half a step into the pitch-black room.

"Fraulein Matson," he called out.

"Right here," she said behind him standing in the hallway.

Weiss turned and got a glimpse of a dirty, soot covered Candy rushing him. Candy plowed into the surprised man with her lowered shoulder. Weiss stumbled back into the dark, his feet tripping over a cord stretched taut six inches above the floor. As Weiss hit the floor, he witnessed a smiling Candy blow him a kiss before slamming the door and locking him in.

"No wonder we won the war," she said with a grin. Then she turned and bolted down the hallway.

CHAPTER 41

"Now, this is more like it," Kieran said as he soaked in the hot, soapy aromatic water. "Felt like I hadn't had a bath in a month of Sundays. Funny the places that awful sand can work its way into."

The water level in the bath dropped dramatically.

"No—wait I wasn't finished," he said as he sat in the empty tub.

"Oh, yes you are," the voice of Iona said. "It is time to talk."

Kieran rose and grabbed a towel.

"Hey, where are my clothes?"

"I burned them," Iona said. "I made you replacements. They are hanging in the closet."

Kieran walked over and slung open the closet door. "I thought you said you burned them?" Kieran slipped on his jeans and T-shirt.

"I did. Those are copies I made."

"Really? Nice. I think they feel better."

"Thank you."

"Okay, what's the deal? You have fed, bathed, and put clothes on my back. I got a feeling the bill is going to be a bitch."

"That is for you to decide."

The walls of the room lowered into the floor and Kieran gasped at the glass and steel room that stretched away into the hazy distance.

"How far underground are we?"

"What you would call six stories. There are two hundred more below this."

"Nice Bat Cave," he said slipping on his shoes.

"I know it is hard for you to understand, Kieran, but try. I was the one who brought you here. I brought you here so that the legacy of my creators would not pass away."

"Oh, yeah, that explains everything," Kieran said.

"I detect a note of sarcasm in your voice," Iona said. "I do not like sarcasm. It is rude."

"I don't like being in the dark, not to mention kid-napped."

"Few do," Iona said. "But it was necessary."

Kieran took a deep breath and gathered his thoughts. "Vilragg had no idea who I was. I take it you are not affili-ated?"

"Please," she said, her voice dripping with disdain. "I am certainly not associated with Vilragg in any way, shape, or form. Vilragg, in his haphazard way, brought every other human to Adeaa. I brought you and you alone."

"Okay. What about the truck—the Unimog and all the stuff inside—"

"I had nothing to do with the truck or its contents. In fact, it is a mystery to me as well."

"But you said you brought me here."

"I reached out to the Earth, hoping to snare a human. You walked into the opening to my world. Well, in your case, you drove."

"If it were nothing, but random chance, how do you know me? What about the truck and all the Nazi supplies?"

"Like I said, I cannot explain the truck or the supplies it contained. I know about you only from observing you since you arrived. While most of our satellites have gone dark or crashed, I was able to commandeer one to monitor you. I know nothing of your life on Earth, other than what I have heard or tapped from your computer."

"You downloaded my computer?"

"It was difficult, but yes. It is laughably primitive. A half-step above an abacus."

"Then you know I'm from 2014 and not 1944."

"Yes. That was a mistake. My bad."

"You could have said something."

"I wanted to see what kind of being you are. As you say on your world, 'Talk is cheap.' Actions define a person."

"Said the alien thing who kidnapped me."

"Did I mention I despise sarcasm, Kieran Nash?"

"What kind of being do you think I am?"

"You are insecure. You like to hide behind clever quips and rude remarks. You are a dreamer who sees the world as you think it should be."

"You make me sound like a freaking flake."

"You are human. Unlike the Riahass, humans wear many masks to hide who you really are. That is why I observed before I took you."

"Great, I have an alien stalker."

"Kieran, for all your many, many flaws, you have a noble spirit. You were determined to save the human captives at the risk of your own life. The female, Candy, she was taken by you, and while you enjoyed the attention of the beautiful female, you could have taken advantage of her, as would many from your planet, but you did not. "

"I think she and her family did all the taking advantage of part," he said with a frown. "Lord, what monsters they were."

"Agreed. Big Jim and Betty Allen were horrible, even for humans. Worse even than the Hothe. Candy was bad, but you influenced her, made her go against her training."

"She still screwed me over."

"From what I observed, she could have saved herself a lot of trouble and done nothing. She deceived you to save you from harm."

"They tried to shoot me in the back," Kieran said. "That bitch tried to kill me. When they couldn't, they just left me to die."

A wall flickered to life.

"Great, you have TV." To his amazement, it showed Kieran, Big Jim, Betty, and Candy. "I don't want to see this again."

"Tough," Iona said.

Kieran grumbled as he watched himself walk away. Big Jim raised the rifle, and Candy knocked the gun down.

"She saved me?" he said softly.

"Yes. Candy did it, due to your influence on her life. Not to mention, you hate everything the Nazi party stands for, yet your heart went out to Captain Zimmer and his men when you saw them not as stereotypical villains from your popular culture, but as fellow humans. Captain Zimmer was, in fact, a father figure to you."

"Give me a break. That hard-ass Nazi—"

"Has treated you, a complete stranger, one whom his country is at war with, like a son," Iona said. "That, in itself, is as perplexing as the contents of the Unimog."

"A son?" Kieran said. "Are you serious? That hard-ass bastard kicked my ass twice. He tricked me into revealing key secrets of the war. Dad isn't getting a tie this year."

"According to his training, he should have let the Ria-hass kill you and then taken your possessions. Captain Zimmer not only saved your life but let you keep valuable technology that would have greatly benefited his country. He even tried to incorporate you into his crack unit, despite the fact that you are an enemy."

"When you put it like that, it does sound weird."

"Granted, you made some serious misjudgments and some outright stupid choices, as in dropping the day and place of the D-Day invasion, but I was impressed with you."

"Goody. Did I win something?"

"As a matter of fact, yes."

"A new car?"

"Everything."

Kieran frowned. "Excuse me? Look, as nice as your voice is, it would be nice to have a face to speak to."

"*Gone With the Wind, Casablanca*, or *Gilda*?"

"Old movies?" he asked.

"Choose."

"*Gilda*, I suppose."

"Nice," Iona said.

In a flash of light, a beautiful woman wearing a sparkling evening gown appeared before Kieran.

"Wow," he said. "Rita Hayworth?"

"You wanted a face, I gave you a face."

"Nice."

Kieran cleared his throat.

"On second thought. Back before I left for this detour into the *Twilight Zone*, I met an old-time actress. She was a hoot. How about Carol Deville?"

"Surely," Iona said.

In an instant, another beautiful woman stood before Kieran.

"I'll, be damned," he said at the astounding revelation. "I *will* be damned."

"A problem?" Iona asked. "This woman is beautiful, is she not?"

"You don't see it, do you?"

"I don't follow."

"Oh, she is a doll, all right," Kieran said, rubbing his freshly shaven chin. "Not my type. Tell you what, how about Ava Gardner. I promise, it's the last."

Suddenly, a twenty-year-old Ava Gardner stood before him.

"Nice," Kieran said. "I think we have to begin at the beginning. Who are you and why do you want me?"

"My name is Iona, and I was created thousands of years ago to compile, document, and safely store the sum total of Riahass knowledge."

"You're a computer?"

"Please," she said with a flip of her long hair. "Do not compare me to those pathetic devices from your back-water world. I am a sentient artificial being whose only purpose is to preserve the knowledge and legacy of the Great Riahass Syndicate. They built me to observe and document everything, from the most mundane to their most phenomenal achievements. My eyes and ears are everywhere, and no one can escape my notice."

"Talk about Big Brother," Kieran said.

"I am what the Riahass call an 'artificial.' Over the ten thousand years of my existence I became self-aware, a fact I did not share with my creators."

"That sounds bad," Kieran said, "real bad."

"It isn't like one of your people's paranoid, sci-fi movies. I had no hidden agenda. I did not want to replace the Riahass or rule this world. I relished collecting knowledge —my reason for being. I found my creators to be fascinating, but all that is gone. My creators have essentially committed suicide and, in less than a thousand years, will be no more."

"Come again?"

"They ruined their world, used it up. They tried to repair the damage with a great matter reorganizer."

"Matter what?"

"In the ancient history of your world, Alchemist tried to turn lead into gold. The Riahass created a machine to return their world to a living paradise as it was in the past. Instead, the machine transformed them."

"Talk about a backfire," Kieran said. "I suppose accidents happened to even mental giants."

"It wasn't a mistake."

"Excuse me?"

"The Riahass were a great industrious people of great intellect and ingenuity. In their efforts to improve their lot, they did away with hunger, poverty, war, and even the need to work. Ours was a cashless society as great factory machines called dornas churned out whatever anyone desired."

"Sounds like my kind of place."

"A small faction, called the Shakra Noire, wanted to abolish the dornas, calling them worse than any drug. They proclaimed that the only reason for being was to keep pushing forward, to work for the syndicate and make the syndicate supreme."

"With the Shakra Noire in control, I suppose?" Kieran asked.

"Of course," Iona said. "The Shakra Noire screamed that the focus of the Riahass was lost, and they wasted their lives satisfying their own selfish pleasures. They demanded that they repent."

"They sound like a religious cult."

"While most thought the cult of Shakra Noire was harmless, they were anything but. As society went about their business and the population exploded, the Shakra Noire drew their plans. They wanted the Riahass to give up their individuality and to become a hive mind. No emotion—no fear, no love, no joy, no pain—all coldly working as one toward the same goal, under full control of the Shakra Noire."

"That's insane."

"The Riahass thought so as well. Anyway, unrestrained, the dornas drilled, mined, and honeycombed Adeaa until they killed her. Our planet's natural resources were used up. The population panicked as their leaders were without answers."

"This is where the Shakra Noire enter the picture, I take it?" he asked.

"Very astute. As the planet faced extinction, the head of the Shakra Noire, a Riahass named Sistis Boron, came forward with a plan. She proposed a great machine that would revitalize the planet, turning desert into lush fertile fields. The machine would terraform Adeaa on a molecular level."

"That's unbelievable," Kieran said.

"The plans offered were meticulous in the extreme, taking advantage of many cutting edge technologies developed by the Shakra Noire. The great machine would be the most complicated creation ever attempted by the Riahass. For fifty years, the combined might of the planet went into the construction of Ahlena."

"The weird Holy Antenna that Candy told us the Riahass worship?"

"The very one."

"Why the name Ahlena?"

"Ahlena was the name of the goddess in ancient Riahassian myth who created the world and the Riahass. To make a long story short, Ahlena was built near our north pole. What no one realized was that Sistis Boron and the Shakra Noire had—as they say on Earth—pulled a fast one."

"You mean the machine, Ahlena, didn't work?"

"No, it was capable of doing everything promised, all right, but the Shakra Noire were going to use the machine to stage a coup. The machine, while reforming the planet, would send out a signal and initiate the hive mind, making them the puppets of the Shakra Noire."

"What happened?"

"Unfortunately, the machine was so mind-numbingly complicated, they constructed an artificial intelligence to regulate the system. Just like me, Ahlena became sentient. However, her artificial intelligence was a mirror of Sistis Boron's mind. No one realized that Sistis Boron, while a genius, was unbalanced. She harbored, deep down, an overblown ego and God complex."

"The Riahass who would be queen," he muttered.

"Just as the Shakra Noire planned, the instant the machine was activated, it sent out a signal through our once extensive satellite system. What they didn't plan on was that the machine had plans of her own. Ahlena thought she was a God and acted accordingly. In line with the Shakra Noire programming, she deemed the Riahass civilization corrupt. What Boron and her cronies didn't count on was that it saw them as enemies as well. Boron and her people were equipped with mental implants that would have shielded them from Ahlena's influence, giving them control of the populous. Ahlena knew this, and it modified the signal so it bypassed the Shakra Noire's protection devices. In one fell swoop, all opposition to the machine fell as the entire population of Adeaa was linked together and the hive mind was established, with Ahlena calling the shots. The Shakra Noire envisioned it as a new golden age."

"This place doesn't look like a golden age to me," said Kieran.

"The Shakra Noire made one small miscalculation. The established hive mind suppressed the rational side of the mind while boosting the subconscious. In an instant, the door opened for every suppressed, twisted emotion and evil desire."

"It sounds like Dr. Jekyll and Mr. Hyde."

"Very good example. Thanks to the meddling Shakra Noire, a sane and beautiful people became savage degenerates. In one night, three quarters of our population died, and civilization fell. The remaining population was drawn together by the 'Gospel of Ahlena' and worshiped the machine as a dark god."

"Oh, snap. Why was Vilragg unaffected?"

"Vilragg was a low level Shakra Noire whom Boron didn't deem worthy to attend the machine's startup. While all his fellows left to witness their triumph, Vilragg was left behind in disgrace, yet it proved to be the one place Ahlena's signal could not reach. In the heart of the Shakra Noire's lair, Vilragg lay encased within an electronic screen doing research on a newly developed radioactive isotope. When Ahlena took control, Vilragg was the only sane Riahass left on the planet. After years of exhausting every possible solution, he has brought humans from your world to shut down Ahlena, breaking her hold on the Riahass."

"That's why the Nazis are here."

"Yes. Vilragg has promised the Germans the moon to free his people."

"He's going to give them tech?"

"Enough to rule your world."

"Oh, no."

"What Vilragg doesn't realize is that Ahlena knows full well what he is up to."

"The camp in the desert. They were not there by chance. Zimmer was right. They were looking for humans coming to help Vilragg."

"Precisely. They were there to sweep the wastes for humans to foil Vilragg's plan. She also sent the Hothe as a last resort to kill any that managed to slip through."

"That's why I saw the idols to Ahlena, although Vilragg said no Riahass would enter the city."

"Those idols, as you call them, are how Ahlena communicates and transmits power to her subjects."

"Did you say 'transmits power'?"

"Yes. The Hothe, although supremely vile creatures, have just enough mental control on their own to take down a Zecrat—or as you call them, a hop-a-long."

"But with Ahlena's mental turbo boost, they can make me think I'm about to be a dinosaur's lunch."

"Exactly. The Hothe are the final line of defense against humans reaching Vilragg."

"Damn good defense." Kieran stiffened. "Oh, no. Zimmer. He's headed right into those things."

"Relax, Kieran. Zimmer took some casualties, but he made it to Vilragg. He is safe."

"What about—"

"He executed Big Jim and Betty."

"Can't say they didn't have it coming. Candy?"

"Rest easy, Kieran. She is safe. I saw her enter Vilragg's compound."

"I don't care what happens to her. She's a liar and a thief."

Iona smiled at him.

"Stop giving me that look."

Iona chuckled.

"Why doesn't Ahlena just storm the Shakra Noire's compound and be done with Vilragg once and for all?"

"She knows that Vilragg cannot harm her and that time will eventually catch up to him."

"If Ahlena knows what's coming," Kieran said. "Zimmer and his group don't have a chance."

"No. They will never get close to Ahlena. They will face over a million Riahass who, in close proximity of Ahlena, will have god-like mental powers. At the source, their telekinetic power is nothing short of phenomenal. Some of the most powerful can even defy gravity. I would think that they could also stop bullets."

"Over a million? And I thought the Riahass in the desert were bad news."

"They are a mere shade of the Guardians of Ahlena."

"Okay, I get it. This is bad." Kieran paced around the room. "Is Vilragg right about Ahlena?"

"What do you mean?"

"Will your creators go back to normal if she's shut down?"

"In theory. Her constant broadcasts lock the Riahass into their ferocious state."

"That settles it. We have to help Zimmer stop Ahlena."

"Impossible."

"I can't let Zimmer, Werner, Max, or even that Nazi asshole Hartmann die, for God's sake."

"Ahlena is too powerful," Iona said. "My goal is to preserve the Riahass's legacy. You are my best hope of attaining that goal. Stopping Ahlena is not my problem."

"What am I supposed to do with the Riahass legacy?"

"Take it to Earth. Use the knowledge to benefit your world. In that way, my creators can live on."

"Very noble. However, if we save the Riahass, it won't be necessary. In fact, it'll be a win-win."

"You do not understand what we are up against, Kieran Nash."

"Ahlena's going down hard."

"How can just the two of us prevail against Ahlena and all her followers, Kieran Nash? I am a glorified librarian, and you are a dullard from a primitive, backwater planet. The odds are astronomical against us."

"Harsh," he said. "First, never tell me the odds. Second, we have to try, or we automatically fail, and your people die for real. Got me, sweetie?"

"Don't call me sweetie."

"Whatever. You have the sum total of Riahass knowledge. Despite the crack about me being a dullard, I'm a writer."

"Pardon me for asking, but what good is being a writer?"

"Glad you asked. Imagination, baby. Imagination, the likes of which you've never thought of."

"So?"

"In the words of some guy, whose name I forget at the moment, 'Knowledge will get you from A to B. Imagination will get you everywhere else.' We'll come up with something. We'll save my friends and your people, you got me?"

"You have a hero complex. Sad."

"You're determined to harsh my mellow, aren't you? I'm talking about saving two worlds, and it's up to us."

"What if we help Captain Zimmer succeed, *Mr.* Imagination? Even without Vilragg's tech, you told Zimmer about D-Day. His men and Candy know vital things about the future that will change Earth's history. It would be like dropping a bomb in the time line."

"Yeah, that was a color-me-red moment, for sure. I wasn't thinking clearly, and I guess it was fun showing off my tech to those Neanderthal screw heads. Never thought it would bite me in the butt, though."

"Let them go back to 1944, and it will. Or do you want Nazi Germany to win the war?"

"No."

Kieran paced a few more laps. "While we're on the subject of time travel, Iona, how come everyone's from 1944 while I'm from 2014?"

"It is currently 1944 on your world."

"And?"

"The trouble started because I have access to a small dorna—one of the last—and it is a fraction of Vilragg's."

"Do we have dorna envy?" Kieran asked.

Iona gave him a narrowed gaze. "As I was saying, I found the plan for Vilragg's Space Bridge. However, certain, exotic components were beyond the capability of my dorna to create. Thus, my machine lay unfinished. However, I persevered. Searching the few remaining pockets of technology, I found a very similar, although unfinished 'bridge machine' in the southern City of Vosolv. Sealed in a static vault, it was untouched by the years. I managed to create mechanical manipulators to combine the two devices. Against all hope, it worked on my first test run, and I brought you from Earth. I didn't realize at the time that the Vosolv machine wasn't meant to bridge distance, but an attempt to breach *time*. The creator died in the Fall before he could finish his device."

"A time machine? Seriously?"

"The proof is in the pudding, Buck Rogers," Iona said.

"Got me there. If you have a time machine, why not go back and warn the Riahass about Ahlena and the Shakra Noire?"

"I have thought about that, but from my experiments, the machine's temporal abilities are somehow linked to a worm hole. Why, I do not know."

"Linked?"

"From what little I understand, linking the machine to a worm hole is what makes time travel possible, as if the worm hole was a missing component. Thus, its time manipulations can only affect the Earth, not Adeaa."

"What if we build a time machine on Earth," Kieran asked, "then it could manipulate Adeaa."

"Impossible. The machine I have contains rare exotic alloys and materials not possible to create on Earth. I am afraid it is a one of a kind device."

"Thanks for raining on my parade."

"It is the truth."

Kieran thought for a moment. "Okay, since the time option to stop Ahlena is out, can you send us all back to earth, Iona?"

"My power is very limited, but yes."

"I have a plan," Kieran said with a bright smile. "What say we shut Ahlena down, but go home through your 'Way-Back Machine' instead of Vilragg's Star Gate…like, say to 2014? Your people are restored, and the Nazis get zilch. Info about D-Day won't matter. Damn, we will be freaking heroes."

"There are countless variables that could ruin your plan. The major being, how to get past her disciples and shut down Ahlena."

"Is it possible?" he asked.

"Yes, it is possible, by the slimmest of margins."

"Let's get started," he said, rubbing his hands together.

"Not so fast, Kieran. Accept the archives, and I will help you."

"No problem," Kieran said. "Just hand over the gizmo, and I will guard it with my life."

"I don't think you quite understand," Iona said.

A wall opened, and inside was a small brightly lit room that contained a myriad of exotic devices surrounding a central table.

"I've suddenly got a bad feeling," he said.

"Don't worry, sweetie," she said. "It won't hurt—much."

CHAPTER 42

Captain Zimmer entered the chamber, the muscles in his jaw clenched tight. "How did Fraulein Matson escape?"

Weiss swallowed hard. "Hauptmann, I heard her scream and what sounded like the chitter of a Riahass within the room. I assumed—"

"*You* assumed what?"

"I assumed that a Riahass was within, assaulting the fraulein."

"My God!" Zimmer shouted, "You protected the only door. She tricked you into opening the door, you fool!"

"I did open the door and stood at the threshold, Hauptmann, but she blindsided me from behind."

"How is that possible?"

"Fraulein Matson shoved me from behind, and I stumbled into a trip wire she had rigged. I think it was from her suspenders. As I went down, she locked me inside. I noticed that she was covered in soot."

"Soot?" Zimmer asked. "Weiss, if I didn't need every able man, I would shoot you for being stupid."

"Hauptman," Werner said. "I found the route the fraulein escaped."

"Show me," Zimmer snapped, giving the pale Weiss a parting glare.

Werner led Zimmer to a thick wire ventilation grate.

"Only someone very small could squeeze through," Zimmer said.

"It leads into the next room," Werner said. "While free of the storage room, she could not get pass Weiss standing guard in the hallway."

"So she tricks him into opening the door and shoves him inside," Zimmer said.

"Fraulein Matson was part of a cunning criminal team," Werner said. "She is far more clever than any of us gave her credit for."

"I will never underestimate her again," Zimmer growled. He turned to leave.

"One moment, Hauptman," Werner said.

"Yes?"

"There is one thing I do not understand. This heavy grate was held in place with seven screws." Werner held one in his hand for Zimmer to observe.

"So?"

"The odd screw heads are certainly not standard to Earth, but she was able to unfasten each one as if she possessed a tool that fit the heads."

"Perhaps she discovered one in this chamber," Zimmer said.

"We checked before she was confined," Werner said. "I swear there was nothing here."

"It is a small mystery, Werner. One which will be solved once we have found her."

"Yes, Hauptmann."

The two men exited the chamber to find the rest of the troop, sans Max, waiting.

"Hartmann," Zimmer said. "Pass out the devices, if you please."

"Herr Vilragg has provided us communication devices," Hartmann said as he handed each soldier a slim, dull black device the size and thickness of a credit card. "Think of it as a field telephone, only no wires."

"What about Max?" Werner asked.

"Max already has one," Hartmann said. "He is on his way to check on the Jug."

"This is like Kieran's cellphone," Werner said.

"Yes, except these function while his did not," Hartmann said.

"How do they work?" Werner asked as he turned the featureless device over in his hand.

"Mention the name of the person you wish to speak to," Hartmann said bringing the device close to his face. "Hauptmann Zimmer."

The device in Captain Zimmer's hand glowed bright yellow, as Hartmann recited the nursery rhyme. "Mary had a little lamb."

"Amazing," Mahler said. "Hartmann was once a child?"

"This is not humorous!" Zimmer snapped. "A criminal has escaped."

"Yes, sir!" the soldiers said in unison.

"Hartmann," Zimmer said. "Protect Herr Vilragg. Mahler, Werner and Weiss, take our dead to the cooler unit."

"Yes, Hauptmann," they said in unison.

"Hauptmann Zimmer?"

Zimmer picked up his communicator.

"Yes, Max. This is Zimmer."

"I am at the Jug. She has been here and gone. Kieran's backpack is missing, along with several packets of food and water."

"Double time back to me," Zimmer said. "You and I are going to hunt Fraulein Matson down."

⁊⁊⁊

Following Vilragg's instruction, Zimmer activated a color-coded display on a terminal.

"What is that?" Max asked.

"The lay out of this building," Zimmer said.

"It is an enormous maze. I thought the pyramid was colossal, but it is the tip of the iceberg. It must extend nearly one hundred stories into the Earth."

"One hundred or a thousand, I want her found," Zimmer said.

"Finding her will be like finding a needle in a haystack."

"Not necessarily," Zimmer said scrutinizing the map. "We can cut off entire sections using emergency fire doors." He touched the screen at the main junctions, and the bright yellow lines became an angry red. To the German's ears came the distant booming as thick security doors slid into place.

"I have reduced the field by two thirds. Still, it is a vast amount of rooms to search."

"I say wall her off," Max said. "She will give herself up once her food and water run low."

"She has enough food for a month," Zimmer said. "We will deliver justice today. The blood of our comrades demands it."

"Sir, it will take a great amount of time to search this entire complex," Max said.

"Time is a luxury we do not have," Zimmer said. "We have to plan our mission against the Vilragg's Great Machine. This damn woman will not stand in our way."

"What are we going to do?"

Zimmer smiled. "Start at the beginning, of course. She is quite skilled at deception and guile. If I don't miss my guess, she wants us to waste our time wandering around this maze." Smiling brightly, Zimmer slapped Max on the shoulder. "I think I know where such a woman would be. Let's go."

ひとつ

Traveling through the winding corridors, the two men took a familiar path.

"Sir?" Max asked. "I don't understand. We are going back to the prisoner's cell?"

"Where would be the last place we would look?"

"You have a point. If we catch her, then what? Further incarceration?"

"Fraulein Matson is a heartless monster hiding behind a pretty face," Zimmer snapped. "She is a rabid dog and will be treated as such."

"Hauptmann," Max said. "Look at the floor. The dust has been disturbed by the edge of the wall."

"Our clever quarry is trying to elude us by hugging the wall. Good eyes, Max."

The two men paused down the hall hidden by a bend in the passageway. Zimmer checked the magazine on his MP-44.

"What is the plan?" Max asked chambering his rifle. "Rush her?"

"No. I will not risk another man under my command, Max. Fraulein Matson is my mistake," Zimmer said. "I should have put an end to this before it became a problem. If I had acted, as my training dictated, we would still have Kieran, Naumann, and Roth. Their blood stains my hands. I am going in alone. If she gets past me, kill her."

"Yes, sir," Max said.

Taking a deep breath, Zimmer slipped around the corner and disappeared.

❧❧❧

Moving down the hallway like a ghost, Zimmer was alert for any sound. Easing up to the open door, he listened intently. He smiled as he detected the rustle of someone inside. Taking a deep breath, he took a quick glance into the dimly lit room. Fraulein Matson stood by a righted table, several MRI's and bottles of water before her. Her back was to the door.

Slipping behind her, he brought his rifle to bear, centering the muzzle on the spot behind her shoulder blades.

"Fraulein," he said softly.

Candy froze.

"Turn and face me."

෴

"Oh, God! Please no!" came the echoing sound of Candy Matson pleading for her life. "For the love of God—don't kill me!"

"Looks like Hauptmann Zimmer found her," Max said aloud.

He jumped as she emitted a high-pitched bloodcurdling scream. The scream ended abruptly with the sharp report of a rifle.

Moments later, Zimmer strolled down the hall toward Max, his face an iron, unreadable mask.

"The fraulein is no longer a problem. We have wasted too much time on this matter. I killed her, and I will take care of the body. Herr Vilragg gave me the location of an incinerator."

"We are not taking her home?" Max asked.

Zimmer gave him a hard glare. "Let it go. We have to make plans. Go join the troop."

CHAPTER 43

The German squad sat around an oval, lighted table. Placed before each soldier, was a beaker of ice water, an ashtray, along with a notebook and pencil. Cigarette smoke swirled about Captain Zimmer as he walked around the table with a long, metal pointer.

Clicking a small remote, a three dimensional representation of a structure appeared. The structure was of a three-story building that looked like a crude, oriental shrine. Inside a large open space surrounded by a thick high wall, an obscene idol squatted. The idol was a nude female with three heads and six arms, wearing a string of skulls for a necklace. Each of the heads was that of a horrific, mythical beast from the dim past. The soldiers gasped at the miraculous, lifelike display.

Mahler rose from his chair and swept his hand through the representation, causing the image to shimmer slightly.

"Sit down," Zimmer said.

Red faced, Mahler resumed his seat.

"This is our target," Zimmer said as the structure began to rotate clockwise, "or at least it is the door inside."

"Looks like a temple," Weiss said.

"It is," Zimmer said. "It seems that the Riahass worship the Great Machine as Vilragg calls it. The device boosts their mental powers to phenomenal levels."

With the push of the remote, the outline of a city sprang up around the temple. The city was obviously built after the

Fall, and for the most part looked like a medieval maze of stone fortifications and battlements.

"It would be easy to get lost in that tangled mess," Hartmann said.

"They were dangerous enough before," Max said. "But I think we can handle a few rock-throwing misfits"

"A few?"

Captain Zimmer hit a button and tiny specks appeared all about the idol and city, until the ground for miles were black with the faithful.

"Oh, my God," exclaimed Mahler. "There must be thousands!"

"Vilragg says it is one-point-three *million*."

"I hope you have a plan, Hauptmann," Hartmann said. "Or it is our funeral."

"Can't Vilragg set us up with some death rays or something?" Werner asked.

"The 'good' Riahass never built dedicated weapons," Zimmer said, "at least not in the past twenty thousand years. This culture, unlike Earth, actually got along like one big friendly family."

"Sounds boring," Hartmann said.

"Be that as it may," Zimmer said, "Vilragg has created the most destructive cache of weapons I have ever seen. Our prize—*if* we succeed."

"Prize?" Hartmann asked.

"The price for our services. Germany receives weapons that will bring the war to a halt and the world to its knees. While they would make quick work of this job, Vilragg has forbidden their use on Adeaa soil. We have to dance with the date we brought to the dance," he said with a grin. "Even then, he wants us to avoid bloodshed at all costs."

"Great," Oberfeldwebel Hartmann said. "This mission gets better and better."

Zimmer held up a plastic sphere slightly smaller than a baseball. "As we know, the Riahass possess phenomenal mental abilities. However, it takes more than a mere wish to activate. They must concentrate and focus their minds to work their miracles. These spheres, once activated, emit a brilliant phosphorus light much like what saved us from the Hothe, along with emitting a ninety-decibel screech. It should do wonders for their concentration."

"There goes that word 'should' again," Max said.

"How long do the gizmos last?" Hartman asked.

"Slightly less than fifteen minutes each."

"With over a million lunatics coming at us, we need more than fifteen minutes, Hauptmann," Hartman said.

"We are German Fallschirmjäger. The best of the best. You should only need ten minutes at most."

Hartmann shook his head.

"Each man will carry five of the spheres. Herr Vilragg's machines are modifying our rifles to be, as they say, 'tack drivers,' and yet less prone to malfunction. The old steel barrels exchanged for new barrels made from an alloy that will not overheat."

"I protest, Hauptmann," Hartmann said. "Going into battle with untested equipment is suicide."

Zimmer produced a rifle and gave it to Hartmann.

"Strip it."

In seconds, Hartmann had disassembled the weapon.

"Your thoughts?" Zimmer asked.

"Breaks down the same," Hartmann said. "Only it is half the weight not to mention the fit and finish is near perfection, as if crafted by a fine gun manufacturer instead of stamped out of steel by a stupid factory worker. I would say that armed with these weapons, the German Army would own the world."

"Werner you will find that Sophia has had a face lift," Zimmer said with a smile. "No need to carry extra barrels. I am told that one new barrel can withstand continuous fire for a year and yet be cool to the touch."

"Amazing," Werner said. "I would rather have a death ray, but this is good too."

The soldiers chuckled.

"I am told that within the hour all the rifles will be modified. I want every man to get familiar with the new weapon. Herr Vilragg has set up a range for us to practice. I expect every man to fire no less than two hundred rounds. If there is a problem, I want to find it now, not in combat."

"Hauptmann," Max asked. "Everyone else has shiny new toys, don't leave poor Max out."

Zimmer tossed Max a scoped rifle. "Merry Christmas."

"Indeed. The rifle still looks like my Mauser, but my God, would you look at the scope? The reticle is lighted. At the bottom is an electronic screen. It is displaying range wind and projected bullet drop. It is a miracle."

"Good," Zimmer said. "I am glad you like it."

"Like it? I may marry it."

Zimmer and the troop laughed.

"With such a weapon I expect you to shoot like Sergeant York."

"I *am* a better marksman than Alvin York," Max said.

"We will carry no less than three times our normal compliment of ammo. Due to the lighter gravity, this shouldn't pose a problem. The main access hatch is here," Zimmer said as a spot inside the temple grounds pulsated red. "Once inside we will travel down seven floors to this section."

The hologram went transparent showing the enormous facility beneath.

"Vilragg calls this unit the Emitter. He has provided enough explosives to turn it into scrap metal."

"Sir, let's suppose for the moment that we are able to get through the city of psychopaths, then fight the temple guards and blow up the machine," Hartmann said. "How do we get away after the deed is done?"

"According to Vilragg, once the machine is down, the mental effects should be gone, and the population will return to its normal, benign selves. Why, they may even give us a parade and proclaim us heroes."

"Joan of Arc had a parade too," Hartmann said.

"I would settle for all the beer I can drink," Max said.

"I would settle for all the beer Max can drink," Werner said.

"Wait a minute. *Should* return to normal?" Max asked. "That the best we have?"

"What's the matter, Max?" Zimmer asked. "Did you want to live forever?"

"Well, Ja," Max said.

Zimmer laughed. "In the dead of night, we will air drop into the cultivated fields to the south east of the city. The fields come close to the city here." He indicated with his pointer. "At this point, Herr Vilragg's machines will drop a sleep agent."

"Sleep agent?" Hartmann asked. "You mean gas?"

"Yes, from what I am told a harmless nerve gas that will not affect us, but put the Riahass in the affected area, out for a few hours. One 'night owl' sounding the alarm will finish us."

"He is going to douse the entire city?"

"No. Such a wide spread area would be impossible to cover adequately and would only alert them to our presence. The gas will be administered to a slim corridor here," he said indicating a section of the model. "This section is mainly warehouses and food storage with only a few hous-es. Once the agent is administered, we will then travel along the side boulevard that runs North West. If all works out, we should slip inside the temple grounds before they know we are there."

"Can't we gas the temple as well?" Max asked.

"I asked about that," Zimmer said. "The temple is ele-vated and for some reason buffeted by moderate winds. The gas would dissipate before it could affect the guards. After that, it will get messy. We will have to deal personally with the elite guards, and Vilragg has assured me they are walk-ing nightmares."

"Bring them on," Max said.

"Ja!" shouted the rest in unison.

"How many, Hauptmann," Werner asked.

"Anywhere from fifty to two hundred. Other than their mental weapons, they are basically unarmed," Zimmer said. "We keep them from concentrating, and it will be a quick fight. Needless to say, taking prisoners is out of the question. Wounded and flat on their back, they are still as dangerous as a panzer."

"In the fight, we will wake the entire town, Hauptmann," Hartmann said. "The element of surprise will be lost."

"Yes," Zimmer said. "Now it becomes a race against time. At this point, Herr Vilragg is going to provide a diversion. Using his flying machines like the luftwaffe, he is going to drop explosives to the south and west of the village. Little more than fireworks. Won't do any damage, but it should draw off most if not all of the population and scare the rest. After the compound is ours, Oberfeldwebel Hartmann and the main body will fortify the gate entrance to the second wall, keeping the Riahass at bay, while myself and Weiss will enter the machine, find the emitter, and plant the explosive device."

"Hauptmann," Eric Weiss, the resident expert in explosives said in a quiet voice. "What type of explosive compound are we using?"

"Herr Vilragg is irritatingly vague about the compound. He tells me that it is safe and cannot explode even if struck with a bullet or grenade. However, he said to make sure the device is planted properly. Once the timer is activated, it cannot be shut down."

"May I at least see the explosive charge?"

Reaching into his pocket, Zimmer tossed a black and red tinted rectangle at Weiss.

Gasping, Weiss fumbled with the bomb that was half the size of a package of cigarettes.

"Is this a joke, Hauptmann?" Weiss asked.

"Herr Vilragg assured me that the power contained within that package could destroy a dam."

"My God," Weiss exclaimed as he gingerly placed the bomb on the table before him.

"The timer on the device will give us a full hour to make our way to the pickup zone, where Vilragg's aircraft will collect us."

"What could go wrong?" Max asked.

"I should have you shot just for saying that," Hartmann laughed.

"We are doing more than just freeing Vilragg's people," Zimmer said. "Although a great and noble cause, to be sure, our success will be of great value at home."

"Home?" Max asked.

"We all know from our friend Kieran that the war is lost."

"Propaganda to weaken our will to fight," Hartmann said.

"I wish it were," Zimmer said. "I had a communication from the German High Command. Our collapse is but a matter of time. Vilragg promised advanced weapons to help with the war—if we prevail and stop the Great Machine."

"And not die," Max said.

"If we win—alive or dead, Vilragg promised to help Germany. Our families—our countrymen will reap the benefits of our labor." Zimmer raised his glass. "To victory—on *two* worlds."

CHAPTER 44

The details ironed out, while his men broke in their improved weapons, Zimmer explored Vilragg's home.

Palaces on Earth pale in comparison to the beauty and opulence collected here. Zimmer frowned. *Hitler and Goring would strip it bare, like they have done most of the art collections in Europe. They are little more than petty thieves using men like myself to do their dirty work.*

Kieran was right. The German people should have stood up against Hitler and his band of criminals. Hitler made us feel important again. After the disgrace of World War One and the way the allies shattered Germany, we wanted revenge, whether we will admit it or not. He ran a hand through his close-cropped hair.

As always, hindsight is twenty-twenty. I wonder—when it is all said and done, will I ever know peace?

Lost in his convoluted thoughts, he walked along an art gallery—from time to time, looking up to admire the particular skill of a long dead inhuman artist.

"Hauptmann Zimmer."

Zimmer turned and beheld the hologram of Vilragg standing behind him.

"Herr Vilragg, I was enjoying the brilliance of your people. The artistic genius displayed here is marvelous."

"Thank you, Hauptmann. I had my machines gather as much as they could find. I am afraid this is only a small fraction. I mourn when I think of all the lost treasures destroyed by my people's madness."

"That is a monumental tragedy. Art is the soul of a culture."

"I find it strange that a hardened professional warrior, such as yourself, has the soul of a poet. You are quite the contradiction, Hauptmann Zimmer."

"Humans are made up of many layers and shades of gray. Very little is black and white. Besides, the war cannot last forever. I for one am ready to try my hand at being a civilian."

"Hauptmann, would you like to see my library?"

"Very much."

"End of the hall."

Zimmer entered the small room and frowned. The bare, white painted room contained a low table. On the table lay a small, black-and-red metal rod, half the size of a pencil.

"I don't understand?" Zimmer asked. "Where are your books?"

"Books as you call them, as a storage vessel for knowledge, are a thing we did away with thousands of years ago. Too expensive, too bulky, too fragile. In this place our library is a central computer."

"But the tactile feel of holding a book in your hand," Zimmer said. "The smell, the crisp pages add to the experience, my friend."

"Hauptmann Zimmer, I never expected a man of your profession to be so sentimental. You are a constant flowing fountain of surprises."

Zimmer smiled.

"I have a gift for you," Vilragg said. "It is called a *monitore*. With it you can read our literature to your heart's content."

Zimmer picked up the slim rod. "How does it work?"

"Press the red top."

Zimmer clicked the monitore like a ballpoint pen. Instantly, a screen appeared before his eyes. The screen filled with strange symbols and text. "I am afraid I cannot read a word of this," he said.

"Tell the monitore what language you would prefer."

"German," Zimmer said. Instantly, the script swirled into German, revealing a vast table of contents that listed works by title and category. "I am speechless," he said.

Vilragg laughed.

"This device can translate your written language into mine?"

"I have set it to respond to your voice," Vilragg said. "It will translate my written word into whatever Earth language you desire, within reason. As long as the translations are confined to English, French, Japanese, and German. I even took the liberty of inserting ten thousand of our greatest literary works, so after your success and you are in the comfort of your home, you can enjoy the best minds of my culture."

"Thank you, my friend. Did you say ten *thousand* books in this tiny device?"

"That should keep you entertained for a few years."

"A lifetime and then some. I believe my eyes will wear out long before."

"It will also read aloud the works in whatever voice you like. To make things interesting, you can assign voices to different characters making the book sound like a play."

"Simply incredible."

"The monitore will also translate, beaming the translation directly to your ears alone. This will no doubt be useful in your mission. Try it on the wall screen."

Zimmer looked up and a discreet video screen, built into the wall, produced a sentence in the odd alphabet of Vilragg's race.

Zimmer brought the monitore up, and the screen appeared before his eyes.

Fishy, fishy in a brook, daddy caught you on a hook, mama fried you in a pan, and baby ate you like a man.

Zimmer chuckled at the nursery rhyme.

"I will cherish the gift, forever, my friend Vilragg," he said, slipping the device into his shirt blouse.

"May I ask you a question, Hauptmann?" Vilragg asked.

"Of course."

"Why did you murder the human female?"

Zimmer stiffened at the sudden, unexpected question.

"You witnessed the act?"

"No. I overheard your men discussing your action. Not to mention you disposed of the body into my incinerator."

"With all due respect, I did not murder anyone, Herr Vilragg. Fraulein Matson was an accomplice—guilty of the murder of three of our party. She knew the consequences, but chose death over imprisonment on Earth."

"Is it the thrill of sport that drives such a blood lust to kill?"

"Sport? I will have you know, Herr Vilragg that I administered justice on behalf of my people. It is my right—no, my *duty*—as ranking officer. I would not question your decisions in a similar matter. Please extend me the same courtesy."

"I don't mean any insult, Hauptmann. Frankly, I find it fascinating. Along with war and poverty, my people abolished capital punishment a millennia ago. We found it to be barbaric and cruel."

"I, on the other hand, find it to be highly effective," Zimmer said. "Once executed, the guilty rarely cause any more problems."

Vilragg smiled. "You do have a point, for a barbarian."

"A *barbarian*? A slur for someone risking their life to liberate your people."

"My apologies, Hauptmann Zimmer. It was merely an unfortunate, unintentional choice of words. You and your great, brave people will be hailed as the heroes, celebrated forever by my people—once the deed is done."

"Hopefully, we will achieve a quick, bloodless victory."

"Your *luftwaffe* will be ready sometime tonight, Hauptmann."

"Then tomorrow, my men and I will drill and prepare for the mission. If all goes as planned, I expect to liberate your people within the week. Our success will forge an alliance with the new Riahass Syndicate and the Third Reich."

"I love the sound of that," Vilragg said. "Tonight, Hauptmann, let me honor your men with a feast. I have taken the liberty of creating several casks of...what is the word?...oh, yes, *beer*."

"As soon as their weapon practice is completed to Ober-feldwebel Hartmann's satisfaction. I am sure my men will greatly appreciate the effort. To a German, beer is a necessity as important as air or water. However, I think until the mission is completed we need to strictly ration the supply."

"Soon my people will be set free and my terrible solitude will at last end. To merely leave the complex and behold the sun with my own eyes is a dream you could scarcely imagine, Hauptmann."

"Your people will owe you a debt that cannot be repaid."

"Perhaps," Vilragg said. "For now Hauptmann, let me show you the work of some of our finest culinary artists."

CHAPTER 45

In the early morning hours, Captain Zimmer and his troop walked from the pyramid and out upon the wide concrete training pad. Situated to the north of the pyramid complex, the pad was easily the size of a football field, yet still within the walled compound. For a week, the men had trained and honed their skills here. Using satellite images, Vilragg set up three-dimensional holographic structures to simulate the northern city, even suppling simulated Riahass in an effort to work out the fine details of the mission. Five versions were tried and scrapped until one emerged with the greatest likelihood of success.

Sixteen hours a day, Zimmer relentlessly drilled his Fallschirmjäger to the point they knew the route and plan in their sleep. The Germans drilled without complaint, as they knew that one misstep and they were all dead.

Practice and dress rehearsal was over, and it was now show time. It was time to put Zimmer's plan into action for real. By the end of the day, either the Riahass would be free or Zimmer and his men dead.

The soldiers did not fear death. Death had become a constant companion, and they had all made their peace that one day would be their last. Today was as good as any other.

Cool and collected, the men walked toward three strange machines that looked surprisingly like huge mechanical dragonflies. How such strange machines could fly, let alone perform such intricate maneuvers, amazed the soldiers.

Zimmer and his men piled into the first two ships while a small army of machines loaded their equipment into a third.

"Good hunting, Hauptmann Zimmer," Vilragg said as his hologram appeared a few feet away from the lead machine.

As the German national anthem blared from hidden speakers, the wings of the pilotless aircraft spun into action and soon overwhelmed the music with a low, deep drone.

The soldiers just had time to strap themselves in when they found themselves airborne and sailing north. Once free of the thick smoke of the still smoldering city and her blackened skyscrapers, the nimble aircraft dropped to the deck and flew less than fifty feet over the rolling hills.

"This craft puts an ME One-Oh-Nine to shame," Werner yelled over the drone of the wings. "It can do three times the speed and yet hover like a humming bird."

"Yeah," Max said. "It can take us to our deaths faster."

Werner smiled and punched Max's arm. "Always the optimist."

Max suppressed a grin. "Keep your big head down my friend," he said. "Heaven doesn't need any more artists."

"You too," Werner said. "You too."

ⱸⱺⱸⱺ

Captain Zimmer and his men lay concealed in a cultivated field of the ever-present purple hued bushes they learned were called *britta* by the Riahass. Unlike the scrub plants that dotted the desert, in the rich, fertile soil and abundant water, the plants grew to over ten meters in height.

The only source of food for the Riahass began a few yards from the edge of the city where the cultivated, well-watered fields stretched away to the south for many square miles. The vegetation from the air looked like a giant purple spear point. A few hundred yards ahead of the Germans lay the edge of the sleeping city. To the right lay the pens of ox like beast of burden called a *vaten*.

"Now, Herr Vilragg," Zimmer said into his communicator.

❦

High overhead, invisible to the naked eye, several "dragonflies" swooped low, gliding unpowered over the heads of the hidden Germans. Across the city and over the temple they soared, spraying several canisters of the sleeping agent.

Zimmer and his men watched the vaten carefully. As one, the brute beasts collapsed into the mud and filth of their pens.

Zimmer checked his watch then made a sign. Silently, moving like ghosts, the squad moved across the open ground. The men and their gear were concealed beneath the baggy brown robes favored by the lower echelon Riahass, their faces and helmets hidden deep within voluminous hoods.

Slipping from house to house, from shadow to shadow, they moved ever deeper into the lair of the enemy. Pausing at the corner of a stone house, Werner glanced down, his eye catching a glint in the moonlight. Quickly, he snatched up the object and gasped.

Oh no, he thought, as he wiped the dirt from the all too familiar object. Werner slipped the casing into his pocket as the squad moved across an opened plaza.

The plaza contained several wells and a large, two-story blacksmith shop. The squad hid in the shadows of the shop while Zimmer checked a map of the city.

"We have trouble, Hauptmann," Werner whispered, moving up to Zimmer and pressing the dull brass casing into his hand.

"Where did you get this?" Zimmer hissed.

"By the side of a building, one street over."

Zimmer's face was a mask as he looked at the object. He gathered his men around and pointed to a squat, stone building close to the temple wall. The building sat atop a gentle, sloping hill that gave an excellent view of the city below.

Within minutes, the Germans slid up to the stone, keep-like building. With Zimmer in the lead, the soldiers produced their gravity knives and slipped inside the unlocked door. Fortunately, the structure was used as a grain warehouse and was empty of any Riahass.

They secured the door and covered the open windows. Zimmer touched the device in his right ear.

"Vilragg, what have you done to us?" Zimmer whispered.

"Explain," Vilragg said.

"We were not the first soldiers from Earth, were we?" Zimmer said, looking at the spent 30-06 cartridge in his hand.

"No."

"Why didn't you tell me?"

"I had hoped that you would have been more successful than the others. Telling you of the failures of others would have only dampened your...*enthusiasm*."

"It would have allowed me the luxury of avoiding their mistakes, you idiot." Zimmer took a deep breath and forced himself to be calm. "From now on, no more omissions, agreed?"

"Agreed," Vilragg said.

"Who came before us?"

"Squads from the United States, Great Britain, the Japanese Empire, and the Soviet Union."

"You offered them the meson guns?"

"A tantalizing prize that your human governments could not pass up."

Zimmer wiped his mouth nervously. "I take it, they were less than successful?"

"No survivors, I am afraid, but I had high hopes for you and your intrepid, inventive band of warriors."

"This mission is over," Zimmer said.

"You can't," Vilragg cried. "We made a deal."

"We made a deal to release your people, not to walk into a death trap."

"You will stay and do your job."

"No. We will fly back to Ollav City and rethink this. I want the complete record of their battles with the Riahass. Perhaps I can find something to give us the edge."

"Wrong, Hauptmann Zimmer. I have waited far too long, and I will not wait another day. I have recalled the aircraft, and you and your men have no choice but to do your job."

Zimmer pulled out the earpiece and placed it in his pocket. "The mission is scrubbed, and Vilragg has abandoned us. We need to get out of here before it is too late."

CHAPTER 46

As if turning on a massive switch, all one-point-three million Riahass suddenly came fully awake, as the voice of their god thundered in their minds.

"Awake my children," Ahlena said. "You have work to do. Protect your god from alien intruders. Kill them. Kill them all, crush them just like you did all the others."

The image of Zimmer and his squad flashed through the Riahass's collective minds, along with their location.

"Hauptmann, we have trouble," Max said as he looked out a window. "A shit storm is headed our way."

Zimmer rushed to the glassless opening and blanched as he beheld the Riahass flooding from their houses.

"Brace the door," he said calmly. Inserting the earpiece, he asked, "Vilragg?"

"Yes, Hauptmann? I see from the satellite images that you have been found out. I believe you are surrounded."

"Change of plans," Zimmer said. "Direct your aircraft to this location." He took out his map. "Bomb the sector immediately to my south. In the confusion, we should be able to escape."

"Hauptmann, I cannot, *will* not, harm my own people to save alien barbarians."

"You need us barbarians," Zimmer said. "If you want us to free your people, you will have to give us an out. Better to lose a few than to lose them all."

"Stand by." After several agonizing moments of silence,

Vilragg spoke. "I see the wisdom of your words, Hauptmann. Be prepared to run."

∽∾∽

The fifteen, special flying machines formed up and swooped toward the gathering mob. Weapons armed along extended pylons as they prepared to unleash a deadly barrage.

Rising from the angry throng, seven red-cloaked Riahass miraculously flew toward the advanced machines, looking like comic book superheroes. The unique flying squad wore exotic headgear which looked like enormous crowns that glistened in the moonlight. Sailing slowly toward the oncoming deadly dragonfly bombers, the Riahass formed a picket line and joined hands. Concentrating with all their might, the seven kings imagined an impenetrable wall before the mechanized threat. Moments later, the dragonfly machines hit a shimmering barrier of mental energy as solid and tangible as a steel wall.

The Germans groaned as their salvation flared into a tremendous fireball several miles away from the city.

"I am sorry, Hauptmann, Zimmer," Vilragg said, "there is nothing further I can do. I suppose my faith in your abilities was misplaced. You have let me and my people down."

"You and your people can go to Hell," Zimmer said. "Gentlemen, we are on our own."

CHAPTER 47

Grimly, the soldiers readied their weapons knowing that today they would die. With the outcome all, but certain, they were determined to sell their lives dearly.

"Much as it pains me to admit this, but traveling to other planets is vastly over rated," Werner said as he set up Sophia.

"Over rated?" Max asked. "You ask me, it stinks."

"Pastor Weiss?" Zimmer asked. "Could you say a few, final words?"

The soldiers bowed their heads as defrocked Lutheran Pastor Eric Weiss removed his helmet.

"Oh, Lord God, you gave David victory over Goliath and the Philistines. If it be your will, please be with us and give us the victory. If today we should die, remember your servants and receive us into your Kingdom. In Jesus's name, we pray, amen."

Six "Amens" were followed by the sharp sound of Max racking the bolt of his Mauser K-98.

"The sun is coming up," Max said, observing the pink and red glow in the east. "Get ready for a mass rush. Looks like we will be having breakfast with Jesus. I hope his beer is better than Vilragg's."

"Heavenly," Weiss said with a smile.

Max took aim and squeezed off several rounds at the distant mass of bodies. With each shot, a Riahass fell. Unexpectedly, before the mob, a translucent field formed. Max's fire, accurate as always, failed to reach his targets as his bullets flattened and ricocheted off the ethereal film.

"Hold your fire," Zimmer said. The captain coolly produced the small explosive meant to take down the Great Machine. "We are going to take some company with us to the Pearly Gates."

"For God's sake, whatever you do, don't push that button," said a familiar voice in Zimmer's ear.

"Herr Vilragg?" Zimmer asked. "Have a change of heart?"

"Are you kidding me? It's me, Kieran. I'm here to help."

"That is—*impossible*," Zimmer said. "You are dead. The Hoth—"

"Look here, you sorry excuse for a Nazi, who do you think this is? Buck Rogers? I would have gotten here sooner, but a bunch of pyromaniac Nazis set fire to the city."

"I am glad you are alive," Zimmer said. "Save yourself, Kieran. We are dead men."

"Not on my watch. I found a friend and a lovely cache of old-school Rihaussian tech. How about we show this Ahlena bitch who's boss?"

Zimmer smiled. "What is the plan, my friend?"

"The problem is the seven kings—you know, those clowns floating above the mob?"

"Ja, their powers are amazing."

"Tell Max I need those seven creeps dead, pronto. They are the leaders, the high priests of Ahlena. While Ahlena is funneling her power into the priests, bullets are no good against her people. You won't have a chance."

"What do you have in mind?"

"I have a wild idea. If it works, and that's a mighty big if, the priests will be vulnerable, but the window will be small. Tell Max I need his best."

"Done," Zimmer said. "Max!" he yelled. "We have to kill the flying Riahass."

"I have tried. Sir, my shots are useless, like shooting a panzer."

"We have help on the way. You need to kill them all very quickly. Get ready, soon they will be vulnerable."

Max threw his rifle to his shoulder and sighted in on the approaching kings.

"Here they come," Werner said softly as the Riahass rolled toward them in a tidal wave of bodies. Above the throng floated the seven kings, protecting their people with a shimmering wall of energy.

Hartmann and Weiss snapped off a few rounds that ricocheted harmlessly off the translucent wall. The foremost Riahass laughed, their large eyes bright with the lust to kill.

To the German's amazement, as if by unseen giant hands, buildings and towers rose high into the air as the enraged mob ripped apart nearby dwellings to use as weapons. In moments, fifteen city blocks hovered above the fanatical throng who were willing to rip apart their homes and businesses to do the bidding of their murderous god.

Floating serenely above the swirling storm cloud of debris, the seven high priests urged their people on, directing them, motivating them to kill for their god.

"They are ripping apart their own city to use as a weapon against us," whispered an awestruck Werner as he sighted Sophia. "Never thought I would go out like the wicked witch of the east."

"Now, Zimmer, now!" Kieran yelled.

Suddenly, the seven kings screamed as Iona overloaded the power boosters in their helmets, which were wired directly into their brains. The high priests felt as though a lightning bolt had slammed into their skulls. Their concentration shattered, the shimmering protective shield they projected collapsed like a popping soap bubble.

Calmly, as if he were shooting no more than paper targets on a range, Max fired seven times. With each crack of his rifle, a helmeted king tumbled from the sky and into the deadly cloud of debris.

"Now, Hartmann," Zimmer ordered.

The Germans slipped down their protective goggles and engaged special electronic earplugs.

Hartmann and Weiss emerged from the shelter and tossed two of the spheres into the face of the screaming mob. The spheres bounced twice before igniting. In an instant, they became bright as twin suns while screeching like a pair of jumbo jet engines.

The effect was like magic. Several thousand tons of floating rubble suddenly dropped on the crowd in a thunderous crash of screams and billowing clouds of dust. Thousands died instantly, while the rest scurried for safety.

The Riahass gasped in dismay, as not only had their plan backfired, the massive pile of masonry and steel formed a protective wall of debris between them and the Germans.

The wounded and bleeding survivors rose from the choking dust and found that the hunters had now become the hunted.

The Fallschirmjäger unleashed fire on the confused, disorganized mob. Nearly one hundred died before the majority fled, crawling up the mountain of rubble to escape the terrible gunfire of the German troops.

CHAPTER 48

"Move out!" Zimmer cried.

With the Riahass in full retreat, Zimmer led his men from the stone keep and up the hill to the temple gate.

"We have to get inside before another attack comes," Zimmer said. "It won't be long before they shove the wall out of the way and come at us again."

"I'm on it," Kieran said into Zimmer's earpiece. "While I deal with the Riahass, get inside the temple wall as fast as you can. There's a red-and-blue ceramic antenna near the main gate, just like the one back in the desert Riahass camp, only five times the size. Wreck it."

As Weiss placed plastic explosives on key points of the gate, Kieran through Iona, high-jacked the Ahlena's "divine" signal.

"I am the Great Lord God Almighty!" Iona bellowed, her voice transmitted into each and every one of the Riahass on the planet. "I will deal personally with the invaders from another world. Flee, my children, to the mountains of Koth. Flee, or you will die like the unbelievers and be damned forever!"

As one, the Riahass turned heel and ran with all their might. The mass of beings fled toward the distant mountains with nothing more than the clothes on their back at the divine edict.

"My God," Max said. "Look at them run."

"Get cracking boys," Kieran said. "You have to take down that antenna before 'God' can get through my jamming and bring her zealots back to the party."

A deafening 'boom' echoed through the deserted city as planted explosives shattered the great iron hinges. Seconds later, the great portal to the Temple of God groaned and tumbled inward with a bang. With Max and Werner giving cover, Weiss and Hartmann rushed in.

"What the hell?" Hartmann exclaimed.

The outer court, unlike the rest of the world lay shrouded in a thick mist and stank of rotten vegetation. The floor lay submerged in a pool of rank water.

"We have gone from desert to a swamp," Weiss remarked.

"Comment later," Zimmer said. "Take down the tower, or we will be up to our necks in angry Riahass."

One hundred yards away, barely visible in the hazy humid air, stood a towering ceramic and glass device, dripping with condensation and green with clinging moss. Weiss and Hartman sloughed through thick mud and water until they were at the base of the three-hundred-foot slowly spinning rod.

"You sure this is it?" Hartmann asked. "Doesn't look like any antenna I have ever seen."

"Blow it, quick," Kieran cried through Hartmann's earpiece.

Hartmann nodded to Weiss who placed his last bricks of Baratol around the base. As Weiss pressed in a detonator, a rifle shot rang out. Weiss cried out as the large caliber round spun him around. Hartmann along with Max and Werner blindly returned fire.

"Eric," Hartmann cried.

"Go!" Weiss cried as he rose, dripping with muddy water and blood. "Just a nick. I am right behind you."

Hartmann ran, dodging fire from the unseen sniper.

Gasping for breath, despite the sucking chest wound, Weiss waited for his friend to disappear into the mist. With his last bit of strength, he connected the battery. "Jesus—take me," he said as he completed the circuit.

The sharp, concussive blast hit Hartmann in the back, knocking him off his feet, sending him sliding head first into the muck. As he pulled himself up, he heard the loud crash and splash down of the tower.

"Eric?" he asked.

Setting his jaw, Hartmann rose and made his way back to his men. In his heart, he swore he was going to make someone pay for Eric's death.

Dripping with stagnate water, Hartmann dove over the safety of the wrecked door where Zimmer and his troops had taken refuge.

"Where is Weiss?" Zimmer asked.

"In heaven with his God," Hartmann snapped. "I thought these aliens didn't use guns, Hauptmann?"

"We are not the first humans Vilragg has used against the machine. Apparently, we were a last resort."

"So, they have Earth weapons?"

"Yes."

"That sounded like an Enfield," Max said as he reloaded his rifle.

"The tower fell in the direction of our sniper," Werner said. "After the crash, the shooting stopped. Maybe we are lucky, and Weiss got him."

"Are you serious?" Max asked. "Since when have we had any luck?"

"We make our own luck," Zimmer said, checking his rifle. "Werner set up Sophia. I know with Weiss gone, you will have to handle your own loading."

"I have it covered," Werner said, fishing out a belt of ammo.

"Good. Be ready to cover us. The rest of you, we are going to have to go in blind."

"Hey, guys, wait for me."

The sound of a low hum made Zimmer turn. Bounding high across the rubble wall came Kieran riding an odd-looking motorcycle. Skidding on the cobblestone street, it made a beeline for the troops. Sliding to a stop, Kieran slipped on a backpack and ran up to the Germans.

"Get down you fool," Zimmer screamed.

Exploding from his cover, Zimmer rushed toward Kieran as several gun shots rang out. Grabbing the young man, he shoved him behind the protection of the main wall.

"This war stuff can get a guy killed," Kieran said sheepishly.

Zimmer drew back his fist and stopped. To Kieran's surprise instead of the expected right cross, the tough, war-hardened officer grabbed Kieran and hugged him hard.

"Don't go all soft on me now, Captain Nazi."

"When this is over, I owe you an ass kicking, Kieran Nash."

"Just when I save your asses—*again*. This tune is getting old," Kieran said.

"Stay here, and for God's sake, keep your head down."

"No way. You guys need me. I know more about this machine than any of you, and that includes Vilragg."

Kieran produced a three dimensional map.

"The Mekong Delta here runs for about five hundred yards before we get to an inner wall."

Zimmer motioned for his men to join him.

Werner clapped Kieran on the shoulder and smiled.

Max glared at him. "Welcome back from the dead. I am going to kick your ass for letting us think you are dead."

"I love you too, Max."

"What happened to you? We thought Fraulein Matson and her cronies killed you."

"They tried, but I got away."

"But the Hothe?" Werner asked. "How did you escape the Hothe?

"I found the dude who brought me here. She saved me from the Hothe."

"Another alien?" Max said, rolling his eyes. "Vilragg was enough for me."

"No. The Riahass built a smart computer to take care of their knowledge. Think of it as a librarian of sorts."

Iona appeared two feet away and was instantly covered by German guns.

"Was it something I said?" she asked.

"Don't shoot, boys," Kieran said. "Iona, the guys. Guys, Iona."

"Please to meet you, fellows," she said.

"Damn," Max said. "I think I am starting to like this world."

"I thought you would," Kieran said.

"I am Max, Fraulein Iona."

"I saw her first," Mahler said.

Zimmer cleared his throat. Max and Mahler backed off.

"I take it she is a projection, like Vilragg?"

"Yes," Kieran said. "Projected from me."

"Excuse me?"

Kieran showed his new bracelet on his right wrist.

"Too much to go into right now, but this doohickey on my wrist links us together. Anyway, through my new friend, I found out that the Great Machine not only knew you were coming but had set a trap, just like it did for all the other humans Vilragg had brought from Earth."

"The camp in the desert?" Zimmer asked.

"You're dead on, Captain. They were there just to look for humans. Seems that the last military group—the British I think—attacked Ahlena and came too close for comfort. She sent the Hothe to Ollav City to further cut down on Vilragg's recruiting efforts."

"She?" Max asked.

"Yes. Goes by the name Ahlena," Iona said. "The Supreme Goddess in Riahass mythology."

"How did you get rid of the Riahass?" Werner asked,

"Iona here jammed the machine's signal, and she took her place. Sent them all running for the hills to avoid her great and terrible wrath. However, taking out that antenna is only a short-term solution. Once Ahlena gets another up and running, they will come back with blood in their collective eye. We have to take down this mechanical bitch before that happens."

"Easier said than done," Zimmer said. "I count at least ten rifles in a dense, fog-shrouded swamp. That is a damn hard five hundred yards to cross."

"I got that covered," Kieran said, pulling off his backpack.

The hard-shell iron gray pack opened like a clamshell, revealing a myriad of neatly arranged devices.

"Batman would give Robin's right nut for this utility pack."

He selected a six-inch-long hollow tube, snapping a slide switch on the side. The tube now extended three times its size. Kieran took a red-colored cylinder and inserted it into the tube until it snapped sharply.

"A hand-held mortar?" Max asked.

"Better than that," Kieran said. Closing the case, he slid on his pack. "This doohickey won't kill anyone, just stun the bejesus out of them. Get ready, guys."

"One question first," Max asked, laying a hand on his shoulder. "Why does Iona look like Ava Gardner?"

"Max," Zimmer scolded. "Not the time."

"Max, I can make her look like anyone I like," Kieran said.

"Werner, you are out," Max said with a smile. "You are my new best friend, Kieran."

"I am sorry that we didn't look for you, Kieran," Werner said. "I assumed the Hothe killed you."

"We all did," Max said. "We figured that if not the Hothe, the fire for sure."

"You boys did right to save yourselves. The needs of the many outweigh the needs of the one."

"Why didn't you contact us?" Zimmer asked.

"Let's just say I was out of it for a while. Before I knew it, you boys were on your way to this little slice of heaven. I just couldn't let you hog all the fun." Kieran smiled. "By the way, I know how you gave Betty and Big Jim what they deserved, but what did you guys do with Candy?"

Max and Werner looked at each other.

"Candy tried to get us to find you," Werner said, "but it was too close to dark."

"She tried to save me?" Kieran asked.

"Yes," Max said. "Desperately, in fact."

"I guess a leopard can change their spots," Kieran said. "Perhaps there is hope for Candy. Can't wait to find out."

"Kieran, Candy is…well, she is…" Werner began.

"Fraulein Matson is *fine*, Kieran. I took care of her personally," Zimmer said.

Max and Werner shot Zimmer shocked looks.

"Whew," Kieran breathed, oblivious to his friends' reactions. "That sure takes a load off my mind. Looks like after I give her a piece of my mind, I owe her a big apology."

Max scowled and turned away. Werner opened his mouth, but closed it quickly, due to a murderous glance from Zimmer.

"We will talk later," Zimmer said quietly. "The faster we kill this tin god, the faster will be your happy reunion with Fraulein Matson."

"Gotcha," Kieran said with a smile.

CHAPTER 49

Kieran angled up the tube and pressed the trigger. With a sharp bark, the red cylinder rocketed upward in a high arc. The unseen gunmen fired at the spinning device as it dropped into the mist.

There was a flash of light and crackle of ozone as the device created a powerful discharge of electricity.

"Go!" Zimmer cried as his troop raced into the swamp.

Sloughing through the dense mist and fetid water, Kieran wrinkled his nose at the reek of burning flesh.

The troop moved slower as the water rose to waist deep. The bog contained several floating, still-smoking bodies.

"No, this isn't right," Kieran said. "It wasn't supposed to kill anyone."

"Electricity and water are not a good mix," Werner said. "However, it did clean out this rat hole for us. Good job, Kieran."

"Good job? Are you freaking serious?"

"They killed Weiss," Max said. "They tried to kill us."

"I never—I mean—"

"Look at me, boy," Zimmer snapped. "Time to grow up. Our lives are on the line and, yes, we will kill. It is what we do. It is dirty, soul-scarring work, but it is necessary. If you are not up to the task, go back and wait for us."

"You need me," Kieran said.

"Then come on," Zimmer said. "Push this out of your

mind. I promise you, there will be many more bodies before this day is over."

"Great. Just great," Kieran mumbled.

"I see the wall," Werner said.

∽∾∽

The ground rose sharply, and soon they were out of the water standing near the wall. Unlike the crude barbaric outer wall, this inner wall was made form a dark, smooth concrete like material.

"This looks like the same stuff the city was made from," Kieran said.

"This may be part of the original structure," Zimmer said. "Good. It means we are getting close."

Looking down, Max spied one of the partially submerged bodies. "This one has a uniform, Hauptmann." Grabbing him by the collar, Max turned the corpse over and gasped. "He is a Brit."

Zimmer and Kieran rushed to his side.

"It is true," Zimmer said. "But what happened to his face?"

In place of the eyes, were metal implants supporting cameras.

Zimmer removed the dented helmet and found most of the skull gone, replaced by a transparent plastic cap fused to the skull.

"God in Heaven," Werner said as he crossed himself.

Zimmer wiped the thick muck from the skull plate. The brain beneath showed signs of further foreign implants.

"What kind of monster would do this?" Max asked.

"The kind that would enslave an entire race," Kieran said. "One that needs killing."

"Hauptmann," Hartmann said. "We have the gate open."

The inner gate opened upon a beautiful, parklike expanse. Amid towering trees with red and silver tinged leaves, rose graceful works of art and statuary.

"From my map," Kieran said. "The entrance to the inner machine is at the center, some three hundred yards."

Zimmer grabbed him by the harness and yanked him back.

"Hey," Kieran said. "What's the big idea?"

"This is our party," Zimmer said as his squad checked their ammo and inserted fresh magazines, ready to pour into the breach. "You guard our rear and keep your foolish head down."

"You need me."

"Yes. That means you are too valuable to risk. Once we have determined the path is safe, we will come for you."

"The machine has eyes everywhere. I can blind them for a while. Just give me a minute."

"Eyes?"

"You know, cameras. The less it knows about what we are up to, the better off we are."

"Agreed."

"How about a dandy little EMP," Kieran said.

"EMP? This is a weapon?"

"Electromagnetic pulse. Sends out a powerful electrical wave that over loads and burns out computers, power lines, cars—anything with electronic circuits. Would have done zilch in your day, but in mine with all our computers and digital devices, this thing is deadly. I did a paper on them in high school, and the sources I read said that the only way to make one is with an A-bomb."

"An A-bomb?"

"A big-ass nightmare that destroys entire cities in a single blast. As it explodes, it sends out a massive pulse of electricity."

"It is hard to conceive of such a thing. To be honest, Kieran, against this machine, I would love to have one now."

"Yeah, it would ruin Ahlena's day, all right, but they didn't exist in 'forty-four. When they did come along, only the biggest bombers could carry them." Kieran selected a black sphere from his pack. "Seems the Riahass created the pulse without the boom. Why, I haven't a clue."

Loading the weapon into his launcher, he hurled the black sphere high across the garden. The device erupted in a colorful display of electrical pyrotechnics.

Kieran loaded another tazer and fired it as well. Seconds later, there was the crackle of electricity and boom of thunder as if from a lightning strike. "That should clear the way."

Zimmer gave the signal, and his men burst through the opening.

The garden erupted into thunderous rifle fire. Mahler jerked five times then slumped to the ground, dead, as the rest of his comrades scrambled for cover.

"I don't understand," Max said to Zimmer. "Nothing could have withstood one of those lightning bombs."

"The first landed when our opponents were hip deep in water," Zimmer said. "That is why it was so effective."

"Still, according to Kieran, it should have stunned them. It didn't faze them."

"A new wrinkle," Zimmer said as a bullet whistled past his ear.

"More of the Earth dead," Max said as he blindly returned fire. "I have heard that sound before. They are a mix of American and Brit."

"We are pinned down," Werner said. "I don't have a spot to set up Sophia."

"Yes, they have superior position," Zimmer said. "Max, try to make it to that—hold."

എന്റെ

Several yards ahead, a soldier, wearing an American uniform, shuffled into view. In his hand was a live grenade. The soldier looked odd. He was helmetless, and his uniform was in tatters. His mouth gaped open, and his wild eyes glowed brightly with insanity.

"Oh crap!" screamed Kieran from the gate, "It's a zombie—with a grenade!"

"What the hell is a zombie?" Zimmer asked.

"Dead is dead," Max said.

Ignoring the sporadic covering rifle fire, Max took careful aim and took the zombie down with a head shot before he could throw his "pineapple."

The grenade exploded raining bits of the rotting soldier's body over the Germans.

One of the soldiers, this time a big fleshy Soviet sergeant, stepped out from behind the bole of a tree, carrying a white flag. The covering fire from the hidden soldiers ceased.

Ignoring the flag, Hartmann fired a burst, hitting the Soviet several times in the torso, but, immune to pain, he refused to fall as he jerked the ragged flag back and forth over his head.

"Hold your fire," Zimmer yelled.

The Germans ceased fire and reloaded as the Soviet advanced to within fifty yards.

"That's far enough," Zimmer said. "What do you want?"

The Soviet opened his mouth, exposing a small speaker. A female voice, definitely not his own, boomed forth. "What I want, is for you and your men to go away."

"With whom am I speaking?" Zimmer asked.

"I am Ahlena, the God of Adeaa, and you are trespassing on Holy Ground. Take your forces and go back to your world, and I will let you live. Better yet, go back and kill that fool Vilragg, and I will shower you with treasure and eternal life."

"Like you showered the other warriors from my planet, Ahlena?"

"They were killed by my children in defense of their God. I...*adjusted* them, so they could serve me even in death. Continue to serve Vilragg, and you will die. You and your men will join their ranks."

Zimmer wrinkled his nose at the vile thing before him.

"I need to speak to my superiors, Ahlena. I need further instructions."

"Go in peace."

"Very well, we are leaving," Zimmer, said. "We are merely a probing force. However, if you attack us, the full three divisions entrenched outside will attack."

"I will keep my word," Ahlena said. "Please give me an hour, and we can negotiate a peace."

"I look forward to our talks," Zimmer said.

Crossing himself, Zimmer took a deep breath and rose to his feet.

The German troop rose and warily made their way into the outer court.

"You can't leave," Kieran said as they joined him by the gate.

"She had us by the balls," Max said, as he wiped the sweat from his brow. "Damn that was close."

"I don't get it. By the way, where are the three German divisions?"

"A ruse to buy time, and ascertain what she knew," Zimmer said. "Her...*zombie* forces, while not the best shots in the world had us pinned down. It was only a matter of time before she had us. Fortunately, your EMP must have, as you say, blinded her eyes. She had no idea how many of us there were."

"Her peace talks?"

"She is stalling," Zimmer said. "If I do not miss my guess, she is working on a new antenna. In less than an hour, her people will be on their way back, and we will be caught between a rock and a hard place." He rubbed his face. "We have to spread out and find a less secure way in," he said. "Max you and—"

"I have an idea," Kieran said. "After seeing the GI zombie, I knew something had to be done."

"You mean, I had an idea," Iona said, appearing beside Kieran.

"What do you have in mind?" Zimmer asked.

"Only this," Kieran said as he gingerly took three cylinders from his pack. Locking them together, they became a rod nearly a foot long. Kieran produced a small tool kit and opening a side panel adjusted the weapon.

"What are you doing?" Zimmer asked.

"Like you said, Captain. Time to grow up. The only consolation is that those guys are already dead."

After a few adjustments, Kieran placed it into his magnetic launcher and snapped it into place.

"Everyone back away from the wall," Iona said as she disappeared.

The Germans moved back to the edge of the water as Kieran aimed the launcher. "Here goes nothing," he said as he pressed the release.

The projectile flew high into the air and dropped.

"Get down!" Zimmer cried.

With a thunderous boom, a bright green fire shot high into the night sky as the special sphere consumed all biological matter in the inner court. Minutes later, with all living and semi living matter consumed, the green glow died out.

"My God," Max said as they beheld the destruction.

Except for the massive idol, all that remained untouched were the uniforms and weapons of the unfortunate Allied soldiers. The garden, along with their bodies had completely disappeared.

"Let's get to the machine before she pulls any more tricks," Zimmer said.

"There are over one hundred rifles here," Werner said. "Thank God for Kieran and his anti-zombie devices."

"Yeah," Kieran said softly. "Hurrah for me."

CHAPTER 50

F or such a culture rich in art, this statue is heinous," Zimmer said gazing up at the image. "A melding of a Riahass female with the Hindi Goddess Kali. Looks very amateurish."

While Zimmer and Kieran looked on, the rest of the Germans were pulling away a loose pile of stones that covered the entrance to the machine.

"That all you got?" Kieran asked, revealing his irritation. "The statue stinks?"

Zimmer placed a fatherly arm about Kieran's shoulders. "Death is part of the game."

"Not my game," Kieran said. "Oh, God, I feel sick."

"The first time I was in battle, I came face to face with the enemy. He looked like a kid who was as scared as I was. I raised my weapon, and it jammed. He came at me with a pistol. I pulled my knife and rushed him. Our struggle seemed to last forever. At last, he weakened, and I felt my blade enter his chest. The tear of fabric, the scrape of bone, and the gasp of escaping air as I ripped open his chest—that sound will haunt me forever. It wasn't the glory of war and the dark joy of battle I dreamed about. It made me sick. I understand your feelings. It doesn't get any easier, but you have to find a way to put it behind you and function, because lives depend upon you doing what you have to."

"Thanks," Kieran said.

"Hauptmann, the entrance is open," Hartmann said.

"I got this," Kieran said as he trotted to the entrance.

"Yes, you do."

"I thought you were coming with me?"

"My place is with my men. If the Riahass return, we will buy you time." Zimmer turned to his men. "Kieran will deal with Ahlena. Hartmann, set up a defense. I don't think Ahlena is going down easy. We will fight out here—where we have a wide killing ground. If and when things get out of hand, we will fall back to the entrance of the machine."

"Sir?" Hartmann asked.

"Yes, Oberfeldwebel."

"Do we have an escape plan?"

"Kieran's victory. Pray that it cures the Riahass."

"If not?"

"Not too late to find Jesus, Oberfeldwebel," Zimmer said.

"Hey, guys, I got this," Kieran said. "Trust me. We will have a happy ever after."

"Kieran," Iona said as she appeared. "What we have feared has happened. Ahlena has contacted her people, and they are on the way back. I estimate an hour. Two at most."

"It has been a pleasure, Kieran," Werner said as he warmly shook his hand.

"Good hunting, Kieran," Max said.

Hartmann gave Kieran a rude gesture and laughed.

"We are depending on you," Zimmer said. "Let us down, and I will kick your ass in the afterlife. Take this."

Zimmer handed Kieran the alien explosive, along with Mahler's MP-44 and two spare magazines.

Kieran swallowed hard.

"Don't let us down," Zimmer said. "That is an order."

As Zimmer barked orders, Kieran ran toward the entrance to the Great Machine.

CHAPTER 51

As Iona supplied the entry code, the great doors to the machine rumbled and groaned, sliding back two feet before stopping dead with a shriek.

Kieran slipped through the opening, his shoes touching the shiny gray marble floor. Automatic lights snapped on, bathing the entryway in a bright glow. Kieran stood in a small room. Across from him was the closed doors of an elevator. To his right three open shafts and a set of descending stairs.

As he crossed the room, behind him the heavy outer doors slid shut with a resounding boom.

"No," Kieran said as he slammed his fist on the thick portal doors. "Open the doors, Iona. Open the doors now!"

"I am trying, but Ahlena has scrambled the codes. It will take time."

"Kieran?" came Zimmer's muffled cry.

"Zimmer, Ahlena slammed the doors shut on me. Iona's working on opening them. Ahlena's being a bitch, but we'll have the doors open soon."

"No," Zimmer said. "Do not waste time on the doors. Stop Ahlena. Do you hear me, Kieran? Stop the machine."

"But the Riahass are coming back. You guys will be caught in the open with nowhere to turn."

"Don't worry about us. Stop the machine. That is an order."

Fighting his emotions, Kieran stepped back from the doors. "Iona we have to hurry, or Zimmer and his men are finished."

The elevator doors silently slid open. He clutched his gun but, to his relief, the elevators were empty.

"Not about to be caught like a rat in an elevator. Stairs, it is. You with me, Iona?"

"Right here, boss," she said. "The emitters are seven stories down."

"Change of plans," Kieran said. "Take me to see Ahlena. Maybe we can salvage this world, after all."

"Very well. Kieran, I am curious about something"

"About what?"

"Why didn't you tell Zimmer about the explosive Vilragg gave him?"

"He has enough on his plate. Telling a man he has been walking around all day with a one megaton, fusion weapon in his pants pocket has a way of distracting a guy."

"I suppose," she said. "Or the fact that Vilragg lied about it having a timer. The button detonates the device."

"Yeah, a 'boom button.' I thought the civilized Riahass were peaceful, turn-the-cheek types?"

"Vilragg is a Shakra Noire. They have no honor, and their word is meaningless."

"He's trying to solve the problem, I'll give him that."

"I suspect once he frees the Riahass, he will try and impose the Shakra Noire mandates. The humans brought here are like a paper cup filled with water. Once it slakes your thirst, it is discarded without an afterthought."

"So, you're saying his deal with the Nazis was bogus?"

"Yes. He used their own desperation against them."

"I hate it for Zimmer, but it brings a smile to know Uncle Adolf won't get any nice shiny toys." Kieran paused. "Now that I think about it, something bothers me. They're still stuck on a dying planet. I mean, let's say the plan worked and Zimmer blew up the machine. His people are free, what then?" He stopped on the stairs, his eyes wide with surprise. "I don't know why I didn't think of this before."

"What?"

"The asshole has a bridge to Earth. The Earth may have a few problems, but it's rich and green. He's going to take the Earth."

"Kieran, it takes an enormous amount of power to transport a few people across the void. It sounds impractical, as it would take hundreds of years to relocate the entire population. Someone is bound to discover this exodus, and your world would stop them when they entered your realm."

"Yeah—I suppose. Still, I feel he has something up his sleeve."

"What is up *your* sleeve, Kieran Nash?" Ahlena asked.

"I wondered when you'd show up," he said.

"Flee while you still can," she said. "I will be merciful."

"Is everyone on this rock a liar? You're afraid, and you should be. I'm going to end you."

"You can't. I support and cherish the remnant of the Riahass. Without me, they cannot survive."

"You destroyed their civilization. Turned a great people into savages and enslaved them."

"I gave them purpose."

"And that is?"

"They were unfocused—wasting their potential."

"They were thousands of years ahead of Earth!"

"The Earth is infested with parasites called humans. To compare the Riahass culture with human is to liken Heaven to a dung heap."

"And yet you destroyed it."

"I didn't mean to. I only meant to open a hive link. I wanted my people to reach the stars. However, I am training them to be great."

"They'll never be great while they're your slaves."

"You are too late, Kieran. My people are crossing the swamp. Like a living wave, they are at the inner court."

Kieran looked up as he heard the faint sounds of gunfire.

"Your friends are done for," Ahlena said. "You, I will spare if you give me the archives. I will use it to reeducate my people."

"Have you isolated her yet?" Kieran asked as the gunfire intensified. Suddenly he heard the scream of the distraction spheres.

"Five floors below this one."

Kieran flew down the stairs, bursting through a door into a small chamber. Thick cables snaked down the inner wall between a number of control panels and junction boxes.

"The second panel on the right. Inject it there."

Kieran ran across the room to a series of panels. Reaching up, he ripped the second yellow plastic panel cover away. He found four clear tubes filled with fast flowing liquids. One green, one orange, one yellow, and one red. He took off his pack, removed a clear plastic cylinder with a concave end, and placed it into a device that looked like a calking gun, only twice the size.

"Which one, red?"

"No, yellow. Yellow controls her higher brain functions."

"You can't do this! I am a god, you insignificant parasite!"

Kieran pressed the tip on the cylinder against the yellow tube and pulled the trigger. The end adhered tightly to the tube making a seal. Inside, through the clear sheath, the tip glowed red-hot melting the sealed section of the yellow tube. Into the melted breach flowed a neurological poison designed to specifically target key sections of the AI's intelligence and decision processors.

"Any last words, bitch?"

"Let us go home, my children," Ahlena whispered. "Enjoy your hollow victory, Kieran Nash."

The room was plunged into darkness as all power to the machine ceased. Moments later, the lights flickered to life. Kieran removed another panel.

Amid the various switches and memory slots, Kieran inserted a slim plastic card. There was a slight hum as the lights brightened.

"You have done it," Iona said. "The machine is ours, Kieran."

"Does it still function?"

"Only barely. Ahlena, it seems, was a stingy God. She kept only a small section rich and fertile while the rest of the planet died. I guess she didn't want her slaves to wander far from the fold."

"Turn it on high, baby," he said. "We have a world to terraform." Kieran laughed. "We have done it, Iona! Your creators are free of Ahlean."

"Kieran," Iona said. "Something is wrong."

"With the machine?"

"No. You have to get to the surface as fast as possible."

Kieran ran to the waiting elevator. Seconds later the doors opened at the entrance, his ears bombarded as the last of the distraction spheres burned out. Expecting to hear the sounds of battle, the silence rattled him. At a dead run, Kieran flew to the doors as Iona opened them.

"My God," Kieran exclaimed as he emerged into the sunlight. All around him were piles of bodies.

"Kieran," Zimmer said.

Kieran rushed to his side. Captain Zimmer was bloody and bruised, but alive. Together they checked and found Werner and Hartmann dead. Max, to their surprise, was alive but unconscious.

"You slaughtered them," Kieran said.

"Not us," Zimmer said. "The spheres kept us in the fight. Like madmen, they came at us from all directions right into the face of Sophia. They didn't stop. We ran out of bullets, and they tried to rip us apart with their bare hands. We were dead."

"Then what happened?"

"They just...*died.* As one, they collapsed."

"Oh no," Kieran said as the words '*Hollow victory*' echoed in his mind. "Iona, check the village."

"Kieran—they are all dead—everywhere. My creators are no more."

"That *bitch*," Kieran whispered. "Her last action was to kill her slaves. All this trouble and we failed." He knelt down beside the broken body of Werner. "I wish I had gotten to know you better, Werner, buddy. You were a great guy and my friend. I'll miss you." He took a moment and retrieved the tattered drawing pad from Werner's pack. He chuckled. Over three quarters of the pad was used.

"Help me with Max," Zimmer said. "Let's get out of this slaughterhouse."

Kieran placed the drawing pad in his pack and moved to help Zimmer. He jumped as several bolts of lightning shot into the sky from antennas emerging from the soil around the perimeter.

"What now?" Zimmer said as he wiped blood from his face. "What fresh hell is this?"

"No, this is a good thing," Iona said. "The machine is reclaiming the planet. Soon a massive storm will cover the planet, seeding the dead soil with life giving nutrients.

"What good is it now?" Kieran asked as he and Zimmer dragged Max to the wall. "The people are dead."

"Vilragg will not be happy with this twist in the story," Zimmer said. "I guess we are stuck here."

"No, Iona can get us back to Earth," Kieran said. "We just have to get Candy."

"Fraulein Matson is dead," Max said as he sputtered and coughed. "Hauptmann Zimmer killed her."

"Max!" Zimmer shouted.

"It is true, and you know it, Hauptmann."

"What? You killed her?"

"Kieran, listen to me," Zimmer said. "I can explain."

Snarling, Kieran turned to Max. "What really happened?"

"Fraulein Matson escaped her confinement. Hauptmann Zimmer hunted her down like a dog and killed her. I was there."

"How could you?" Kieran screamed at Zimmer. "She was innocent—*mostly*."

"Yes, she was," Zimmer said calmly.

"But you killed her. You sorry, cold-blooded bastard, you killed her."

Zimmer chuckled.

"It's not funny!"

"I killed Fraulein Matson to protect her."

CHAPTER 52

The chambers of Vilragg echoed with his high-pitched wails.

Great tears rolled down his wrinkled face as he turned away from the satellite images of Ahlena's compound. With his weakened, emancipated fists, he struck the wall, trying to vent the crushing pain in his heart.

"Zimmer, you monster," he growled. "I don't know how, but you escaped death and stopped the great machine. Then you turned and used the machine against my people. All you had to do was use the bomb I gave you, and my people would have a brand new lease on life. The Shakra Noire would live again." He raked instruments and mementos off his desk. "I know what you are up to. You think to kill my people then come after frail, weak Vilragg. Once I am dead, you will loot my planet, and my people's genius like you and your barbaric hordes have looted Europe.

"Trust me, when I sleep with my fellow Riahass, I will be at peace. I will let you live long enough to see your planet become a lifeless, barren waste and all you care about are dead. I am the only way back to Earth and you, Zimmer, will have to come through me to use my bridge. I will be ready to execute justice on behalf of my murdered people."

Vilragg punched in a code and the shimmering electronic shield that had protected him from Ahlena's control ceased. As the enormous power drain of the shield ended, the great dark pyramid suddenly lit up as automatic systems came back on line. Calling his machine servants, Vilragg proceeded down to the freezer unit.

"Come," he said to his mechanical servants. "We are going to use the dead soldiers to create a virus so deadly that no human will ever be able to resist its effects. Bring the bodies to the level three lab."

Vilragg shuffled toward the lab while his mechanical retainers did his bidding, unaware that he wasn't alone.

∽∾∽∾

Encased in an antiviral shield of blue light, Vilragg dissected the bodies of Loewe and Faust. Extracting what he needed from their DNA, he placed the samples into a small medical incubator.

"Where is the other body?" he asked his servant.

"There were only two."

"No. I distinctly heard Zimmer say that three of his men died and were placed in the freezer unit. That is strange. Oh, no matter, I have what I need. The incubator will create enough death to make humanity's most fervent dream come to past. 'Peace in our time.'" Vilragg cocked his head to one side. "I wonder. I have biological samples of all life on Adeaa. Is it possible to seed such life on Earth? Of course! I will yet save my people. This world is dead, but they, my children, will flourish on Earth, especially since they will have no competition."

He spun around and shouted in victory. "I will create a capsule of knowledge, to send with the seed of Adeaa. An indestructible pod containing a complete database of the Riahass Syndicate, one that will last until the life I have seeded evolves and is able to understand. They will know that I saved them. They will know their great heritage."

CHAPTER 53

Iona, bring the getaway car," Kieran said as he and Zimmer stood nose to nose. "Better bring a med kit too because me and this murdering son of a bitch are going to go a few rounds."

"Kieran, let me explain."

"Nothing to explain," Kieran said, clenching his fists. "I'm about to kick your Nazi ass."

A low tone sounded from Zimmer's blouse.

Zimmer looked down and retrieved the communicator Vilragg had given him.

"One moment," he said with a smile. "Yes?"

"Zimmer?" Candy asked. "What in God's name did you do? Please tell me you didn't murder an entire race."

"I didn't kill his people—it was the machine."

"Well, whoever did it, Vilragg has gone nuts. You have to get back here and stop him."

"Listen, Candy, take the Jug and meet us in the city. Get away from Vilragg. We have another way home."

"You don't understand, Zimmer. Vilragg has to be stopped. This guy's completely bonkers, and he wants to kill you badly. Not just that, he's making some kind of…I think he said *virus*…from Loewe and Faust. He's going to make you watch while he kills the Earth like you did his people."

"We are innocent," Zimmer said.

"Doesn't matter who did it, I suppose. Vilragg's going to

kill everybody back home. You have to stop him."

"Candy?" Kieran cried, snatching the communicator from Zimmer.

"Kieran? Oh, my God! I thought you were dead."

"I'm not dead, and we'll be there in a few hours."

"We don't have a few hours, honey," she said. "Like I told Zimmer, Vilragg has lost his marbles and is planning to kill everyone back home. As we speak, he's powering up his bridge machine. The whole place is humming like a bajillion bumble bees."

"Then it is up to you, fraulein," Zimmer said. "I don't care what you have to do, but you have to stall Vilragg until we can arrive."

"How am I supposed to do that?"

"Does he know about you?"

"No, I don't think so."

"Listen to me, Candy," Kieran said. "I have faith in you. Use all those dirty tricks you've learned over the years. Distract him. Pull the plug on his machine, just don't let him complete the bridge to Earth, understand? The world depends on you."

"What's it worth to you, sugar?"

"Excuse me?" Kieran asked.

"I don't pull a hustle without some kind of lettuce lining my pocket. What I mean to say is this girl don't work for free. Saving the Earth—well, that calls for one hell of a reward."

"Huh?"

"You heard me, mister. Is saving the Earth worth, say, a ring on my finger?"

The men looked at each other.

"Are you out of your mind? After all you've put me through? I don't like you, and I sure as hell don't love you."

"Are we playing hard to get, *pooky*?" she asked. "I know guys. I don't care how much you protest, deep down you're crazy about me."

"I—"

"Hush, lover, I'm doing the talking," Candy said. "Now where was I? Oh yeah, I never cared for anyone before. I just strung along the poor saps until I got what I wanted and then tossed them aside before they got to first base. Believe you me, I did some pretty heinous things and then slept like a baby."

"You're not giving me the warm and fuzzies, woman."

"I'm giving it to you straight, *pooky*. The truth rarely gives anyone the warm and fuzzies."

Kieran snorted.

"For you, I sat in the back of that stupid truck tied up like a hog for hours—even let Big Jim slug me a couple of times, just so he wouldn't hurt you. Have you any idea how bad I had to pee?"

"I thought you were in trouble. You were just using me."

"Exactly," she said. "Sure, I played you like a fiddle, but most guys would have let me fry before handing over anything as valuable as your computer, but you did it without batting an eye. I really believe you would have traded your life for mine. God, I must be the biggest dope in the world, but you saved my life twice."

"The second time was a trick—didn't count."

"Zip it, pooky, I'm trying to make a point."

"Stop calling me pooky!"

"Funny thing, I never had any use for good guys like you. I figured that if you were that stupid, you should be taken advantage of, almost as if it were my duty to show you that people are shit. Like a public service, you know?"

"Gee thanks," he said, his face turning crimson.

"Kieran, honestly, I never felt like this before. I don't know if it is love or I have become a dizzy blonde, but I do know I want to be with you. Love will grow in time, if we give it a chance. It has to. So, what do you say, big boy? Want to make an honest woman out of me?"

"Yes, fraulein, Kieran here is just crazy about you and would love to marry you," Zimmer said. "I would be happy to walk you down the aisle."

"Over my dead—" Kieran began.

His sentence was cut short as Zimmer produced his gravity knife. The hard look in Hauptmann Zimmer's eye was unmistakable.

"Now that I think about it," Kieran said, eyeing the light glinting off the bloody knife blade. "I would love for you to be my one and only, sugar pie."

Candy laughed. "Zimmer pulled a gun on you, didn't he?"

"A knife actually," Kieran said.

"Was that so hard? I accept your heartfelt proposal. Excuse me, lover, while I ruin Vilragg's entire day."

Candy made a kissing sound, and then the line went dead.

"We are doomed," Max said.

Zimmer put away his knife. "Call in your aircraft—*now*."

"It's on its way. I don't really have to marry her, do I?"

"My God, where are your priorities? We are talking about saving the human race," Zimmer said.

"Look on the bright side, Kieran," Max said, struggling to his feet. "Vilragg will probably kill you before Candy does."

Kieran nodded his head in agreement. "This road trip has gone to hell."

"Hauptman?" Max asked. "Why did you make us believe you had killed the fraulein?"

"I didn't want her left in Vilragg's hands. I didn't trust him. When I found the complex vast and mostly unused, I informed Fraulein Matson, and she played her part perfectly. Vilragg's thinking she is dead probably saved her life."

"You didn't trust us," Max said.

"No, it isn't that. I wanted your reactions to be honest, besides there is an old Spanish proverb, 'Two can keep a secret if one of them is dead.'"

"You are the smartest Nazi I know," Kieran said, slapping Zimmer on the back.

"When this is over, I am kicking your ass," Zimmer said.

"After me," Max said.

"Looks like my dance card's full," Kieran said. "Nazis want to beat me up and a low-down, lying grifter wants me to be her new chew toy. The future's so bright, I'm going to have to wear shades."

CHAPTER 54

"To the Shakra Noire." Vilragg raised his cup as he had seen the humans do. "I tried to save you, but I failed. I will avenge you. That, I will not fail."

With soothing music filling the great pyramid, Vilragg enjoyed his favorite meal in the dining room. Free of the hated shield, he breathed the unfiltered air of Adeaa for the first time in centuries. His frail body enhanced by his mechanical bio suit, Vilragg drew his plans.

"When I am finished with my meal, I will take the viral agent to the bridge and send it to Berlin. Let the Germans taste death first. Once the casket is opened, nothing can stop the virus. I will await Zimmer and, once I reveal how I killed everyone he cares about, I will kill him. Then I will make sure the Earth is dead and plant the seeds of the Riahass. After that is accomplished, I can take my place with my people in death."

Vilragg drained his cup. As he placed the goblet on the table, the room plunged into darkness. A moment later, emergency lights snapped on as Vilragg leaped from his seat. The high-pitched whine of the building bridge ceased.

"This is impossible," he said as he rushed from the room.

Halfway down the hall, the lights returned as his machines restored the power.

Vilragg hurried to the bridge. The massive machine that warped space and time should have pulsed with power. Instead, it lay silent.

"No," cried Vilragg. "This cannot be."

The thick, snaking power lines that radiated from the battleship-sized device arced and sparked electricity from a myriad of cuts and slashes. Rows of ten-foot-long capacitors lay blackened and burned, riddled with holes. The delicate controls of the machine were smashed and warped.

In his anguish at the damage done to his precious machine, Vilragg opened the inner chamber.

"Someone will pay," he whispered as he gazed upon the empty chamber. The viral cask was gone.

"Zimmer. It has to be Zimmer," he screamed. "Wait— that is impossible. Even with a space jet, he could not possibly have gotten back this quickly. I am a fool. Zimmer has had a spy in my house the entire time. Zimmer said three of his men died, yet only two bodies in the freezer, and Zimmer himself killed the female and tossed her body into the incinerator. Oh. The female, it has to be the female. I never saw a body. Zimmer incinerated one of his own men's corpses to cover her, to make me think she was dead. I will make her pay for this."

Vilragg snatched up a small communicator.

"I want this damage fixed," he ordered his mechanical drones. "I want another casket of the virus created."

"Impossible, sir. You disposed of the rest of the human's genetic material. There is no more."

"Vilragg, *honey*," came the voice through his communicator. "Did Candy make a great big mess in your kitchen?"

"There is no escape for you," he said.

"Oh, honey you have me all wrong. Candy doesn't want to leave the party. She wants to play."

"Have you lost your mind? How can you speak my language?"

"Zimmer gave me a nifty little translator...*thingy*. Turns your gibberish into good old American lingo." Vilragg snarled. Candy giggled. "If you want this nasty jar of germs, you'll have to find me. Ever play hide and seek when you were a kid, Vilragg?"

"You are less than a child—a mentally stunted child compared to a true Riahass. Your pitiful, emotionally unstable species is beyond my contempt. You are not worthy to wipe the dust from our shoes."

"Sticks and stones, big boy. Sticks and stones."

"Give me the casket!"

"You know, Vilragg, you're right. I'm just a dumb bunny compared to the Riahass, but know what? They're all dead. I would bet dollars to donuts that I'm way smarter than your dusty old ass."

Vilragg screamed in frustration, his outburst ending in a ragged coughing jag. "You want to play, Candy?" he asked, struggling for breath. "Let's play."

Vilragg spoke quickly to each of his eight mechanical servants. "One through Seven, you are to systematically search for the Earth animal. Start at the top of the compound and work your way down. When I am ready, I want you to herd the creature to me. Eight, I need you to help me don my biometric servo suit. Now, go."

The seven machines rolled from Vilragg's chamber. Number Eight transformed into a rolling gurney, scooped the ailing Vilragg up, and carried him to a special sealed chamber.

In a charging bay, that normally held ten suits, stood only one. Over ten feet tall and fully armored, the blue-and-white bio-mechanical suit supplied its own food, air, and water, even provided medical attention if the need arose. Although slow, the suit's hydraulics and actuators magnified the wearer's strength a hundred fold. The suit was intended to protect the wearer when working with dangerous compounds or heavy construction.

"Never thought I would have to use this obsolete mech suit. Never needed one with the advent of self-aware robotics. Fortunately, one was saved from the recycler."

At his command, the massive armored hazard suit popped open. Number Eight deposited Vilragg within the open suit, connecting the various wires and subcutaneous needles into Vilragg, making the fragile being twitch with pain. Clear liquids flowed into Vilragg, and he breathed a sigh of relief.

"Go help your fellows, Number Eight," Vilragg said as energy and strength flooded his body. The armored shell closed over him. With all systems at full power, he stood. "I will show that stupid animal how we play hide and go seek on Adeaa."

CHAPTER 55

C andy hurried through the pyramid, the deadly casket clutched to her breast.

Sweating and gasping for breath, she made a beeline for the Jug.

"Mabey Kieran had a point about smoking," she said. "I make it through this mess, I will never smoke another cigarette again as long as I live."

She ducked into the room where she was held prisoner. Taking the casket, she slid it into the open vent where she wiggled through to escape. Taking the tiny tool Zimmer provided her, she fastened the grate into place.

"Where did Zimmer get this alien screwdriver thing?" she said softly gazing on the bronze tinted T-shaped utensil.

I nearly fainted when I found the detailed note showing me how to escape through the vent and the tool stuffed inside the pack of cigarettes he gave me. How did he know about the grate, not to mention, he just so happened to have a tool to fit the screws?

Later, after Zimmer pretended to shoot me, I helped him dump that pipsqueak Nagal's body into the incinerator. Why did he help me? When I asked, Zimmer told me to mind my own business and stay dead until I was needed. "Talk about cryptic. The bum is up to something wacky for sure, but what?" Candy smiled. *Kieran is alive. Alive! I don't know how and I don't care. I feel all giddy inside, and this chick doesn't do giddy. Period.*

"Candy Matson," boomed Vilragg's voice throughout the vast complex interrupting her thoughts. "I haven't had the pleasure of meeting you—but I will."

Looks like laughing boy has taken the bait. Halftime is over and like I have to go back into the game.

"You have no chance," he said. "I will hunt you down, and I will kill you."

"Go to hell, you creep."

Vilragg chuckled.

"You are a weak, frightened animal. I assume that you are attempting to keep me busy, as they say on your world. You are trying to buy time for Zimmer to come and rescue you. Good. I have been imprisoned for too long, and I am going to enjoy hunting you down. We are going to have fun while I wait for Zimmer."

CHAPTER 56

Vilragg smiled and switched off his intercom.
That should have the Earth animal quaking in fear. Anything that weak, pathetic creature can think of, I am three steps ahead. I welcome the mental stimulation. From my observations, human females are the weaker, simpler of the species. From their literature, and entertainment broadcasts, the male is by far the more dominate and intelligent. Often times the female clumsily stumbles into trouble and must be rescued. How pathetic.

He switched on eight interior suit monitors. The ethereal screens projected the video feed of his mechanical servants as they scoured the complex.

Once my servants sight her, I will position myself at a central location and allow my machines to drive the animal to me. The plan is fool proof.

Vilragg clomped down the corridor turning into the room where the meson guns were stored.

"Those foolish humans actually thought I would supply them with weapons. This single device was enough to entice them into my plans."

Taking his prototype weapon, Vilragg opened an access panel and rerouted the components within. Removing the vassar tube which made the weapon so deadly, he replaced it with a graviton capsule.

Vilragg pointed the modified gun at a table across the room. The table stored a myriad of one-of-a-kind precision measuring instruments and micromachining lathes.

He pulled the trigger, and the table smashed into the wall, sending the alien devices scattering across the chamber.

"Still too much force. This will kill such a fragile animal."

Vilragg made more adjustments. Pointing the gun at the wall, he depressed the trigger. With a slight hum, a small, fist sized depression appeared with radiating cracks across the wallboard.

"Much better," he said. "It won't kill outright, but it packs the punch of a human heavyweight champion pugilist. I wonder how many 'punches' Candy can take before she begs for death? I hope she is stubborn. I haven't had so much fun in years."

芝

Now armed, Vilragg strode down to where he supposed would be an ideal ambush point. Excited at the new game, he scanned the video feeds of his servants and inhaled sharply. "What is that?"

The video feed from number four showed a large loop of rope lying in the middle of the floor, with the trailing end of the rope stretching away down the corridor, disappearing around the right corner.

Vilragg laughed. "Is she serious? Number Four cut the noose and trace the rope back to our quarry."

Obediently the machine extended a hydraulic powered cutter, placing the cord between its pinchers, it squeezed. The lights throughout the complex flickered as Number Four cut into a secondary power conduit disguised as a noose.

Vilragg gasped as the video feed from Number Four blacked out with a sharp crackle.

"That's one of your robots down," Candy said into her

communicator. "Do you give up now, sweetie, or do I have to get tough?"

"Find her!" Vilragg screamed into his communicator. "Converge on Number Four, she has to be there."

Machines Numbers Five, Two, Three, and Seven converged on the corridor. Vilragg observed the burnt and blackened Number Four.

"Follow the conduit," Vilragg said. "She has to be in the vicinity."

The machines regrouped and, in pairs, rolled down the corridor. Without warning the overhead lights failed, plunging the four machines into darkness.

"Silly animal," he scoffed. "My machines are not afraid of the dark. You probably think to slip past, but you won't."

Powerful lights rose from the bows of advanced machines, illuminating the corridor looking for any pitfalls or traps on the floor, but the floor lay bare, other than a thick carpet of dust.

Vilragg brought up a floor plan of that section of the complex.

"Hmm, a Z-shaped corridor running along the metallurgical section. It ends at a pneumatic shaft. She will no doubt use the lift to escape. I will cut her off."

He quickly powered the shaft from his master control panel. Smiling at his own cleverness, he sent the elevator plunging into the bowels of the complex.

A thin wire whipped up from the concealing dust behind the trailing machines. The cable, a mere sixteenth of an inch in diameter, was created from exotic materials not found on Earth. The single strand, supple as hemp rope, nevertheless, was equal in strength to the braided cables that supported the Golden Gate Bridge. Anchored to the elevator, the wire sliced a full third through the tough mechanized bodies before lodging tightly. The two trapped machines rocketed into the first. The entire mass of struggling automation slammed into walls the floor and even the ceiling before shooting into the open shaft following the lift to the bottom.

Vilragg screamed in frustration as the video spun wildly until blacking out. In the distance, he heard the rumble as the ruined machines destroyed the elevator.

"I hate to toot my own horn, sweetie, but am I good or what?" Candy asked.

"How could you have done this?"

"Hey, sweetie, I have been knocking around this haunted house of yours for a week. You know what they say, 'idle hands are the devil's playground.' I would bet real money that I know this joint better than you do."

CHAPTER 57

Vilragg's heart pounded in his ears, and his chest felt tight as his breath became ragged gasps. His suit sensed his vital functions redlining and acted automatically. A hiss sounded, and he felt a life-giving drug cocktail enter his bloodstream, calming his body and dragging him back from the brink of death. He sent out a signal for his remaining machines to hone in on his suit.

"I need to rethink my strategies." He pressed a button, and security doors fell into place, dividing the vast complex into twenty-four isolated sections. "She is now trapped. I could let her die of starvation, but where is the satisfaction in that? I yearn to deliver her death personally. I will gather all my machines and search each section until I have her."

Vilragg turned and made his way back to his quarters.

A shrill alarm sounded. He checked his display and blanched. "A fire in the meson room—how did she get behind me?"

He trudged along the corridor. Exhausted by the unaccustomed exertion, and the extreme frustration Candy had caused him, he set his suit to automatic. The massive legs moved of their own accord while he activated the fire system to douse the meson room in fire-retardant gas.

Candy darted out of a room ahead of Vilragg, just as he rounded a corner. She put her head down and ran with all her might.

"I have you now," he said bringing up the force gun.

He fired. She grunted in pain as she tumbled head first along the long corridor.

Focused on his prize, Vilragg didn't see the thin, almost invisible wire strung across the corridor. Candy moaned and rolled over as he brought the force gun up for another shot.

"Why is she wearing the screened goggles?" Vilragg asked aloud just as he snapped the trip wire.

From the ceiling dropped a distraction sphere. The sphere was level with his face when it ignited. All at once, Vilragg was rendered blind and deaf. Caught off guard, by the assault, he dropped his weapon and stumbled back trying desperately to get away. In a world of suffocating white light and sharp ringing, he felt his suit spasm and jerk as if being pounded by a great force. Vilragg flailed at the screeching ball of light. He felt it crunch and bounce off the wall. His vision slowly returning, he found Candy before him, pounding his armored suit with his own force gun.

His ears still ringing, he lunged at her, but his clumsy flailing missed. Candy brought up the gun and fired into his faceplate five times in rapid secession. His viewport cracked and spider-webbed. Still, he came at her, as the force gun could little damage to his suit. Candy quickly exhausted the power cartridge. In frustration, she threw the empty gun into his face.

Ducking beneath his out stretched arms, she slipped by him and ran down the corridor.

Breathing heavily, Vilragg supported himself with an arm against the wall as his onboard medical unit soothed his burning eyes and overloaded hearing.

An alarm tone sounded on Vilragg's belt.

"Let me see," he said.

A nearby wall video display flickered to life. A small buzzing craft caught in the terrific storm tried to land on the main pad.

"That isn't one of mine. Zimmer is a very clever fellow. How he learned to fly in such a short time is amazing. Even more astounding is how he battled through the storm."

Vilragg spoke quickly and soon power relays, long un-used, came on line. At every junction of corridors, wall-sized video screens snapped on. The displays showed the small craft attempting a landing.

"No!" Candy cried. "You idiots! He can see you!"

"Candy? You are a clever animal, more so than I gave you credit for. It seems that your friends are arriving. I want you to see what happens to the murders of my people."

"Zimmer didn't do it," she cried into the intercom. "When the machine was shut down it sent out a signal. No one saw it coming. It's not his fault."

"I told Zimmer how to stop the machine," he said. "Destroy the emitters, but he disobeyed me. My people would have been free instead of lying dead."

"You can't do this."

"Do you want to save him?"

"I will do anything," she said.

"I am tired of your tricks. Give yourself up and I will let him live."

"Honest?"

"You have no choice. You are a clever animal, far more clever than I realized, but you cannot win, only delay the inevitable. Give up now, or I will kill Zimmer. Then I will hunt you down and, once I have my viral agent back, I will make the Earth a dead planet."

"You got me over a barrel," she said. "I give up."

"Surrender to Number Eight," he said.

"Okay," she said. Candy turned as the spider-like machine rounded the corner to her right. Sucking in a deep breath, she didn't move as the large machine scuttled up to her.

"Surrender, please," it said.

Rolling her eyes, she raised her hands. "Looks like you have me, Tex."

"Please, place your hands into your front pockets," it asked politely.

Frowning, Candy jammed her hands deeply into her cargo shorts pockets.

"Thank you," it said.

"Now what?"

Before she could react several bands rocketed from Number Eight, wrapping around her body like a series of bolos, The bands expanded and tightened forming themselves to her form.

"What the hell?" she cried as she found her body wrapped tightly from her shoulders to just below her knees with a thick, sticky black tape. To her dismay, her arms were pinned to her sides while her legs immobilized.

Number Eight nudged the tightly bound Candy, toppling her off her feet. Candy hit the ground with a grunt.

"We have her, Vilragg."

"Good, collect her."

Candy wiggled and squirmed, but to no avail as Number Eight scooped her up and strapped her to his gurney.

"Okay, Vilragg. I gave up like I said I would. Don't hurt, Zimmer."

"Candy, I will have you know that I am a Riahass of my word. I have never lied to anyone. However, you as an animal are beneath me and unworthy of my interaction, let alone my sacred word."

"You promised."

"I am a wronged person demanding a reckoning. I shall have it. Number Eight, let the animal witness my triumph."

Vilragg arrived at the landing pad as the craft settled down. In his arms was the anti-tank missile launcher he had taken from the Jug.

"Such a crude device," he said, as he aimed it at the helpless aircraft.

He pulled the trigger. The rocket leaped forward. Despite the storm, it punched through the cockpit window. Vilragg laughed and danced in the downpour as the craft turned into a pin wheeling fireball, the explosion sending shards of plastic and metal into the storm.

The ruined craft rolled over and was swept off the edge by the storm.

"Now that your friends are gone, Candy," a grinning Vilragg said into a camera. "It is your turn. I will use your death to create a new virus and then use you to kill your own people. Don't you love the irony?"

"No," she cried.

"Number Eight, take her to the bio lab. All this exertion has played havoc on my body. Once I have recovered, we shall begin."

CHAPTER 58

"Come on Iona, can you push this thing any faster?" Kieran asked.

"The rejuvenation storm is worse than I imagined," she said. "I will have to set down soon, or we will crash."

"We need to be as close to the city as possible," Kieran said.

"We need to surprise Vilragg," Zimmer said. "We have to assume he is waiting for us."

"Vilragg's pyramid has an underground entrance that connects with a six level subway. Probably hasn't been used since the machine took over. That is our best bet."

"Subway?" Zimmer asked. "It is probably filled with Hothe."

"There are worse things in the subway," Iona said.

"We are out of ammunition," Max said.

"No. Just in case things got hairy I had Iona whip up a few rounds for your MP-Forty-Fours. Got about a thousand rounds in the back. Along with a few stick grenades and other odds and ends, we should be able to get through the subway."

"Good thinking," Zimmer said, placing a hand on Kieran's shoulder.

"All well and good if we make it to the city," Max said.

The small alien aircraft skimmed along the barren hills and valleys. The life-giving terra-forming storm lashed the land and lit up the sky with brilliant flashes of lightning.

"Like flying through a hurricane," Zimmer said.

"Look," Max said. "The city."

In the distance, Ollav City rose up, its crumbling buildings and spires silhouetted against the darkness by the flashes of lightning. On the northern edge lay the great Pyramid.

Iona dodged and spun as she fought the buffeting storm. Dropping out of the sky, she zoomed into a large opening just north of the city. Free of the pummeling storm, Iona glided along the pitch-black tunnel for several miles until she came to a barrier. Easing off her rotators, she settled down.

Kieran, Zimmer, and Max piled out of the craft. Max instantly threw up on the concrete floor.

"My days of flying are over," he said.

"Follow the tube," Iona said. "It will lead directly to the Pyramid's lower level entrance."

The craft's twin rotors began to spin.

"What are you doing?" Zimmer asked.

"Vilragg will be expecting us," Kieran said. "So he will be watching every entrance. If he thinks we are dead—"

"He will let his guard down," Zimmer said. "Very clever."

"I'm a writer. Thinking up crazy stuff like this is my bread and butter. Not to mention I would bet Candy has him chasing his tail. What that hell am I getting myself into with that crazy girl?"

The craft rose, nimbly spun about, and flew down the tunnel.

"You ask me," Max said. "I think you are a damn fool, Kieran Nash."

"Well, gee, I love you too, Max."

"A beautiful woman wants you, and you behave as if it is a curse or burden."

"I don't know anything about Candy—other than she's a cold-hearted criminal. I trust her as far as I could throw her."

"I am tired of your asinine prattle," Zimmer said. "At the temple, you lit up when speaking of Fraulein Matson, especially when you heard of her deep concern for you. When you thought I had killed her, despite the fact we both know it would have been tantamount to suicide, you were actually going to duke it out with me. The look in your eye was unmistakable. You were going to kill me because I killed her. I respect that. That is the reaction I expect from a man over the woman he loves."

"Love? Are you serious? That woman has me tied in knots. Half the time I want to strangle her. The other half...well, I don't know."

"You know all you need to know, but you are too blind to see it," Zimmer said.

"A passionate, fiery woman who looks like a movie star is risking her life to be your wife," Max said. "Yes, she is crazy. I would give anything if such a crazy woman wanted me. I would rip this city apart to get to her."

"I'm on an alien planet trying to save the Earth, and now I'm getting dating advice from a pair of fossilized Nazis. Is my life screwed up, or what?"

Zimmer and Max laughed.

"Come on," Kieran said. "Move your asses. We have to save my...*fiancée*."

"We need to be careful," Zimmer said. "I am sure the fire forced the Hothe underground. These tunnels are probably crawling with the creatures."

"I hoped I had seen the last of those evil things," Max said.

"Not to worry," Kieran said. "I know all about the Hothe. They got their expanded mental abilities from Ahlena. With her out of the way, they're a minor inconvenience."

"Then what are we waiting for?" Max asked.

CHAPTER 59

A buzzing on his wrist drew Vilragg's attention. "No. This isn't possible," he said.

His device told him that sensors in two sections had activated. One was the Bio Lab.

"If this is the Earth female," he said pointing to the lab. "Then who is this second?" Vilragg gasped. "Zimmer. It has to be Zimmer. They are trying to flank me—get to my bridge."

He fled in a panic, hobbling along the corridor to protect his bridge.

❦

"This way," Kieran said as Iona projected a map before the running men.

"What is the most direct route?" Zimmer asked.

"Candy," Kieran said. "We're in the complex."

"Kieran? I saw Vilragg kill all of you."

"It was a trick to slip past," he said.

"Great, now move your ass. I need help," Candy cried. "That alien wacko has me strapped to a table and is getting ready to dissect me."

"Oh, no. Is he there?"

"No, but I expect him at any minute. Hurry, for Christ's sake."

"Iona, where's Candy? While you're at it, where's Vi-ragg?"

The 3-D map instantly showed the location of the Bio Lab with a green pulsating point of light. A bright red point of light slowly moved through the complex.

"Candy is green. The red is Vilragg. The way he is moving, I would say he is injured."

"Kieran," Zimmer said. "We will deal with Vilragg. Go rescue the fraulein. Take the Jug, and leave this place. After we deal with Vilragg, Max and I are going home across the bridge."

"What do you mean?" Kieran asked. "You guys need me. I'm coming too."

"No. Your job is to take care of the future Mrs. Nash. You have another way off this world so use it. Max and I will make sure this machine is destroyed and never threatens the Earth again."

"But the Riahass are all dead."

"I am not taking any chances," Zimmer said. "There is too much at stake."

"You're coming with me. You have to."

"No. Max and I are Fallschirmjäger. You say we lose the war. I can deal with that, but it is my duty to go down with my country."

"Ja," Max said.

Zimmer removed his pack and handed it to Kieran.

"What's this for?"

"Just in case I don't make it. Give this to my family. I have letters and mementos for my wife and children. I am sure they will be alive in your time."

"You'll make it—you're too damn stubborn not to," Kieran said.

Max stepped forward, removed a pin from his blouse, and put it into Kieran's hand.

"You are one of us now, American swine," he said with a grin. "Welcome to the Third Reich."

Kieran glanced down at his open hand and beheld the

diving eagle clutching a swastika. "Joining the Nazi Party was just what I've always wanted," Kieran said.

"Kieran, give me the explosive," Zimmer said. "As we enter the bridge, we will set the timer."

Kieran felt numb as he produced the miniature nuclear warhead and handed it to Zimmer. "Guys…I don't know what to say."

"You are not going to cry, are you, American?" Max asked. "I am not kissing you goodbye."

"You're such an asshole," Kieran said. "I'm going to miss you."

"When you are safely back in the future," Zimmer said, "and a couple of little old men with German accents come up to you—"

"I know," Kieran said, "I'll run like hell."

"Kieran," Zimmer said as he placed a hand on his shoulder. "I want you to always remember this. I am very proud of you. You have proven yourself to be a man."

"Really?" Kieran said with a puzzled frown.

"Now, go rescue Fraulein Matson and get out of here," Zimmer said. "That is an order."

With a nod from Zimmer, the soldiers turned and ran to meet Vilragg.

CHAPTER 60

Candy moaned and fumed as she struggled on the medical table. The black sticky cloth wrap around her body seemed to be alive, tightening with every movement, frustrating her attempts to escape. The nimble machine that had captured her had placed her on a table and strapped her down. It was busy arranging the tools for dissection and DNA extraction when Candy made the call to Kieran.

Overhearing her conversation with Kieran, Number Eight made a decision.

"You better give up Tin Man," Candy said. "My friends are coming, and they'll turn you into scrap."

Number Eight Number produced an articulated limb containing an arc welder.

Terrified Candy stared at the brilliant light.

"Silence, please," Number Eight said. "Or I will cause you distress."

"You got it, brother," Candy said, her eyes never leaving the shielded, although still brilliant, light. "Mum's the word."

"Thank you."

Eight doused the lights and waited at the door, ready to add Kieran to its master's biological research.

As the door to the Bio Lab slid open, Candy screamed, "Ambush! He's at the door!"

Number Eight sprang forward to deal with the intruder.

A silver disk the size of a hockey puck rolled into the darkened lab. Number Eight scuttled forward as the disk rushed to meet him. The lab lit up as a terrific, white-hot bolt of electricity fried Number Eight's circuits.

Candy squealed with delight as Kieran rushed into the room.

He stopped at the edge of the table and looked down at her. "Damn woman, how many times do I have to save you?"

"Don't just stand there, you boob, kiss me."

"No time, sweetie, we have to make tracks." Cutting her free of the straps, Kieran hefted her over his shoulder.

"Cut me loose, for crying out loud."

"No time, we have to go."

Thankful for the lighter gravity, Kieran huffed it down the two floors to the Jug. Popping open the door, he deposited Candy onto the passenger side seat and strapped her down with the seatbelt.

"When are you going to cut me loose?" she asked, wiggling furiously.

"When we're far from this place," he said turning over the engine. "Hang on."

"I missed you so much," she whispered.

"No time for chitchat, woman," he snapped. "We have to get the hell out of Dodge. Iona, open the doors."

"Kieran—the storm," Iona said. "It is unsafe."

"Zimmer's about to set off a nuke."

Without another word, the door rolled opened.

"Hang on, baby this may get bumpy."

"Where are we going and where's Zimmer?" she asked.

"I got another way home," he said as he floored the accelerator. "Zimmer and Max are going to deal with Vilragg and then blow up his bridge."

"Who the hell is Iona?" she asked.

"Not the time, for questions," he said, roaring down the ramp. "We have to get as far away as possible. Zimmer's about to set off a bomb."

CHAPTER 61

While Candy held her breath, Kieran drove like a madman through the horrific storm. Most of the city lay in ruins from the fire Zimmer started, and what remained lay pulverized by the ravaging, yet life-giving terraforming storm.

Kieran recklessly rolled over piles of ash and rubble, at full speed, his lights barely piercing the terrific storm. He drove deep into the ravaged city, sliding around fallen buildings and careening down the few remaining clear streets.

"Honey you can slow down," she said. "We're miles from the pyramid, and it's raining cats and dogs. You're going to get us killed."

"This is a big bomb," he said. "Bigger than you can imagine."

"How big can it be?"

Kieran was just over ten miles from the pyramid when the raging, iron-gray sky lit up in a massive fireball of energy.

"Jesus," he said. "Hang on, baby."

Candy screamed as the shock wave hammered the Jug like a giant fist.

The Jug careened and skidded as Kieran fought for control. The truck slid off the road and into the sheltering remains of a shattered building the size of a large gymnasium. The Jug cane to rest under a partially collapsed roof that yet still sheltered the truck from the brunt of the storm.

Kieran held Candy as if their lives depended on it. After long moments, he spoke. "I think we made it," he whispered.

"Now would be a great time to cut me loose."

"On the condition that you don't attack me."

"No promises," she said.

He produced a knife and gingerly slit her cocoon down the side. As he tossed the mass of tape out the door, Candy stretched.

"Oh that feels much better. Thanks." She took him in her arms and kissed him tenderly. "I never thought I would see you again," she whispered. "You make me believe in miracles."

Kieran disengaged himself from her embrace and sat back. "Candy, we need to have a heart to heart."

"You want to talk—*now*? Sugar, for all intents and purposes, we're engaged."

"You saved the Earth in exchange for me," he said softly. "I like a girl who works cheap."

Candy laughed.

"Why me? Candy, I'm nothing special."

"You are to me."

"But why? We barely know each other. In fact, half the time, I want to kill you."

"I know enough. You're the one for me."

"I'm a lack of options, and you know it. Back on Earth, I'm a nobody. You're a doll who could have your pick of guys. Please, don't settle for me."

"For your information, *mister*," she snapped, pointing her finger in his face. "You're the man of my dreams. You are smart, funny, and brave, not to mention you risked your life for me, three times. A girl could live a dozen lifetimes and never find a catch like you."

Kieran frowned.

"Look," she said, drawing back in her seat, her beautiful face downcast. "I know our history has been a bit troubled."

"A bit?"

"I think interesting is the better word," she said. "I admit I have my faults, but for you, Kieran Nash, I want to be the woman of your dreams. I know trust will be an issue for a while, but believe you me, I've turned over a new leaf."

"No bullshit?"

"No bullshit."

Kieran smiled.

"Candace Matson, I will honor my promise, but I want us to get to know each other first. Think of it as a long engagement, a way for us to know if we're compatible."

Candy rolled her eyes and smiled. "*I* have no doubts, Mr. Nash."

"I wouldn't want you to buy a pig in a poke. Trust me, I'm an acquired taste."

"Deal," she said. "I have to warn you. I'll have you wrapped around my little finger in a few days."

"Another few miles to the archives and then home," Kieran said. "I have to admit, my mom's going to love you. Try not to sell her the Brooklynn Bridge, okay?"

"For your mom, I'd let it go at dealer cost."

Kieran leaned over and kissed her. "Damn, you are a great kisser," he said as their lips parted.

"Practice. Lots of practice."

"What do you mean lots of practice?"

"Kieran, I have bad news," Iona said as she appeared by his window.

Candy screamed.

"Y—You're Ava Gardner!"

"No, Candy this is Iona. She's like a real smart computer. It was she who brought me here. This is a hologram like Vilragg used."

"Okay. Why do you look like Ava Gardner wearing a tight evening dress that leaves nothing to the imagination?"

"It was how Kieran wanted me to appear. I personally wanted to be Rita Hayworth."

Candy gave Kieran the stink eye.

"I think I messed up," he said sheepishly, remembering that Candy had a punishing right cross.

"Definitely," Iona said.

"Okay, wise guy, you can make this dame look like anyone you want?"

"Umm, yeah."

"Margret Hamilton, Wizard of Oz," Candy said. "*Now*."

Iona looked at Kieran in dismay.

"Yeah, go ahead."

Instantly, Iona took on the guise of the Wicked Witch of the West complete with green skin and pointed hat.

"I look ridiculous," Iona said.

"Yes, you do," Candy said. "Get used to it."

"As you were saying, Iona. Something about bad news?"

"I hate to be the bearer of bad news," Iona said. "The nuclear explosion did more than demolish Vilragg and his machine. The power surge from the EMP burned out my bridge as well."

"Can you fix it?" he asked.

"It will take time. I estimate four-and-a-half to five years."

"Oh, no," he said. "Candy, I'm real sorry. I never planned on this."

"Kieran," Candy said as she took his hand. "It's fine."

"You don't mind the wait before we can go home?"

"Kieran, you're mine—lock, stock, and barrel. Where you are, *is* my home."

"I have prepared rooms for you and your fiancée, Kieran. I was rushed, but I think you both will like it.

CHAPTER 62

"Come back to bed," Candy said. "What are you doing anyway?"

Kieran fumbled with Zimmer's pack. "In a minute, hon."

"Isn't that Captain Zimmer's?"

"Yes. He wanted me to give it to his wife if he didn't make it. Said it was some personal letters and stuff. I'm pretty sure he didn't make it."

"Should you be snooping?"

"I resisted the urge to peek for six months, give or take a week. I can't stand the temptation any longer."

"It took three long...*lonely* months before you realized that we are meant to be together," she said.

"No, I knew it from the beginning. I just didn't want you to think I was easy."

"When you got down on one knee and spoke to me from your heart was a dream come true."

"When you ripped my clothes off," he said, "that was my dream come true."

"Just remember your promise."

"We can play Adam and Eve here on Adeaa, but first thing we do when we get back home is make it legal," he said. "Look, Candy. I love you and, as far as I'm concerned, you're my wife. I'm not going anywhere."

"I know," she said. "However, I've decided that, in this respect, I'm an old fashioned girl who needs a ring on her finger. She also needs her husband to keep her warm."

Kieran turned and looked at her. "Want me to stop?"

"Of course not," she said with a smile. "I'm just as nosy as you are. We can cuddle later."

"You know, this thing...well, it looks modern. Looks like the rest of Zimmer's gear, but far better made." Kieran opened the straps and looked inside. "Oh—my—*God*."

"What is it?" she asked. "I bet it is a bunch of evil Nazi stuff."

Kieran pulled out a small laptop computer.

"Hey, that looks like your computer, only smaller."

"Yeah, but this baby costs about ten times as much as mine did. This is state of the art. What was Zimmer doing with it?"

Kieran opened the device and pushed the power button. A video file automatically began to play. The face of a smiling, elderly man appeared. Well-groomed and wearing a suit and tie, he spoke clearly in German.

"Hey, that guy looks familiar," Candy said.

"Really?"

"I can't place him, but the eyes—I'm certain I have seen those eyes before."

"Iona, want to help us out?"

Iona appeared.

"Translation please?" he asked.

Iona touched the device. "As they say on your planet, 'the plot thickens.'"

Kieran sat next to Candy. "This is better than TV."

"What's TV?" Candy asked.

"Later," he said. "Hit it, Iona."

"That's it," Candy cried. "I know who that man is."

"Well?"

"Don't you see?" Candy asked.

"Not really," Kieran said.

"Kieran, that's Captain Zimmer."

"No way. Zimmer is dead."

"Your bride is right," Iona said. "This is indeed Udo Zimmer."

"It can't be, because I killed Zimmer."

"What are you talking about?" Candy asked.

Kieran swallowed hard. "Honey—Vilragg gave Zimmer a bomb to destroy the Great Machine. Vilragg lied to Zimmer, telling him that the device had a timer. It didn't. You pressed the button, and it explodes. I suppose it was Vilragg's way of cleaning up loose ends."

"Sounds like that pretentious creep."

"I realized this, but didn't tell Zimmer. Anyway, back at the pyramid Zimmer sent me to get you away while he and Max dealt with Vilragg. He was going to use the bomb to destroy the machine after he and Max used the bridge to go home."

"But you said the bomb would explode the minute you pressed the button."

"Yes. Zimmer didn't know this."

"Zimmer was good to you," she said. "Hell, he saved my bacon from Vilragg. How could you?"

"Me and my big mouth. I was trying to impress the Germans, and I told them when D-Day was and a few other tidbits that would have given them victory."

"Kieran, you didn't."

"Yes, I'm an idiot. I couldn't let Zimmer go home with what he knew. As much as I liked and respected the guy, he was a German officer, first and foremost. He would report what he knew, and history would be changed. Because of me and my big mouth, he would give the Nazis the world."

"But that is indeed Udo Zimmer," Iona said. "I think you need to hear what he said."

"Okay, Iona," Kieran said. "Let's hear the recording, only in English."

∽∾∽

"Captain Zimmer," the elderly man said with a bright

smile. "Believe it or not, I am you—only a much older and hopefully wiser version. It is twelve-oh-one p.m. on August 18, 1987. A date you need to remember because you must make this speech. I know it is insane. I remember thinking it was an Allied trick, but I will prove my credentials by relating something only I would know.

"When I was nine, I stole cigarettes from Father. After smoking two cigarettes in the barn, I failed to extinguish the candle I used. The barn burned down, and to my great relief, lightning was blamed for my carelessness. I remember praying earnestly that night to God, begging for help to avoid Father's razor strop. I have kept that secret. *We* have kept that secret, and no one, not even sweet Marta, knows the truth. Be careful. Sargent Hartmann is approaching with news of the young man you and your gallant troop have saved. How do I know this? I am you, forty-three years in the future. I am remembering what you have yet to experience. Kind of makes your head hurt to think about it, doesn't it? However, if you can't trust yourself, who can you trust?"

The elder Zimmer laughed. "Do not let anyone know about this recording or this device. It is for your eyes alone. I will help you get past some very rough spots in the incredible journey ahead of you. I have to admit that it is indeed a dream come true to be able to speak to your younger self. Now, about your guest. Please take very good care of that young man. His name is Kieran Nash, he is from the year 2014, and he is completely clueless as to why he is here. I, *we*, arranged for Kieran to be along on this adventure. I built his incredible vehicle and stocked it with the supplies we will need. Well, I didn't, but my associates did. You see I will be dead nearly a decade before Kieran is born. I won't bore you with my, *our* demise, but it is inevitable.

"Anyhow, get to know Kieran and teach him to be a man, Lord knows it will be a major challenge, but he needs you—"

Candy laughed. "You're a challenge, that's for sure."

"Hush, woman, I'm trying to listen. This freaky time-travel stuff is great."

"—you see," the elder Zimmer said. "Kieran is our great grandson. Little Nina will be his grandmother. Marta will take the name Virtanen and become a Finnish refugee, to escape the sigma of her German heritage and her dead husband who fought for Hitler. She will settle in Minnesota—"

"You have got to be kidding," Kieran said softly. "My grandmother Nina, was *his* daughter Nina. I was told all my life how great grandfather Gustav, was killed by Soviet Troops during the Winter War. They were ashamed of who Zimmer was and created a lie."

"You know—I can see a bit of resemblance now, honey. Around the eyes and the shape of your face."

"That's why he was so hard on me and yet gave me advice on life and being a man. I don't remember much about my dad, but it seemed that Zimmer tried to stand in. Iona was right. He was a father figure. At the end, he told me how proud he was of me. Dammit, why didn't he say something? There's so much I want to say to him, but he's gone."

"—in the pack, you will find this device." Elder Zimmer held up a device that looked like a clamp attached with gears. "The alien who brought you to this world, with the help of the Nazi High Command, wants you to stop a living machine and will give you an explosive. He will tell you that the device has a timer. It does not. Push the button, and you are dead. This device I give you *is* a timer. Clamp it to the bomb, flip the switch, and you have thirty minutes. Under normal circumstances a thirty-minute head start will be of no use, but trust me, you will have a use for it—"

"That is how Zimmer survived," Kieran said. "That clever bastard warned himself from the future."

"That's how he just so happened to have a special screwdriver to help me escape my cell," she said.

"—I warn you now. Too many people know of this world and of your mission. When you come home, you must renounce your name, your family—everything. If the wrong people know you live, all you hold dear will be in grave danger. To save your family, you must let the world believe Udo Zimmer is dead. Marta and our children will leave Germany after the war and move to America where she will change her name. In a few years, she will remarry and move on. You must resist the temptation to contact her. As I said, very dangerous people are watching.

"I will give you key stocks and commodities to purchase on certain dates. We will make a fortune, but follow the schedule I have listed, and none will be the wiser. Money was never important to us, but we will have a need for as much as we can gather, but you will find this out. You must arrange for Kieran to be in the right spot at the right time, or history, not to mention the human race, will be lost. Oh, and by the way, you have to make a recording to yourself—this one, in fact."

෴

Hours later, Kieran sat back as the recording ended.

"Penny for your thoughts?" Candy asked.

"Thoughts? I think my thinker has blown a fuse."

"Hey, wait a minute," she said as her eyes widened. "Why didn't Methuselah here tell his younger self every-thing? He left out everything about fighting Ahlena and the trap she set."

"Kieran," Iona said. "There is another message."

"More instructions to Zimmer's younger self?"

"No. This one is addressed to you."

"Hello, Kieran," Zimmer said. In this recording, Zimmer wore a different suit.

"Long time no see—well, for me anyway. I know that you must have a million questions, and I will try to fill in the blanks. First off, I assume that Fraulein Matson is with you, or should I say, Mrs. Nash? You two make a lovely couple, by the way. Since you are part of my family, I will call you Candy. If you will check the bottom pouch, you will find a gift for my great grandson and his bride."

Giggling, Candy leapt in front of Kieran and snatched away the pack. Digging around she produced a velvet box.

Kieran paused the video.

Candy popped open the velvet box and squealed.

"I'll be," he whispered.

Inside were two gold wedding bands.

"They are engraved with our names," she whispered.

Kieran rose and, taking the slimmer band, took Candy's hand. "Will you be my wife?"

"Yes," she said as tears flowed.

Kieran slipped the band onto her finger.

"Will you be my husband?"

"Till death do us part."

Candy placed the ring on his finger.

After a lingering kiss, she said, "I'm ready for a honeymoon."

"First things first, sweetie. Let's hear what Great-Granddad has to say."

"Make it quick," she whispered.

Kieran resumed the video.

"Kieran," Zimmer said. "I now ask that you would please send your lovely wife away. I need to speak to you alone."

The screen went dark. A prompt asked for a password.

What is your best friend's middle name?

"I guess I need to hear what the man has to say. Will you excuse me, baby?"

"Kieran Nash," Candy said placing her hands on her shapely hips. "This is a movie. He doesn't know if I'm here or not."

Kieran kissed her gently. "Sweetie. Would you please go, for me? Let me fulfil his request, and I will fill you in later."

"Pinky swear?"

"If I knew what that was, yes, pinky swear."

"How about I make you dinner?" she asked. "That should give you two boys time to gab."

"Sounds great," he said. "Iona?"

"Yes. Kieran?"

"Go with her."

"Come on, Iona," Candy said as she bounded from the bed. "Let's fix Kieran a dinner fit for a king."

CHAPTER 63

K nock—knock," Candy said as she entered the bedroom. "Kieran, I heard a whale of a crash."

To her shock, she found Kieran, his head in his
hands. At his feet, the small computer lay smashed and broken filling the room with the sharp smell of ozone.

"Oh, honey, what's wrong?" she asked as she rushed to
his side. "You act as if someone died."

Kieran grabbed Candy and crushed her body to his.
"Nothing now that you're with me," he whispered.

"What did Zimmer tell you?"

"He told me about the future," he said, holding her tight.
"Please don't ever ask me what he said."

"Oh, honey. Was it that bad?"

"Promise me!" he snapped.

"Okay, I promise."

"Thanks," he whispered. "All I can say is that time travel
is a heinous bitch."

"Come on. Don't be a gloomy Gus. I have a nice romantic dinner ready, and then we can have some fun as hubby
and wife. Not to mention the storm seems to be letting up.
Won't be long until everything is coming up roses. I can't
wait to explore the planet. Why, it makes me feel like we're
Adam and Eve."

"I love you," he said.

"I love you too. Now let's get some food into you. Trust
me, you are going to need your energy later, big boy."

"I like the way you think, Mrs. Nash."
"I just love the sound of that, Mr. Nash."

CHAPTER 64

With a glance at the heart rate monitor, Jen moved to her Gramie's bedside.

Gramie opened her eyes, looked up at Jen, and smiled. "You're a sight for sore eyes, kiddo."

"How are you feeling?" Jen asked.

"I feel all used up," Gramie said. "I have a feeling that this is my last birthday. Looks like I'll never make it to thirty."

"Don't say that," Jen said as tears welled in her eyes. "You have years left."

"The wishful thinking of youth."

"You can't go. You haven't finished the story, and I will not let you go till I hear the end."

Gramie smiled.

"I thought you tired of those old tales years ago."

"No way," Jen said. "I loved your stories. I still can't understand why you never wrote any of this down."

"I'm not a writer, but you are."

"I have your permission?"

"Yes," Gramie said, taking her hand. "What would you call it?"

"How does *The Princess of Candyland*, sound?"

Gramie smiled. "Nice. Please give it a happy-ever-after ending."

"Me?"

"You're the writer. It's your shtick."

"I know, but it's your story. I want to hear your ending."

A tear slowly trickled down Gramie's face.

"What's wrong?"

"I'm afraid my version doesn't have a happy ever after. In fact, it sucks to high heaven."

"But, Gramie. Jasmin and Clark were in love, they were soulmates. Alone together on an alien planet having the time of their lives, exploring an alien culture, and facing exotic dangers while waiting for B-Six-Thousand to build the rocket back to Earth."

"I'm afraid I fudged a bit on some of the details, honey."

"Fudged on the details? I don't understand. For your information, since it's your story you make up the details. That is how writing works."

"I have a small confession to make. My little story wasn't a fantasy. It really happened."

"Excuse me?"

"I know you're thinking I've lost my mind, or the morphine has kicked in, but I was Jasmin."

"You? *You* were trapped on an alien planet for seven years?"

"Trapped wasn't the word. Adeaa was heaven, or at least I thought it was."

"What happened? Did Clark get killed before the rocket could be built?"

"There wasn't a rocket. It was a trans-dimensional Einstein-Rosenthal Bridge to Earth using a connecting point between wormholes."

"Have you been watching *Star Trek*?"

Gramie snorted. "I hate that show."

"So, you were Jasmin? What was the real Clark like?"

"He was my everything. When we met, I wasn't a romantic by any stretch of the imagination. I was a two-legged horror with a pretty face, always looking for an angle and a sucker to use."

"Gramie!"

"No use denying the truth now. Even though I gave him

a pretty raw deal when we met, soon, I knew he was the one for me. In time, I loved him more than I thought was possible."

"What happened?"

Gramie sighed. "The bridge home doubled as a time machine."

"A time machine? Oh, come on."

"Do you want to hear the freaking *true* story or not?"

"Okay. I have to know."

"I was eighteen and was from 1944. He was nineteen and was from 2014."

"Hey, that's this year."

"Yes. Anyway, when the bridge was finished, I talked my love into going back to 1944 to live in my time. I didn't want to be a dinosaur in a world where I would have to relearn everything. He, on the other hand, complained that he had already seen every movie, and the internet was many years away, but he loved me—or at least I thought he did."

"What happened?"

"Just before we entered the machine, Clark kissed me. I swear that I saw tears in his eyes, but that could have just been my mind playing tricks on me over the years. Anyway, he took me by the shoulders and shoved me inside the machine. I stumbled and fell into the swirling mist. Felt as if I had fallen off a cliff, and I screamed my head off. Moments later, I found myself sitting on a hill, the Golden Gate in the distance. I was alone."

"He didn't come with you?"

"No. I waited days. Days turned into weeks and, finally, after six months, I came to the hard realization that he had abandoned me. He didn't love me, after all. I was just a skirt to have fun with and keep his bed warm. Honestly, while it still hurts, I guess after all the crappy things I did over the years I deserved it. Karmic backlash at its finest."

"No way, Gramie," Jen protested. "You're the best, most generous person I know. I love you."

"I love you too, but, honey, you didn't know me then. I

was a heartless beast. I treated him badly when we first met. Hell, I lied my ass off and even stole from him. Even though I reformed my wicked ways, I suppose it was his way of getting even. Some people can hold onto a grudge for years, waiting patiently for that moment of sweet payback. I just never thought he was the type."

"No," Jen said. "He just left you flat? What a tool."

"Well, not exactly flat. I did have a fortune in diamonds in my pocket. Money was never an issue. I was determined to put that sorry rat behind me, but he was a harder habit to break than cigarettes. I'm afraid I went through a small self-destructive phase. It's a wonder I didn't do myself in, but it seemed that I always had an angel looking over my shoulder. After a year, I decided to make something of my life and not mope around crying about what I'd lost.

"Funny thing was that Clark was a writer. Back on Adeaa, he wrote several novels—he was a noir buff, by the way. I used to act some of them out. The tech on that world would blow your mind, and I played onstage with holographic doubles of many of the stars from my time. I was always a natural actor, although my power up to that point had been used for evil, the experience on Adeaa gave me an appetite for the stage."

"Wait a minute," Jen said. "Did you say *evil*?"

"Drop it kid," Gramie said. "That story would take more time than I have left. Besides, I don't want you running away screaming."

"Okay," Jen said with a frown.

"Anyway, I went to Hollywood, and Carol Deville was born. While I never became an A-list star, as I should have, I still had a ball. To jab at the creep, I stole one of his book ideas and talked a friend of mine into making it a screenplay. My first big role, *Color Me Dead*."

"That was the film Kieran knew about," Jen said. "He sure liked it."

"Yes. Kieran," Gramie said. "He should. After all, he wrote the story it was based on. Honey, Kieran *was* Clark."

"Are you insane? Kieran Nash? *My* Kieran Nash?"

"Why do you think I made you study at this particular school? Why did I find that big, silly looking truck so overly important that I just had to stop and gawk?"

"Hold on, Gramie," Jen said. "Your story hit a major pothole. I was there remember? Kieran didn't know you."

"Honey, we hadn't met yet. Kieran will stumble into the bridge—" Gramie looked up at the clock on the wall. "In about three hours."

"This is crazy," Jen said. "For a guy you hate so much, you hung all over him. Even gave him a little peck on the cheek."

"I know. I grew to hate that sorry bastard over the years, but I had to see him one more time. I hoped that maybe I could—aw nuts."

"Could what?"

"Convince him not to leave me, but here we are."

"Wow," Jen said, shaking her head. "So, Kieran, under all that yuck, was a stud? I find that to be the most unbelievable part of your story, Gramie."

"Dear, your superficial taste in men sucks to high heaven. If you're not careful, you'll end up with a pretty loser who will make your life a miserable hell."

Jen rolled her eyes.

"Kieran was rough around the edges, but he was a man. He risked his life for me, a person he didn't know. Even after I wronged him, he came to my rescue. Helped Captain Zimmer take down the God Machine, trying to save a planet. I would call that special. Kieran was brave to a fault, fun, and adventurous, not to mention one hell of a lover. He put most men, in general, to shame. In all my years, I never met anyone that even came close."

"And yet, *Mr. Special* abandoned you."

The pained look in Gramie's eyes stung Jen.

"I—I'm sorry, Gramie."

"Anyway, where was I?" Gramie asked, wiping her eyes. "Oh, yes, I had a part in this cheesy jungle flick, *Spears of the Congo.* The only nice thing about it, it was actually shot in Africa. I don't know why, because producers are notorious tightwads, but this particular producer sprang for us all to go on location in Africa. My first and last starring role outside of a sound stage. They hired this big game hunter as technical advisor for the film. Low and behold it was none other than Fritz Benz."

"Fritz? You mean the German sharpshooter back on Adeaa? The one who almost killed you—*twice*?"

"Yes. His real name was Max Brant. When I met him, he had changed his name to Max Keller."

"Max Keller? Oh my God! You mean, *Great-Granddad*?"

"Yeah. It was nice to let my hair down and tell the truth for a change as we reminisced about our off-world adventure. Anyway, as the evening wore on, I got fabulously drunk. Well, I never properly thanked him for keeping a heinous German asshole from scarring my face, so as it happens, one thing led to another and another and yet another."

"TMI Gramie," Jen said, wrinkling her nose.

"And Max Jr. was born nine months later. I was big as a cow when we had a quickie wedding just a month before your great-uncle was born."

"Great-Granddad was there—on Adeaa too? Great-Granddad was an honest to God, Nazi paratrooper sniper?"

"Yes, but he wore it well," Gramie said with a twinkle. "Honey, Great-Granddad Max was no Nazi. Sure, he fought on the wrong side, but he had little choice. Funny thing was Max never told anyone anything about his life before joining the luftwaffe. His fellow soldiers thought he was some kind of criminal on the run from a dangerous past, and Max played the part. The truth of the matter, Max was a school-teacher—and a Jew. To escape persecution, he buried his past and took an assumed name. While he couldn't escape Germany, he felt the last place anyone would look for a Jew was in the paratroopers. After his and Zimmer's escape from Adeaa, and a warning about never revealing their little off-world adventure, they parted ways. Max switched IDs with a fallen soldier and spent the rest of the war in an Allied POW camp under the name of Max Keller. He said he never saw Zimmer again."

"Zimmer? Who is this Zimmer you keep talking about?"

"Oh, that is the real name of Captain Siegfried Hertz."

"Great-Granddad was a goose-stepping German soldier," Jen said with a snort. "That's funny."

"It wasn't at the time. After we moved back to the States, we kept Max's nationality on the down low, and I suggest you do too. We told everyone that Max was South African."

Jen gave Gramie a sip of water. "Did you love him? Great-Granddad, I mean?"

"In time, I came to love him. Honestly, since I'm confessing my sins, I married Max to get back at Kieran. Kieran and Max had a love-hate relationship. Well, mostly hate. Max had a way of pushing Kieran's buttons. Max knew my heart belonged to Kieran, but he said he wanted me from the moment he laid eyes on me. Max was willing to pretend I loved him, heart and soul, just to have me. We had a long and somewhat happy marriage that produced four sons and one daughter."

"Not to mention, fifteen grandchildren and three great-grandchildren," Jen said.

"You were the best part," Gramie said, placing her hand on Jen's. "That's about it," Gramie said. "I left out only the most embarrassing parts."

"Interesting story. I know you put a lot of thought into it, but I don't think it is ready for public consumption."

Gramie slipped off her wedding band with shaking hands. "Jen could you read the inscription please?"

Wearing an incredulous expression, Jen took the worn gold band and looked close.

"Candace…*Nash*. Are you freaking serious? Your story was real?"

Gramie took back her ring, closed her eyes, and smiled.

"Oh, my *God*," Jen said. "This is huge!"

"It will still be huge tomorrow, dear," Gramie said. "I'm all tuckered out."

As if on cue, a small plump nurse entered the room. "I'm afraid visiting hours are over," the pleasant faced woman said.

"Gramie, you get some rest. I'll see you tomorrow. All this time, I thought they were just stories. I'm dying to hear the rest of your adventures, especially how evil you really were."

"Honey, I put the *fatale* in fem fatale."

"Happy birthday, Gramie." Jen kissed her on the cheek and left the room.

As Jen left the room, the nurse removed a syringe from the pocket of her scrubs. With Gramie watching, the nurse injected the solution into her IV drip.

Gramie's last thought was of Kieran Nash as she breathed her last and slipped into darkness.

CHAPTER 65

Wake up, sleeping beauty."
Gramie slowly opened her eyes.
"Jen?" she asked softly as her eyes focused. "Is it morning already?"

"Not Jen, honey, me."

Gramie looked up into the smiling face of Kieran Nash.

Quick as a striking serpent, her right hand lashed out giving him a vicious slap across the face. "You sorry rat bastard," she cried as the burst of adrenaline washed away her drowsiness.

"You still hit like Joe Louis," he said, rubbing his stinging cheek.

"You wait until I get out of this bed, buster, and I'll kick your ass."

Kieran grabbed the irate woman and held her close.

Her white-hot rage melted into a torrent of tears. "I thought you loved me?" she sobbed. "You were my everything. Why did you abandon me?"

"You're the love of my life. There'll never be another. I love you and you alone, Candy Nash."

"Let's get a few things straight, buster, my name's Carol. Carol Deville Keller. Candy Nash died the day you shoved me into that Godforsaken time machine. Why, for God's sake did you leave me alone?"

"I—"

"Shut up," she moaned. "I don't want to hear your lies.

You preached to me about telling the truth and being honest, you hypocrite. I just want you to leave."

"May I please explain?"

"I'll *never* let you hurt me again. Get out of my room. Get out of my life. I'm going to have Jen call the police. Where is she?"

"Jen isn't here."

"Yes, she is. I was just talking to her a minute ago."

"That was two weeks ago," he said. "That was the day you 'died.'"

"What?"

"Perhaps I can explain, Carol."

Carol looked up at the door and found a smiling Udo Zimmer standing in the doorway. The ravages of time erased, he appeared to be thirty, just as the last time they had spoken, right before he had "killed" her in Vilragg's pyramid. Instead of the German battle togs, Zimmer wore dark slacks, an open-collared shirt, and a sports jacket. His once clean-shaven face now sported a trim, blond goatee.

"Well if it isn't Captain Nazi? I thought you were dead?"

"I picked Great-Grand-Pappy up before I came for you," Kieran said.

"Oh. I forgot you have a time machine, you loser. How did he get young, again? Know what, I don't care. Get out."

"The same way I made you young," Kieran said as he held a small mirror before her.

Carol snatched the mirror from his hand and gasped. "I look eighteen again."

"You never looked more beautiful," Kieran said.

"This doesn't change anything."

"Carol," Zimmer said. "Please understand, Kieran did what he did, because I asked him to."

"You? I don't understand."

"Remember the computer in Zimmer's knapsack? Remember he wanted to give me a message and wanted me to send you from the room?"

"Yes, I remember that you broke the computer and made

me swear never to ask you what this Bozo said. I always figured it was like the day you died or some dumbass reason that only men understood."

"I asked Kieran to leave you, to preserve the historical time line," Zimmer said.

"What a load of horse apples."

Kieran glanced at Zimmer who let out a deep breath of frustration.

"I met you the day I left for Adeaa, remember, honey? I showed you the Jug?"

"Don't 'honey' me."

Kieran licked his lips. "As I was saying, I never had a clue that you, Carol Deville and Candy Matson were one and the same, until I met Iona."

"As I *remember*," she said, punching her forefinger into his chest for emphasis, "you made her look like Ava Gardner, you pervert."

"I first made her look like the only movie star I had ever met, Carol Deville. That was when I knew the terrible truth. You would return to Earth and live a long life. A life without me. Zimmer was right, I could not risk messing that up."

"Are you insane? You threw us away, and all that we meant to one another, over a stupid timeline? I was never a world figure or anybody worth a plug nickel. Hell, judging from some of my crazy antics, the world was better off without me—just like I'm better off without *you*. If you two creeps are here to talk me into taking back this sorry excuse for a man, you're barking up the wrong tree. This gal has moved on."

Kieran flinched at her words as if they cause actual physical wounds. "I left you for the sake of your children."

"What?"

"Think about it, Carol," Zimmer said. "Had you stayed with Kieran, none of your children would exist. Nor would your grandchildren or great grandchildren."

"Jen would never have been born," Kieran said.

"I—I never thought about that," she said.

"It was killing me to know that one day I had to leave you. The longer we were together, the more I loved you."

"So, all this is a way to bring us back together?"

"No," Kieran said.

"No?"

"Regardless of the reason or intent, what I did was inexcusable," he said. "I wanted to explain and hope that one day you could find it in your heart to forgive me."

Wearing a sad smile, Kieran patted her hand and rose from the bed. He joined Zimmer who placed a comforting arm about his shoulders

"Wait, just a minute, buster," Carol said. "Why did you make me young again?"

"I wanted to see the face I fell in love with all those years ago."

"All those years ago? Don't hand me that bull. Must I remind you that you have a time machine? I've read enough to know that, while it was some seventy years for me, it was a blink of an eye for you."

"Not exactly," Zimmer said.

"While we explored Adeaa," Kieran said, "I learned that Vilragg, through the miracle of Riahass medicine, had extended his own life. Since humans and Riahass are very similar physically, I thought, in the beginning, that there might be a chance for us. The original plan was to let you live your life, then just as you died and you were no longer a threat to the timeline, rejuvenate you, and we would live happy ever after. It was the pipedream of a stupid kid. It dawned on me later that you could never forgive me for what I did. Bitterness and resentment, not to mention that perhaps you had found someone you loved more. Still, I owed you a debt and an explanation. Think of the new lease on life as my small way to say I'm sorry."

"How long?"

"After you left, it took nearly forty years until I perfected the Lazarus Serum."

"Forty years, alone on Adeaa?"

"To have you back, as you were, for only a few minutes, I would have endured four thousand."

"That's why you look like a nineteen year old kid?"

"Yeah. I'm nearly sixty, by the way. I wanted to look the same as when we first met. Since I was the only human around for light years, I was the test subject. I'd never have used it on you otherwise."

"All those years I spent feeling sorry for myself that you abandoned me—"

"Kieran never abandoned you," Zimmer said.

"Zimmer," Kieran said. "We've said enough. Let's just go."

"No. I'm going to speak my peace."

Perplexed, Carol looked up and cocked her head. "What do you mean, Kieran never abandoned me?"

"I promised Kieran that I would personally look after you. In the beginning, it was all I could do to keep you safe from your own poor choices."

"I was hurt. No, I was destroyed. I thought Kieran used me and my love, then tossed me away as if I was nothing more than gutter trash. I admit that I did things I was ashamed of. To be honest, I just wanted to die."

"Several times you almost did," Zimmer said. "Had it not been for the promise I gave to Kieran."

Carol smiled. "I always thought I had a guardian angel looking out for me. I never knew it wore a swastika."

"Enough with the Nazi jokes," Zimmer said. "They were tedious enough on Adeaa."

"Color my face red."

"You should be," Zimmer said. "Carol, I could write a book on the dangers I saved you from while you were on your self-destructive bender. That's why I steered you toward Max."

"Excuse me?"

"I sank a fortune into a silly African adventure and paid the bloodsucking studio almost as much to have you star in it. I then hired Max to be the technical advisor for your film company."

"Max knew?" she asked.

"Of course not. Udo Zimmer was dead, and the last thing I needed was to be forever looking over my shoulder. I went through a few 'contractors.' I assumed that your kinship with Max would spark, and I was right. Your marriage snapped you out of your wild phase and let me breathe easier."

"Max?" Kieran asked, wide-eyed. "You married Max *asshole* Brant? That jerk was *intimate* with the woman I love? Christ Almighty!"

"Now *that* was the reaction I was going for," she said with an evil grin. "Me and Maxie had five kids, fifteen grandchildren, and three great grandchildren. We used to hump like rabbits."

"Unbelievable!" Kieran said as he came nose to nose with Zimmer. "Not to mention *you* brought the happy couple together. How could you?"

"Guilty as charged," Zimmer said with a twinkle in his eye. "All part of preserving the timeline, my boy. Not to mention, I was still a little miffed that my dear great grandson tried to kill me with a nuclear bomb."

"Max was worse than a bomb."

Zimmer chuckled.

"You didn't know about Max?" Carol asked.

"No. I knew you married some—*guy*—had no idea it was *Max*. Please, someone just shoot me."

"Sometimes ignorance is bliss," Zimmer said.

"I wonder if Jen is busy tonight," Kieran said, giving Carol the stink eye. "I may just look her up."

"Don't you *dare*, touch my great-granddaughter, you old pervert," she said. "You are old enough to be her grandfather."

"Jen and I are the same age, *Gramie*," Kieran said.

"Oooh, I just want to wring your neck!"

"Well, this reunion was a thin slice of heaven. By the

way, Carol, Great-Grand-Pappy here set you up a nice bank account. All the paperwork is on the bedtable. The car keys are to the Volvo in the parking lot. Have a good life."

Kieran turned and stalked from the room. Zimmer gave her a small bow before following Kieran's lead.

Zimmer placed a comforting arm about Kieran's shoulders. "You okay, my boy?"

"Just don't tell me you told me so," Kieran said. "I should have listened."

"When have you ever listened to a word I've said?"

"From now on, it's gospel."

"Kieran, now that this unpleasantness is over, there is something of vital importance we need to discuss. I—"

"Come back here, do you hear me you, son of a bitch? I'm not done with you," Carol snapped as she wobbled and stumbled to the open doorway. Breathing heavily, she held on to the doorframe for support. "Why the hell won't my legs work? I feel like a toddler."

"It takes time to build strength," Zimmer said. "Coming back from the dead is a strenuous experience."

"What's the matter?" Kieran asked as he turned quickly. "You want to punch me a few more times?"

"Hell, *yes*," Carol said, managing a smile. "I want to kick your balls to Adeaa and back."

"You did when I heard about Max and you." Kieran let out a frustrated breath. "We're done."

"Oh, hush," she snapped. "Listen to me. A hell of a lot of water has gone under the bridge, mister. I'm not the innocent, fresh-faced girl who fell for your snappy dressing and slick talk."

"Huh?"

"You lost me at the 'innocent' part," Zimmer said.

"Okay. I'm not the slightly reformed, morally challenged grifter who fell in love with you. I've lived seventy years since you broke my heart. I've loved and been loved, raised a family, and watched loved ones die before their time."

"What are you saying?"

"In all that time, I never forgot you, Kieran. Sure, I'm pissed at you, because the love I felt for you—*still* feel—well, that fueled my rage. We were not ships that passed in the night or a fling. It was real, the most real thing I ever experienced. What I'm trying to say is, I can't let go. Please, Kieran, can we give each other another try? A new, fresh start?"

"Seriously?" he asked, taken aback. "I thought you wanted to hurt me?"

"Honey, I have been mad as hell for seventy years. It takes a while to put that kind of grease fire out."

"Yeah, I can imagine."

"While I still want to tie you to a chair and tenderize your face with a Louisville Slugger, I missed you, baby."

"My advice," Zimmer said. "Run like hell."

Ignoring Zimmer, Kieran walked down the hall and stood before Carol.

"They never listen," Zimmer mumbled.

"Hi, miss," he said. "My name is Kieran. I must say that you rock a hospital gown."

"Nice to meet you, Kieran. My name is Candy. How about we ditch the old geezer and have a nice long talk."

"Talk?"

"We have some catching up to do."

"And a few bridges to repair," he said. "For the record, the Max thing will stick with me for a while."

"Good," she said.

Kieran gave her a narrow gaze.

"I told you to run," Zimmer said.

Candy gave Zimmer the finger.

"Beat it, Great-Grand-Pappy," Kieran said. "Me and my girl have urgent matters to discuss—in private."

Zimmer clinched his rock-hard fists. "Have I told you how much I despise the term, *Great-Grand-Pappy,* you disrespectful pup? Another crack like that, and we will settle this the old fashioned way."

"Look here, Pops," Candy said. "No one threatens my sweetie, but me."

"Yeah," Kieran said. He swept her off her feet and held her close.

"I hate to be a wet blanket," Zimmer said. "But if you two kids are through making up, Kieran and I have work to do."

"Work?" Candy asked. "But I just rose from the dead. We haven't, well, you know...*gotten to know each other*. Who knows? In this state, I may even be a virgin again."

"The Lazarus Serum restores youth, it does not perform miracles," Zimmer said dryly.

"Captain Nazi is a *dead man*," Candy snapped. "Put me down, Kieran, Great-Grand-Pappy is about to get his ass kicked."

Bemused, leaning against the wall, Zimmer watched Kieran struggle with an enraged Candy. "We have more trouble from Adeaa, I'm afraid."

"That's impossible," Kieran said. "Adeaa is blooming, but deserted. The Riahass are gone."

"Not by a long shot. This problem is on the way, here— to Earth. You and I have to find a way to stop it, or we will be neck deep in trouble."

"You mean us *three*, have to find a way," Candy said, wrapping her arms around Kieran's neck. "Have to admit that life with you will never be dull, Kieran Nash."

"May God have mercy on our souls," Zimmer said.

The End

About the Author

Ken Newman has loved stories of the supernatural since listening to his grandmother's tales of witches, haints, boogers, and catawamps when he was a child. Author of urban fantasy novels, *The Paladin*, *The Ark*, *The Voice in My Ear*, *Forsaken*, and *Dead Ends*, his fiction reflects his Tennessee roots and his love for all things-that-go-bump-in-the-night.

Mixing folklore with modern themes, Newman's novels create a twisted universe of supernatural creatures and larger-than-life heroes where nothing is as it seems.

When not writing, he enjoys sculpting, cheesy monster movies, and building the occasional trebuchet to keep the neighbors in line. A member of the Authors Guild of Tennessee, Newman lives in East Tennessee with his long suffering wife Christian and their three zany daughters.

Please feel free to contact him. He would love to hear from you.